Sue MacKay lives with he▨ ▨▨▨ ▨▨ ▨▨
New Zealand's beautiful M▨▨▨▨▨▨▨ ▨▨▨▨
with the water on her doorsṯẹp and the birds and
the trees at her back door. It is the perfect setting
to indulge her passions of entertaining friends by
cooking them sumptuous meals, drinking fabulous
wine, going for hill walks or kayaking around the
bay—and, of course, writing stories.

Born and raised just outside Toronto, Ontario,
Amy Ruttan fled the big city to settle down with
the country boy of her dreams. After the birth of
her second child Amy was lucky enough to realise
her lifelong dream of becoming a romance author.
When she's not furiously typing away at her
computer she's mum to three wonderful children,
who use her as a personal taxi and chef.

FAKE FIANCÉE TO FOREVER?

SUE MacKAY

NURSE'S PREGNANCY SURPRISE

AMY RUTTAN

MILLS & BOON

First published in Great Britain 2023
by Mills & Boon, an imprint of HarperCollins*Publishers* Ltd,
1 London Bridge Street, London, SE1 9GF

www.harpercollins.co.uk

HarperCollins*Publishers* Macken House, 39/40 Mayor Street Upper,
Dublin 1, D01 C9W8, Ireland

ISBN: 978-0-263-30610-1

06/23

This book is produced from independently certified FSC™ paper to ensure responsible forest management.
For more information visit: www.harpercollins.co.uk/green.

Printed and Bound in the UK using 100% Renewable Electricity at CPI Group (UK) Ltd, Croydon, CR0 4YY

FAKE FIANCÉE TO FOREVER?

SUE MacKAY

MILLS & BOON

I dedicate this book to my special group of friends
who go on wonderful trips away together.

You ladies rock.

PROLOGUE

TILDA SIMMONS BLINKED. A bright light shone on her eyes. 'Go away,' she muttered.

'Hello, Matilda. I'm Toby, a nurse. You've been in an accident.'

Her head was throbbing something awful. 'I remember. I think.' Hadn't she lost control of the car on black ice while driving to work? Slammed into a brick wall or something?

'You've been sleeping since coming up from Recovery to the general ward after having surgery to your face. The surgeon will explain everything as soon as he's free.'

Hence the headache. 'Thanks.' The nurse wouldn't give her the details. Not his job.

Toby continued. 'Tell me the pain level in your head.'

One to ten, with ten being the worst. 'Six.'

He raised an eyebrow in disbelief, but only said, 'I've got strong analgesics here that the plastic surgeon insists you're to take now you're on the ward.'

In other words, this nurse would make sure she swallowed them, and didn't ignore them.

'I understand. To be honest, I'm happy to have the relief. I feel woozy.' The after-effects of anaesthesia were clouding her mind a little. A new state for her, but as a theatre nurse she'd seen it happen more often than she could recall.

'Glad to hear it.'

Hang on. 'Did you say plastic surgeon?' That meant tissue damage and scarring. On her head? Her face? 'What happened? Am I all right?' Was she going to look like something that scared the pants off little kids? A breath stuck in her throat. She sucked in hard, coughed out, aggravating her tender throat. Breathed in again, ignoring the increased pounding behind her eyes.

'Easy.' Toby touched her upper arm. 'Everything's going to be fine. You've been lucky. The wound is on the side of your face by the hairline. Not to mention your surgeon is one of the best.' He was watching her closely, no doubt keeping an eye on her vital signs. 'You're in Western General Hospital, by the way.'

'What's wrong with me?' Panic struck. She was a nurse, so she should know what was going on. Shouldn't she?

Again the nurse's firm hand pressed her upper arm. 'Steady. You've had a knock to the head. This is a normal reaction to shock and surgery.'

True. She nodded and pain stabbed behind her eyes. 'Can you break the rules and tell me what my injuries are?' For the life of her, she couldn't remember what she'd been told before being carted off to Theatre. Probably nothing too detailed at that point, if she was even conscious.

'Think this is where I come in.' A man stepped around the nurse. 'I'm Gary Cook, your plastic surgeon today.' Standing beside the narrow bed, he continued. 'It appears that your head hit the steering wheel and the side of your left cheek split wide open. I've put everything back together with layers of suturing. Your forehead also needed stitching. Your left clavicle's fractured but according to the orthopaedic surgeon who read your X-ray earlier you don't need surgery for that. Time and rest will take care of it.

From your GCS I'd say you've got severe concussion so no partying for a few weeks.'

Fat chance of that even if she wasn't in here. James didn't like her going out and enjoying herself with friends. So her Glasgow Coma Score had been low. 'How low?'

'Four. But it's normal now. You came through surgery without a hitch. From here on it's all about getting better. I'm recommending you stay in hospital for at least two nights, but we'll monitor you before that's a definite.'

Right now this was all too much to take in.

'Thank you.' Her eyes were closing of their own volition and she couldn't find the energy to raise her eyelids again. She'd prefer to do without the after-effects from surgery, but it seemed she'd stuffed up driving and this was the price. An image of racing towards a brick wall filled her head. Something like a groan fell over her lips. It could've been a lot worse. A hell of a lot worse.

'You're safe, Matilda.' The nurse touched her hand.

The next thing she was aware of was waking again with a monitor beeping somewhere behind her head.

Toby had a blood pressure cuff around her arm. 'Welcome back, Matilda.'

'Hi,' Tilda managed. From now on she'd try not to be so damned cheery with her patients. It seemed a bit OTT while lying here feeling utterly useless.

'One to ten, with ten the worst, what's the pain level in your head?'

Twelve. 'Seven.'

'I'll talk to the duty surgeon and see if we can give you something stronger for that. In the meantime, do you want a drink of water?'

Her mouth was a desert. 'Please.'

'I'll go get it. I'll also tell your husband he can come in. He's pacing the floor of the waiting room, desperate to see you. He's not happy we wouldn't let him in until you woke up, but as you'll know sleep's the most important thing for you right now.'

James was here? When he'd been heading to Banff for business? When he'd left in a foul mood because she hadn't picked up his dry-cleaning yesterday?

'How long ago did I crash?'

'Roughly four hours.'

So James had turned around to come back and see her. After the massive argument they'd had she half expected him to have stayed away on purpose. Her heart softened. They mightn't agree on much these days but he had returned home to see her. Something was going right.

'You wrecked my car.' James stood at the end of the bed, glaring at her. 'It's ruined. After all the hard work I put in to get it up to speed and looking the best on the road, you go and drive it into a wall.'

Forget it. They weren't getting on. Why had she thought they might? Those days were long gone.

'It was an accident, James,' she said wearily. 'I struck black ice.' Nothing wrong with her memory after all—unfortunately.

'So what? If you can't handle a powerful car then you shouldn't have been driving. Don't you even care about what you've done?'

Didn't he care about her and if she was going to be all right?

'I am sorry.' She truly was because he loved that car, but she'd also like some recognition as his wife, who he was also supposed to love. She wasn't just some woman who'd crashed his favourite vehicle.

'Sorry?' he yelled. 'You think that makes everything all right? You stupid woman. Sorry doesn't begin to cover it.'

'Go away, James. I don't need this right now.' Proof that he really didn't love her enough. Not enough to be worried after a serious accident had landed her in hospital anyway. 'Go.'

Lachlan couldn't believe what he was hearing from the room where a woman was recovering from surgery. What sort of man would tear strips off his wife in that situation? Or at any time. Not once had the guy asked how she was feeling. He hadn't shown even a hint of concern. To Lachlan, it seemed to be all about the car.

Leaping up from the desk, he strode across to the room where the woman lay looking upset. Along with tired and defeated. Quite a sorry picture. 'Excuse me, Mr Simmons?'

'Who wants to know?'

'James, quieten down, will you?' Matilda Simmons gasped.

Lachlan intervened before the guy started ranting again. 'I'm Lachlan McRae, another plastic surgeon on the ward,' he told the distressed woman. 'I couldn't help overhearing your husband.' The whole ward probably had.

'James' surname is Connell, not Simmons.'

'Mr Connell, your wife's had serious surgery this morning. She needs to rest.' He paused, waiting for the guy to ask how she was and how the op had gone.

'Hope you knew what you were doing. Her face looks terrible.'

For the first time in his career, Lachlan wanted to plant

his fist in someone's face—this man's in particular, so he'd feel the pain his wife was dealing with. It took a long, deep breath to keep his anger at bay.

'I didn't perform the procedure but I know there'll be scarring for some time to come, but long-term Matilda will barely see where she's been injured.' Yes, he did add emphasis to 'injured' because someone had to get through to this man that his wife had been seriously wounded.

'Think you could put my car back together in the same condition it was when I left home this morning?' Connell was yelling again, glaring at his wife.

She winced, embarrassment now the most obvious emotion on her bruised face. 'James, shut up,' she whispered.

'What? You don't want people knowing what an idiot you've been?'

Lachlan watched the patient roll carefully onto her side, her back to her husband, and he said, 'Mr Connell, I have to ask you to leave now. Your wife needs to rest,' he repeated a little louder than before.

'I'll stay as long as I want,' the man shouted. Was this his only way of making a point? To shout so loudly everyone within a hundred metres heard?

'Please stop yelling. There are other patients in need of quiet. This is a hospital. People are here because they're unwell. We do not tolerate behaviour like yours, Mr Connell.' Now *he* was raving. His anger was unusual. Something about his patient's vulnerability had him wanting to protect her from more than a damaged face. 'I am advising you to go. Now.'

'Need a hand in here?' Toby stood in the doorway. A large man with shoulders like a brick wall, he could make people quiver with a stare should he feel the need. He was also the gentlest nurse on the surgical ward.

'I think we're fine. Mr Connell was just leaving.'

Absolute silence fell. All eyes were on the husband. Even Matilda had turned just enough to see what her husband did. She appeared to be holding her breath.

'See you later.' The man stomped out of the room as Toby stepped aside.

Lachlan's chest rose and fell normally and the tension in his gut eased. 'Thanks, Toby.'

'You had it under control.' The nurse came into the room, speaking softly. 'Matilda, I'm back to harass you. How're you feeling? Pain level?'

'Five,' she uttered. 'I'm good. Truly. I'm a nurse and know about these things.'

'Where do you work?' Lachlan asked. He didn't recognise her, but then her face was swollen and bruised.

'I'm a theatre nurse at St Michael's, Gastown.'

'That'll be why we haven't come across each other then. I don't do ops there.'

'It's a good crew there.' She was fading. Everything catching up with her once more?

'Anything I can get you?' he asked, wanting to help any way he could.

'My phone?'

Toby spoke up. 'If it's in your bag which is on the bedside table then you're in luck. The paramedic found it in the car and brought it in with you.'

Lachlan stepped closer. 'Like me to pass you the bag?' He didn't want her moving any more than necessary. *And* he wanted to offer her a hand getting what she required. Which at the moment didn't include a ranting husband. Instead she needed to relax and sleep off the shock resulting from the accident.

'Can you get my phone out?' She managed a wobbly smile. 'There's nothing in there that'll bite, I promise.'

Her smile nudged him on the inside. Which shouldn't happen. This woman was a patient, no more, no less. But he was still angry at the way her husband had treated her so could be he was being a little soft.

'Good to know, since I need my fingers for work.' Delving into a woman's handbag seemed a bit like stepping onto a minefield. Not that he'd ever done that, but when he'd worked in the States he'd put a soldier's hand back together who had, and triggered a small bomb as he did so. 'Here you go.'

He handed the phone to Matilda before stepping out of the room, where he sucked in a lungful, then let it go. No one should be abused by a loved one. The way Connell spoke to his wife was appalling. While she was still recovering from surgery and shock, at that. He leaned against the wall, eyes closed, and breathed out his bad mood. Time to move on. The woman's relationship woes were not his problem.

Suddenly he was thinking of Kelly, his late wife. Not once had he spoken to her like Connell had to Matilda. The man should be holding onto his wife for dear life. He had no idea how lucky he was she'd survived. Four years ago when a driver fell asleep at the wheel of his car and drove into Kelly, she'd died instantly. *His* arms had felt empty ever since. An emptiness he doubted would ever be filled again.

'Janet? It's me, Tilda.'

Lachlan straightened at the sound of the distressed voice coming from the room behind him.

'I'm in hospital. I had an accident on the way to work.'

Pause. 'I'm all right. Promise.' Pause. 'Because I had surgery on my face.' A longer pause. When she spoke next her voice was full of tears. 'I can't take any more, Janet. I've tried and tried to be good enough for him.'

Lachlan hissed air over his bottom teeth. Love had been easy for him and Kelly. From day one, they'd had each other's backs and both their plans for the future and their hearts had been completely in sync.

In the room behind him Matilda was getting worked up. 'When I get out of here, can I stay with you for a while? Just until I find my own place. I'm done with James.'

Lachlan walked away before he heard any more. Matilda Simmons seemed to be moving on from her marriage, but that might only be temporary. She had yet to get over what had happened earlier in the day, and right now her mind would be all over the place. Whatever she did, it was none of his business.

CHAPTER ONE

Twelve months later

HER PACK SLUNG on her back, Tilda stepped through the main doors into the arrivals hall at Phnom Penh Airport and looked for a man holding a card with her name on it. She presumed that was how he intended getting her attention. Or would he rely on memory? If he even recognised her name. It'd been a surprise to read who'd be meeting her at the airport. Showed just how small the world could be. And how her mind hadn't been a complete blank at the time, because she was sure she'd recognise him.

Matilda Simmons.

She checked out the relaxed man holding the piece of card and laughed. Mr Lachlan McRae, plastic surgeon, hadn't changed a bit since she'd last seen him on the ward where she'd recuperated from the accident that changed her life for ever. He mightn't have been her surgeon but he'd been in and out of the room she'd shared with a patient of his. She hadn't imagined the good looks. That face was chiselled and now sported a light stubble that was even more attractive. Sexy came to mind. She shoved that thought away fast. She was done with men except for the occasional one-night stand just to remind herself she still had some appeal to the male species. James had killed her need to be loved.

Growing up with only her grandmother, she'd always longed for more family and thought she was on the way to finding it when she and James fell in love. Turned out his idea of loving was telling her how to live her life in a way that suited him. She'd believed in him, loved him to bits, and that was how he'd repaid her. If that was what men wanted from her then from here on out she was going solo. Even once the divorce became final she wouldn't be rushing out to find a man to give her heart to.

That included this particular man, who was smiling as though he did recognise her. Might just be his friendly nature. She'd looked different back then, with her face red and tight around the glaring scars. These days her hair was longer and hung loose to cover the worst of those, though they had already faded some, as Mr Cook had assured her they would.

Crossing over, she held out her hand. 'Hello, Lachlan. Funny how we've ended up working for the same charity at the same time.'

'Hi, Matilda.' He shook her hand, his fingers warm to the touch. Or was that because she felt tired and a little chilly after the long flight, despite the humid air here? 'I did get a surprise when your name came up on the list. A nice one, I have to say.' That made her feel warmer but no more interested, other than as a colleague. He continued, 'I'm meant to pick up another guy as well, but his flight's been delayed and he won't be here until tomorrow morning.'

'So we're going out to the medical centre now?' From what she'd read online it might be about an hour away, and right now she'd really had enough of sitting in one seat for any length of time. A shower and a walk would be preferable, except she understood that wasn't happening until she got to the Hospital Care Charity's staff quarters.

'Can I carry your pack for you?'

There were a few too many clothes and shoes inside, plus some books to read when she wasn't on duty or out sightseeing, but that was her problem.

'I'm good, thanks.'

'Okay. Over here.' He led the way outside. 'In answer to your question, we're staying in town overnight. I hope that's all right with you? There're no surgeries scheduled for tomorrow morning so Harry, he's the administrator, suggested that since I have to be at the airport first thing to pick up Dave we might as well stay at a hotel in the city. It'll make it easier for you to unwind and get a decent night's sleep as it's kind of noisy where our quarters are, right next to the clinic on a main road. I say let's make the most of the opportunity.'

Seemed someone was looking out for her.

'Perfect.'

'Harry booked us rooms at a small hotel one street back from the Mekong River. I wondered if you'd like to take a walk and maybe have a meal so that you can stay up to a reasonable hour and get your body clock on track for normal as soon as possible.'

It came back in a rush. This man's deep voice, full of kindness when James had been so outrageous. Seemed nothing had changed. Still deep and kind. But there *was* a difference; he had a twinkle in his eyes and a lightness in his face that she hadn't seen then. That was professional. This was friendly. He made her feel welcome in Cambodia when it wasn't up to him to do that.

'That was my plan—stay up until about ten. Not sure if it actually works, but I intend trying.' They'd reached a large parking area and were weaving through slow-moving vehicles of all descriptions. Lachlan seemed focused on both traffic and her. She liked him already. 'How long have you been in Phnom Penh?'

'Three weeks. Two to go. It's a wonderful place. The people are so open and pleasant while busy trying to make ends meet. I've never done anything like this before and I'll definitely volunteer again. What about you?'

'First time too.' Two years ago she'd applied to work for a month at a charity clinic in Laos but James had hated the idea of her going away to help others. He'd said she had no right to leave him alone for a month. In the end she'd capitulated because it made life easier. 'I'm hoping it'll be a great way to meet locals and get to understand their lifestyle a little.'

'You'll get to do that, for certain. Here we are.' Locks pinged on a dented car in front of them. 'The car belongs to the clinic.'

'It's seen better days.' She laughed through a deep yawn. The long-haul flight was catching up with her big time.

'Sure has. Did you get any sleep on the plane?' Lachlan took her pack and stashed it on the back seat.

She couldn't remember him being so intriguing before, but her mind had been on other things. James and his damned car. Anyway, she'd been married then and wouldn't have looked twice at another man. Now she was single and still not looking twice. For different reasons though. Marriage was a total commitment. Running solo meant looking after her heart, and she no longer trusted herself to know when she'd found a good man.

The man beside her seemed more relaxed and casual away from work. It suited him. To get to know him a bit more might be interesting if she was on the lookout for someone to have fun with, but she wasn't. Not even for a one-night stand? Maybe. Despite the heat bouncing off the tarmac she shivered. Where did that idea come from? He was only here for another two weeks. It could work. Or not. Another yawn widened her mouth. But there was no denying her life had been a bit dull lately. Was she only just realising that when there was a hot man beside her?

'I dozed a little. Bit hard when I had a wriggly ten-year-old on one side and a woman on the other who spread out over more than her own seat.' The joys of flying economy class. She'd never flown any other way.

Lachlan winced as he opened the door for her. 'Hate it when that happens. Climb in and we'll head into the city.'

A gentleman. Why wasn't she surprised? She recalled his tact with James when he was berating her for wrecking his favourite car. It had been apparent even in her post-op state that the surgeon hadn't been happy with her husband but he'd remained cool, calm and collected as he should, even though she wasn't his patient. Which was more than she'd been.

She'd cried after James had gone that day, lots of tears of frustration and disappointment. Of course, shock from the accident had added to her distress too, but reality had finally set in. James was never again going to be the loving, kind man she'd fallen for.

The longer they were married, the more selfish he'd become and the more controlling he'd tried to be. It hadn't helped that he'd taken to drinking as a way of drowning his woes, the biggest of which was apparently her. He'd been furious when she'd learned she was pregnant. That was not in his plans. He'd demanded she get an abortion. She'd refused, which had really rocked the boat as she was not meant to go against his demands. He didn't like it when she stood up to him. Which hadn't been often enough, she reflected grimly. But when it came to the baby, she'd refused to give in. Except, in the end, he'd won in a roundabout way. She'd miscarried at eleven weeks, and to this day still missed her baby and all the promise that would've come with him or her. She'd never hurt her child, before or after it was born.

Her mother had died from a haemorrhage giving birth to her, and her grandmother had told her often how much she'd wanted to be a mother even though the father had refused to acknowledge the pregnancy. To the point that he'd threatened to hurt her mother if she'd tried to stay in touch.

'Where are you? Not nodding off, are you?' Lachlan's deep voice cut into her thoughts.

'Not at all.' Looking out at the chaos that was the traffic, she asked, 'What's it like driving here?' There was lots of tooting as drivers dodged around other vehicles. Add in tuk-tuks ducking and dodging amongst the faster vehicles and it was bedlam.

Lachlan tossed her a wry grin. 'I won't talk a lot for the next little while. It's kind of crazy, yet I admit I get a thrill out of making it from A to B in one piece.'

'That sounds scary.'

'It's really not that bad, and the speed's fairly slow despite how it looks.'

'Tell me about the clinic. How many people are working there?' Should she be asking him questions when he'd said he wouldn't be talking much? 'Don't answer if you have to concentrate.'

'I can do two things at once, despite being a man and saying I wouldn't talk much. There're ten volunteers at the moment, though that number changes almost weekly. Along with me, there's a general surgeon doing small ops, nothing major. There's one anaesthetist and everyone else is a nurse or paramedic from various countries. You and I are the only Canadians at the moment.' He did talking and driving at the same time very well.

No doubting he *was* a man either. Muscular without being overly so, his strength apparent in his firm body. Throw in good looks and he was quite the package. If she was looking for a guy to get close to—but she wasn't, she chastised herself. Remember James. Usually she never forgot, even for a moment.

'I've been in Toronto for the past ten months. I had another nursing job lined up in Quebec starting two months ago, but the nurse I was replacing changed his mind about leaving. That's when I saw an article about the charity hospital here and how they needed a nurse urgently.'

Her mouth was getting away from her. She wasn't into sharing about herself since she'd walked away from James. Hadn't been inclined to do so before that either. People didn't need to know anything about her other than she was a highly capable nurse. But talking about work had little to do with her private life, so why not be friendly? There was nothing to lose and maybe something enjoyable to gain.

'You moved away from Vancouver after the accident?' He didn't sound too surprised. Did that mean he remembered James ranting about the car?

She'd started this, so she might as well get it out of the way. 'After I left hospital I never returned home. My marriage was over. I stayed with a nursing colleague until I'd fully recovered, then headed east for a change of scenery and to sort out my stuff. Now I'm here in Cambodia.' It was exciting, to say the least.

'What's next for you?'

'I've sent a couple of applications for theatre positions to hospitals back in Canada, but I'm not holding my breath as it's at least a month before I'll be available and most places want an immediate start.'

'My partners and I do most of our work at Western General and they're always looking for theatre nurses.'

'I'll keep that in mind.' She might've had enough of working with Lachlan by the time he finished up here. Then again, they might well hit it off and she could want to see more of him. At work. Nowhere else. Lachlan might be kind and considerate, and built like a basketballer, but so what? Throw in how she felt more than a little bit hot sitting beside him, and she did feel a slight connection to him, but nothing would come of it.

She was well and truly over James, but the thought of another long-term relationship gave her the shivers. She intended remaining independent from now on. No one was ever again going to tell her how to live her life. Growing up with only her grandmother to share her achievements and failings with, she didn't need a man at her side all the time. Didn't need one, but would love to have some fun, just so long as he wasn't a control freak.

In the beginning James had been so loving and devoted that she'd wondered what she'd done to deserve him. Only after they'd got married did his true colours start to show. He had to be in charge of everything, and expected her to run round after him whenever he demanded. Belittling her grew to be his favourite pastime. Whenever she'd done something he deemed wrong he'd acted like a toddler throwing his toys out of the pram.

His total disregard for her after the accident had been the final blow. Not once had he asked if she was going to be all right. Not once. He had returned to visit her in hospital after his first outburst, but only to give her a full rundown on the damage done to his precious vehicle. His spiel hadn't lasted long. The nurses had overheard—hard not to when he was shouting so loudly—and this time they'd removed him from the ward with the warning not to return. She'd backed them on that. Coming not long after his reaction to her pregnancy and miscarriage, it'd been the last straw. He'd been shocked when she'd walked away from their marriage without a backwards glance, stunned she didn't kowtow to him.

Surprise, James. I am stronger than you gave me credit for. Something to remember at all times.

Lachlan was still talking. 'Did you enjoy Toronto? I specialised there. It's a massive city.'

'Too big, I reckon. I felt lost without the sea nearby.' Going down to Kitsilano Beach for a swim or a spot of paddleboarding had been one of the highlights of living in Vancouver previously. 'The lake was far too cold for anything but walking along the bank.'

He nodded. 'Vancouver felt almost tropical when I returned home, though that feeling didn't last into winter.'

'I won't have to worry about chilly temperatures for a few weeks.' She'd packed one jacket and a jersey just in case, but doubted they'd ever come out of her bag.

'Here it's the humidity that gets to you. It can be quite draining.'

She could listen to him talking all day. His voice was

smooth and had her imagining his fingers moving just as smoothly on her skin. Might be time to get out there and have some short-term fun. Not with Lachlan though. Why not? Um, because…they had to work together? Because… She had no idea, other than a strong instinct to look out for herself and something about this man suggested he could make her feel vulnerable if she wasn't careful. And careful had been her middle name since the day her grandmother had been injured in a freak accident at the amusement park she'd taken Tilda to for her sixth birthday. She'd had to stay in social welfare care for a week as there was no one else to look after her. Since then she'd been careful about getting close to people, afraid they could get taken away from her. Seemed she'd dropped the ball when James came along. That wouldn't happen again. She knew better now. Should've known better the first time.

'Did I mention parking is a pain in the backside?' Lachlan did a loop of the block where the hotel stood.

His passenger laughed, a warm, happy sound, touching him in an unexpected way, making him feel cheerful, and not looking for a hidden agenda. It was more than a relief.

Meredith, a friend he'd known all his life and who'd married his best mate, Matt, had begun playing on his kindness ever since Matt's death eighteen months ago. She'd like Lachlan to move in and become her husband and father to her three boys because it would make life easier for her. He'd told her no. He understood she wanted to have one big happy family so they could move on from the tragedy, but it wouldn't work the way she'd suggested. Anyway, it was her parents and his who were really behind the idea of them getting together, as they'd always hoped he and Meredith would marry one day.

What no one understood was that while losing Matt had rocked him big time, losing Kelly a few years earlier had already broken his heart. He couldn't love again, and while Meredith claimed that was fine and she'd care for them all, he still could not do what she'd asked. What if someone else died? Him? Where would that leave the little guys then? Up a creek without a paddle didn't begin to come close. Which was why he wasn't getting into a relationship ever again. Losing Kelly had decimated him, and just when he'd finally started getting back on his feet Matt went and dropped dead. Go figure. He clearly could not trust those he loved to stay around for ever.

Someone tapped his arm. Matilda. She said with a cheeky smile, 'Do one of those Italian parking tricks I've seen online where you put the front to the kerb and the back pokes out into the street.'

'It's tempting, but think I'll go with legal and safe.' He didn't want a parking ticket turning up at the clinic after he'd left the country. A hassle no one needed.

'There.' Matilda pointed. 'It'll be a tight squeeze, but we should fit in.'

Was she setting him up for a fail? He loved a challenge, and this one would be a breeze. 'Watch this.' Better not make a mess of it. He didn't. The space was small but so was the car. Driving was one thing he was good at. Along with repairing scars and making patients feel better about themselves.

'Not bad,' she drawled, and shoved open her door. Her dark brown hair fell across her cheek as she turned to smile at him. He ached to reach across and run his fingers through it. Stunned, he gripped the steering wheel hard. Where did that idea come from? It was so not like him. He had to work with Matilda. She'd probably have slapped him if he had reached over and touched her. She should. It would be too intimate an action. He vaguely remembered her hair had barely come below her ears a year ago. He preferred the shoulder-length style she wore now. It suited her better and softened her features.

How had she coped over the intervening time? At least she'd dumped that scumbag. Best thing she could've done. Not every woman had what it took to walk away from a control freak like her husband. The guy had been beyond horrible. That day in the ward, overhearing him raving at Matilda, his protective side had come raging to the fore and had him wanting to intervene. Fortunately his professional side had won out or he might've found himself before the hospital board explaining his behaviour, even when she hadn't been his patient. To his credit, it would've only been a verbal confrontation. He didn't go around hitting people, although his fists had tightened at one point. But there was no denying how much he had wanted to keep his colleague's patient safe, and that had nothing to do with his medical calling.

'You're looking good, a lot more relaxed than you were in hospital.'

Her eyes widened. 'I would hope so.'

Make him feel foolish for mentioning it, why didn't she?

'Moving to Toronto helped, I presume?' He was digging a bigger hole by the minute, but he couldn't help himself. There was so much he wanted to know about Matilda. Which was strange since he didn't like getting involved with people and knowing too much about them, then feeling protective of them. Might be better to remember he'd only add to her problems with his determination to keep his own emotions safe. If she even looked at him twice.

There were already enough people relying on him back home and he'd needed some time out for himself, hence being in Cambodia. The time had come to start living his own life again, only he didn't know exactly where to start. When this opportunity had come up his two partners in the plastic surgery clinic they'd started five years earlier had been blunt in their insistence he take it and have a complete change. They were covering for him back home, which added to his guilt. He'd let them down. Sure, he worked hard but he'd changed from the cheerful specialist to a surgeon who turned up for work just because it was where he was meant to be. After three weeks here he already felt the thrill for his work coming back. No pressure, just doing what he loved. Exactly what he needed and enjoyed.

Getting out of the car, Matilda paused. Looking at him, she nodded. 'I didn't know anyone when I landed in Toronto, yet I fitted in with flatmates and work colleagues easily. That showed me I wasn't incompetent or useless without James to point me in the right direction.'

'Your confidence grew.' He'd have thought she was already confident if she'd left her husband while recovering from a major accident.

'I'd say more like it returned. I got back most of what I'd lost over the years of my marriage. I'm very happy now being single.' Her lips clamped shut as a stunned expression crossed her pretty face. Perhaps she thought she was talking too much? She opened the back door and reached in for her pack.

So she wasn't rushing to find a new life partner. That surprised him. She seemed open and friendly, and he couldn't imagine her being on her own for ever. Though he understood how hard it was to move on after being hurt so badly.

As she slung the pack over her slim shoulders she said, as though speaking to herself, 'I'm dying for a shower.'

He tried to not think about that image. Instead he led the way inside the small hotel and up to the counter. When they'd checked in and had keys in their hands, he asked, 'How about we meet back down here in an hour and go for a walk alongside the Mekong before heading to the Correspondents' Club for a meal?'

'Can we make that half an hour? I'll fall asleep if I have to wait around, and then there'll be no waking me. I do want to stay awake for a few more hours.'

'Dave gave me your phone number in case we missed each other at the airport so I can call you in thirty minutes if you don't show up.' For some inexplicable reason he was pleased to have the number so he could get in touch with her if they weren't both at the clinic at the same time. They might get to spend time together outside the clinic over the next couple of weeks. He'd been sightseeing a few times with other volunteers whenever they had free time, and he'd like to show Matilda the places he'd already seen.

'Thanks.'

'See you shortly,' he said as she headed for the stairs, looking lovely despite the exhaustion coming off her in waves. She wouldn't be running solo long, or without friends. She was *too* lovely not to be popular.

Careful, Lachlan.

'There is an elevator, Matilda.'

Her hand waved at him over her shoulder. 'It's only one

floor and I can't wait for that shower. I must stink something awful after so long in the air.'

'Can't say I noticed.' That might be because he'd been too busy keeping an eye on the road as well as Matilda's physical attributes and everything else about her except her aroma. So far, she'd come up trumps in every respect. Unfortunately.

The woman disturbing him paused, one foot on the first stair, and turned to face him. 'It's Tilda, by the way.'

'Right. Tilda.' Not Matilda.

A tired grin split her face. 'See you shortly.'

Kapow. Right in the solar plexus. He felt it like a physical blow. Hard. Swift. Sexy as hell. Nothing to do with the image of her as a naughty child, and all to do with this stunning woman staring at him, blinding him to reality. What reality? The one where he wasn't looking for a partner? Although if he did find one for himself, that might make Meredith wake up to what she was trying to make him do and realise it was never going to work. But that wouldn't be fair on any woman he got even a little bit close to.

'Back here in thirty.' The clock should start ticking now, as right at this moment he needed as long a break from Matilda as possible. *Tilda.* Time to get his breath back and put his sensible head on. Throw the other one away before he got in too deep, wondering what lay behind that friendly façade. He needed to remember the pain when he'd lost Kelly and admit he was not going to be setting himself up for more of that any time soon.

Tilda trudged up the stairs, exhaustion pouring off her in waves. Not a fan of long-haul flights then. But who was? Not him.

He could suggest they take the car to the club but she'd

said she needed to walk and get some fresh air. Fresh air. Bring it on. Thirty minutes. He followed her up the stairs, confused and not liking the fact he was getting so stirred up by Tilda.

Coming to Cambodia had given him space to look at his home situation more clearly. When he'd introduced Matt to Meredith at a party they'd instantly fallen for each other. A wedding and three sons later, Matt had died. A fit, energetic man, his heart had just quit on him at the 10K mark in a local half marathon. Despite all the medical help on hand for the race, nothing could be done to save him. He was gone, leaving everyone devastated. Leaving Meredith and their three young boys for ever. It had been hell. Still was some days. There were times he struggled to accept what had happened.

He'd done everything possible for the boys so they had a male role model to rely on. He adored the little guys. They were awesome. They came and went in his house as they wished. Living just around the corner made it easy for them to pop in and out. Too easy maybe, but no way could he turn them away. Nor could he marry their mother simply for their sakes. He'd never been attracted to Meredith. In the long run that would be a mistake that would affect everyone, and he'd find it almost impossible to come back from.

Up ahead, Tilda turned right along the hallway to her room.

Lachlan turned left. He could already tell she was beautiful inside and out. Who'd have thought a year ago he'd ever think that about another woman? Not him, that was for sure. He didn't usually get side-tracked so easily.

CHAPTER TWO

'I FELL ASLEEP in the shower,' Tilda told Lachlan as they strolled along the riverside. Right after she'd rinsed the conditioner out of her hair she'd leaned against the wall to let the warm water slide over her achy muscles and the next thing she knew she was sliding downwards to land on her butt, water pouring all over her.

Lachlan walked with his hands in his pockets, his shoulders loose, like he had all the time in the world. He probably did tonight. A well-earned break in a hectic schedule?

'Just as well I didn't panic when you were a few minutes late coming downstairs and send someone in to check up on you.'

That would've been interesting.

'They'd have got as big a shock as me,' she said with a laugh. Looking around, she sighed with happiness. The smells of street food wafted past her nose, making her hungry, while the sounds of traffic and people laughing, talking and shouting in languages she didn't understand filled her head. 'This is awesome. To think I'm walking on the bank of the Mekong River. It's an icon for this part of Asia.'

Her companion laughed. 'It's muddy.'

'And very wide. Bet nothing gets in its way.' She pinched herself and looked around at the city behind them. 'I can't believe I'm really here.'

'It's so different to home.'

'Vancouver is your home town?'

'Yes. I did time in different places while qualifying but returned once I was ready to establish my career. My family's there, and my closest friends. I've no desire to move away when everything and everyone I want is nearby.'

'Fair enough.' She'd grown up in Vancouver but had no real attachment to anywhere except the little house in Langley where her grandmother and her mother had also grown up. It had been a sad day when the house had been sold to pay for Grandma's room at a rest home.

'We cross the road here.' Lachlan looked in both directions. 'Any rate, I think we do. We'll give it a go and see what's on the other side.'

'You haven't been to the club before?'

'Once. The first night I arrived in town, Harry picked me up and brought me into the city for a meal before driving us out to the clinic. He seemed glad to get away for a few hours and was in no hurry to return to base. There was no mention of staying over for the night though. He takes his responsibilities very seriously. Quite happy for everyone else to get away for a few hours or more, but rarely does he do the same.'

She was terrified of stepping off the footpath into the crowded road. 'They're all out of control.' There was nothing orderly about where the vehicles went or how close they came to others as they passed with horns blaring nonstop.

He grabbed her hand. 'The rule is once you step off the sidewalk and out into the traffic, don't stop. The drivers will see you and dodge around you, but if you try avoiding them they haven't a clue where you're heading and things can get messy.'

They reached the other side of the road, alive and in one piece.

'See? We made it.' Lachlan was laughing like he'd just had the most exciting experience of his life. If that was the case he needed to get out more often.

With me? she wondered. Might as well since she was here to have fun as well as help people. Huh? Hadn't she already admonished herself for thinking he was different to other men? As in turn-up-the-heat different.

'What's that building up ahead? Two storeys, big windows, lots of lights.'

'Our destination. Well spotted. Let's get inside and away from all the jabbing elbows.' He let go of her hand.

Despite the loss of connection, Tilda didn't try to put any distance between them. It felt good to be walking alongside him, close but not quite touching. As if they were an item. Obviously they weren't and were not likely ever to be, but she could pretend for a little while. There'd be no consequences when Lachlan wasn't falling over with eagerness to get to know her better.

Being happy walking to a club for a meal with him didn't mean she was giving up her hard-earned independence. The time in Toronto had made her realise she could once more rely on her choices and judgements when it came to where she lived and worked and who she went out with, so long as nobody was looking for anything permanent. She'd become a toughened-up version of the Matilda who'd married James. He'd been her one big mistake and she wasn't willing to make another.

Lachlan opened the door and nodded for her to go first. She quickly scoped him out, felt her eyes widen.

Settle down, Tilda. This is a man you're going to be work-

ing with for a couple of weeks. You do not need to create any complications because you're tired after a long flight and excited to be in a new country.

A light hum of voices reached her as they climbed the stairs to the main floor. Mostly Westerners, she realised. Made sense, given the name of the place.

'Is this a public club?'

'Yes. Known for its great food and cold beers.' Lachlan led the way to the bar. 'No Cambodian food. They leave that for the locals and the markets. This is more your burger and pizza stop.'

Her mouth watered. 'I can't wait.'

'Didn't you eat on the plane?' he asked with that mischievous twinkle in his eye. 'Or do you like four meals a day?'

'Since I don't know what day I'm on I'll go with the message from my stomach and eat.' Tomorrow she'd get back to normal, whatever that might be here.

When they left the club an hour later Lachlan texted for a tuk-tuk to take them to their hotel. 'Might as well make the most of the city by night while we're here. The driver I'm contacting is Kiry, a local man who picks up most of our patients to bring them to the hospital and then takes them home when they're ready to leave. He also hires out his tuk-tuk in the city at night.'

'Busy man, by the sound of it.'

'Very. Here he is.'

They squeezed into the back, their thighs, hips and arms pressed against each other.

'Is your child a boy or girl?' Tilda asked about the small child sound asleep in a safety seat at the front after Lachlan introduced her. A tiny screwed-up face was just visible from its cocoon of blankets.

'Is boy. Phala. My first son.'

'He's lovely. You bring him out with you every night?'

'My wife works. A cleaner at hospital. Nights.'

They both worked nights, meaning someone had to look after their son. It couldn't be easy.

'You're busy people.'

The driver relaxed a little. Because she hadn't criticised him? 'We are. Have to keep roof over heads.'

'Show us a little of the city,' Lachlan said to him.

Tilda settled back to watch the town unfold before her. 'This is amazing.' Her first trip outside Canada and the USA was turning out to be an adventure already.

Tyres screeched on the tarmac. The tuk-tuk spun around, slammed into a car, then bounced across the road.

Tilda flew out of her seat, saw the road racing up to meet her, just like the brick wall from the past. Her heart pounded and she opened her mouth to cry out, but a strong hand grabbed her wrist, tugging her upward. She jerked her head sideways and skidded along the rough surface on her arm and hip, and banged to a stop against the kerb. Not a brick wall, but it'd hurt all the same. The hand still gripped her wrist.

'What the hell?'

'Tilda? You all right?' The grip loosened but didn't let go entirely.

'Lachlan? That you? What happened?' She pushed up onto her hands and knees.

'Easy. Let's check you out first.' He was right beside her, reaching to take her shoulders in those firm hands.

'I'm good. Might have lost some skin on my arm.' A quick glance. 'Not much.' But her shoulder was beginning to hurt. 'What about you?'

'Took a knock on the hip, but otherwise think everything's in working order.' He winced as he stood up, rubbing his right hip.

'Seems we got lucky.' Her hands were shaking as she took Lachlan's to pull herself up onto her feet. Her head was light, causing her to sway. 'You caught me.' He'd prevented her face-planting on the road.

'It happened so fast. Hey, I've still got you.' He wound an arm around her waist as she drew deep breaths and her balance returned. 'A car hit the tuk-tuk. Then I think the tuk-tuk banged into another vehicle.'

'What about Kiry? His son?' No, not that cute little boy. He *had* to be unharmed. 'Where are they? Are they all right?'

Lachlan looked over to the vehicle. 'Kiry's inside the upturned tuk-tuk. He looks dazed but okay.' He moved across to him. 'Where's your boy?' he asked urgently, peering around.

'Here,' Tilda called. 'On the road. Under the tuk-tuk.' Dropping to her knees, she leaned close and felt the child's head, then his upper body where the blanket had fallen away. 'Hello?' What was his name? 'Phala?' Was that it? The way she pronounced the name, he probably wouldn't recognise it. Hopefully he'd recognise her tender touch on his cheeks, then his head. 'Lachlan, Phala's unconscious.'

'Kiry's foot is jammed between the pedals and he's also got a trauma injury at the front of his head.' A crowd had sprung up around them. 'Anyone speak English?' he called.

'Yes.' More than one answer.

'I'm a doctor, this lady's a nurse, but we need urgent help for the little boy. Can someone phone for an ambulance?'

The moment the question was out, people were saying

they'd already done that. Lachlan got down beside her, those fingers that had been so gentle on her arm now touching the boy's head, searching for impact injuries. 'There's a soft patch behind Phala's left ear I don't like, and another, smaller one on the back of his head.'

'His breathing's erratic. So's his pulse. Wait...' She touched the boy's cheek. 'Do it again, Phala. He opened one eye for a millisecond,' she told Lachlan in an aside. After waiting a moment she sighed. 'Nothing. Must've been a reflex reaction.'

'Ambulance coming.' A local stood near to them.

'Tell them we have a little boy and his father needing help,' Lachlan said. 'Two stretchers are required—if they've got them,' he added quietly so only she heard.

'Yes, I tell them.' The man pushed through the crowd surrounding them.

'Shall I check the father?' Tilda asked. 'He might be in a bad way too.' He hadn't called out for his boy, and that should've been the first thing this loving dad would've done if he was fully aware of what was going on.

'Do that. We can triage who's worse off, though the paramedics will no doubt do the same. I'll stick with this little guy. He's in a bad way.' Lachlan was lifting an eyelid. 'No one home.'

Her heart filled with worry for the boy, Tilda crossed to the tuk-tuk driver. 'Hello? Can you hear me?'

Kiry talked rapidly in what she presumed was Khmer, leaving her clueless.

'Talk to me in English. I'm a nurse. I was in your tuk-tuk when that car hit,' she reminded him.

More useless words flowed out of his anguished mouth but she only recognised the word Phala.

She shook his arm to get his attention. 'Your son is with a doctor. I need to help you so you can go with him in the ambulance.'

'What's wrong with Phala?' Just like that, he'd flipped languages.

'He landed on the road and has some wounds.' The father frowned. Didn't he know that word? 'He's hurt his head.'

'Alive?'

'Yes.' That was all she was saying. Not that she knew much more, but this man didn't need to be upset any more than he already was. 'Is your leg stuck?'

Tears were pouring down his face. 'Phala hurt? I want to see him.'

'As soon as we get you out of the tuk-tuk.' She looked around, saw two men watching them. 'Can you help, please?' she asked without thinking about languages.

They moved forward.

'This man's leg is caught. We need to pull that steering bar back. Can you do that while I try to move his leg?'

'Yes, we help.'

Between them they managed to move the bar enough for Tilda to pull Kiry's leg free. 'Broken shin bone,' she told Lachlan when he appeared beside her minutes later. 'But I think it's a clean break. I can't feel any splinters under his skin.'

'The paramedics are here and have taken over Phala's care.' He touched the injured leg, and nodded.

'Phala?' demanded the driver as he gasped with pain. 'Where my son?'

'With the ambulance medics.' Lachlan glanced at the two men she'd got to help and raised an eyebrow.

One nodded, and spoke firmly to the driver.

Tilda then asked him, 'Where do you hurt, other than your leg?'

Again the other guy translated, and then told her, 'In heart. For his son.'

'I'm sure he does.' She blinked back tears as Lachlan began checking over the man's upper body, and saw no reactions to his probing fingers. 'Looks like it might only be his leg that's injured.'

'It'll be enough, considering he needs to be able to drive to make his living. But if it's a clean break it'll only be a few weeks until he's back at work.' Lachlan straightened up as a paramedic joined them. 'This man had his leg caught and Matilda says it's broken. I concur with her diagnosis,' he added crisply. 'She's a nurse.'

'Thank you for helping him and his son.' The paramedic spoke slowly and clearly. 'We take over now. Another ambulance is coming.'

'Of course.' They both stepped out of the way.

'How's your arm?' Lachlan asked.

'Forgotten all about it in the moment,' she muttered.

Again his hand was on her arm, lifting it to see clearly. 'You've taken a fair bit of skin off. I need some wipes to clean it.' He went over to the paramedic. 'Matilda was also hurt when she was thrown out of the tuk-tuk. Do you have some antiseptic wipes and plasters we could use to clean her up?'

'You were in the tuk-tuk too?' The paramedic looked surprised. 'That's not good. Yes, there are bandages in the ambulance. Come with me, I'll get them.'

'We'll wait until you've got this man on board.'

'No, no. I need a stretcher for him so I'll get what you want at the same time.'

'Want help with the stretcher?'

'These men will do it.'

Within minutes Tilda was walking down the road, once more feeling light-headed now that she wasn't concentrating on helping the driver.

'Welcome to Cambodia,' she murmured.

Lachlan took her arm, drawing her close to that awesome body. 'Been quite the day, hasn't it?'

'Y-yeah.' Her teeth had begun chattering. Probably shock setting in, now that she wasn't focused on helping the little boy. Closing her eyes didn't help. That brick wall from the past returned to her mind. No, it was the road surface. Racing at her, only for her to be jerked sideways. 'Th-thanks again for grabbing me.'

'Sure you're okay?'

'Nothing another hot shower won't fix.' Soaking under warm water to soften her tense muscles had to be a good idea. As long as she could get her clothes off over her head. Her arm was pounding and moving it only aggravated the aches.

'Or a stiff drink,' Lachlan added.

'That also sounds like an ideal remedy.' Might be better than the shower, because then she'd still be with Lachlan.

The hotel receptionist looked up as they entered the front door. 'Hello, Dr McRae, and Miss Simmons. Have you had a nice night?'

I've had better.

Then again, sharing a meal with Lachlan at the club had been pretty darned good. So relaxed and easy.

'It's been great, thank you.'

'That's good. We like guests to enjoy Phnom Penh when they stay here.'

'At least she didn't say guests should have new experiences,' Lachlan chuckled as he kept the elevator door from closing as Tilda stepped inside.

'Your first time being thrown out of a tuk-tuk then?' she asked. Then laughed and couldn't stop, gulps of laughter bumping up her throat and over her tongue.

'Tilda? Hey, take a deep breath. You're in shock.' He stood before her, holding her upper arms. 'Come on. Breathe in slowly.'

He must think she was hopeless. Might even be wondering how she managed to remain calm in the difficult situations nurses often encountered.

'Sorry,' she gasped. 'I'm fine, really.' She took a deep breath before continuing. 'It's catching up with me. That's all. I keep seeing the road racing towards me before you grabbed me.'

'The same pictures are flashing before my eyes too.' He was staring down at her, his eyes locked with hers.

All laughter vanished. Instead, she was overwhelmed with a sudden need to replace that vision of the road with something warmer, kinder, pain-free. She pressed into his hands still holding her, her head spinning, her breathing slowing. 'I...'

Need to kiss you.

Stretching upward, she began sliding her arms around his neck as though holding onto him would save her from the frightening pictures in her head. She wanted to obliterate the accident from her mind.

Lachlan lowered his mouth to meet hers, touching lightly at first then pressing into her firmly, covering her mouth, sending thrills of anticipation up her spine. His tongue came into her mouth, met hers, caressed. His lips owned hers. She kissed him back with everything she had, and her head spun as she tried to taste more of him. To feel his heat in her mouth. To be one with him. To forget a lot of things from the past. To—

What was she doing? Jerking back, she dropped her arms to her sides. A mortified flush bloomed on her cheeks. 'I'm so sorry!'

The elevator rattled and shook, bumped to a halt. The door squeaked open.

Lachlan loosened his grip on her. 'Tilda? It's all right. It's not every night we get thrown out of a tuk-tuk.'

Tilda. Her head shot up and she stared at him. He'd used her abridged name often. Only those she was close to called her Tilda. Yet she'd told him to use it when they'd only just met. Tilda sounded more special than ever in his deep, sexy voice.

She stepped out of the elevator while digging into her bag for her room key.

He took the key from her shaking fingers. 'I'll clean those abrasions for you.'

A bucket of cold water would've been more useful than that calm voice of his. She'd lost control, he hadn't, and now she needed to get back to how it had been before. They were going to be working together, not having a hot but short fling.

'I can manage, thank you.' She grabbed the key back off him and hurried to her room.

Idiot, idiot, idiot.

CHAPTER THREE

TILDA ROLLED OVER and stretched. She touched the other side of the bed. Empty. Good. She had walked away in time before she'd done something even more stupid. Though how she'd resisted the temptation to ask him back to her room when that kiss had been so intense and exciting she wasn't sure.

Lachlan was not the right man for a fling when they'd be working in the same team over here. The accident had brought them together. Work should keep them apart, other than as doctor and nurse. The thing was, she already liked being with him. They were relaxed together and that was enough. Except she'd gone and embarrassed herself last night by throwing her arms around him and kissing him. How would he react to her this morning?

Sitting up too fast, she groaned as aches fired up, letting her know she hadn't come out of yesterday's accident totally unscathed. Her upper arm was colourful and a little swollen where she'd skidded across the road. She was sore where the skin had been scraped off and there were other aching bruises on her hip and leg, but nothing major. The consequences could've been a lot worse.

Her phone pinged as a text came in.

I'm heading to the airport to pick up Dave. Will let you know when I'm coming by the hotel to collect you. Make the most of the break. We've got surgery this afternoon. Lachlan.

Nothing short about his message. A little smile curved her mouth. He was rather gorgeous, even when she wasn't looking for a man to get all up close and personal with.

She decided she wouldn't even think about last night. At least she hadn't talked too much about herself or exposed her heart and the dreams for her future. But then she never did—other than to James, and look where that had got her. Her dreams for the future were in lockdown, and they were staying there. She so wasn't ready for a rerun of her marriage. Not every man was like him, but how could she tell for sure? She'd stuffed up well and truly once, and once was more than enough for her.

Still, she'd better answer Lachlan. He didn't deserve to be ignored because of her determination to remain single.

I'll be ready when you get back.

Right now a soak under the shower followed by coffee and breakfast were top of the list to get her day started. Glancing at the dishevelled bed, she laughed with a lightness in her chest that was new. Little more than twelve hours in Cambodia and she'd had dinner at the Correspondents' Club with a man who was rattling her a little too much for her liking, then she'd been involved in a crash and attended to a little boy who'd been seriously injured. If that was how this trip started out, what lay in store for the coming weeks?

In the shower, she soaped her aching body, unable to stop thinking about last night and being with Lachlan, then the accident. How was Phala? And his dad? Was there any way of finding out? She could wait until she got to the charity hospital since he worked there too, but she needed something to distract her from Lachlan.

'Where's the nearest hospital?' Tilda asked the receptionist when she went downstairs in search of coffee.

'The main one's a few streets away. Why—do you need to go there? Are you sick?'

'No. There was an accident with a tuk-tuk last night and a little boy called Phala and his father were hurt. I'd like to know how he's getting on.'

'I know what you say, I heard about it. I will find out where they are and let you know while you have breakfast.'

'Thanks.' It was strange not being able to make a call herself but the chances of finding someone at the hospital to talk to her in English, let alone tell her about their patients, were remote.

The girl came into the hotel café half an hour later. 'The boy is very sick, and the father broke his leg. He's with his son.' She handed Tilda a piece of paper. 'This is the hospital where they are.'

Tilda blinked away the tears threatening to slip down her face. What a kind person this girl was. 'Thank you so much.'

A text arrived. Lachlan.

Twenty minutes away.

Time enough to finish her coffee and eggs, and go upstairs to get her bag. Lachlan seemed as friendly as he'd been before the accident, didn't appear to be keeping his distance since her random attempt to get close and lose herself for a while. If he was willing to forget about it she could relax and enjoy his company, and get on with being a nurse working with him without feeling awkward.

'Stop looking for trouble,' she growled.

Her mouth dried when he sauntered into the hotel lobby a short time later. *Drop-dead gorgeous* came to mind. How well did he live up to that look in bed? It would be fun finding out...

For heaven's sake, Tilda, how are you going to cope for the next two weeks until he leaves?

With difficulty, she suspected.

'Morning.'

She'd manage—by being sensible.

'You look a lot more rested than last night.' His smile seemed tired. Or was that tight? Was her kissing him getting in the way of the easygoing manner they'd established before the accident?

Nothing she could do but get on with the reason why she'd come to Cambodia.

'I'm feeling great. Ready to do some work.' She'd paid for the room, despite being told the charity would take care of it. In her book, money donated to the charity was for the locals in need, not her. The girl on the counter had told her after she'd paid that Lachlan had done the same for his room. Another thing to like about him.

'I'll take that.' Lachlan reached out to lift the pack from her shoulder. 'You must be sore this morning.'

'Not too bad. You?' The aches were still there but nothing she couldn't handle.

'Great.'

As they headed outside she told him about Phala and his father. 'I'd like to visit and see if I can do anything for them.'

'I agree,' Lachlan said. 'Right now we need to get back to the clinic. Dave's plane was late landing and our patient's already waiting for us, no doubt getting more nervous with each passing minute. Be aware that often these people we're helping get very agitated about their operations.'

'Thanks for the heads-up.' It sounded like a different nervousness to what she'd seen with people at home, who were used to regular medical care. For the people the charity was helping, being in the care of foreign doctors and nurses might be a little frightening.

'I haven't forgotten what an eye-opener it was when I first arrived here. Thought I was done with surprises as a doctor. Got that wrong.'

He could admit to being wrong as well? *Go, Lachlan.* James was always right, no matter what.

The front passenger seat was empty. 'Dave's sitting in the back so you can get a good look at where we're going,' Lachlan said as he opened the door for her.

'I've been here before.' The man in the back of the car smiled. 'I'm Dave, by the way. You're Matilda?'

'Thanks, and yes, that's me.' Lachlan's arm brushed against her shoulder as she pressed past, making her feel like cheese melting into a puddle.

The car dipped as Lachlan slid into the driver's seat. The air rapidly evaporated as he shut the door and turned the ignition on.

'We'll drive past the palace on the way out of town. It's worth a visit. I went last week and would like to go back. You want to join me? And anyone else keen to go,' he added almost as an afterthought. Didn't he want to be alone with her? she wondered.

'You bet. If I get the time I've got a list of places to visit, including the palace.' First priority was working at the clinic but she'd been told there'd be occasional days when staff could grab a few hours for themselves. Having Lachlan for company would be a bonus. As long as they remained friendly.

'It's just around this corner,' Lachlan said. 'There—isn't that amazing?'

'Sure is.' The golden roof and spires were beautiful against the blue sky. The gardens were neat and pretty, the stairs leading up into the palace inviting. 'Wow, I've got to see that. But you don't need to go again. I've got weeks to do some sightseeing.'

'Sure, but if you change your mind and want a ride, let me know.'

That'd be a weak moment if she did, she warned herself. Staying safe and single was her new mantra. Tilda sat staring out of the window, drinking in all the sights that unfolded with every turn. People everywhere, vehicles vying for space on the roads, the Mekong on its relentless journey south.

'Maybe I should take up travelling permanently. This is fantastic.'

'You wouldn't miss home? Family and friends to drop in on whenever you wanted some company?'

There weren't a lot of friends to miss. She'd run solo most of her life. While in Toronto she'd been putting her marriage behind her, not moving on. She hadn't missed James at all. Seemed her marriage hadn't been what she'd believed and the freedom in realising that had given her the strength to live on her own while staying in touch with everyone who mattered.

'I don't really call anywhere home.'

'You don't have a home of your own? Nowhere in Vancouver?' Lachlan pressed.

'No.' She wished he'd stop asking questions. They made her uncomfortable.

'Are you returning to Vancouver after this spell here?' He wasn't giving up.

'Depends on where I land my next job.'

'Hmm.'

She waited for more but Lachlan was suddenly not very forthcoming. She shrugged.

A snore came from the back seat. Dave was out for the count.

'I've bored him to sleep.' Tilda smiled with relief. She didn't want everyone knowing she'd become a bit of a wanderer, and that she had no reason to settle in one place any more now that her grandmother had passed, no other family to stay close to. Her one close friend was taken up with the love of her life at the moment and she wasn't going to intrude on them and spoil things. 'Where's Dave come from?'

'Florida,' Lachlan replied as he concentrated on the car in front, which appeared determined to squeeze through a gap only wide enough for a bike. He winced. 'Only in Asia.'

'You think?'

'I'm guessing. You going to get behind the wheel over here?'

'I doubt it.' She'd far prefer to pay a local or go with Lachlan. He handled driving here with aplomb. Did he handle his plastic surgery cases the same way? Of course he did.

'That's Boeung Kak Lake.' Lachlan pointed beyond the

road. 'There're places you can walk along the edge and get some great photos while you're at it.'

'I'll do that next time I'm in this part of town. When I get a day off.' It was taking a while to get very far. 'Walking might be quicker than going by car, though.'

'You're not wrong there. Here we go.' He zipped through a string of stalled cars and swung around a corner onto another road. 'This eventually takes us out of the city centre.'

Shuffling her butt further into the seat, Tilda watched out of the window, enthralled by the different lifestyle unfolding in every direction. People appeared to be constantly on the go, heading in all directions, laden with food bags or children or whatever else they needed.

'The girl I'm operating on this afternoon has third-degree burns to her hands and legs.' Lachlan brought her back to why she was here. 'I am hoping to relieve some of the tightness in her hands today and, if it goes well, next week I'll tend to her legs.'

She couldn't imagine Lachlan not making certain it went perfectly. 'That'll take some recovery time. Will she stay at the charity hospital the whole time?' They wouldn't be able to send her home until the risk of infection was all but gone.

'She's booked in for a minimum of three weeks. Her grandmother will stay with her until she's ready to be discharged. You'll get to show Grandma how to dress the wounds and what to look for in case of infection.'

'Do they speak English?'

He shook his head. 'Not a word, but there's an interpreter at the centre. Anyway, these people are very astute and seem to pick up on anything we need them to understand.'

They were moving along at a steady pace now and the traffic was thinning out, making it easier for him to negotiate his way. He seemed to know exactly where he was going, whereas she knew even if she came the same way once a week over the next month she'd still be none the wiser. Navigation was not her strong point. It was why she had maps galore and a GPS on her phone. Grandma had always teased her by saying she could be spun around in her own bedroom and still wouldn't be able to find the door when she opened her eyes.

Another snore sounded from the back.

She grinned. 'Glad I didn't fall asleep last night when you brought me in from the airport.'

'Think you could compete?'

'I hope not.' She was still tired after her flight and a night that hadn't contained much quality sleep, thanks to recurring images of being thrown out of the tuk-tuk and Lachlan grabbing her in the nick of time.

She glanced sideways again, this time admiring Lachlan's strong chin covered with dark stubble. He looked even better unshaven than he had with his smooth face last night. Sexy as. He was quite the distraction she didn't need. No wonder she'd thrown herself at him.

Squirming with mortification once more, she returned to watching the scenery, feeling a buzz at being in a country so different from Canada. Travelling was starting to look exciting, even when she knew she'd be spending most of her time working. Maybe because of that. Being a nurse was her ultimate career and she never tired of helping people requiring care. There was something so satisfying about seeing a child going from unwell or injured to upright and smiling, or an adult getting back on their feet, ready to face the world again after being knocked down by an accident or illness, and knowing she'd had a hand in that.

A yawn rolled off her tongue. More sleep required—when she had time. Sunlight spilled over her thighs through the windscreen, warm and comfortable. A dog ran across the road, weaving between vehicles, impervious to the danger it was in. She held her breath until it reached the pavement safely, then sighed with relief. Thank goodness for small mercies.

Someone was shaking her gently. 'Wake up. We're here.'

'I didn't snore, did I?'

Lachlan's ensuing grin didn't tell her yes or no.

'Suppose it means I'm boring if both my passengers fell asleep,' Lachlan chuckled as he lifted Matilda's pack from the car. No, she hadn't snored, unlike Dave and the noise he'd made. But to be so relaxed that she'd just drifted off seemed to prove that he didn't affect her the way she'd got to him. He should take heed. He wasn't ready to get close to any woman. Might never be. He hadn't yet let go of Kelly enough for that.

'Welcome to the centre.' Harry held his hand out to Matilda. 'Glad to have you with us.' Then, 'Good to have you back as well, Dave.'

Matilda shook Harry's hand. 'It's great to be here. I've been looking forward to this ever since I got the acceptance email. Thanks for the info pack. I looked things up online but it's nice to get first-hand knowledge of the area where I'm going to be.'

'You're welcome. I'm sorry about last night's accident. Glad you're all right. Lachlan filled me in this morning. Kiry and Phala are doing as well as expected.'

'Kiry was devastated his boy got hurt.'

'No surprise there, he's a devoted dad,' Harry said. 'Did Lachlan warn you you're up for surgery in a little while?'

Matilda grinned. 'No rest for the wicked, eh? Yes, he did mention it.'

Lachlan's toes curled at the sight of that wide grin. She'd had him wondering if they might become more than colleagues. Careful. A one-night stand was all well and good, but taking it any further than that was not going to happen. He might eventually want another relationship when he'd sorted himself out a bit more, but he doubted it. The fear of losing someone else was still too raw. Anyway, Matilda wouldn't be the right woman. She might be friendly, but she'd clearly been hurt by that horrendous husband of hers, and was probably wary of getting involved again, however briefly. 'I'll show you to your room and leave you to unpack before getting down to business in Theatre.'

They all headed in the same direction. The rather basic staff quarters were in a small block next door to the hospital. There were two wards, one for males, the other for females, one theatre and two rooms used for consultations and every other job required with patients. He waved a hand in the direction of a grassed area with outdoor seats. 'Those are some of our patients and their families,' he told Matilda. He was deliberately sticking to calling her Matilda this morning, even inside his own head. Tilda felt too intimate and intimacy between them was not happening, despite the persistent itch under his skin. 'They prefer being outside than in the wards whenever possible.'

Some of the people waved back. 'Hey, Doc.'

Lachlan veered over to them. 'Hello, everyone. This is Matilda, another nurse for you to get to know.'

'Hi, I'm happy to meet you all.'

Everyone chattered at once, then stopped and laughed.

The engaging woman at his side joined in the laughter. 'I'll learn a few words as soon as I can.'

'We say some English,' Kosal told her. 'Not lots.'

'Good. I'll try your language too.'

Lachlan smiled. 'Right, let's get you sorted.' And away from him for a moment or two while he got himself together. Matilda had a way of knocking him sideways when he wasn't even looking for a deeper connection to anyone.

An hour later he was again distracted when Matilda walked into Theatre dressed in blue scrubs, her shiny long hair tied in a ponytail swinging from side to side as she looked around the small but well-equipped room. There was nothing more bland than a nurse's uniform and yet his hormones were doing a frantic dance.

'I'm impressed,' she said. 'I hadn't expected such an up-to-date operating room. We've got all the equipment we need and more.'

'Due to very generous sponsors, I've been told.'

'Talk me through what's happening.'

In other words, cut to the chase. He could manage that. Bringing up the patient's file on screen, he proceeded to outline the procedure he was about to undertake. 'Charlina suffered burns when a pot of boiling oil was accidentally tipped over her. I want to make it possible for her to be able to bend her fingers again. I'll be taking skin from her buttocks to graft onto the fingers.'

'More scars to fix others.'

'Yep. No other choice, though. It's the downside to this work.'

She touched the back of his hand. 'But you're making things better for her.'

His chest swelled with pride, even when she hadn't said anything more than how it was. 'Thank you.' Right, it was time to get on with doing what he was here for. 'Tilda, this is Sally, our current anaesthetist. She's from Bristol.'

Matilda turned to the other woman in the room. 'Hi, Sally.'

'Hello. Right, are we ready?' Typical Sally, always abrupt and ready to get started. But she was good and he wouldn't want any other anaesthetist—if there had been another—for the operations he did here.

Two and a half hours later he had to say the same for Matilda. She was alert the whole time, never missed a step and had the scalpel or suture thread ready almost before he knew he wanted them.

'Start bringing Charlina round,' Lachlan told Sally. 'I'm finished. Well done, team.' He could look forward to working alongside Matilda over the coming fortnight. She knew her job and did it well. What else could he look forward to with her? He had mentioned going to the palace on a day when they weren't in here with patients. But what about going out for a meal one evening, just the two of them?

Hello? Lachlan? What are you thinking?

She was clearing away the needles and threads, scissors and used swabs. 'Charlina's going to be very sore for a few days.'

He agreed. 'Keep an eye on her pain levels and let me know if she doesn't improve.' Not that he wouldn't be checking on the girl regularly himself, but a second pair of eyes and ears never went astray. 'Her grandmother might talk to you more easily.' He was aware the older women that came to the centre were often wary of talking to foreign males.

Hands on hips, Lachlan stretched up on his toes to ease

the tension in his back that came from a long time standing over the operating table.

'You need a massage?' Matilda asked.

Surely she wasn't offering? An image of her hands on his lower back, her fingers rubbing and digging in, turning him on, filled his head.

He hurriedly wiped his mind clear before he embarrassed himself. 'There's a spa just along the road and they're very accommodating of us and the hours we work.'

'I'll check them out. Nothing beats a good massage.' She was suddenly looking everywhere but at him.

'I know what you mean.' Truly. A deep massage fixed a lot of kinks in his body, and after last night's crash there were some new ones to tackle. 'You seem to attract vehicular accidents.'

She blinked. 'Hope I've had my share of them by now.' Looking around, she asked, 'Is that it for today or do we have another patient lined up?'

'That's it, unless Harry has forgotten to mention something, and he's usually on the ball so I think you can safely head out of here and take a well-earned break.' He paused. *Don't ask. Move away.*

But his feet were glued to the floor. Words fell out, unimpeded by common sense. 'Want to go for a meal later and try the local food? Wat Danmak is a short walk down the road.'

Her gaze was intense as she looked at him. Over a simple question? Or was she weighing up whether she should spend more time alone with him?

He waited, his heart pounding a little harder than normal. Say yes. Say no. Matilda had got to him when he wasn't expecting her to. But then he had been thinking about her almost non-stop since last night.

'Nearly everyone will come along. It's something of a Sunday night ritual, to download the week with a few laughs over a wine or beer.'

Her smile was tired. 'Then I can't say no, can I?'

Pleased she saw it that way, he suggested, 'Go take a shower and unpack your gear, if you haven't already. One of us will come and get you when it's time to go.'

Her smile was thanks enough. 'Perfect.' With a toss of her head that sent her ponytail swishing across her shoulders, she headed out of the door.

'She fits in well already,' Sally commented.

'Seems to.' Yes, and here he was, wanting her to fit in well with him. When it had looked as if she might turn him down about going out to dinner he'd been reminded to be cautious, yet the moment she'd changed her mind, even if it was to go with the group and not alone with him, his heart had soared.

Showed how much Matilda was getting to him. Too much, too fast. He needed to pull sharply on the handbrake to keep these rampant emotions under control. Just the idea of a fling with her brought him out in a sweat. Sure he wanted one, but it was too risky. What if he couldn't walk away at the end of his time here and forget all about her? He'd have to do that, though. His heart wasn't strong enough to be broken again. What if Matilda's wasn't either? He couldn't do that to her any more than he could make himself vulnerable again.

CHAPTER FOUR

'MORNING, CHARLINA.' TILDA studied the girl curled up against her grandmother and smiled. They looked lovely together. 'How are you feeling?'

The notes showed the last time she was given painkillers was at six that morning. She told the interpreter, 'I'll get her something for her pain in a moment. Can you explain that I am going to change the dressings now?' She was due in Theatre in half an hour but first had to see to Charlina and another patient also post-op. 'Hold your hand out for me. That's it.' This multi-tasking gave a new take on theatre nursing as she got to follow up on how their patients were faring.

Charlina seemed to understand what was required without the interpreter telling her as she held her arm out straight. Apprehension tightened her face and she grabbed her grandmother with her good hand.

'It's all right. I'll be very gentle.' Unwinding the dressing, Tilda exposed the wound. It looked good. No redness or any new swelling to suggest an infection. After cleaning the area around the wound she smoothed on ointment and replaced the dressing with a new one. 'There you go. You're very brave.'

Grandma touched Tilda's arm. *'Saum arkoun.'*

'Thank you,' interpreted the woman standing on the other side of the bed.

'No problem.'

'Charlina seemed uncomfortable when I saw her earlier. How did you find her?' Lachlan asked when Tilda stepped into the pre-op room.

'It's more like a cupboard in here.' She laughed when her arm brushed Lachlan's back as she squeezed past. 'She was very stoic. Her hand hurts a lot so I've given her more analgesics, but when I changed the dressing she didn't flinch once. A little toughie, really.'

Lachlan was reading a file on the computer. 'You get a decent night's sleep?'

'What with the dog fight and those people having an argument outside the building?' It had been very noisy out on the street on and off throughout the night but she had still managed a few hours' rest.

He looked up at her with a wry smile. 'Better get used to it. I don't think there's been one quiet night in the time I've been here. That was a good meal, wasn't it?'

'Good meal, good company.' Just saying. Probably shouldn't have, though, in case he thought she was specifically referring to him, as she'd sat beside him at the restaurant. So much for keeping her distance. Her good intentions didn't work very well around this man.

His eyes widened slightly. 'I agree.'

She really needed to put the brakes on how much she enjoyed his company—and how her body reacted whenever he was around. Unfortunately, she just couldn't stop thinking about how sexy and good-looking he was, and feeling heated and ready for some fun.

'I love the food here.'

'It's not bad,' he agreed. 'Now, our first patient this morning is a thirty-one-year-old man, Dara, with a deformity in his calf muscle after an accident when he was in his teens. The original trauma was put back together too tight and over time it has got worse, making walking difficult and painful.'

'Thirty-one? He's lived with this all that time? That's harsh.' Her heart went out to the man she hadn't yet met.

'That's reality when you're living on the poverty line and have a family to fend for.' Lachlan stood up. 'Somehow he's slipped through the cracks until now. Probably too busy working and looking out for his kids to have time to see a doctor. He's also got a scar on his face I'm going to tidy up.'

Taking a step back from Lachlan, she drew a breath. He *was* too sexy. He tore at her resolve to remain only friends. Another deep breath. If she lifted her hand from her side she'd be touching him. She wanted to. Too damned much.

Turning around, she stepped over to the cupboards and found a set of scrubs to wear. Far more practical and sensible than touching the man who'd tipped her sideways right from the get-go. She could not afford to ignore how James had changed towards her over time. Passion was all very well, but it was the rest of what relationships involved that usually caused the heartbreak.

'Glad he's come to the centre. You'll make things so much easier for him, and he'll be better-looking too.'

'He won't believe what's happened when he tries to walk again,' Lachlan agreed.

'Have you got a physiotherapist lined up?'

'Harry has. She works in the city but does extra work here on the side for nothing. She's a local who trained in Bangkok before returning to her family home.'

'She sounds awesome.'

'No different to everyone here. Including you, with the way you have that relaxes your patients with just a touch or a word, even when they don't understand what you're saying.' He paused, seemed to reflect for a moment, then, 'You're so good at what you do, Tilda. It's early days working together, but I don't see you changing your approach to people.'

Which touched her like nothing had in a long time. Because Lachlan had said it? Perhaps. She couldn't imagine feeling as sensitive about those words if it had been another doctor saying them. But then she'd become so used to James putting her down for most things that for anyone to compliment her was like being given the best present ever.

'Thank you.'

Despite it being a compliment about her work, the excitement tripping along her veins had little to do with work and the doctor, and far more to do with the man delivering it. Did this mean she was opening up to the possibility of another relationship? Of getting close to a man again? Lachlan? Because no other man had made her even start to feel good about herself for a long while. Because she didn't let them. Hadn't been ready. That might be changing, though...

She repeated, 'Thank you.' For what? Being honest and kind? Or for waking her up to a future she'd given up on? Face it. Just because James had turned out to be so controlling didn't mean every man would be the same. Yes, but how did she trust her judgement after getting it so wrong with her husband?

A shiver ran through her, lifted the hairs on her arms. A glance at Lachlan and she was confused. He was a great guy, and this time she wasn't only thinking of his body and how sexy he was. He came across as honest and forthright, genuine and caring. Enough to risk getting closer to? To find out more about him? Not likely. The only way to keep her heart safe was by not putting it out there in the first place. She'd grown up independent, had been strong enough to leave her husband, so why change now?

Because I'd love to have the family I've missed out on so far. Such a short time in this man's company and she was already looking for that? *Give yourself a break, Tilda.*

'Time to get on with the job, Matilda.' He spoke in a steady, serious voice. Probably to bring her back to reality, because he must've guessed that she'd wandered off into a private world of her own. Hopefully he wouldn't realise he had a starring role in her tumultuous thoughts.

Grabbing a clean set of scrubs, she closed the cupboard with a bang. 'I'll be right there.' It was far too soon to be thinking about him like this. Any time would be too soon.

In the bathroom she ignored the persistent worries and ideas her brain was raising and quickly swapped clothes. It was time to go help change Dara's life. Her contribution might not be huge, swabbing and monitoring, but it all added up. So good, Lachlan had said. She hugged herself for a moment. Really? He'd sounded genuine. What was surprising was he had no qualms about saying it.

Sally was talking to Dara, who lay on the operating table when Tilda joined them. The interpreter stood next to her, explaining everything Sally said.

When they paused, Tilda said, 'Hello, Dara. I'm Matilda, your nurse for the operation.'

He blinked, his eyes full of worry.

She touched his arm and smiled. 'I'm going to look after you. I'll be with you when you wake up too.'

'Hello, Dara.' Lachlan had arrived, oozing calmness.

His patient instantly relaxed a little.

Picking up the syringe with a dose of fentanyl, Tilda said quietly, 'Dara, just a little prick in the back of your hand. Start counting to ten.'

The interpreter barely got the words out before Dara said two words, presumably *one, two*, and then nodded off.

'Good to go,' she told Sally.

'Onto it.'

Only the beeping from the monitors made any sound as everyone waited for the anaesthesia to take effect.

Watching the monitors, Tilda saw his heart rate settle, the peaks brought on by the man's fear quietening down. 'Blood pressure normal.'

'He's ready,' Sally said.

Lachlan picked up a scalpel. 'First I'll deal with the facial scar by making an incision to remove the old scar.' He didn't have to say what he was doing, but after yesterday, when he'd operated on Charlina, Tilda understood it was his usual way to discuss the operation with the staff working alongside him.

She liked that, liked knowing what was going on. She hadn't worked with plastic surgeons very often, and it fascinated her what they could do.

'Swab.'

She dabbed the area he indicated. Checked the monitor. Swabbed some more. Held a small basin out for the scar tissue. Swabbed again.

'I'm doing an incision layered closure. It takes time and is tricky—especially on the face—but gives the best result.'

Didn't she know it? 'He'll be like a new man.'

The theatre went quiet as Lachlan concentrated on repairing Dara's face.

Tilda watched closely as he deftly sutured delicate layer

after delicate layer, handing him needles with thread as he required. His fingers never faltered. What would those deft fingers feel like on her skin, winding her insides tighter and tighter with need? The moisture in her mouth dried. She had to get over this obsession with him. One hectic kiss did not change anything.

But it had made a difference to her mindset.

When Lachlan moved onto Dara's leg, time started moving again, and it wasn't long before their patient was wheeled out to the recovery room by another nurse who'd said she'd take over so Tilda could grab a drink before the next operation began.

'What's next?' she asked in general when she returned to Theatre.

'Ten-month-old with a cleft palate,' Lachlan answered as he scrubbed his hands under the hot tap. 'She's been sent here by a local GP.'

'Poor little tyke. What a way to start life.'

'We've got her early and will soon have her fixed up and looking good. Not to mention able to start to learn to eat normally for her age.'

The moment she saw little Bebe, Tilda fell in love. She was tiny and oh, so cute with big brown eyes watching every move anyone made near her. She didn't cry when picked up and placed on the table, nor when she was injected with a drug to relax her ready for anaesthetic.

'She's beautiful,' Tilda sighed. 'I could cuddle her all day.'

Her hand touched her belly softly. There'd once been a baby in there. Gone in a flash of pain and a load of anguish. It had broken her heart to lose her baby and she'd refused to think about having another. It had hurt too much losing hers to want to risk that pain again. Though that longing for a family had never quite left her, so perhaps one day she might step up and try to get pregnant again. Women had miscarriages and went on to see the next pregnancy through to full term. She couldn't deny she'd love to have a child to love and cherish and watch over as he or she grew up. To have a wonderful man at her side as well would be the best thing ever, but the chances were remote unless she let go of the past and moved on.

'Isn't she just.' Lachlan stood beside her, looking down at the wee girl with longing in his eyes. Did he have similar feelings to hers? What was his background when it came to family?

She hadn't a clue, she realised. Had he been married? Divorced? Children? Still married? No way. He couldn't be. He wouldn't have let her near him at the hotel if he was. Would he? Even when she'd been desperate to get over her shock after the accident in the tuk-tuk and prove she was alive and well, not lying in a hospital or morgue, she didn't think he'd have transgressed if he was in a relationship back home. He didn't seem the type to play around. But what would she know?

'Have you got children?' She had to know. Had to find out a little about him or she'd never sleep again.

'Not really.'

'Huh?' Meaning?

'Wrongly worded. I don't have any of my own. But I do have a lot, and I mean a lot, to do with my friend's three young boys. My best mate died eighteen months ago from a heart attack and I've become their male mentor and role model. Poor little blighters,' he added sadly.

Sorrow swamped her. 'I couldn't think of a better man for the job,' she said huskily.

'You don't know me that well.' His smile was wonky.

'True, but I can't see you as a control freak or you wouldn't be here. Nor can I imagine you're a mean, tough man who expects the boys to jump every time you speak.' Of course she had been wrong before...

'No, they've had enough to deal with without me adding to the pressures they face.' The vinyl gloves snapped as he pulled them on. 'Right, let's get this underway. The sooner we operate, the sooner Bebe is on the road to recovery.'

Personal conversation over. Fair enough. He'd given her enough to think about for now. But she still didn't know if he was single. He'd said *he'd* become part of their lives in a big way, not *we*.

'Fair enough.'

'Are we ready?' Sally appeared at the head of the table.

'Yes.' For once Lachlan didn't talk much.

She could go along with that. She was here to work, not focus on her personal life.

'Bebe,' she said, looking for any response. 'Out for the count, I'd say.' The monitor showed a steady heart rate, normal BP and temperature.

Sally took over, sending the wee girl into a comatose state. 'There you go, Lachlan. All yours.'

He picked up a scalpel. 'Swab her face, please, Matilda.'

They were underway.

'That was a long day,' Lachlan said to the room in general. It was after six and they'd just finished the last scheduled surgery. He was used to long days back in Vancouver, but here the hours seemed more drawn out. Probably because there were fewer medical staff picking up the odd jobs that always came with operations. Nor could he deny the stress from seeing these people's suffering that he didn't often come into contact with at home.

Glancing across the lounge room to Tilda, he saw her covering a yawn. Was it getting to her too? She hadn't held back at all when it came to looking after their patients.

'It seems busier than what I'm used to,' she agreed. 'Yet it's not really. Guess I'm still getting over jet lag.'

Harry opened a bottle of wine and began filling glasses. 'This might help,' he suggested.

'Or send me to sleep at the dinner table.' Tilda laughed.

Her light laugh caught Lachlan's breath. She *was* lovely. When he'd learned who he was picking up from the airport the other day there'd been an inexplicable flutter of anticipation in his gut he didn't understand. A flutter that was getting stronger all the time, despite him constantly reminding himself he didn't want another relationship.

'There you go.' Harry pointed to the glasses. 'Or there's beer in the fridge.'

Tilda took up the offer of wine, as did two other nurses and Sally.

'I'll have a beer,' Lachlan said. 'Anyone else?'

After handing round some drinks, he sank onto the chair furthest from the woman screwing with his mind. She was beautiful, inside and out. Her manner with patients, no matter their age or sex, was what he'd want if he was lying helpless in an operating theatre. Caring and concerned without being OTT. Genuine too. She'd obviously fallen for wee Bebe. A loving look had filled her face as she'd watched over her like a mother hen. There'd been a moment when she'd touched her own abdomen. He wasn't even thinking about why.

His heart squeezed. He and Kelly had discussed having

a family once their careers were established. If only they'd known what was coming they might've gone ahead and to hell with their careers. He mightn't have been quite so lost without Kelly if he'd had their child to raise. A mouthful of beer did nothing to soften that thought.

Turning to Harry, he asked, 'You think you'll ever go back home to work in a public hospital?'

'Funny you should ask. I think I'm about ready to give it a go again.' He stared at the floor between his feet for a moment. 'I went through a particularly nasty divorce a couple of years back and took on this position to give myself time to calm down and think about what I wanted for the future.'

Lachlan knew where the guy was at. Different reasons, similar results. 'Sometimes a bit of space works miracles on the mindset,' he said. It was certainly helping his. Even his heart seemed to be shifting, opening up a little—when it really shouldn't.

'Your head needs sorting?' Tilda chipped in, her cheeky grin firmly in place.

'Whose doesn't?' he shot back. But when he looked closer he saw there was a real need to know behind her question. Was that grin her way of hiding her pain from her broken marriage? Or was there something else disturbing her?

'True,' she replied, before sipping her wine. Then she continued, 'I feel as though I've left everything behind in Canada and for now I can get on with doing what I like best without worrying about the future—or the past.'

That was unexpected. Seemed she didn't mind being honest, even if it exposed her inner thoughts.

'I know what you're saying.' That was all he was saying on the topic. He'd said too much already. She didn't need to know about the pressures he faced back in Vancouver.

'After you mentioned there were jobs going, I've just applied for a theatre job at Western General. If I get it, I'll have to start looking for somewhere to live. I'd like to buy a place of my own now that the house James and I owned has been sold.'

He answered without thinking. 'There's always a spare bed at my place if you need somewhere in the meantime. Lots of them, in fact.'

Her eyes widened. 'You want to think about that first?'

See? She read him like a book. He shook his head. 'Not really. I rattle around in a large house and it would be good to have some company. Temporary company, I know, but the offer stands.'

She breathed deep, then smiled. 'Accepted.' Added, 'Thank you. I will get onto looking for a place of my own once I get home. If I get the job, of course.'

'I can't see why you won't.' And that wasn't because there was a shortage of decent nurses. He'd hoped she'd apply to Western G, and had already pre-empted her application and put in a good reference for her via his partners.

A light hue coloured her cheeks. 'Let's wait and see.' Then she looked around the room in general. 'Has anyone here been to Angkor Wat?' she asked.

'I have,' said Harry, sounding grateful for a change of topic. 'It's a bit of a trip to get to Siem Reap but well worth the effort. You can fly, which saves a lot of hassle on the road, but then you'd miss out on seeing so much along the way.'

'It'll come down to whether I have time once I'm finished here. I read that you've got to be careful of the monkeys. They have rabies, so getting bitten isn't wise.'

'That's true, but I don't believe it happens very often. Everyone's warned about the dangers, though there are those who think the monkeys are cute and want to pat them.' Harry laughed. 'Besides, you had a vaccination for rabies before you left home, surely?'

'I did, along with a load of other things.' Tilda turned to Lachlan. 'I'm thinking of going to see Kiry tomorrow when I'm not needed here. I presume he's still in hospital. His boy will be anyway, and where Phala is, I suspect Dad is.'

'Good idea. Mind if I join you?' Lachlan asked. Might as well get to know her better since they might be sharing his house in Vancouver for a little while.

'Of course not.'

'Take the car,' Harry told them. 'Go in the afternoon. The schedule's light tomorrow.'

'Thanks. I can start operating earlier in the morning to make up for it. The patients are already here tucked up in bed.' Lachlan looked at Tilda.

'I'd like that, as long as I'm not causing someone else to have to do extra duties in the ward.'

'Grab the opportunity,' Harry said kindly. 'Someone will want you to cover for them soon enough. That's how it goes around here. All work and no play is not recommended. I work on the belief that if our volunteers get to see something of the country they've come to help in, then later on they'll put their hands up for more chances to do the same.'

'Makes sense,' Lachlan agreed. However, he wouldn't think about 'playing' with Tilda. It was just about checking in on Kiry and his son to see if there was anything he could do for them. Nothing like playing but, come to think of it, any time spent with Tilda was relaxing and enjoyable, and yet at the same time she could wind him up something terrible. That kiss hadn't been relaxing at all. It had been intense and exciting, and probably wasn't going to happen again. She might be happy to spend time with him, as he was with her, but getting too close to one another mightn't be wise. If she did get a position back home at Western General then it would be best for them both to have maintained a purely professional relationship here.

Home. All the problems that he'd needed a break from rushed into his head, reminding him nothing had changed, that they were still there waiting for him. Maybe he should sign up for another twelve months here. Except that wouldn't change a thing. No, in less than two weeks he'd be back in Vancouver, dealing with everyone's persistence about him and Meredith getting together permanently. He knew Meredith was also struggling to stand up to the pressure from her parents. She wasn't a strong woman and desperately wanted someone to take charge of everything for her. Her parents would be ecstatic if they moved in together, as would his. Even when they were kids both sets of parents had wanted them to get married when they grew up. Neither he nor Meredith had ever thought it was a good idea, but with Matt's passing Meredith seemed incapable of fighting them about it.

Tilda was laughing at something Sally had said, a soft, rolling sound that filled him with a sudden longing for love. A love that wasn't conditional on anything, with no demands to do what someone else felt was right. A love that came with genuine care for one another, an understanding that each of them was entitled to be themselves while backing their other half in their life choices. Like he'd had with Kelly. And most likely wouldn't ever experience again. It was too scary to risk his heart again, now he knew how it could all go so horribly wrong.

A tune rang out. Tilda tugged her phone from her pocket and stepped over to the doorway. 'Hi, Janet. How's things? Andy bought you the sideboard? The one you've been hankering after for months? He's in love, for sure.' She was laughing as she talked.

Then Lachlan saw the laughter slip, only to return again a moment later.

'Me? Having a brilliant time. Great people to work with.' Her gaze flicked his way, then away. 'Yes, absolutely. Okay, it's not cheap phoning offshore, I know. Talk again. Bye.' She returned to her seat and picked up her wine, a furrow between her brows.

'All good?' he asked.

Her eyes widened. 'I don't know where Janet—my best friend—finds the time to go to work or fill the pantry, she's so taken with all things Andy. Long may it last.' She turned to answer something Sally asked, sipping her wine with a serious look on that exquisite face.

Lachlan turned away. The longing for more time with her refused to back off one bit. If anything, it had grown. Was Tilda a woman he could have another chance at love with? He felt goosebumps rise on his skin. It was far too soon to be wondering about that, he knew, but hope was a fickle thing. It appeared when he least expected it, and didn't go away when he wished it to.

A clatter of plates being placed on the table dragged him out of his reverie.

'Dinner smells delicious,' Tilda said as she stood up. 'I'm starving.' She looked strong and in charge of her life.

But he'd seen another side to her, seen the despair on her face when her husband had abused her for crashing his car, had seen the hurt at not being cared for, cherished, or even asked how she'd fared in the accident. Was her apparent strength a camouflage for what was going on inside that beautiful head? Was she anywhere near ready to move on to another relationship? Or had she sworn off men for ever? Of course that happened in the early days after a relationship ended, but from what he'd seen with friends in similar situations, it didn't last long. They'd all found new partners and were happy again.

Take note, Lachlan. You too can move on and be happy.

He shuddered. Not likely, with the loss of Kelly forever reminding him how even the strongest love could be shattered. Did that make Meredith's idea a better option? He didn't love her as more than a friend but if anything happened to her it would still be painful for him. No, it wasn't fair to any of them to marry her without love on either side. So he'd return to Vancouver and his career, and the little guys, all on his terms. He wasn't deserting the boys, but neither was he going to be their permanent father figure. Fingers crossed that the man Meredith had mentioned dating a couple of times lately might turn out to be right for her and the boys.

'Coming?' Tilda called from the other side of the room, a laden plate in her hand.

He laughed, putting aside everything but the here and now. 'You really are starving, aren't you?' This relaxed feeling came so easily when he was around her. It made him happy. He'd enjoy it over the coming days, and to hell with anything else.

As he placed a full plate on the table next to her, his phone pinged. Sitting down, he swiped the screen and saw a photo of the boys. They were laughing, and no doubt shouting, with their arms in the air as they leapt off the deck.

His heart melted at the sight of the guys. He did love them. Matt's lads were very special.

'You okay?' Tilda asked softly.

He held the phone so she could see the picture. 'My mate's kids.'

'Aren't they gorgeous? Wow.' She looked away. 'It must be so hard for them to lose their dad.'

'Sure is.' Another ping and another photo arrived. Meredith dressed to the nines in tight jeans and an off-the-shoulder blouse, a wide, determined smile on her overly made-up face. No, he wasn't being nasty about her, he was just over it all. 'His widow,' he told Tilda tiredly. Though why he'd shown her the photo was a bit of a mystery. He didn't want her thinking Meredith meant more to him other than as Matt's widow.

'She's lovely,' Tilda said, sounding thoughtful. Trying to figure out where he fitted into the picture?

'Matt fell for her in a blink.'

'I can see why.' She forked up a mouthful of rice and vegetables.

'She's been struggling to move forward since he died, and likes me there for her a little too much.' There, he'd put it out there. Some of it anyway.

Tilda took his phone out of his hand, and flicked the screen back to the photo of the boys. 'These are the ones who get to you, who've touched your heart. It was there in your face the moment you saw the photo. They're important to you. I might be wrong, because I know nothing about you and what's been going on, but I think they're lucky having you on their side. Nothing else is as important.'

Was it all right for a man to cry? In front of his colleagues? All over a few words this woman had said. Because she'd somehow got to the heart of his woes without digging for information. She seemed to understand him instinctively.

'Thank you.'

She shrugged eloquently. 'It's true.'

Shoving up to his feet so fast his chair crashed to the floor behind him, he swore. 'Damn it.' Tilda read him way too easily and he didn't like it. Returning the chair to upright, he headed for the door and air that wasn't tinged with Tilda's scent. Sweet with a little bit of sharpness. Tilda to a T.

Outside, the air was hot and stifling, vehicle and other smells real and unattractive. Just what he needed to get back on track. Matilda Simmons could not become a part of his future. He wasn't ready to let her anywhere near his heart.

Even if it felt like she'd already started knocking on it.

CHAPTER FIVE

'HELLO, KIRY,' LACHLAN said to the man stretched out on the hospital bed with Phala swathed in a small blanket tucked against his chest. 'How are you?'

Tilda watched Kiry's eyes widen and a lopsided smile begin to spread across his mouth. 'How's Phala?' she asked. It had been a busy week since the accident and today was the first time they'd been able to get back into town.

The smile faded. 'He's still sick. I'm sorry for crash. Are you hurt?'

'Don't say sorry. It wasn't your fault that other car hit the tuk-tuk.' At least she didn't think so, but then she had to admit she hadn't seen the car coming and was only going on what bystanders had told them at the time. 'We didn't get hurt,' she added.

'That's good. I worry.'

'Don't worry any more.' Lachlan stepped closer. 'How's your leg?'

'My leg break but already mending well. Phala much worse. His head hit and he sleeps a lot.' He twisted his head to look over to a small woman curled up on a mattress on the other side of the bed. 'My wife, Bopha.'

The woman blinked sleepy eyes. 'Hello.'

Kiry rattled off something in his language and the woman pulled herself upright.

'Hello.' Tilda held her hand out. 'I'm Matilda, and this is Lachlan.'

Bopha's hand was small in hers as Tilda squeezed it gently. 'Sorry if we woke you, but we wanted to see how your husband and baby are.'

Again Kiry talked to his wife, and she reached up to hug Tilda.

'My wife work here at night.'

And was sleeping beside her family by day. It must be exhausting, Tilda conceded. Not to mention what worrying about her little boy did to her. Lachlan had already talked to a doctor and learned Phala had suffered concussion and a small skull fracture. The good news was that he should recover relatively quickly with no serious side-effects.

She returned Bopha's hug. 'Can I do anything for you?' she asked instinctively.

Bopha looked to her husband, who spoke to her.

He interpreted her reply. 'You have been kind coming to see us. Thank you.'

'How long before you can work?' Lachlan asked him.

Tears welled up in Kiry's eyes. 'Few weeks to fix leg. Tuk-tuk broken.'

'Where is it? At a garage?'

A frown appeared on Kiry's forehead. 'Garage?'

'To fix tuk-tuk.'

'Ahh. Yes, at garage. But no fix. No money.'

Tilda's heart plummeted. These two worked so hard to make ends meet and now they'd lost one important source of income. 'Can—'

Lachlan caught her hand, squeezed lightly. 'Mind if I talk to him about this? Man to man,' he added quietly.

She got it. Male pride was important here. Whatever

Lachlan was about to say, it would be better coming from him. 'Go for it.' She moved nearer to Bopha, who was hugging Phala close 'He's lovely,' she said. Just as cute as the first time she'd seen him, despite the crepe bandage wound all over his head.

His big brown eyes followed her every move, his little mouth curved into a smile that sent ripples of longing through her. Why, here in Cambodia, were little children tripping her heart and making her wish for another chance to have a baby? It wasn't as if she was in a position to have a child. No permanent job, even if that would be easy to fix. No home—again, a little effort would sort that. She had some savings and although she couldn't afford to buy the place of her dreams, she could buy a small apartment for the two of them. No family to support her and love her baby. Her heart sagged. No easy answer to that one.

'Tell me where the tuk-tuk is. I'll go and see if they can fix it now,' Lachlan was saying. 'I will get it done for you.'

'No, not for you to do. I had accident, you and lady hurt.'

'We are all right,' Lachlan reiterated. 'No broken bones, no cuts or sore places.'

Phala chuckled when Tilda tickled his chin, careful to be gentle. When his mother held him out to her, she happily held him against her, his small, soft body tucked against her as though she was used to holding little ones so close. If only. This sudden drive to have a baby was a little overwhelming. Realistically, she wasn't sure she was even in a position to become a mother. She'd have to keep working should she choose to have a baby and she'd want to be at home with it all the time, but then other women managed to be single parents, so why not her? Choose being the operative word here. Becoming a parent needed to be thought about in depth to make sure she was in a position to give her child the life he or she deserved.

Lachlan's steady voice cut through to her. 'I'll see what needs to be done to the tuk-tuk. I… We—' he inclined his head towards Matilda '—we would like to help your family.'

Relieved to be distracted from her rather unsettling thoughts, she concentrated on what he'd just said. They hadn't discussed this but he'd picked up on her need to do something for these people. She gave him a nod, although whether he noticed she wasn't sure, as he was focused on Kiry. Was this why she was suddenly thinking about babies? Because Lachlan was touching her so deeply? It was a huge leap to go from feeling a little closer to him, to then having a baby on her own. A gigantic leap. One with no certain landing.

'So would other people at the hospital where you work,' Lachlan continued.

'No. We manage,' Kiry told Lachlan stubbornly. Kiry didn't know he was up against a determined man who she suspected was used to getting his way. How long before the father gave in? Her eyes on Phala and her ears listening to Lachlan and Kiry dispute the matter, she smiled and waited. Bopha seemed to be waiting too, though how she understood what was going on was anyone's guess.

'I know, but let us help.' Lachlan waited with the air of a man who would stay there all day, if need be.

The silence stretched out.

'I get nurse to write address for you,' Kiry finally said with a sigh.

'Thank you.' Lachlan glanced across to her and the child in her arms, and a smile split his face. 'He's beautiful.'

He might've said *he*, but she got the feeling he was including her in that comment. Or was that too much to expect? Whatever, she'd accept how his words made her feel warm and happy, and leave it at that.

'Phala's gorgeous,' she agreed.

'Do you mind if we go and see the mechanic who's supposed to fix the tuk-tuk while we're nearby?' Lachlan asked Tilda as they headed back to the car from the hospital, already guessing she'd say yes. She was just as invested in looking out for the driver and his family as he was.

'Of course not. Getting the tuk-tuk back on the road is important.'

'Exactly.'

'Want me to put the address of the garage in the GPS?' Tilda asked once she was in the car.

'Here you go.' He handed her the piece of paper the nurse had written the details on. 'Hope it's easy to reach. I don't fancy ducking and diving in this traffic for too long.' It seemed more chaotic than usual.

A pert eye-roll came his way. 'Pull up your big boy pants, will you?' She tapped the address into the GPS and ping, there it was.

As simple as that. 'How did anyone get around cities before GPS was invented?'

'By dogged determination and pulling their hair out.'

'That'd work well here when we don't know a word of Khmer.' Starting the car, he indicated to pull out and then went for it. It was the only way to get around here, he'd decided on his first time behind the wheel. Hairy, but it got the right results. Seemed the locals had six eyes in their heads because they usually managed to avoid banging into other vehicles. Hopefully they'd keep an eye out for him so he'd be safe. And Tilda. He didn't want her getting hurt again. She'd had enough knocks in the past year.

'In one hundred metres turn left.'

'Yes, ma'am.'

'In fifty metres turn left.'

'Onto it.'

'Turn now. Then in two hundred metres turn right.' The clear American voice continued directing him and within fifteen minutes they were pulling up outside a shed with tuk-tuks and cars parked in all directions.

'This looks like it.' Lachlan sighed with relief. 'Now to find out what's being done about Kiry's tuk-tuk, if anything. I presume you're coming in with me?'

'What if there's no one who speaks English?' was her answer as she opened the door.

'Then we're in trouble.'

'Hello, can I help you?' a man called out in English from the shed as they approached.

'Problem number one sorted,' he said to Tilda. 'Yes, we're looking for the mechanic who's got a tuk-tuk that was in an accident several nights ago. Kiry owns it.'

'I have it here. What do you want to know?' A tall, slight man sauntered across. 'It's badly damaged. It will cost a lot to fix.'

Holding his hand out to him, Lachlan explained. 'We were in it when it crashed. Can we have a look at it?'

'Of course. Come around the back.' The man led the way past other vehicles to the one they'd come to look at. Inside the large shed there were five mechanics at work on various vehicles.

'You're busy,' Lachlan noted.

'Always accidents on the road,' replied the man mournfully.

So much for thinking driving was reasonably safe if he just paid attention! 'I am constantly on edge when driving here.'

Beside him, Tilda gave a laughing huff. 'Now he says it.'

'Here it is.' The man pointed. 'See how the front is completely crushed in? That can be straightened but the strength will be compromised.' The metal frame had bent and twisted, underlining what the man said.

'So another hit at the front would have even worse consequences?' He hated to think how that little boy would fare then. The wrecked tuk-tuk gave him the heebie-jeebies just looking at it. An idea was already slipping through his mind.

'I can replace the whole framework but it will be expensive for Kiry. I am going to see him tomorrow and ask what he wants done.'

'He needs it to be repaired so he can get back to work once his leg is healed, or how else is he going to earn a living?' Tilda's voice sounded full of tears.

A quick glance her way showed he wasn't far wrong. She was a softie through and through.

Turning to the mechanic, he asked, 'How much to fix it properly?'

The sum he was given didn't help, because he had no idea if it was a good quote or not. Doing a quick calculation in his head, he then asked, 'How much is a new tuk-tuk?' There was a yard full of shiny new ones next door.

The man smiled and told him.

Again Lachlan had no idea if that was good or crazy high. 'Thank you. I'll do some research and get back to you.'

'Would you like to use my office?' The guy wasn't giving up easily. He had a living to make too and, despite the busy garage, he'd want every sale he could make.

Tilda had her phone out and already had information popping up on the screen. 'Nothing in English that I can find.'

'I'll ring Harry, get him to look up what I want to know. He can get the interpreter to tell me prices.'

It took a while but finally he had the answers he needed. 'I need to check that Kiry's okay with this before finalising the deal. I'll phone you tomorrow,' he told the garage owner.

They shook hands, and he headed back to the car with Tilda.

Lachlan held the door open for her, happy to be able to solve Kiry's problem for him. It might take a bit of convincing to get him to accept that this was the better way forward, but he'd leave that to Harry to sort out since he knew the man way better.

'Feel like stopping in at the club for a drink?'

'Yes, I do.'

As simple as asking. No hesitation for once.

'Good.'

So much for holding Lachlan at arm's length. Tilda sighed as they entered the club. She'd said yes without thinking and, to be honest, she was happy spending time away from the hospital with him. It had been a busy week, with the list of patients never seeming to get any shorter. She could go for a meal with any of the staff but it was Lachlan she most wanted to be with. For now she'd run with that and give up questioning her every thought.

'I'll have a water. What would you like?'

'Beer.'

Leaning forward, she gave the barman their order and sat back. 'What you've done for Kiry and his family is special.'

Those firm shoulders shrugged. 'No big deal.'

It was, but she knew when to shut up. Or what to be quiet about anyway.

'I can't imagine how hard it must be for them at the moment without half their income.'

'Very difficult, I'd say.' He picked up the glasses the barman placed in front of them. 'Let's sit by the windows and watch the city going by.'

Okay, so he didn't want to talk about Kiry.

'Good idea.' She followed him to a table overlooking the street below with the river beyond. 'Are you looking forward to getting back home? Seeing those gorgeous boys?'

He took a large mouthful of beer and set the glass down carefully.

A topic she shouldn't have raised? 'Tell me to shut up if I've touched on a sensitive subject.'

'Tempting as that is, I'll restrain myself.' His smile was tight, but it was still a smile, and directed at her what was more. 'I'm getting so much out of being here and the work I'm doing. It's been an eye-opener. In that respect going home will feel a bit like deserting the cause.'

Funny, but she had a feeling it was going to be much the same for her when the time came to board the plane headed back east.

Lachlan gazed outside as he continued. 'I came here because I needed to do something for myself. The past year and a half have exhausted me.' His chest rose on a breath. 'No, that's not true. I was shattered before that. My wife died two and a half years before Matt.'

Whoa. How much could a man take and not break apart completely?

'I don't know what to say, Lachlan.' She placed a hand on his arm. 'It's beyond comprehension.' His skin was warm, while hers was heating up. At such an inappropriate moment too. She gently removed her tingling hand.

'It was. Often still is.'

'I bet.' She sat quietly, leaving it up to him to continue talking or to leave it alone.

'I decided to take a little time out to come here so I might figure out what I want for myself in the future. I haven't come up with all the answers yet, but it's been good getting away from everyone for a break.'

'You look happy and keen to be doing things, like you've recharged your batteries.'

'I do feel marvellous. I get up in the morning smiling. It's been a while since I did that.'

'So what's the problem?'

His mouth flattened. 'Meredith emails and texts regularly, keeping me up-to-date with every little detail about the boys.'

'Why?'

'She wants more than I'm prepared to give. I thought me coming away would give her time to think it through. Focus on dating this other guy she's been telling me about.'

'What does she want from you?'

He drained his glass. Plonked it on the able, looked around, nodded at the barman before looking back at her.

'She'd like us to get married. It would make everything easier for her.'

Her heart thumped. No way. Talk about putting unfair pressure on him. But then what did any of it have to do with her? She and Lachlan had nothing going on between them. The fact she couldn't stop thinking about him night and day did not constitute a relationship. Just a messed-up head on her part.

'You're not keen on the idea?'

'Not at all. She's not my type and, if she's being honest with herself, I'm not hers either.'

What is your type? Down, girl. Wrong place and time for that question, if there'll ever be a right one.

'Why's she so adamant on marrying you, then?'

'She's a bit lost. Trying to pick up the pieces and keep moving forward is hard. We grew up with each other, saw one another all the time. Our parents are best friends,' he added. 'They'd all love it if we got together, and are adding to the pressure, which only makes it more difficult to get Meredith to back down.'

She grimaced in sympathy.

'That still doesn't make it right though. I'm just not interested in her that way.' He sighed. 'I've probably added to the problem by keeping a lot of things going in that household. Too much. But Matt was my best mate. He'd have done the same for my family.'

Tilda found herself sighing with sadness for Lachlan. To have to deal with this must be like walking a tightrope. 'What a position to be in.' Her hand was lying on top of his without her realising she'd reached out to him. 'Stay true to yourself, Lachlan. Otherwise it's a recipe for disaster.'

'I know. Still doesn't make it any easier. It doesn't help that our parents are backing her.'

'Stay true to yourself,' she reiterated.

'I intend to.' Did he realise he'd turned his hand over and was now holding hers? Was he being true to himself?

Or was that simply wishful thinking on her part? Whichever, it felt far too good. So she removed her hand and picked up her glass. 'Cheers to better things ahead for us both.' Her future career was at least looking up. 'I heard first thing this morning that I got that position at Western General. That was quicker than I'd expected.'

'I knew you would. Well done. Guess that means I've got a roommate for a few weeks at least.'

'You bet. I have looked at places to buy online but it's going to be easier to sort that out once I get back to Vancouver.'

'Take your time. The spare rooms aren't going anywhere. Are you looking forward to returning home?'

'Yes. It's time.'

'I'm glad for you.' He drained his beer and nodded to the barman for another one.

'Looks like I'm driving back to the centre tonight. Should be interesting.' She dug deep for laughter, needing to lighten the atmosphere. Now he'd told her about Meredith she felt defensive for him, and for herself. She liked Lachlan a lot. Possibly too much after such a short time, but it was how it was. Funny how she wanted to support him when she didn't really know him that well. It was an instinctive feeling, same as the one that told her she should trust him. That he would never be like James, demanding everything be about him.

'Hope you're good at looking out for all those vehicles that'll be coming at me,' she said when they got back in the car.

'It's a bit like walking through the traffic as you cross the road—stick to your plan, don't suddenly veer off in either direction and you'll be fine.'

It wasn't anywhere near as simple as that. Tilda held her breath as she manoeuvred between a tuk-tuk and another car, and still couldn't relax her lungs as a woman walked out in front of the car. Eyes right, left, right, steer left, straighten, steer left again, straighten.

'You've got this.' Lachlan was back to being relaxed. 'You're a natural.'

'You think? I'm shaking.'

'We're still in one piece, and once you turn the next corner the traffic will thin out.'

'What corner? Which side?' Her head spun one way, then the other. 'Tell me.'

'Easy.' His hand touched her thigh, making her jerk sideways. 'Move towards the right. You've got about two hundred metres to the corner.' His steadying hand gave her confidence.

She could do this. 'There? Where that truck is turning?'

'That's it.' Lachlan was alternating between watching her and checking out the traffic ahead. There was laughter in his voice as he removed his hand.

Come back, she thought.

'You should be terrified,' she muttered.

She was. Though not quite so much now she was getting the hang of all this uncontrolled traffic. When in Phnom Penh, she thought and laughed aloud, pressing the accelerator harder. Then they were around the corner and she could see gaps in the traffic and wasn't being cut off from all directions. Her breathing eased and the thumping in her chest began quietening.

'I'm beginning to enjoy this.'

'Look out for that dog,' Lachlan said sharply.

They both jerked forward when she braked.

'Hell, and here I was thinking this was fun. Maybe not.' The dog was running between two cars and horns were blaring and arms waving. 'Don't tell me if it gets hit.'

Silence.

Oh, no. Please don't let it have been hit.

'He's made it. Now he's racing along the footpath.' Lachlan grinned and returned to watching the road. 'Next turning on the right.'

It might've become fun driving through the mayhem that was Phnom Penh's roads, but when she parked outside the clinic she heaved a massive sigh of relief. 'Phew. We made it back in one piece. Think I'll stick to letting other people drive me around from now on. I've probably grown a few grey hairs in the time it took to get here.'

Lachlan leaned over and looked at her head. 'Can't see any. Still looks dark brown and shiny to me.'

Her eyes met his, and again her breathing stalled. There was a heady mixture of caring and heat in his gaze. The need to kiss him, to be kissed in return, swamped her. 'Lachlan—'

'Shh.' He took her face in his gentle hands, his thumbs making small circles on her cheeks. Leaning closer, he placed his mouth over hers. His kiss was soft and warm, and then it wasn't. It became hard and hot, stealing the air out of her lungs and setting her heart alight with desire. Waking her up fast, underlining why she'd been attracted to him right from the start.

She sank into him, returning his kiss with all she had. It was so easy to give him everything. It was what it was, and she couldn't be more relaxed—and tense—as her lips felt his, her tongue warred with his. And her body heated up and tightened everywhere.

Then he was pulling back, locking an intense gaze on her. 'We'd better stop while it's possible.'

She didn't think it was. 'But—'

'But we're outside the clinic's sleeping quarters, and there's no way we can follow through without everyone knowing. That might not be the best idea we've had.' Longing was blazing in his eyes and going straight to the centre of her desire. 'Plus anyone walking by can see us and that might not go down too well with the locals. We are meant to be a little circumspect around here.'

Flopping back into her seat, she nodded. 'You're right.' But did he know how to get her going, or what? One touch of those lips on her mouth and she'd melted—needing him, wanting him, having to have him. Only she wasn't going to be able to do that.

Damn, damn, damn. They also couldn't do this when they were going to share his house for a while. Platonic was the only way to go.

'Tilda—' Lachlan's hand covered hers '—I'm really sorry. I want to follow through with more kisses and whatever else you're comfortable with, but at the same time you're coming to stay with me and we're going to be working in the same hospital, and that could get a little too intense for both of us.' He continued looking at her, and she could see his mind working overtime behind those intense blue eyes. 'It's probably for the best.' He sounded as though he was trying to convince himself more than her.

'I have no intention of getting deeply involved with you or any other man.' Though she knew very well that she'd already begun to wonder if she'd got that wrong.

'But…' The word hovered between them, filled with temptation.

He was still watching her. The tip of his tongue appeared between his lips, and then, as though he couldn't bear not to, he leaned back in and his mouth covered hers once more.

She froze. Damn, but she wanted to kiss him back. But

she also wanted to protect herself and walk away. Kiss him. Walk away. Kiss him.

He jerked his head back. 'What am I thinking? I've got to stop this. I've got enough problems as it is.' He elbowed the door open.

'So I'm a problem now?' she snapped.

He turned to look at her. 'Tilda—Matilda, unfortunately, yes, you are.' Then he got out, closed the door quietly and walked away.

What sort of problem? A good one? A bad one? Hell, he'd been talking about his problems at home and that had sounded bad. Now she was a problem, so that had to be bad too. Great. Tilda shoved the door open and leapt out. Her head was pounding with frustration and disappointment.

One minute they'd been kissing like there was no tomorrow. Turned out there would be no follow-up. Lachlan had called it quits on their kiss. The fact he'd probably done the right thing didn't make her feel any better. She'd wanted him. Longed to go to bed with him. To have hot, mind-blowing sex with Lachlan. She mightn't want a man in her life permanently, but she could spend the night with one for a few hours, enjoy some relaxation and fun. With this man in particular.

But it wasn't going to happen. That hurt. Being turned down stung. When it had no right to. Tomorrow she might be grateful for his action, but tonight she was peeved and hurt and frustrated. Tomorrow she'd agree with him, but not tonight. If they had followed through on that kiss it would only add an unbearable tension to their relationship. From what he'd told her about his home life, more tension was the last thing he needed. She could accept that, and support him as necessary. She could also feel sad and disappointed they hadn't succumbed to temptation. She was only being human.

'Damn you, Lachlan McRae. Damn you to Vancouver and back. You're not walking away from me. Not tonight.' Tilda ran after him. 'Lachlan. Wait.'

He slowed but didn't stop.

She caught up and grabbed his hand, kept walking at his pace. 'You're right. Neither of us wants a relationship. But we both want each other.' She could've gone on but was suddenly overcome with a rare shyness.

Lachlan remained silent.

'I'm not trying to force myself on you.' She hadn't got through to him; instead it sounded as if she was begging. She stopped and pulled her hand away. Tried to, but suddenly she was being swung into his arms and held tight against that solid body.

'You're right, damn it. I do want this.' His hot lips claimed hers, devouring her, making her knees weak.

Corny, but too true to ignore. Her head spun with the hot sensations swamping her. Pressing into him, she kissed him back like there was no tomorrow. Gave him everything she had with her lips and tongue.

Then he was pulling away again, his arms still holding her but not so close. His chest was rising and falling faster than normal. 'Damn it, Tilda. Where did you come from?'

'From a broken heart,' she whispered.

'Me too.' His hands fell away. 'We're rushing into this, Tilda. It might only be kisses, but when I kiss you I feel like I'm opening myself up to being vulnerable, and I'm not sure I'm ready to do that just yet. I don't want you to be hurt either.'

She got the message loud and clear. They were not following through on those blinding kisses. Not tonight. But she wasn't letting him go either. Not yet.

'I understand. It is a little scary.'

'You think?' His laugh sounded more like a bark as he took her hand and led her back to the hospital, and relative safety from her need to throw caution to the wind and leap on him, pull him to the ground and have her wicked way with that stunning body.

Lachlan was right about one thing. They could both get hurt. Neither of them needed or deserved that. But he was still holding her hand. Did that mean he wanted to follow up on those kisses and get closer to her, despite his misgivings? Only time would answer that.

She had to know more about him before giving into the longing filling her. A longing she was coming to suspect would take a lot to fulfil. A fling mightn't do it. If they even got that far. There was a lot more to Lachlan she had yet to learn, and that was needed to keep her heart safe from another mistake like James had been. She'd be an absolute fool to think another man wouldn't hurt her. She wanted love and a family so much that she was at risk of ignoring the clues and leaping right on in. There'd only be herself to blame if she got it wrong again.

'Time will tell.'

'It's been great working with you, Lachlan. I hope you put your hand up to volunteer with our charity again.' Harry raised his glass and everyone followed suit.

'To Lachlan.'

Tilda swallowed a large mouthful of wine and set her glass down.

To Lachlan.

She was missing him already. 'Time will tell,' she'd declared. But it hadn't changed a thing so far. The past week since those heart-stopping kisses had whizzed past in a blur of work and more work, with a few more kisses thrown in. Holding back the passion bubbling inside her had been the most difficult thing she'd done in a while. She had to constantly remind herself she wasn't ready to let go of the deep mistrust of men she still carried.

Lachlan hadn't been forthcoming in giving more of himself either, and seemed to easily rein himself in whenever their kisses got too intense. Now he was heading home.

He was talking to Harry. 'I most certainly will volunteer again. It's been a great adventure and I've got so much from it.'

Pick me.

Tilda shivered. He was everything she wanted in a man—if she could let go of the fear of making another mistake.

'No more than you've given.' Harry grinned.

Lachlan flicked her a quick hot look. Reciprocal heat flared in her cheeks. She reached for her glass to down something cool. So much for staying in control of her emotions. But then she hadn't been very good at that whenever Lachlan was around. Who'd have thought only a fortnight ago she'd be so easily flustered by him? She'd be lonely once he'd gone.

Sally was unpacking platters of takeout food.

'Want a hand?' She reached for a brown paper carry bag. 'Cheers.'

Time was flying past. Before she knew it the taxi would be here to take Lachlan to the airport and the next time she saw him he'd be her temporary landlord. Should've had a fling while they could. A short-term arrangement that would've finished tonight and at least she'd have satisfied the restlessness in her heart.

As the meal came to an end Lachlan came across to her. 'Come and join me outside for a few minutes before my taxi arrives?'

Breathing in that sexy male scent that was him, she nodded. 'Going to give me the rules for living in your house?' she teased.

He took her hand. 'I really wanted to have a few minutes alone with you without everyone else around.'

'Are you ready to go home?'

'Sort of.' His chest rose slowly on a long intake of air. Then he let it go and gave her a blinding smile that sent heat rushing to her toes and everywhere else. 'I should warn you that the boys and Meredith drop in and out of my place a lot. As though it's their own house, really.'

'That's fine, I understand. Is Meredith still pestering you to marry her?'

'A little.'

This Meredith thing had to stop. It wasn't fair to Lachlan. 'How will she react to me being in your house?'

'Probably won't make any difference to her end goal.'

An idea was forming in her head. Dare she put it out there? Chances were Lachlan would think she was crazy and immediately withdraw the offer of a room, but she badly wanted to help him. He deserved to be left in peace, if that was what he wanted.

The words fell from her mouth in a rush. 'Won't me staying there really make any difference at all?'

'I doubt it. I've been completely blunt in the past and it still hasn't changed a thing.'

'What if we pretended to be getting married? Say that's why I'm moving in?'

Lachlan stared at her, shock widening his eyes for a long moment. Then he gave her a small, heart-tugging smile. 'You're serious?'

'You're helping me out with an offer of somewhere to stay. I want to do something for you.'

'But pretending to be my fiancée? You'd really go that far?'

'It's more about how far *you're* prepared to go. It's your family and friends we'd be facing up to. Of course it doesn't totally fix the problem, because it would only be a fake engagement, but it might give everyone time to stop and think about what they're wanting of you. Or give Meredith the incentive to focus on the guy you told me about that she's supposed to be dating.'

The next thing she knew, she was being swung up in his arms as he spun her around the deck. Then he placed her on her feet and leaned in for a kiss. 'Oh, Tilda, you are full of surprises.'

'That's a yes then?'

'A very big yes. But if I—or you—change our mind before you get home then that's fine too.'

Her heart was thundering in her chest. What had she done? Funny how she didn't really care. She was stepping out of her comfort zone for Lachlan and it felt good. There might be no stopping the kisses and where they could lead once she reached his house, but that might be for the best. She could find out how she really felt about him. She shrugged off the insidious thought that she already knew and was making herself dangerously vulnerable.

'Tilda?'

'Yes?' Then she spoilt the seriousness by grinning. 'One day at a time, eh?'

He held his hand out, ran a finger over her lips. 'Done deal, Tilda.' There were sparks in his eyes as though he was trying not to smile too much.

Tilda. Her nickname sounded so sexy coming off his lips. A softening started expanding inside her heart, raising hope for more between them than just a room in his house. Because if they were pretending to be engaged then they'd most likely need to share a bedroom, wouldn't they? So maybe they should just go ahead and have a real fling? Get this desire out of their systems and move on.

'You're wonderful, you know?'

'Absolutely.' She laughed, feeling on top of the world. Then she suddenly sobered. 'Are we doing the right thing? It does seem a little OTT. I'd hate for anyone to get hurt by our actions.'

'You're helping me out of a difficult situation that just won't go away. I hope when we come clean and admit what we did, everyone will finally accept how serious I am about not wanting to settle down with Meredith. Honestly, I don't believe she really wants it either. It's just the easy option for her.'

Reaching up, she kissed him. 'Then we'll see it through and, who knows, maybe we might have some fun along the way.'

More kisses, because fiancées kissed their guys, didn't they? Even fake ones? She'd make sure they did.

CHAPTER SIX

Hi. How's it going over there? Been to see any other tourist sites? I miss the city and all the noise and smells. It's strange being back at work here after the charity hospital. More papers to sign off, for one. Looking forward to you getting here. Lachlan.

HE WAS? GREAT, Tilda thought, because she missed Lachlan far more than she would've believed.

Hitting reply, her fingers began answering his email.

Sally and I went out to the Killing Fields yesterday. Very confronting. We've got a lot of general surgery patients this week as that's the specialty of the surgeon who replaced you. Charlina was discharged successfully, so that's good. And Phala and his family are now back at home too.

My start date at Western G is the Wednesday after I get to Vancouver. I've got a very good deal with management.

Cheers, Tilda.

PS It's not the same now you've gone. Too quiet.

Not that Lachlan was noisy, but his presence always made her feel more alive.

* * *

Lachlan pulled on clean clothes, threw his dirty scrubs into the theatre laundry basket and headed out to the car park to call Tilda. With a bit of luck she wouldn't be helping with an operation right now.

'Hi, Lachlan. How are you?'

Just hearing that chirpy voice sent tingles down his spine. 'I'm great. How's it going over there?'

'Much the same, busy, busy. You know how it is.'

So she wasn't missing him too much. Whereas he hadn't stopped thinking about her since he'd boarded the plane out of Phnom Penh.

'Everyone's pleased you're coming to work at Western General. Seems your reputation as being cool and calm in tricky situations has beaten you here.'

'Accepting the position was a no-brainer. Back in my home town and a great pay rate to boot.'

'So you're ready to settle here then?'

Say yes and we can have some fun together.

'Yes.'

He fist-pumped the air.

Tilda continued. 'Toronto was never going to be a permanent move. Nor anywhere else I might've ended up. I can't wait to find somewhere to live and unpack all the furniture and other gear I've got in storage. Could do with some different clothes too. Kind of tired of what I brought over here.'

'You'll have friends and family to catch up with too, no doubt.' The silence was suddenly deafening. 'Tilda? Did I put my size ten in it?'

'Not really. I don't have any family. My grandmother brought me up as my mother died in childbirth. Having me.' Her voice was low and sad. 'She never told anyone who my father was, and as she was an only child I don't have any relations that I know of.'

'I can't imagine what that's like.' There were times when his brother was a pain in the butt but he couldn't imagine not having him there to talk to and share a laugh whenever possible. Now that Ian lived in Quebec they mostly ribbed each other by phone.

'I'm used to it. My best friend and her fiancé live in Seattle. We met at school and have always been close.' A sigh came over the airwaves. 'Anyway, enough of that. Have the boys been pestering you?'

'Can't keep them away. They've heard about you and keep asking when you're coming to stay with me.'

'Really? You've already told everyone we're an item?'

'I bit the bullet at the weekend. Figured it would be easier for you if they'd already heard about our engagement before you arrived.' It hadn't been as hard to do as he'd expected.

'You might have to hold my hand through the meet-and-greets.'

'No problem. I like holding your hand.' He drew a breath. 'I'm missing you, Tilda. A lot. We got on so well it seems strange not having you around.' Maybe they could have a fling while she was here. He still wasn't sure he was ready to settle down again, but it seemed he was open to having a short-term relationship with her.

'Know what you mean. I miss not hanging out with you too.'

'I want to kiss you again.'

Her gasp came over the airwaves, sending a thrill of need down his spine. 'You do?'

'Of course I do. I can't stop thinking about those few kisses we shared and wanting more.'

A kissing sound reached him. 'Not quite the same, I know,' she said quietly. 'But I admit that it feels like I've been tossing and turning in frustration all night, every night. I can't get home soon enough.'

'Tell me something I don't know,' he growled.

Tilda put the phone down and hugged herself.

Tell me something I don't know, he'd growled. That had to be the sexiest voice she'd heard him use yet. Lachlan wanted to kiss her some more. And she was desperate to kiss him back. And follow up with something more. Her hands itched to touch his body all over. To feel his pulse under her palm, his heat against her body, his sex between her fingers as she rubbed him. To hear that sexy voice talking to her, his lips caressing her skin.

Her fake fiancé was getting closer to her by the day, more so since he'd left here. As if being apart was a catalyst to needing to be together.

Picking up her phone, she scrolled through the numbers and tapped Lachlan's. 'Just wanted to say I'm dreaming of kissing you right now.'

'Tilda…' He groaned her name out, sending longing sky-rocketing throughout her.

'Got to go. Talk again later.' She tossed the phone into her locker and headed into the ward to check up on a patient with a bounce in her step. It was strange how she and Lachlan seemed to be ratcheting up the tension and the desire to be together when they were so far apart. When he was here they'd kissed, and had begun to take tentative steps towards getting closer, but this was something else far more exciting. It was quite sudden how they were talking more intimately to each other, almost as though his leaving here had been what they'd both needed to see they cared for each other and wanted each other.

'When does your flight get in to Vancouver? I'll be there to pick you up,' Lachlan asked two days before she was due to leave Cambodia.

'I'll email you my ticket so you have the details.' Tilda sounded breathless. Keen to catch up?

He hoped so. There'd certainly been no hesitancy from her when they'd talked about kissing. He grunted a laugh. Their last phone conversation had been right on the edge of phone sex, only stopping when Tilda had heard someone call out for her.

'I'll be waiting for you.' No doubt impatiently.

He'd probably be at the airport waiting for her before her flight had even left the ground in Asia, he was so desperate to hold her in his arms. Almost from the moment he'd walked away from her at the charity centre he'd become more and more aware of how much he longed to have her in his bed. But that was getting ahead of things. So far they'd only kissed, and hinted at more, and yet now he couldn't imagine that not happening. His fake fiancée was coming home and he wanted nothing fake about their time together, however limited that might be.

'I'd better go. Dave's calling for me. Surgery's about to start.'

'See you on Saturday. Take care.'

'You too.' One of her squishy kiss sounds came through. 'Lachlan?'

'Yeah?'

'I can't wait to see you.' Click. She was gone.

Leaving his chest thumping and his head spinning with hope.

His finger moved fast over his phone screen.

Same back at you. xx

Lachlan stood outside the doors in the arrivals hall, tapping the floor with the tip of his shoe as he waited for Tilda. Two weeks never used to feel as long as the last two had. He'd been busy with work, and seeing the little guys and giving his house a lick and a polish for his guest, but each day had felt as though it lasted at least forty-eight hours long.

Where was she? Judging by the number of people coming out of Immigration, at least two planeloads of passengers must have disembarked since the arrival of her flight came up on the arrivals board.

His heart lifted. There she was, walking straight towards him with a wide smile on her beautiful face.

'You waiting for someone?' Her pack slid off her shoulder to land at her feet.

'You bet.' He wrapped her in his arms, making the most of that divine body pressed against him. Had he missed her, or what? Not quite how this was meant to pan out. Whatever *this* was.

Leaning back in his arms, her pelvis pressing into him was a reminder of how horny she made him feel with barely a touch. Then she looked up at him. That smile reached inside him to grab his heart so tightly he almost gasped out loud. Her hands were on his chest, making him just plain happy to be with her.

'Come here,' he groaned. His mouth found hers, and when she opened under his hungry lips he melted in an instant. 'I've missed you so much,' he murmured into her sweet, mint-flavoured mouth. Had she heard him? It was one thing to tell her over the phone, he discovered, but quite another to say it to her face.

Holding Tilda tighter, closer, he savoured her, his whole body smiling. She was home, with him, and he couldn't ask for anything more right at this moment.

Her mouth left his.

He leaned in to find hers again.

She tipped further back, her hands splayed wide on his chest now. 'Lachlan.' His name was rough and sexy on her tongue.

'Yes?'

The blue topaz of her eyes shone at him. 'I missed you too.'

She had heard him. Or was she reading him too easily? That was something she was very skilled at. From the moment she'd walked out of Immigration he hadn't tried to hide his feelings. He'd been too overwhelmed with the excitement of being with her to be able to cover his emotions.

'Let's go home. I think we've put on enough of a show for everyone here.'

Her laugh made him even harder. 'You think?'

Bending down to pick up her pack, he tweaked his trousers, then slung the pack over one arm so it fell in front of him. With his other hand he reached for Tilda's. 'Your ride awaits.'

'Not in a tuk-tuk, I hope.' Her smile further ramped up the need in him.

'Don't tell me you've already had enough of those?'

'I never really felt comfortable in them after my first experience. Kiry took me and Sally to town in his brand-new tuk-tuk one day as a way of saying thank you for chipping in to buy it, and I couldn't relax entirely. He still had his lower leg in a cast!'

'Everyone put money towards it.' Kiry was popular with the staff and, as Lachlan had expected, they'd refused to hear of him buying it for the man on his own. Something he'd totally understood because he'd have done the same if another person had come up with the idea. 'Has he been giving them all free rides?'

'Each and every one of the staff. I had to take a second ride for you. Kiry said we were in the accident together, we should have to ride together, and since you weren't there I got two goes.' Tilda shivered. 'I chose somewhere very close to the hospital for the second one.'

Lachlan leaned in and brushed a kiss on her cheek. 'I owe you.'

Her finger ran along his bottom lip. 'I'll take it out of your hide. It hasn't been the same since you left. Not for me anyway. The one highlight was seeing little Phala pretty much fully recovered.'

He grinned. 'I bet. I'm thrilled the little guy is better.' He was glad to hear how much she'd missed him too. Somehow, it gave him the confidence to go forward with their plan. 'Let's get out of here.'

Her smile widened into a full-blown hello, great to see you look.

Did this mean they would continue having a great time together for a little while? Have a fling of epic portions? Or risk becoming more involved?

Digging a bigger hole to get out of when our time is inevitably up, warned the sensible side of his brain.

Even if it only ended up being a fling, it would still be

devastating when it ended, he suspected. But right at this moment it seemed he couldn't care less. He was so glad to see Tilda and to be able to touch her, hear her laugh and chatter away happily. Tomorrow was another day for the worries to resurface.

As they headed into the city Tilda said, 'Thanks for the upgrade to first class. I had the best sleep I've ever had on a plane. Couldn't complain about the service either,' she said with a laugh.

'Guess that means you won't be falling asleep as soon as we get home.'

She faked a yawn. 'Want to bet?'

His fingers drummed on the steering wheel as an image of Tilda in his bed filled his head.

Whoa. Slow down.

But hell, he'd missed her so much more than he'd have believed possible. He wanted her. In all ways possible.

Again, slow down.

They had to be so, so careful.

Tilda breathed deep, relishing the scent that was Lachlan. Bumps rose on her forearms and her fingers tightened as she fought the urge to reach over and grip his thigh, to feel his heat under her hand. He might pull over and leave her on the side of the road if she did that, although after their last few phone conversations and the welcome she'd received at the airport she somehow doubted it.

When he'd hauled her into his arms and kissed her senseless when she'd walked up to him in the terminal she'd known where she wanted this to go. And suspected he felt much the same. He'd got horny—fast. Yes, she'd noticed. Hard not to. She laughed at the corny pun. Hard. Yep.

He wanted her all right. She wanted him too. All caution seemed to have been hurled to the wind.

His thigh was tense under her palm.

She pressed it a little harder. Her fingers clung to the taut muscles. Her mouth dried while her heart rate hit the roof.

How far was it to his house? She knew how to get to his suburb but had no idea how long it took. Only that it would be too long. A tense, teasing, long time.

Lachlan gently lifted her hand away and placed it back on her lap. 'I've got to concentrate.' His voice came out all husky and low and upped the level of heat in her core to what felt like volcanic proportions. It was nothing like she'd heard from any man before.

'Sorry.' She wasn't really. He hadn't thrown her out of the car. She was only sorry it was taking for ever to get wherever they were going.

'Don't be.' He leaned forward as though to focus on the road and ignore her. But then he gave her a quick glance and that beautiful mouth curved into the most tempting smile, and she relaxed.

A little. Not so much that the pounding in her chest disappeared, but she could sit back and watch him as he drove. As long as he broke every speed limit on the way.

What had happened to change everything so fast? When they'd kissed before she'd wanted him, but not like this. Not with the feeling that if she didn't have him she'd shatter into a million little pieces. Two weeks without seeing Lachlan, only hearing him talking in that low, nerve-tingling voice, and she'd been hot for him the whole time. Then the moment she'd set eyes on him again today she was completely lost. It was something to think about, but not now. That would be impossible. Thinking of anything sensible at all seemed beyond her.

If only she could touch his stubble with her fingertips. But the last thing she needed was to distract him and be in another car accident.

It was going to be strange walking into his home as his fiancée, staying until she found a place for herself, though she supposed that might change in the short-term if they started a fling. When Lachlan had gone home she'd begun to realise just how badly she wanted him. The worry that she might be making a big mistake still remained, as did the concern that he might hurt her more the deeper in she got. Yet not seeing him every day had been pure torture.

What did he feel about her? Before he'd left Cambodia he'd told her he wasn't interested in getting into a relationship. She'd said much the same in reply. She'd meant it and still felt that way. They might be hot for each other, but that was a whole different ball game to thinking about anything permanent. Apart from kisses and sex, because sex was foremost in her head at the moment. She wasn't ready for anything more.

But, whatever played out between them, she had a role to play in his life at the moment. For the first time she wondered if she'd taken on more than she could deal with by pretending to be engaged to him. The ending could hurt if she let these new feelings of want for him take over. So the sensible answer was to keep the brakes in place and enjoy whatever unfolded slowly. She could stand up and be accountable for her own needs while giving back something to the man who'd inspired these feelings in her. Starting with making love. Yeah, well, if he didn't hurry up, she was going to explode with need before they got to his house.

Finally, when it felt as though she was just about to expire from sheer frustration, Lachlan turned into a driveway and drove up into a garage, barely waiting for the door to lift high enough to go under.

He pressed a control hanging from the sun visor to close the garage behind them. As he braked and turned the engine off he was already reaching for her to start kissing her hard and deep. How had he managed to drive with all that passion simmering in his veins?

Glad they'd made it, she kissed him back without reservation. This was what she'd been looking for, wanting so badly.

'Tilda, we'd better get out of the car before one of us gets bruised.' The gear stick was digging into his thigh.

Her seatbelt was uncomfortably hard against her breasts. Without pulling her mouth away she felt behind her for the door handle, then opened the door and abruptly jerked upright. 'Come on.'

They met again at the front of the car, eyes only for each other, hands reaching out. Then Lachlan was grabbing one of hers and racing her through the internal door into the house, where he headed for the sweeping staircase.

They were all but running. Tilda held his hand tight, not wanting to lose touch with him for a second.

'In here,' he gasped at the top of the stairs as he turned them into a big room with a massive bed beckoning.

'Pinch me,' she whispered as she slowed. She'd never seen a bed so big.

'Let's go for a kiss instead.' Lachlan was already holding her face gently and lowering his mouth to hers.

'Any time you like,' she replied softly, before stretching up to wind her arms around his neck and hold on. Her legs were running out of strength as desire soared through her, and the last thing she wanted was to land on her butt on the floor. 'Lachlan.' She breathed his name slowly.

'Tilda, slow down. You're winding me up so tight I'm going to lose control and it'll all be over in a minute. And that's the last thing I want.'

He scooped her up in his arms and turned for the bed, where he laid her down with excruciating slowness, kissing her neck and driving her insane with need for him.

'Lachlan,' she gasped through a haze of longing. Her fingers were clumsy as she worked on the buttons in front of her, trying to focus so she could last longer than a few seconds. Her body was crying out for him, for release with him inside her.

'Let me.' He tugged his shirt over his head and tossed it aside, exposing the wide muscular chest she'd only felt under her palms and through his shirt when they'd kissed before. She traced his muscles, feeling his hot skin, wanting, wanting, wanting more.

'Can I remove your blouse?' His voice was husky with passion, his eyes dark with lust.

She pushed up and began to pull her top over her head.

'I'll help…' His hands replaced hers on the blouse and as he removed it he leaned in to place a line of kisses from her waist up to her ribs, to first one breast, then the other.

She was crying out with the sweetness and the agony of it all. Bring it on. 'I can't last, Lachlan.'

'Yes, you can.' Fingers flicked her nipples, and then his mouth headed south, licking, kissing, over her stomach and on down to her womanhood. Her legs trembled and her hands were fists at her sides and her back was arching upward in agonised ecstasy.

'Take me, Lachlan. Now. Please,' she begged.

He replied with a hard stroke of his tongue.

She shuddered. Unable to wait any longer, she slipped under his body and exhaled with the thrill of his weight on top of her, the feel of his blood pounding through his veins.

'No, Tilda. Let me bring you to the brink first.'

'I'm already there.' She moved her hand down his hot, hard length and then squeezed him gently.

His eyes widened, his face tensed and then he gasped, 'Hang on. Condoms are on the bedside table.'

Oh, yes. Rolling a condom down that hard shaft was as good as anything so far, her fingers played with him, teasing all the way.

Then he was taking her hands away and plunging deep inside her, pulling back to push in gloriously again, and again.

Tilda's body tightened as waves of desire rocketed between them, and she cried out as she shattered into a million pieces. She also felt whole again for the first time in a long time.

'Where is she?' Lachlan's mother strode into the kitchen an hour later, his father right on her heels. 'I want to meet this woman who's put a smile on my son's face.'

'Tilda's having a shower, Mum.' Sometimes he wished they didn't have an open home policy where the family came and went as they pleased. To be fair, there'd never been an issue before, but what if his parents had turned up thirty minutes ago? That would've been awkward.

His mother walked over to the door and tilted her head as though listening to something. Then she smiled again. 'Your en suite shower, by the sound of it. You haven't wasted any time, then.'

I'm thirty-seven, damn it, he thought moodily. *Not a kid needing supervision.*

'We'll see,' he muttered. He wasn't quite sure where he and Tilda were at after that mind-blowing sex. It couldn't be a one-off. No, it wouldn't. From her response, there'd surely be a lot more where that came from.

His mother walked past, patting him on the arm. 'I'll make some coffee while we wait.'

He should've warned Tilda his mother could be a bit OTT when it came to her son, and now he was supposedly engaged she wouldn't be quiet about it. Apparently, he'd never stopped smiling since arriving back from Cambodia, which had her overly excited. He felt his mother was exaggerating. He admitted he was happier than he'd been when he'd left to go to the charity hospital, but hardly enough to suggest anything deep and meaningful was happening here just yet. Only great sex. But there was some truth in the fact Tilda had changed him and made him see there could possibly be a future for him at some point that involved love, and even a family, even if it wasn't with her.

Big step there, Lachlan.

True. The fear of losing another loved one still gripped him when he wasn't being careful. So slowly, slowly was the only way to go. How about going back to bed with Tilda— after he'd sent his parents packing and locked the doors?

Need to change the locks for that to work.

'See? He's daydreaming again,' his mother said with a laugh.

'Give the man a break,' his father grunted. 'He doesn't need his mother interfering in his love life.' He winked at Lachlan.

'Oh, hello.' Tilda stood in the doorway, looking hesitant.

'Hey, Tilda, these are my parents, Faye and John.' He crossed to be with her, to show solidarity. After all, Tilda had come up with the fiancée idea to support him.

'Hello, Tilda, nice to meet you.' His mother gave her a quick hug before stepping back, sussing out the woman before her. 'This is a bit of a surprise for all of us, I have to say.'

Tilda blinked, then smiled, looking almost at ease. 'For both of us too.' She turned to his dad and held out her hand. 'Hello, John.'

'Welcome home,' his dad said with a cheeky smile.

Parents. Lachlan grimaced. Had he really been such a sad sack for so long that these two were so desperate to see him happy again they'd go along with anything he did? It had been devastating losing Kelly, and then Matt, but surely he'd managed a few laughs in the intervening time?

'It's been a bit sudden, you two meeting and getting engaged,' his mother commented pointedly.

'We first met a year ago,' Lachlan said to throw her off the scent.

'You did?'

Tilda blinked, then straightened her shoulders. 'Yes, but I've been working in Toronto for a lot of that year.'

'I see.' It was obvious his mum didn't, because he'd never mentioned Tilda before returning from Cambodia. No reason to when he hadn't expected to meet her again.

'How do you like your coffee, Tilda?' his mother asked.

'White, no sugar, thanks.'

'I hear you're starting work at Western General this week,' John said. 'You're going to be in the same area of the hospital as Lachlan.'

'Small world, isn't it? But then I think Lachlan might

have had some influence there, though he's denying it, of course.'

Lachlan shrugged. 'The department's been looking for a really top-notch theatre nurse for a while. There's a nationwide shortage at the moment.'

'Top-notch, eh?' His father grinned.

This was getting worse by the minute. 'Mum, Dad, back off, will you? At this rate you'll scare Tilda away.'

His mother passed Tilda a mug of coffee. 'I see you haven't got an engagement ring yet.'

Another blink from Tilda. 'We'll get around to that once I've settled in here and at work. There's no hurry.' She gave him a desperate look.

It was only supposed to be a temporary situation. Why would they have thought about getting a ring?

'That's something we'll do when we're ready. It's meant to be a special time and I'm not dragging Tilda to the jeweller's while she's still getting over jet lag and unpacking her belongings from the storage unit she's using.' Lachlan put an arm around Tilda's shoulders and drew her closer.

His mother smiled softly. 'You could wear Lachlan's grandmother's ring in the meantime, Tilda. It's a diamond solitaire. Quite beautiful, and it needs to come out of the box where it's lain for a few years.'

Tilda tensed a fraction. 'Um…thank you, but that won't be necessary.'

'My family do like to interfere in my life,' he told her with a tight laugh. 'We'll talk about it later, Mum.'

Tilda looked up at him and smiled. 'It's okay. I understand they want you to be happy.'

'We do,' his mum agreed. 'It's been a long stretch since

he was, and so it's natural to think you are the cause of those smiles.'

His father cleared his throat. 'We'd love you to come to the charity lunch we're putting on at our home in a fortnight, Tilda. No doubt Lachlan would be bringing you anyway, but I'm making it an official invite. We do this once a year to raise funds for children with leukaemia. I'm a pathologist, by the way.'

'Hence the charity.' Tilda nodded. Her shoulders lifted as she drew a breath. 'Thank you for the invitation. I'd love to come, though I'll need to find a suitable outfit. I take it this won't be a casual affair?'

Not within an inch.

'We'll talk about that later too.' Next thing, his mother would be offering to take her shopping and that might lead to more problems. His mother's idea of where to shop for clothes was nothing like what he'd seen of Tilda's wardrobe so far. But then she might have a load of expensive outfits in that lockup where her things were stored. There were still a lot of things he didn't know about this wonderful woman. But he was going to enjoy finding out, if his parents didn't scare her off first.

His mother opened her mouth.

He shook his head warningly at her.

She closed her mouth and went back to making coffee for the rest of them.

What have I walked into? Tilda asked herself as she looked around the expansive kitchen and dining area. The house was massive, and furnished beautifully. There was real money behind Lachlan, something she hadn't even considered. Why would she? It wasn't on her radar when meeting people.

'It won't be difficult to stay out of your way, Lachlan,' she teased in an attempt to gain some control over her mixed-up feelings about where she was and what they were doing.

'Why would you want to do that?' he teased.

She had walked out of Immigration and into his arms like they were an item. They had gone straight to his bed when they'd arrived here.

'You know. Those days when you're way too busy and feeling grumpy and everyone's a nuisance.' Not that she'd seen one of those days affect him yet. She was talking for the sake of it.

His mother might be making coffee but her ears were like revolving radar, picking up every word and nuance. Best keep calm and steady, try to forget how her feelings for the woman's son were erupting all over the place.

Lachlan grinned. 'Haven't got time for those.' Then he added, 'I do rattle around in here. It's better when the boys come round. Though they like hiding and it takes for ever to find them. Or it would if they ever stopped giggling.'

'They're still at the giggling age? Love it.' Starting tomorrow, she'd get to know the boys a little. How many weeks would she have here? She should get onto finding an apartment ASAP, but it was hard to get excited about that at the moment. After making love with Lachlan, the only place she wanted to be was in this house where that large bed beckoned. His lovemaking had been a game-changer. Before, she'd thought a fling would be exciting. Now she wanted more where that came from, along with getting to know him in so many more ways.

'Campbell, the oldest lad, likes to think he's too old for

little boys' games, but that doesn't stop him partaking if there's an ice cream at the end of it,' Faye was telling her.

'Kids, eh?' Strange how the longing for one of her own had started growing since Lachlan became part of her life. It couldn't be because her body clock was ticking down. There were years to go. She was thirty, not forty. Plenty of time to get her life running smoothly before doing something about finding a surrogate father—if she didn't go and fall in love. A sideways glance at Lachlan had her straightening up and moving to put a small gap between them. It would be all too easy to hand her heart over to him if she wasn't very careful. But he'd never indicated he was open to anything but a temporary fling.

Both John and Faye were looking at her with something like hope in their eyes. What had happened to them wanting Lachlan to marry Meredith? Was it just that they really wanted him to be happy and it didn't matter who that was with?

This was crazy. She wasn't their son's partner, and suddenly the lie was becoming overwhelming. Gulp.

'I'm sure Lachlan has lots of ice cream in that freezer just waiting for the boys.' She nodded to the upright freezer by what she presumed was the butler's pantry.

'Every flavour you can imagine,' he answered with something like relief in his voice. So he'd sensed her unease and was hoping she'd keep quiet about the truth?

Putting her coffee mug down, Tilda faked a yawn. 'Sorry, but the flight's catching up with me.'

Suddenly everyone was busy drinking coffee. Lachlan gave her a small smile, knowing what she'd done and thankfully wasn't cross with her.

'Right, we'd better be going. I need to drop by the garden centre,' John said.

Faye gave Tilda a hug. 'It's lovely to meet you,' Lachlan's mother said quietly. 'I mean that, even though we've been taken by surprise at how quickly you two have got together.'

'I understand.'

More than you know.

Okay, she and Lachlan needed to have a talk about dealing with this, because she clearly hadn't thought it through properly when she'd made the offer to be his fiancée, but right now that was the last thing she felt like doing. She *was* suddenly very tired. Hardly surprising given the long flight and then making energetic love with Lachlan. Right now she wanted quiet time with him and no one else. No discussions about a pretend relationship. No talk about outfits for a glamorous luncheon. Only time to absorb where she was, and who she was with, and how well their bodies had reacted to each other.

'I'm sorry everything's suddenly caught up with me.'

'You get some sleep and I'll see you again before the luncheon.'

'Mum means she'll be around here early in the week, if not tomorrow,' Lachlan told her after his parents had left. 'She likes to be in charge.'

'I hate that we'll eventually disappoint her.'

'That'll be for me to deal with.'

'Still, it won't be easy. She's being so kind to me.'

'I bet she turns up with the boys tomorrow. It will be an excuse to talk to you some more.'

'I can't wait to meet the little guys.' But as for his mother? That was tricky because she already liked Faye. The woman was warm and caring, and very open. Yes, Tilda was happy to see more of her, as long as she wasn't too intent on sussing her out about every last little thing.

Looking at Lachlan, her heart lurched. He was awesome, and she was starting to care for him, despite her own warnings. Another surprise was how much she wanted to see Lachlan playing with the boys. She'd bet he was a great father figure to them. Another side to him that would only make her admire him that bit more.

'Bet they're adorable.'

'They are. Two of them are so like Matt, it freaks me out sometimes.'

'It must be wonderful having children and watching them grow up.' Damn. 'Sorry, that came out wrong.'

'Because Matt won't see his boys become young men? Don't apologise. You're being normal and, to be honest, I'm tired of people tiptoeing around the fact he's gone.' He'd watched her closely as they'd talked about the boys. 'You didn't think of having children when you were married?'

As much as she didn't like talking about herself or her past, if they were going to become closer then she had to be completely honest about everything so there'd be no comebacks later if anything went pear-shaped. 'I fell pregnant once. It wasn't planned but I was so excited. It made me realise how much I wanted to have a complete family.' She stood beside Lachlan, looking out across the front lawn. Kids would love playing here. 'Then I lost the baby.'

His arms wrapped around her. 'That's awful. How did you cope?' He breathed the question against her neck.

For a distraction it wasn't bad, but she needed to finish this conversation. 'It wasn't easy as I was devastated. But the worst part was that James was pleased. He didn't want a baby in our lives. It would mean he didn't get all my attention.' She hugged Lachlan back and then stepped out of his arms. 'I really am better off without him.'

'I agree. Never liked him from the moment he started shouting at you in hospital.'

As far as she knew, it was the only time he'd ever seen James. But his support had surprised her. So unlike anything James would've done.

She looked around, taking in what she could see of the house from here. The kitchen was state-of-the-art with white walls, tiles and benches. Everything shone enough to blind her if she stared too hard. 'Are you into cooking?'

'My thing's strictly heating up take-outs,' he said, laughing. Then stopped and turned to take her hands in his. 'Welcome to my house, Tilda. Make yourself completely at home with everything. I want you to be happy here.'

That wouldn't be hard. 'From what I've seen of it so far, you have a lovely home.' She spun around and gazed out of the big windows onto another large lawn edged with perfectly laid flowerbeds. 'Who looks after all that?'

'I have a gardener and a cleaner for inside the house, in case you think I might put you on cleaning duties.'

'I wouldn't know where to start.' Her apartments were usually boxes with one bedroom and no space to swing a cat. Crikey, not once had she considered Lachlan might be this well-off. It didn't make a bit of difference to how she felt about him, but it still came as a bit of a shock. Should've realised when she saw his top-of-the-range car at the airport. And the upgrade to first class for her flight home. That had been special.

'Here, take a pew.' He pulled a stool out from under the counter. 'I'll get another coffee on the go.'

Elbows on the counter, chin in her hands, she watched

him and for the first time since she'd walked out of Immigration into his hug she truly relaxed. First the build-up of need that had pulsed between them all the way from the airport to his bed, and then his parents arriving and keeping her on her toes with their ideas about their relationship. No wonder she'd got a bit tense. Now, sitting here as though she'd always been here felt good. She'd got wound up on the flight home, thinking about where they were at and if there might be any awkwardness between them after two weeks apart. She didn't want that. Lachlan was easygoing, not into making demands of her. Yet.

He won't. But… *He could.* So much for relaxing.

'How's work been since you got back?'

'Great. I have felt different since Cambodia. Felt more comfortable from the moment I got away from here, really. Now I look forward to going into work every morning, and when the boys come around I join their games without worrying if I'm doing the right thing by them and hoping Matt would be happy about how I look out for them. I've been to dinner with Mum and Dad twice since I got back. We've talked about Matt, and Kelly, and the road trip they're planning. I've also made it clear I'm moving on, so when I mentioned this woman I met again in Phnom Penh I figure they thought she was the reason I'm suddenly coming to terms with the past and am now looking forward. The engagement knocked them sideways, but they've taken it on board quite quickly.'

'And Meredith?'

'She was stunned at first, but has since told me she'll back me in whatever I do. Says she's trying to sort her life out too, and that maybe she'd pressured me too much.'

'That's exactly what you wanted to hear from her. Now

you—we—just have to keep this going for a bit longer, and not get sidetracked.'

'You're definitely part of why I am where I am now.' Lachlan came over and took her hands in his. 'I'd like to spend more time with you, get to know you a little better. What do you think?' He was grinning in that way that went straight to her knees and made her legs useless at holding her upright. Just as well she was sitting down.

'I think we're on the same page.'

His grin got bigger. 'The relief is enormous.'

He wasn't trying to control her. Big point in his favour. Standing up, she hooked her hands around his neck. 'What say we go back to your bedroom?' she asked.

'Don't you mean *our* bedroom, fake fiancée?'

CHAPTER SEVEN

'LACHLAN, WHERE ARE YOU?' a boy shouted from the back door. 'We've brought the new soccer ball to play with.'

Lachlan grinned. 'Here we go. Your peace and quiet is over for the morning.'

Tilda looked up from her laptop on the counter. 'You, playing soccer? This I must watch.'

'Not good enough. You've got to join in too. Ground rules. Everyone here has to play the game that's happening.'

Faye burst into the room. 'Hello, Lachlan, Tilda.'

Lachlan gave Tilda an apologetic look. 'See you outside shortly.'

Thanks. Leave me with your mum and her questions, why don't you?

'Morning, Faye. Come to play soccer, have you?'

'Me? Not likely.' Faye sat at the table opposite Tilda, giving her the uncomfortable feeling she was in for an inquisition. 'I'm more the sideline ref type.'

'Isn't that true.' Another woman joined them. Tilda recognised her immediately from the photo on Lachlan's phone.

'Tilda, this is Meredith, the boys' mother. Meredith, meet the woman who's got Lachlan twisted around her little finger and making him smile every day.'

Tilda looked around for Lachlan but he was nowhere in sight. Had he heard that last comment? He surely wouldn't have walked away if he had. Would he? No, she didn't believe he'd leave her in the lurch with his mother and the woman who'd wanted him to marry her. But then she could be too trusting when it came to men she cared for.

'Hi, Meredith. I'm Tilda, and no, I am not responsible for *all* Lachlan's smiles.' She wanted to downplay all this as it made her somewhat uneasy.

'Actually, you caused a fair few of them,' said Lachlan from the doorway. He grinned at her wickedly.

He hadn't abandoned her after all. But what he'd just said only added to the pressure of trying to keep everything as open and honest as she could without blowing the cover on what she was doing for him. Raising one eyebrow in his direction, she said, 'Go and play soccer.' They'd talk later when no one else was around to suck up every word and rearrange them to suit their own wishes.

'On my way. Meredith, I need some adult support out here.'

The boys' mother shook her head. 'Like you can't manage my three all by yourself.' But she stood up. 'It's good to meet you after hearing all about you these past couple of weeks. And yes, he does seem happier.'

Tilda could feel her face reddening. This was way more than she'd expected when she'd offered to stand beside Lachlan against his family's pressure to remarry. Somehow she'd thought she'd just be in the background. Silly girl.

'Spending time working in such a different environment probably has something to do with that too. I found Cambodia stimulating myself.'

Meredith smiled knowingly. 'I can see that's what's happened to Lachlan.' Then she headed outside.

Faye pulled out a chair and sat down opposite Tilda.

Here we go. She's not going to let me off the hook so easily. Best get in first and cut her off at the pass.

'Faye, I understand you want Lachlan to be happy and find love again, but that our engagement has come as a shock to you all.'

'We weren't expecting it, that's for sure. Didn't even know he'd met someone. But if he's happy then so are we.'

'I think I understand.'

'Tell me a little about yourself. If you don't mind, that is.'

'Of course not.' It was normal to want to know about the woman her son had got engaged to.

'Are you a Vancouverite born and bred?'

The tightness in her gut eased a fraction. She could answer these sorts of questions, even when she usually avoided them. It might help Faye accept Lachlan was moving on in his own way.

'Yes. My grandmother brought me up in the eastern suburbs.'

'No mother?'

'She died in childbirth.'

A soft, warm hand covered hers. 'I'm sorry, Tilda. That must've been hard living with, growing up.'

'It was. But Grandma was the strongest, most loving woman I could've wanted. I didn't miss out on the basics either.' She still missed her, and always would.

'I suppose our family and how we all tumble through each other's lives must seem daunting to you. Even Meredith and her lads are part of the scene. Her family's always been friends with ours, and Matt hung around with Lachlan since they were teens.' Faye sat back. 'We all sort of slot together, if you know what I mean.'

'Lachlan's mentioned that. He's so lucky in that way. He also told me about Kelly.'

'It was a huge shock for all of us, but especially Lachlan. He was devastated.'

'I can't begin to imagine what he's been through. Then to lose his best friend as well.' Okay, it was time to tell Faye some of her history. 'I was married but I left my ex a little more than a year ago, after I was in a serious car accident and he was more upset about the car than me. He was a bully and I'd had enough.'

'Sounds like you're a strong woman.'

'I try to be.'

'Divorced?'

'It's in the pipeline.'

'Thank you for telling me this. It helps to know a little more about you.' She stood up. 'Let's go and watch the boys playing.'

'Faye, I understand you need time to absorb the fact Lachlan's moving on without your help, but believe me, he is happier than he was previously.'

Not necessarily because of her, though she hoped she was helping. He was always cheerful when he was with her. He also ticked a lot of her own boxes when it came to a man she wanted to spend time with.

For a moment the smile faded from the older woman's eyes. Sudden sorrow for her struck Tilda. All Faye wanted was for her son to be happy, but her idea of how that would happen hadn't come to fruition.

I want it to happen too—but his way, not yours.

'Let things take their course.' Whichever way that went. The same could be said for herself. Wait and see how this new—fake—relationship unfolded. She wanted to be with

Lachlan and find out if they were starting out on a new adventure or if the fling they'd engaged in was all there was to be had.

'You're right. It's just that I feel rather useless. I'm his mother, and I haven't been able to fix everything for him.'

'He's getting there.'

'He and Kelly had something very special and losing her took the ground right out from under him. I only want him to be just as happy again.'

Tilda reached across and took her hands. 'He knows that. He also worries for all of you, but I think he's looking forwards now.' She didn't know him as well as these people but he was strong and focused and ready to go after what he wanted. A small piece of her heart would like to become a part of that, but she was still wary of it being too much, too soon.

'Thank you, Tilda.'

'Come on. Let's see how the game's going.'

Outside, the boys were chasing Lachlan around the lawn as much as they were the ball. 'Their energy levels are high. I wonder how long Lachlan will last?' Tilda said aloud, knowing how much energy he'd used *playing* with her that morning.

Meredith laughed. 'He's good at this. They think they're winning, but Lachlan's in charge.'

He was having fun, no doubt about it. Shouting and laughing as loudly as the boys as he dashed up and down, kicking the ball whenever it wasn't too close to anyone. Tilda watched with a growing sense of longing. Family. Standing here, it seemed so simple. A ball, three boys and Lachlan, their mum and Faye—and herself—watching and enjoying. Family. She'd watched her school mates' families from the outside, dreaming of sharing noisy meals and arguments over whose turn it was to set the table or feed the dog, looking out for each other when other kids tried to pick fights with them. Growing up with Grandma had been safe and loving, but awfully lonely at times.

Yet today it all seemed so easy. These people had it sorted. Of course, that wasn't right. The boys didn't have a father any more. Their mother was struggling with getting on with her life. But Tilda would swear they were happy in their own ways.

Can I have this?

She could if she put aside her fear of making the same mistake she had with James and allowed herself to fall head over heels in love with Lachlan. Getting ahead of herself, surely? Maybe, but, for the first time, she wasn't about to run from the idea either.

He looked her way and smiled that big smile of his that curled her toes and set her heart racing. Did he have ESP? Was he telling her yes, she could have it all? With him? Not likely.

'You have changed him,' Meredith said quietly. 'There's a new calmness about him I haven't seen in for ever.'

That probably had little to do with her, given they hadn't known each other for much more than four weeks, even if they did meet a year ago.

'It's been a long time for him, hasn't it?' These people were so open about things, they made it too easy for her to respond in a like manner.

'Yes. Sometimes I wondered if he'd ever get over losing Kelly. Then I lost Matt, and now I totally understand.'

'Lachlan said you've met a man you like.' Going too far?

Even when Meredith seemed so open. They'd barely met, after all.

'We've been out for coffee a few times. He's nice, but I'm not sure if he's the right man for me. You know what I mean? I've got kids to think of, and I'm afraid of falling for someone and losing them again.'

Did anyone come without baggage?

'Take your time, Meredith.'

Says the expert here.

'Have some fun, and enjoy yourself first. Getting back out there onto the dating scene is scary.'

'It's worked for you.' When Tilda turned to look at her, she added, 'Yes, Lachlan did tell me you'd been married and that you'd left your husband last year.'

Did that mean he cared enough he wanted those close to him to accept her in his life as more than a *fake* fiancée? She couldn't see him talking up the engagement too much when they were meant to call it off later if he wasn't at least thinking they might have something going between them. Or was she just projecting her own desires onto him?

When Tilda didn't reply, Meredith added hurriedly, 'It's okay. He was only explaining why you didn't have your own place to return to. He wasn't filling me in on all the personal details, only that it seemed right for you to move in with him. Lachlan doesn't do tell-all. Especially about a woman he's keen on.'

Tilda felt her face warm. She'd been so thrilled when Lachlan took her to bed the first time, pleased he might have some feelings for her, even if only desire, but now Meredith—and Faye—seemed to think he was truly invested in her, which was the plan, but in reality was scary. They were lying to his lovely family and it had been her idea.

She returned to the original topic. 'Go on another date, and just enjoy it. Don't question every minute of your time with this guy who has got you wondering what lies ahead.'

'Did Lachlan tell you I'd hoped that he and I might eventually get together?'

Tilda nodded. 'He did.'

'He was right to push me away. We've always been close friends, but the X-factor never existed between us. Settling down with him would've been an easy way out of my difficulties. We would've regretted it long-term, I know that.'

'And possibly lost a close friend along the way.'

'True,' Meredith agreed. 'Thanks for listening to me. I can see why Lachlan cares for you. I hope we get to spend more time together. That's when he's not monopolising you.'

'When's the coffee break?' Lachlan appeared in front of her, understanding in his eyes. Had he overheard them talking?

'I'll go and make it now,' Meredith offered and walked off.

His hand was hot on her arm, and he leaned close so only she heard him. 'It's okay. We'll ride this out. Promise.'

'I'm feeling a little guilty.'

'I get that too. Let's give it time. Give ourselves time. Who knows? We might find we want more than a quick fling together.'

Her heart lifted. They appeared to be on the same path, wherever that might lead.

'I'll go and help Meredith with the coffee.' *And get my breath back.*

Lachlan brushed a light kiss on her mouth. 'Can you bring out some lemonade for the boys too? That'll win them over in a flash.'

* * *

'Scalpel.' Lachlan held out his hand.

Tilda obliged by placing the instrument in his hand, grinning at the command. Because, yes, in Theatre Lachlan could be curt because he was focused entirely on the job and nothing, nobody, would deflect him unless there was a problem with his patient's vitals.

'I'm making an incision around the nipple.' A breast reduction coming up.

'Can you do anything to hide those grooves in Annabel's shoulders?' she asked as she watched every move he made. The weight of their fifty-year-old patient's breasts had caused a deep trough-like hollow on her shoulders where her bra straps sat.

He was so precise as he made the cuts ready to remove excess tissue and fat from the breast. 'I can't fill them in, so no. Physio and massage therapy will ease the aching but that's the best we can do. She will feel less and less aching as time goes on.' He nodded at the right breast. 'Clean that area.'

Tilda swabbed beneath the incision, then changed swabs in preparation for more bleeding as Lachlan continued.

It was Friday and the first time she'd worked alongside him at Western G. Wednesday had been mostly an orientation day, and then yesterday she'd been rostered in Theatre One while he'd been operating in Theatre Three. They'd crossed paths in the tea room once, and had to wait until they got home to catch up on each other's day over a glass of wine. It had felt cosy in a way she hadn't known since she was a kid and talking to Grandma about her day at school.

'Do you give your patients a choice on the size their breasts are reduced to?'

'Of course. It's not my place to say what they should have, though I do point out the pluses and negatives of going too small. Or too large.'

'I hadn't worked with plastic surgeons before Phnom Penh.'

'Nothing different to other surgeries for us,' the other nurse on this case said.

'I guess you're right,' Tilda agreed. 'But it's interesting. I like that Lachlan's making people feel better about themselves, not only pain-wise but visually. So many have hang-ups about their looks, it's like a circus out there sometimes. Too big, too little, ugly, beautiful. The list goes on and on. It's crazy.'

'You're not wrong there,' Lachlan said. 'Right, I need to see how I'm doing for size. We're aiming for a twelve.' Lachlan spoke to the room generally.

Tilda handed him the measure. And squeezed her shoulders together. Just the thought of having a surgeon cutting into her breasts made her eyes water. She was lucky hers were average-sized. Lachlan seemed to like them, though.

Behave, Tilda. That's out of place.

Yeah, but he was so hot, even dressed in the ghastly blue work garb that did nothing to highlight the amazing body underneath.

'Looking good. The first one's the easiest, it's making the second match as perfectly as possible that takes more time.' His brow creased as he concentrated on the second breast.

'Heart rate's dropping.' The anaesthetist spoke across everyone. 'Fifty-five.'

'What's up, Jeremy?' Lachlan asked, his hands suddenly still. 'Bradycardia?'

'I'd say so. I'm administering five milligrams of ephedrine.'

'I'll keep going until you say otherwise. Can't leave her like this.'

Tilda swabbed regularly and handed Lachlan whatever he required as soon as he asked.

'Heart rate fifty-nine,' Jeremy reported.

Relief filtered through Lachlan's eyes as he concentrated on removing more tissue from the second breast. A lowered heart rate wasn't a physician's fault, but they always felt it was.

Tilda felt the same. Bradycardia wasn't uncommon but it still scared her to bits when it occurred with a patient she was nursing. People came into surgery nervous but trusting everyone to see them come out the other side better off than they went in.

Four hours after Annabel was wheeled into Theatre, Tilda rolled her bed out into Recovery. 'All done,' she said to Annabel, who was still out of it.

'Any problems?' asked the recovery nurse taking over.

'Yes.' Tilda filled her in. 'But Annabel came right as soon as the ephedrine was administered.' She rolled onto her toes and stretched upward to ease the kinks out of her back and shoulders.

'Go grab a coffee and something to eat.'

'Think I will. I'm on again this afternoon.' Not with Lachlan. Her next patient was in for a knee replacement.

'What have you got this afternoon?' she asked when he joined her on the way to the staff tea room.

'Eighteen-month-old with a cleft palate.' He picked up the bagel he'd bought. 'You like working here?'

'So far it's good. The staff all seem friendly.'

'Aren't they in every theatre?'

'Mostly.' She wasn't going to tell him that some surgeons

could be a bit up themselves. This one certainly wasn't. 'What time do you reckon you'll be finished?'

'That's like asking what the weather's going to be like in a month's time.' He grinned.

'Want to go out for something to eat tonight? Since I can't cook to save myself and it is my turn to put food on the table. My shout,' she added, in case he thought she was taking advantage of his generous nature.

'You're on. I'll text when I'm leaving for home. Got any idea where you want to go?'

'What's that bar on the corner of Toll Road like?' It had looked okay from the outside when she'd walked past on the way to the bus that morning.

'Good basic food. Better music at the weekends.'

'We have a plan.' She stood up. 'I'd better be getting back. Can't have everyone thinking I'm a slacker.'

Lachlan laughed. 'As if.'

'I know, but I'm only a few days into the job and first impressions count.' Not that she'd made a mistake with anyone yet, and didn't intend to in the future, but it was best to tread carefully. One hang-up left over from the James days, she supposed, as she didn't used to be like this.

'Tilda, let it go. You are better than that.' Lachlan leaned back in his chair, watching her with an intensity that said he had her back.

She loved how he supported her, no questions asked, just like a real fiancé. 'You can be bossy when you choose.' Her smile was wide and genuine.

'Not that you take any notice,' he said with a laugh. 'Okay, see you later. I'll pick you up from home. We could walk to the pub but rain's forecast.'

'No surprise.' The clouds had been heavy when she'd

come to work. There was a bounce in her step as she left the room, brought on by the ease with which she and Lachlan got on. It was as though they really *were* in a relationship. But they were in one of sorts. A fling maybe, but they'd still spent time together sharing the everyday things. She felt happier than she'd been in a long while. No way was she about to toss that away when it seemed as though she was finally getting her life in order the way she'd hoped.

'What do you think about taking the boys to Stanley Park next weekend, give Meredith time to have a coffee with the man she's seeing?' he asked.

'Sounds good. It wouldn't make for a good date, dragging three boisterous boys along as well.'

'You two hit it off quickly on Sunday,' he said casually.

'I like Meredith. She's open and honest.'

'Always has been.'

She should be too. 'Are you as happy as everyone thinks?'

'Absolutely. You've touched me in ways I never thought would happen again.' His face became serious. 'We're good together. I only hope we're not racing blindly into something that might backfire on us both.'

She nodded. 'I try not to think like that. I mean, I came to stay with you while I looked for a place of my own, and have I done anything about that? No.' Was she meant to when she was supposedly his fiancée? Did she want to? It was all very well to think she might be falling for him, but reality mightn't work out the way she hoped. 'We've leapt into this with no discussion about what we actually want out of it.'

'It's not the normal way to start a relationship, for me, anyway, but I like what we're doing. Getting together and seeing how we go. We've clicked in so many aspects it feels good to just go with the flow.'

'I know what you're saying. But then I think back to James and how wrong I was to believe he would never hurt me.' She'd never opened up much to Lachlan about her marriage. Right or wrong, it felt like the ideal time to now get some of this out there.

'Yes, and you left him when it got too much. That day he ranted at you for wrecking his car highlighted his true colours. He never stopped to ask how you were. He didn't talk to the surgeon or caregivers about your condition. He was only concerned for his car, for himself. You did the right thing, Tilda.'

'I don't doubt that for a moment. Never have. But sometimes I'm still shocked at how something he did or said can slam into my head. I can't help worrying that I might not be ready for a relationship yet, Lachlan.'

'You wouldn't be normal if you didn't think about the past,' he said with a smile. 'I think about Kelly and the agony of losing her. She was a big part of my life and is never going to go away completely. We both need to take our time with this. Neither of us wants to get hurt again. But meanwhile we can have a blast. Continue having amazing fun together, and get to know more about each other along the way.'

Just like that she relaxed again. Lachlan had a way of making her feel good about herself and her decisions. 'You're on.' They'd fallen into a fling, and now it seemed to be expanding into something more promising.

'He can't breathe!' a man shouted.

Tilda looked around and saw another man outside the elevator doors, clutching his throat while trying to gasp for air. She was at his side in seconds and pushing aside the first man, who was slapping his back. 'Stop that. Bend over,' she told the choking man. 'Now.'

The man's face was red and his eyes filled with fear.

'Thought you're supposed to hit them between the shoulder blades,' the other guy said.

Lachlan was there. 'He's got to bend over first or you could dislodge whatever's blocking his throat and make it drop further down his throat.'

Tilda pushed the man forward. 'Bend.' At last, he did.

Instantly she gave him a back blow, followed by four more.

Lachlan moved in beside her. 'I'll do the abdominal thrusts. He's a big man.'

And she was small against him. She got it. 'Go for it.' Grabbing the man's wrist, she felt his pulse. 'Weak. His lips are turning blue.'

As Lachlan gave the fifth abdominal thrust the man collapsed in his arms, and he staggered to hold him.

Tilda grabbed an arm to help lower the man to the floor. 'He's lost consciousness.'

'Someone call ED and ask them to send up an orderly with a bed,' Lachlan said as he straightened the man's body on the floor. Glancing at Tilda, he said, 'I'll start compressions.'

'I'll be ready to give him the breaths.'

Lachlan's nod was brief but there was satisfaction in his eyes. 'Good.'

At every thirtieth compression he sat back so she could give two long breaths into the man.

He did not react.

Sweat broke out on Lachlan's forehead. Compressions were no picnic. 'Thirty,' he called for the fifth time.

Leaning down, she breathed into the man again.

He hiccupped. Then coughed.

She grabbed his shoulders, rolled him onto his side as whatever had been blocking his throat finally came out. 'Phew.'

'I agree.' Lachlan was appraising the guy, reaching for his wrist to check his pulse.

'Has anyone got something clean to wipe his face with?' she asked over her shoulder. Taking the handful of paper tissues a woman passed her, she cleaned the man's face, keeping an eye on his chest to make sure he didn't stop breathing again.

'Pulse's good.'

'Lucky he was at a hospital,' the same woman said.

'He was very lucky,' Lachlan said to Tilda once the man had been taken to ED. 'You were onto the problem fast.'

'It still gives me a jolt when someone goes down like he did, but I do go straight into nurse mode.' It was instinctive, thank goodness.

'Confident and competent. Think I've said that before, mind.'

She blushed. Which was silly, but she couldn't stop the heat rising and expanding on her face. Compliments didn't come her way very often, and she especially liked those Lachlan gave her. 'Give over. You were equally competent and confident.'

'I'd better get back to Theatre or I won't be acting competently at all,' he said with a grin. 'See you later.'

CHAPTER EIGHT

A WEEK LATER, Lachlan did a double take and swallowed hard as he watched Tilda coming down the stairs in red heels that would've tripped him up on the first step.

The red dress she wore accentuated the amazing figure underneath, bringing thoughts of satin skin to his fingertips. He wanted to rush her back upstairs and tear it off her, to have her naked body under his again.

He took a step back. It wasn't happening. There wasn't time.

She swung a white jacket in one hand. Her hair hung loosely over the sides of her face, shining in the light. Her make-up was enough to accentuate her good features without looking like she'd plastered it on. Red lipstick highlighted those full lips, bringing more memories of exactly where those lips had performed their magic last night.

'You look stunning.'

'I haven't overdone it?'

He'd never seen her dressed like this. In Cambodia she'd been all about casual and comfortable. Nothing had changed since she'd returned home. It showed she had a few more surprises up her sleeve.

'Not at all. I don't want you to change a thing.'

She made it harder by the day to hold back from committing once and for all to her. As if he'd managed to hold back since the day he'd met her again. She'd sneaked in under his radar, become an essential part of his plan to grab a future for himself. A plan that increasingly included her at his side. He was falling for her, and it petrified him. It might be a very hard landing if she wasn't ready to commit. She'd been honest in telling him James had damaged her belief in herself. She was afraid of making the same mistake twice. He knew where she was coming from. He was deathly afraid of losing another person he loved.

For Tilda this was essentially a fling. No more, no less. It should be the same for him. Safer that way. Backing off and giving them both some space was the way to go, but it was impossible. Being with Tilda had brought him to life again and he was going to make the most of it. Who knew? His fears of being left alone again seemed to be subsiding but they weren't out of the picture yet. That would take more time, which he hoped he had.

'There again, we could go back upstairs and shuck all those clothes for another half an hour.'

She shook her head. 'I am not going to be the reason we're late for your parents' charity lunch.' Her laughter dried up and a frown appeared, but she said nothing.

'Don't be nervous. Everyone will be well behaved. Except maybe the boys. They love running around and making a racket, but they won't attack you. Normally they wouldn't be at one of these events but Dad figured they'd make things easier.' He grinned in an attempt to cheer her up. It must be daunting, given she knew no one apart from the boys and his parents and Meredith. And then there was the engagement factor. He might've made a big mistake accepting Tilda's idea for keeping his family at bay.

Tilda winced before lifting her head and locking a fierce look on him. 'I'll be fine.'

'I know you will.' He'd like nothing more than to carry her back upstairs and make love to her, but that was only delaying the inevitable. 'Dad always backs Mum with these charity occasions but he likes to have a bit of fun too. You're just an excuse to have the kids there.'

His father wrapped Tilda in a hug when they arrived. 'You look beautiful. No wonder Lachlan's fallen for you.'

Tilda blushed, but hugged him back. 'Stop it, John. You're embarrassing me.'

'Get on with making the most of what you two have started. It's right there in your faces and eyes whenever you look at each other. Everyone can see it.'

So much for thinking he could hide his true emotions. But he hadn't noticed Tilda being so transparent.

'You're just making it up.' Then he reached for Tilda's hand and got laughed at by his father. 'Come on. I'll show you round and introduce you to some people you might bump into at the hospital.' Anything to get away from his father right now.

Tilda squeezed his hand and made him feel needed. 'Let's get it over with.'

'It's not that bad.' Not really. They were having a fling with a bit more going on in their spare time. They made love every night. They shared not just his house, but his bedroom. They ate together at the end of the day and swapped stories about what they'd been doing at work. They were in a temporary relationship that might possibly expand into something more.

But she's worried she isn't ready for that.

She'd said so. She still didn't trust her own judgement

and thought she might make the same mistake as she had with her ex.

But I would never, ever treat you like that, Tilda. You are your own woman.

'Hello, you two. You look lovely, Tilda. That dress is perfect on you.' His mother was beaming at them.

Right from one overenthusiastic parent to the other. Loving parent, he admonished himself. They cared so much about him, but couldn't they leave him to make his own decisions about what lay ahead?

'Hello, Faye.' Tilda sounded as though she suddenly wished she was anywhere else but here. Then she rallied. 'Is there anything I can do to help?'

'Not a thing. It's all organised and we get to relax and have some fun.'

'I'm looking forward to it.'

Lachlan doubted that. 'Let's grab a glass of champagne.' That'd help settle her nerves. He nodded at a passing waiter and handed Tilda a glass before taking one for himself. 'Come and meet my partners and their wives. They're all normal, nice folk and won't bite.'

She flicked him a small laugh. 'I'll be fine,' she ground through her teeth.

'Susie, Jason, I'd like you to meet Tilda.'

Tilda stepped up, shook hands all round and was soon talking to Susie about her time in Cambodia, and looking more relaxed by the minute.

'She fits in well with everyone,' Jason said.

Most of the time. 'She does.' He'd seen how easily she'd slid into the team in Phnom Penh, and from what he was hearing she was doing the same at Western G, but today was different, which could be because she'd never been to anything quite so extravagant. Hopefully that wouldn't put her off his family because these events were common amongst their friends. 'How's the house coming along?'

Jason and Susie were having a complete makeover done on their home and living in an apartment downtown while it was happening. Not something he could imagine doing. He and Kelly had loved the house when they'd bought it, though it did get a complete repaint job inside and out, along with new curtains, carpets and furniture. It still suited him. What if Tilda didn't like the décor? Was he prepared to change anything she didn't fancy? It would be a finish to all things Kelly. Not such a bad idea if he was starting out in a new relationship, though? Too many questions he wasn't quite ready to answer. Time to shut them down and get on with enjoying the luncheon party.

'Not fast enough, but when do building projects go to schedule?'

'When does anything?'

'When does anything what?' Tilda asked as she joined them.

'Go right when altering houses.'

'Not something I know anything about, I'm afraid.'

His mother appeared at Tilda's side and took her arm. 'Come on. There's someone I want to introduce you to. I think you'll find her delightful.'

Thirty minutes later Tilda returned, a woeful expression on her face. 'I've met the best dressmaker in town. An expert on wedding dresses apparently.'

Lachlan had to laugh. 'My mum can be OTT but she means well.'

'This is getting out of hand now,' Tilda sighed.

She was right, yet his heart felt heavy. If only they were a genuine couple, about to make plans for the future.

Back off, Lachlan. That's rushing things and you know you're not ready to do that either.

'I'll have words with Mum after this function is over, tell her you want to make your own decisions about anything we do.'

'Good. But go easy on her.'

Not everyone left at the end of the auction that raised thousands of dollars for the children's charity. Lachlan was tempted to hang around until the last two couples left but as they were his parents' closest friends he knew that could be hours away yet, so he took Tilda home and made coffee before discussing what to do.

'It's simple,' Tilda said. 'Tell your family we aren't getting married for a while and so there's no need to make wedding plans yet.' Then she sighed. 'Except weddings take a lot of planning, don't they? Couldn't we elope?' Her eyes widened. 'If we were really getting married, that is.'

Her words bit into him, slicing apart his tentative hope for more with her.

'Lachlan…'

Here it comes.

If not the decision to stop the fling before it got out of hand, then at least a request to slow down while they grappled with what they'd started.

A wobbly smile surprised him. 'I don't want to walk away from what we've got. We're only just getting going.'

A feather could have knocked him down. She was still with him, and wanted more. He should be running for the hills about now, but somehow he wasn't. Yet this was scary territory and he wondered if he was actually as ready as he'd hoped he was. It was as though her words were a warning not to forget how badly hurt he could be if something went wrong. How hurt both of them could get.

'But I can't deal with what your mother wants.'

'Fair enough. I would hate for you to regret being with me for however long we have.' He finally seemed to be moving on from his past to some extent. But he understood Tilda might need some space still. He could do that for her. It wouldn't be easy but it would be worth it in the end. And if it didn't work out? Then he'd move on; he would not go back to being that sad man he'd been before Tilda.

She came around the counter and snuggled into him, arms around his waist, breasts pressed into his chest. 'Thank you for understanding.' She tipped her head back and looked up at him. 'Or at least pretending you do.'

Bending down, he kissed her. Thoroughly. Which led to them going upstairs and making passionate love. For now, everything was right in his world.

The following afternoon the front door burst open and Campbell raced in, quickly followed by Lenny and Morgan. 'Lachlan, where are you? We're ready to go to the park with you.'

Lachlan fist pumped the air. 'So am I, guys. Tilda's coming too.' He still felt incredibly energised after an amazing night filled with truly great sex.

'Yippee,' shouted Morgan.

'Hi, you two.' Meredith appeared in the doorway, looking a little down.

'Meredith, it's good to see you,' Tilda said. Then she frowned in concern. 'Are you all right?'

'I cancelled my date.'

Tilda came across. 'Then you'd better come to the park with us instead.'

'Would you mind?'

'Wouldn't have said it if I did.' Tilda pulled out a stool at the counter. 'Take a pew. I've just made coffee. How do you have it?' She could say what she liked about not wanting to get too close too soon, but Lachlan could see Tilda had made herself at home in his house, as though she wanted to stay.

'Black with one.'

The boys were looking impatient. 'Thought we were going to Stanley Park *now*,' Lenny whined.

'I'm not quite ready,' Lachlan told them. 'How about you go to the shed and get my bag with the soccer balls and rugby ball in it?'

'All right…' Lenny dragged out the words as if it was such a big deal to do what they'd been asked.

'You get cold feet with your date?' Tilda was asking Meredith.

'Sort of. He's almost too enthusiastic, if you know what I mean. Keeps saying we should spend the whole weekend together. He says the boys are included in that, but I don't want to rush them into something that might not work out. They could get hurt if they expect too much, too soon.'

'It seems like you're walking a fine line between following your own needs and looking out for them. Err on the side of caution, maybe?'

Just like she was doing, Lachlan knew. She had said as much, but hearing her now really brought it home to him. Should he be doing the same? The potential to be hurt himself was loud and clear. But they got on so well, and when they made love he felt so close to her it was as though they were one person. They were like that in more ways than one too.

He stood up. 'I'll see how the boys are getting on finding the ball bag.'

'You all right with me joining you?' Meredith asked him with a worried look.

'Of course I am.'

'Why can't I chase them?' Four-year-old Morgan stood an hour later, hands on hips, mimicking Lachlan as he stared down the Canadian geese.

'Because you'll frighten them. If you haven't already with all the noise you're making.'

'They're too big to be scared,' Morgan shouted. He only had one volume when he was talking.

'Come on, let's kick a few balls. Not at the geese either,' he added quickly as a gleam entered Campbell's eyes.

'First one to kick a ball between those two trees is a winner,' Tilda called as she bounced a soccer ball with one hand. 'I'm going to beat you all.' She tipped an assortment of balls onto the ground.

Bedlam ensued.

'I want that one!'

'Can't. It's mine!'

'I'm having it.'

'Boys, no arguing. One each. It doesn't matter which ball you have, I've got the winning one,' Tilda teased, which got the result she intended.

Lenny kicked his tennis ball hard and it bounced in the opposite direction to the trees Tilda had pointed to. He grabbed another ball for a second attempt.

'I'll be the goalkeeper,' Meredith announced. 'I couldn't kick a paper bag to save myself.'

'Watch out, Morgan. Line the ball up so you are looking straight at the trees. That's it.' Tilda knelt down and held the ball lightly. 'Now, kick it hard. That's it. Way to go.'

The ball dribbled about ten metres.

Lachlan pretended to kick another ball and made sure it went in the wrong direction, all the while listening to Tilda laughing and talking Lenny through another kick. She was doing something so simple and yet she was clearly happy. She was making the boys happy too. His chest filled with warmth. She mightn't have had siblings or been surrounded with other kids but she instinctively seemed to know what they needed. Attention and fun.

Did she think about having children? She'd be a great mother. There was a big heart in that beautiful chest, if only she could free it up and start living the life she must've hoped for with her horrendous ex. He remembered that day in Cambodia when Bebe was having surgery and the look of wonder on Tilda's face when she'd picked her up. She'd touched her abdomen and made him wonder if she might've been pregnant some time. Now he knew she had been, and it had ended tragically. She had to be wary of trying again.

'Lachlan, look out!' she yelled.

Instinctively he ducked and a soccer ball flew past his head. He spun around to find Campbell laughing at him. 'You little rotter. I'll show you where to kick the ball.' He retrieved the ball and lined it up with the trees. Fingers crossed it went somewhere near the makeshift goal. Sometimes it paid to get one in, right in front of the kids.

When the boys started tiring, long after Lachlan was ready to give up chasing balls and boys, everyone clambered into the large four-wheel drive and they headed to a take-out for burgers and chips.

'A perfect end to a great afternoon,' Tilda said before biting into her chicken burger.

'I'll say.' It had been fun and, best of all, he was pleased she'd enjoyed herself getting to know the kids. It said a lot to him about her. Another plus. There were getting to be a lot of those. He had finally started to open up his heart again and this was the reward. If only Tilda could see how amazing it could be for them both. In the meantime, he'd try and remain careful. Probably too late for his heart to remain completely unscathed, but hopefully he'd still survive if it all went belly-up.

Then she smiled across the table at him. A big, happy smile just for him. 'I haven't had so much fun since we were in Cambodia.'

Lachlan dropped the negative thoughts. Trying to second-guess all the things that could go wrong was exhausting and only wasted the good times spent with Tilda. 'Here's to more fun times where they came from.'

She nodded. 'I agree.'

'I'm going to look at an apartment on Twelfth after work, so I'll be late home,' Tilda told Lachlan when she saw him coming out of Theatre three weeks later.

'You'll do anything to get out of cooking, won't you?' He might be joking but she could sense that sadness lay behind his words and it gave her hope.

'I'll get pizza on the way home.' She didn't really want to find a place to buy, but ultimately her plan hadn't changed. She had money to invest in a property and, while she was living with Lachlan there was no hurry to purchase something, she'd decided to start looking in case the day came when she had to move out of his home in a hurry. She was only doing what she had to, to protect herself in case things went wrong.

Being engaged to Lachlan should be the best time of her life, but it wasn't real. The negative side of her brain kept preparing for the day when they decided to call quits on the engagement. Though she was giving their fling everything she had, she was worried it wasn't going to last. Lachlan seemed happy enough right now, but there'd been no indication he wanted more than what they had. His family had accepted her place in his life, but soon they'd start asking when the wedding would happen—if it was ever going to. They were supposed to be just *going with the flow*, after all. Having *fun times*. And even though she'd agreed to that, suddenly she wanted much more, and she was deathly afraid he didn't.

'I'd better go. The next patient is in the pre-op waiting room and I just saw Mrs Jackson heading into the scrub room.' That at least was real.

'Tilda…' Lachlan paused, drew a breath. 'How about I come with you to look at the place, and then we go somewhere for a meal afterwards?'

'You don't mind looking at an apartment with me?' It didn't really fit the picture of them together, enjoying a hot, heavy fling.

His shrug was nonchalant, and covering up something. Moving towards the day when they split up? 'If we get to have a decent meal afterwards I'm happy.'

'I'll wait for you after work. My appointment with the agent is for six o'clock. Will you be able to make it?'

'I'm not operating this afternoon, and my last patient is

due in the office at five. Meet you at the car.' He turned and headed away before she could answer.

Not that she had anything more to say, other than to ask where this was going. The idea of looking at apartments for herself, let alone signing up for one, made her feel sick. When she'd left Cambodia she'd been looking forward to getting on with her life back here. That had included finding somewhere nice to live, a place with more space than she'd had in the past because she'd be there long-term. Now the idea of living on her own wasn't cheering her up one tiny bit, but she owed it to herself to at least have a backup plan in place. Falling for Lachlan and having no idea how he felt about her had made her feel incredibly vulnerable. She had to do this.

'Matilda? Are you all right?' Allie called. 'We're ready to go in here.'

Allie, another nurse, was fast becoming a friend at work. Shaking away the gloom in her head, Tilda forced a smile on her face and headed to the scrub room. 'I'm all good.' Then she yawned, feeling sluggish at the same time.

'A late night?'

'Quite the opposite.' She and Lachlan had been curled up in bed by ten, which was early for them. For the first time since she'd returned from Cambodia they hadn't made love, as she'd fallen asleep within minutes of pulling the sheet up to her chin. So why this tiredness? 'Could be the busy weekend catching up with me.' Most likely it was due to the stress of living with Lachlan and loving him while feeling incredibly insecure about where they were headed and frightened she was making a mistake. Throw in unexpected hours yesterday, with two unscheduled operations resulting from a car accident and a man falling off scaffolding at a building site, and she'd all but crawled home afterwards.

Not home, Tilda. It's Lachlan's house.

She was there temporarily.

I don't want to move out. I want to stay. With Lachlan.

But that might not be on the cards. Deep breath. She needed to relax. She was going to see an apartment tonight that, from what was on the website, ticked all the boxes on her need-to-have list. She could ring up now and say she'd take it. But she wouldn't. She didn't step blindly into anything. Especially not love.

'What do you think?' the agent asked Tilda. 'I have to tell you I have two more people booked to view this property tomorrow.'

'It's cosy,' she answered, rubbing her hands up and down her arms. It would be if the heating was on.

'Not too small?' Lachlan asked. He looked a little stunned as he gazed around the top-level apartment, ducking to avoid banging his head on the slanting roof.

Matilda winked. 'It's built for shorties like me.'

'Places like this are in high demand,' the agent advised.

Then how come it was still available after being advertised for two weeks? 'It's a handy location for my work and going to the beach.' Buses ran along Burrard, which was close by, so there was no problem getting to work and back. She returned to the bedroom for another look.

'By the time you put a bed in here there won't be any room for anything else.' Lachlan was right behind her.

Nothing new for her. 'Unless I decide to live further out of town, this is the reality of what I can afford.' He'd probably be thinking his wardrobe was bigger than this room.

'Besides, I don't have a lot of furniture. Just shoes,' she added with a little laugh. Shoes were her new hobby. Two pairs in ten days. Not bad for her. Seeing the look of wonder on Lachlan's face when she'd walked down the stairs on the day they were going to his parents' charity event had made her feel sexy and attractive. All because of a pair of shoes. Maybe the tight red dress with the slightly revealing top had had something to do with it too.

'Seen enough?' He made it sound as though there hadn't been much to see in the first place. But then he did live in a mansion.

'I have.' In the lounge she told the agent, 'I'll think about it and get back to you.'

'You might miss out if you don't make an instant decision.'

'I'll take that chance.' This was the first place she'd looked at so far. The problem being that not many seemed to be available in the areas she'd prefer at a price that didn't bankrupt her. But looking around at the small, tidy space she just didn't feel the vibe. It didn't give her that sense of home. Getting picky? Spoilt after staying with Lachlan? Or not ready to move away from him? 'Thank you for showing me the apartment,' she said brusquely and headed downstairs and out of the front door.

'Where to next?' Lachlan asked once they were settled in his car.

'There's a unit on Burrard I'd like to drive by.'

'It's dark.'

'Just do it, okay?'

He started the car and pulled out. 'Burrard's a main road. It'll be too noisy for you.'

Exactly why the road wasn't her desired location, but

she couldn't afford to be too fussy if she wanted to be this close to the city centre.

'I can wear earmuffs,' she snapped. He had no idea how the other half lived.

'Hey.' Lachlan laid his hand on her knee. 'I got a shock seeing that place. It was clean and tidy, but so small. Even for a shortie.' His smile was tired. 'I know I haven't got a clue what you can afford or what's available, but it really took me aback to see that.'

'Can't fault your honesty.' Her heart squeezed. He was always honest with her. She loved that about him. Most of the time. 'I've been saving hard but I can't afford what I really want, so I'm going for the next best thing, just to get on the property ladder.'

The money she had in her investment account wasn't quite enough for the kind of property she longed for. A small house with a little lawn so she could have a garden and a swing for her child, should she ever have that baby she yearned for. Her mind filled with the picture of Lachlan's huge lawns. She could have more than one child there. Problem with that was she wasn't set up for one child, let alone multiple children. They didn't need wealth or two parents, but she'd have to work full-time to support a child and she knew what it was like to come home to an empty house after school. Grandma had worked long hours to provide her with the basics, and she'd do the same, but those empty hours with a distracted babysitter waiting for her to come home were a constant reminder of what she needed to consider carefully.

'What number Burrard?'

Tapping her phone, the address she'd put in earlier came up on the finder app. 'There you go.'

Within minutes they were pulling up outside a property overgrown with knee-deep grass and weeds. Three old cars were parked at angles on the drive and lawn. The house was in darkness.

'This can't be it.' Lachlan was peering through the windscreen, a frown marring his looks.

Looking from the photo on her phone to the house and back, she swallowed the bile that had risen in her throat. 'They spruced up the photo for sure. The unit is supposedly around the back. Who knows? It might be in better condition, but I wouldn't want to be living behind this.'

Pulling back out onto the road, Lachlan said quietly, 'Like I said, there's no hurry to move out of my place. You've only seen two properties so far. Take your time and get it right.'

Again she swallowed. This time it was tears that needed getting rid of. The problem with his suggestion was that she was more than comfortable in his house and the longer it took to find her own place the harder it would be to go. 'The thing is, despite the last few weeks, I don't really know where we're at, Lachlan.'

Lachlan braked, pulled over and parked. Turning to face her, he said, 'What do *you* want, Tilda? Do you want to move out?'

'It wouldn't mean we won't see each other any more if I did. Would it?' It wouldn't be the same though, if she moved into her own place. They'd have to make plans to see each other, not bump into one another beside the bench or under the shower. Did she want that? Not really, but neither did she want to keep living this way. She needed to sort herself out once and for all. 'I don't know how long I can keep up the pretence that we're engaged.'

'I thought you were happy.'

'So did I. Yet suddenly I'm doubting everything.' It could be a passing fear, the past tripping her up. She hoped so. But she suspected it was more to do with her unrequited feelings.

Lachlan nodded. 'Fair enough. We did start out in a rush. But then flings are like that.'

So it was still a fling for him, nothing more serious. Her heart sank. 'What if we went on some dates? Like we were getting to know each other?'

He flinched. 'You don't think we're already doing that?'

Kind of. 'I'd like time to get used to being in a relationship after striving so hard to sort my life out and get back on my feet.' Reaching for his hand, she gripped it, putting aside some of her doubts. 'Are we in a relationship?' Because she could admit that she wanted to be, even if the thought scared her.

'I am.'

Her heart expanded, opened a little more. 'I'm with you. Just not quite as we've been doing it so far.'

Lifting their joined hands, he kissed hers. 'Here's to us and seeing where we're headed then.'

Relief filled her. Leaning over, she found his mouth with hers and kissed with all her need. She mightn't be certain where they were going but she knew she wanted to find out. If she gave him more time, perhaps he would fall in love with her too?

They never did get to eat pizza. Toast in bed after making out between the sheets was the best they managed.

Lachlan couldn't get that apartment out of his head. It was ridiculously small. How could Matilda even contemplate living in such a cramped space? She was probably used to it, whereas not in a million years could he see himself in something the size of a matchbox. His house was too large for one person, but he hadn't been able to bring himself to sell it when Kelly died.

These days the walls didn't resonate with her laughter. He didn't hear her talking to him, didn't even pause to listen for her. Like her scent on the pillows, the sounds had faded away.

I have moved on.

He was more than ready to start living life to the full again.

Just like that, his gaze lifted to Tilda, curled up beside him under the sheet. Even in sleep she looked shattered. And beautiful. Yeah, but the real reason behind his dislike of the apartment was that Tilda was apparently contemplating moving out of here, into her own place, when he'd thought they were getting on so well.

Sliding down the bed, he tucked her in against his body, holding her like he'd never let her go. Because he didn't want to. But he had to. She wanted a place to call her own. If he didn't accept that she'd probably cut him out of her life completely.

Life without Tilda looked impossible from where he lay. So he'd have to make sure they kept getting on as well as this and hopefully she'd finally stop looking for a home of her own and agree to live here, with him.

Home. At the moment this was his, but he'd like to make it theirs. His breath stalled in his lungs. He'd fallen for her more deeply than he'd known. Tilda was beautiful inside and out. She was everything he wanted for the future—his wife, the mother for his children, the woman he'd come home to every night or be there for her when she arrived back from a day at work. But did she want the same thing after everything she'd been through? He wasn't sure.

And if something went horribly wrong with their relationship, would he ever get back on his feet again? He doubted he could. It had been hard enough when he'd lost Kelly, and then Matt. A shudder rocked him. And here he'd been thinking he'd moved on. Conquered his fears. Maybe not so much after all.

Under his arm, Tilda rolled over, her eyes still closed. Then her hand covered his crotch.

'Damn you to the end of the bed and back, Tilda Simmons. I have to have you.'

She was all over him in an instant, her mouth on his neck, her tongue making hot sweeps on his skin and sending shafts of desire scorching down his body to where it all came to a blinding head.

'Tilda,' he groaned as he lifted her head and covered her mouth with his hungry one. His tongue plunged into her, tasting, searching, feeling her heat, her need throbbing through her.

Her hands were on his butt, kneading and caressing in incredibly sexy moves, making him harder than rock. So hard he was going to explode if he didn't have her right then. *Deep breath. Hold on. Not so fast.* His fingers found her heat, her moist spot, slid over her.

She rocked against him, cried, 'Lachlan…'

'Wait,' he said aloud as he reached for a condom. Then he touched her again, his fingers moving back and forth, back and forth, making her hotter and wetter, and turning himself into a molten heap of need and want at the same time.

'Now,' she begged. 'Now, Lachlan. Please.'

He couldn't deny her. He plunged into her heat, deeper

and deeper, again and again, until she cried against him. Within moments he was following her into a place that had no boundaries or fears or questions, only wonder and amazement and a bone-deep satisfaction.

CHAPTER NINE

SATURDAY MORNING TWO weeks later and they had the week-end all to themselves. Lachlan had no plans at all, other than maybe to take Tilda out to collect some of her gear from her lock-up. Something she'd been going to do ever since she'd arrived home but hadn't quite got around to, other than to get a bag of clothes early on.

'I feel terrible.' Tilda suddenly shoved her plate of toast away and leapt up to run out of the room.

She did look pasty, but they hadn't had a lot of sleep last night, being busy between the sheets, so to speak. He followed her through to the bathroom, getting there as the door slammed behind her.

'Hey, what's up?'

Then he heard a retching sound and shoved open the door. 'I'm coming in.'

She was sitting back on her haunches, holding her hair away from her face, looking rattled. 'Did I eat something off?'

'We had steak and salad last night. I can't see that giving you food poisoning.' But she had been more tired than usual lately. Sometimes she'd even been quite pale.

Oh, no.

'Tilda? When was your last period?'

She stared at him, her mouth an O shape. 'Not that.' She shook her head. 'It can't be that. We've been so careful.'

They had. 'Every time.' Passing her a cloth to wipe her face, he knelt down beside her. 'Condoms aren't one hundred percent guaranteed to do their job.' He'd seen the result of that often enough as a trainee doctor.

'I should've gone on the pill.'

Hindsight was a wonderful thing.

'We're probably wrong, but to be on the safe side we'd better find out for certain.'

She closed her eyes and her hands gripped the cloth as she scrubbed her face and mouth. Then she swore. Opening tired eyes, she stared at him. 'Seriously? Someone— something's having a joke on us. Trying to make this fake engagement real.'

He shot to his feet. 'No way.' This had nothing to do with that. It would not be the catalyst to making their fake engagement real. That would only happen if they both wanted it.

'I might not be pregnant.'

'I think you are. Unfortunately.' His teeth were grinding. Becoming a father should have been a decision for him and Tilda to make, not some random occurrence. But he should know better than most how life threw those out there whenever it chose. This was why he'd been so adamant he was remaining single. Until Tilda came along and rocked him to his core. So much for taking their time while they worked out where they were headed.

Shock replaced Tilda's bewilderment. 'Lachlan, slow down. You're overreacting before we've even found out for certain I'm pregnant. Sure, get a kit and then we will know one way or the other and can make some decisions based on fact.'

He reached down and helped her to her feet gently, remorse for his reaction nudging the shock to one side. 'We can work through this. We *will* work through it.' He wanted to say *together*, but he wasn't certain how she'd react to that. Tilda didn't really do impulsive—other than when they were in bed. She'd want time to figure out how she felt about them together and now there was no time.

'Go. Get the test kit so we know where we stand. I need to know for certain.' She turned away, but not before he saw the despair filling her eyes.

He had the feeling she was referring to their relationship more than the possibility of a baby. Their relationship that was loving and caring and had meant so much more to him than it was ever supposed to. Damn it. Of course he'd support Tilda. The baby was theirs, not hers. He was its father. If there was a baby.

'Tilda, I *am* here for you. All the way.' Again, that mental picture of her with that little girl, Bebe, back in Phnom Penh, and the longing on her face loomed up in his mind. If she was pregnant she'd go through with it. He had no doubt whatsoever. She would love and cherish their baby for ever. As he would. All his previous fears slammed back into his head, waking him up to reality—falling for Tilda had made him vulnerable again. But so was she. And he would be there for her all the way. 'Tilda…'

She spun around and snapped, 'Just go and get the kit.'

A longing to hold her until the raw pain left her face, to tell her how he felt about her, filled him. He took a step towards the woman who'd changed his life and helped him get back on track when he'd believed he'd lost direction for ever. But all he could say was, 'We'll make it work. It will be all right.'

'Sure, Lachlan. Is this when you remind me you didn't want a relationship ever again? Don't want children because you might love them and then lose them?' Agony etched her face. 'I'm not staying around to listen to your answers. I'll pack my bag while you go get that blasted kit.'

His heart split open. All over again. He'd probably just gone and blown any chance he might've had with Tilda. He should have known that it was already way too late for his heart to ever recover from losing her. He loved her to the moon and back. But if he told her that now would she believe him, or would she think he was just trying to claim his baby? Losing her was the one thing he'd hoped to avoid by not getting involved. But there were more ways of losing someone than from a runaway car or a heart attack.

So fix it. Be different this time.

His heart quailed at the thought of stepping off that cliff. It would mean burying his fears for ever. Could he even do that? He had to be sure.

'No, Tilda, I will never leave you to deal with this alone. You matter to me. If you are pregnant our baby will also matter to me.'

She stared at him.

He wanted to admit his love, but at the last second he choked. 'Don't go, Tilda,' was all he could say in that moment.

Don't go, Tilda.

'Meaning? Stay for an hour? A day? For ever?' she asked through the despair knocking at her heart. She so wanted a baby but she wasn't ready in every way conceivable. Bad choice of word, that.

Lachlan wasn't heading out yet. 'I don't know what will happen if we find out for sure we're having a baby, but I can't live with the thought of you walking out of here with nowhere to go. Nowhere that you'll be comfortable staying anyway.'

The intensity in his expression made her pause the whirling thoughts in her mind. 'You're concerned about where I might go? That's it?'

'No, that came out all wrong. We are in this together, regardless of where our relationship is at. You must stay here, at least until we have talked about things.'

Must? Telling her what to do? Sounded familiar to her. Her heart broke into pieces. 'You think?'

'In the end, the choice about where you stay is up to you, but for now can we at least get an answer and then talk about it?'

'Fair enough.' She had been about to run off without talking through the consequences of being pregnant. She didn't know for certain she was yet. Oh, yes, she did. Her hand stroked her belly. It might be churning like a washing machine through nerves and fear of losing everything again, but she was pregnant. She felt it in her heart. She'd known this sense of protectiveness last time. Last time she'd miscarried. That couldn't happen again.

'I'll shift into one of the spare bedrooms.' Until she found an apartment. The first one that was available for rent would do; she didn't have to wait to buy one. But she wasn't being fair to Lachlan. He was in this as much as she was. He hadn't said he wanted nothing to do with the baby. In fact he'd been adamant he'd be there for them. Not a familiar reaction from a man she cared about, then. But enough to make major decisions about her future? Her child's future?

His mouth softened a fraction. 'Thank you.'

What about them? There was a lot to talk about and now the pregnancy could influence their decisions in ways that might not be so good for their relationship. She knew she loved him, but he'd never even hinted that he loved her too. But first things first. They needed certainty about the baby.

'I'll still be here when you get back, Lachlan, I promise.'

'Thanks.'

She watched him go, his steps the heaviest she'd ever known as he crossed the hall to the internal door into the garage. Her heart sank lower and lower by the minute, which had nothing to do with the baby. She loved Lachlan with all her heart. It had taken this to wake her up to what that really meant. Because she already knew, despite his optimism, he wasn't ready for a permanent relationship. He seemed to have changed over the past weeks, accepting her into his life in every way possible, even when she'd had her own doubts. Now reality had slammed into him hard and she suspected marriage wasn't on the cards for them. That would mean putting Kelly aside for ever and he might never be ready to do that. Just as she'd struggled to let go of how James had taken over and controlled every aspect of her life. She doubted Lachlan would ever be like James, but it had been so hard to trust her judgement enough to let the past go.

Lachlan looked like she felt—stunned and confused. Fair enough. She got it. But there'd also been a look of withdrawal on his face, despite saying he'd be there for her. For them. Could she love enough for both of them? Did she want to try? Not really. She loved Lachlan but he had to come to her with his heart in his hands or it wasn't ever going to work. She knew that from painful experience.

And until he was ready for that, whatever they'd had between them was over. Even if the test was negative, she wouldn't be getting back into bed with Lachlan. Nor chatting over a meal about anything and everything, or working together to help others less fortunate. This had been a wake-up call for them both. They'd got on so well, had the same dreams and hopes, but now she realised they both had to work out what they really wanted, emotionally and romantically, to be able to meet each other halfway.

She sank against the basin and dropped her face into shaking hands. What a mess. There was nothing fake about the love for Lachlan filling her heart. Nothing. From the moment the thought she was pregnant struck, her first instinct had been to reach out to him—because she loved him so, so much. Yet while he'd said he'd be there for them, he hadn't sounded like the affectionate, caring man she'd come to know over the past weeks.

Which only went to show she'd gone and done what she'd sworn never to do again—fallen in love with a man who wasn't able to share his heart. Lachlan was everything she wanted and that meant he wasn't a control freak. But he had his own baggage and he still wasn't letting her in, wasn't about to discuss his issues properly and see if they could make it work between them. What would he do if she miscarried? Support her for a while and then disappear out of her life?

Naturally he wanted to protect his heart. Like she did hers, only it was too late for her. But whatever Lachlan felt for her, he wouldn't be admitting it. That would be too risky for him.

So she'd have to get busy and find an apartment, fast. She needed her own space. Avoiding Lachlan in his home would only add to the nightmare.

Straightening up, she studied her face in the mirror. Awful didn't begin to describe her blotchy cheeks and sad eyes. Sad? When she was having a baby? The baby she'd longed for ever since the day she'd lost her first one. Even when she wasn't prepared, financially or otherwise, she couldn't wait to carry this baby through to full term and beyond. She would not lose it this time. Lachlan would love his child too, however he felt about her. He had a big heart, loved his family and friends.

So she'd carry on as though everything would work out and the baby would arrive safely in a few more months, happy and healthy.

Put the baby first in everything you do from now on.

Was she up to that? Absolutely. She loved it already. No argument. This was where tough got tougher. She was strong. She now had to be even stronger for her baby's sake. The baby she refused to miscarry.

The doorbell pealed loud in the empty house. Who was that? Lachlan's parents and Meredith and her tribe always bowled in, didn't stop for a closed door, so it couldn't be any of them. Fingers crossed. She wasn't up to facing them at the moment. Her feet dragged as she made her way to the front door. The bell rang again.

'Coming,' she growled, then pulled the door open.

A courier stood there, holding out a letter pack. 'This is for Matilda Simmons.'

'That's me. Do you need proof?'

'No. Only a signature.'

A quick scrawl and she was back inside, closing the door

as she stared at the envelope. A sticker with the law office logo was on the back. The divorce papers had finally arrived. 'Great timing.' Biting down on her frustration, she went to get some scissors and opened the pack to tip out the paperwork.

As she stared at the legal proof signifying the end of her marriage, tears began sliding down her cheeks. So many failed dreams culminating in a single piece of paper. It wasn't that she missed her ex, or even cared where he was or what he was up to. It was how her hopes and wishes had all come down to this. Would her time with Lachlan end in a similar fashion? Not divorce but over just the same. *Finito*.

'Tilda? What's happened now? What's that paper?' Lachlan was back.

She knew he wouldn't have dallied on the way.

'Tilda?' Worry spilled out of him.

'I'm officially divorced.' Her lawyer had said as much in his email yesterday, but seeing the signed paper brought a large dose of reality. It was what she'd wanted, but it still caused her to ache inside, knowing she'd been so wrong about a man she'd once been devoted to.

'You're free again.' He was tense, and he spoke sharply.

She fought the need to reach out to him for a hug and stepped away. 'I am.'

Not if I'm pregnant, because a baby is a lifelong commitment.

One she wasn't quite ready for, but would do all in her power to prepare for regardless.

'You got the testing kit?'

'Yes.' He handed over a small package.

Her fingers were shaking as she took it. 'Crunch time.' And she didn't mean positive or negative. Whatever the result, their relationship was over, but it was going to get awkward sharing this place, even if only for a few days.

At the bathroom door she turned around to look at Lachlan. He was watching her, his face so sad she had to fight not to rush over and throw her arms around him and promise they could make everything all right. He'd resist and she couldn't face that. He had to want to be a father, to want to be with her. Want her, and love her, not just offer to support her out of kindness or duty. She shuddered. No, thank you. She would manage on her own, no matter what was thrown at her.

'I'll be right here,' he said as he sank onto a stool by the counter.

Supporting her? Or desperate to know the result? Probably both. Lachlan wouldn't desert her at this moment.

'Then let's get this done,' she muttered as she closed the door and tore open the packet. Introspection was only delaying finding out one way or the other what lay ahead. Not that she didn't already know.

A few minutes later she laid the result in front of Lachlan. 'I'm pregnant.' Her heart was pounding, making her throat feel blocked and her head spin.

He stared at the blue line for so long she wondered if he'd fallen asleep. Except that was impossible, given the state he was in.

'You're not saying much,' she jibed as all her emotions gelled into shock.

'I'm afraid to utter a word.'

'Lachlan, this is me, Matilda. I have never deliberately done a thing to upset you, so why not discuss this with me?'

'It's not what you might say that worries me.' He finally turned in his chair to look at her. 'I've screwed up big time.'

She was aghast at the pain and despair in his face. 'I've been a part of everything that's happened too.'

'I tried to stay away from you, Tilda. But you got to me so easily.' He shook his head, despair darkening his beautiful face. 'When you came to Vancouver it was impossible not to get closer to you after our time in Cambodia. You're so beautiful and sexy and you steal my breath away every time I look at you.'

This sounded good. She should be feeling happy and ready for something good to come. But this was Lachlan. He was about to pour cold water on his words. It was there in the way he drew himself up and locked those formidable blue eyes on her. She waited, her heart still pounding so loud it was a wonder she could hear herself think.

'Nothing's changed, Matilda. I'm still afraid of losing someone. But I'll always be here, supporting you, doing what's right.'

Back to calling her Matilda. He couldn't have worded it any clearer. Suddenly she was angry. She didn't want the right thing done by her. She wanted his love or nothing.

'Can't? Or won't? Whatever you think, this is real, and it's not going away. I am pregnant with *our* baby. Get used to the idea.'

He rose out of his chair to lean against the counter. 'I am well aware *we* are having a child. It scares the hell out of me.'

'You think I'm not worried too?' She should be grateful he was being honest, but it would be good to have him with her in everything that lay ahead. Their baby needed its father to be there for it and to love it unconditionally. Not to have him pull down the blinds the moment he learned the baby really existed. 'Has it occurred to you that I'm already afraid of losing it?'

'Oh, Matilda, please don't think that. Baby will be fine. Strong like its mum.'

'Her father's strong too. But I've already lost one.' Her? Yes, she was having a girl. She knew it like she'd known she was pregnant. It was in her genes to have a daughter. 'To lose this one would decimate me.'

He looked at her. 'I know.'

He probably did. 'Talk to me, tell what you're feeling right now.'

Get the problem out in the open so we can deal with it.

'I never believed we'd be facing this dilemma. I just want you to be happy.' He paused, watching her the whole time. 'You can always live here. Permanently,' he added in a rush. 'Or at least until we've had time to really consider all the options and think about our baby's future.' He wasn't saying anything about his feelings for her, which said a lot more than he realised.

It had only been a fling after all. He hadn't stopped fearing the worst would happen again.

'So I can live here as a flatmate and the mother of your child? No thanks.' Impossible when she loved him so much.

She felt her grandmother's hand on her shoulder, as she often had when she was growing up, telling her she was strong and capable of standing alone and raising her child to become strong too. Lachlan would have a part in the child's life but not hers. She was not waiting around for him to reject her. Her heart wasn't so strong it wouldn't break. She did believe she could trust him not to try and control her, but he'd never love her the way he'd loved Kelly. She couldn't live with that.

'You have to do what's best for you, Lachlan. But please don't waste a wonderful opportunity to have the life you might really want.'

With that, she turned and strode away, head high and heart slamming. Her hands were fists at her sides. Her stomach was one large knot of frustration and anger and sorrow. That man held her heart in his hands and didn't know it. She'd started to believe she was ready to chance everything again, to love and be loved. The reality was she was single, and going to stay that way. But there was a baby growing inside her so she'd have to calm down and work at being relaxed, so as not to send sour vibes throughout her body and upset her baby. Her daughter had to stay safe. Her heart didn't matter half as much.

Liar.

Lachlan watched Matilda storm upstairs. His heart went with her.

I love her.

Without a doubt. That didn't stop the fear of losing her ramping up to full speed. Or of something terrible happening to their baby. It was terrifying. First Kelly, then Matt. If that happened again to Tilda or their baby— Then he'd be lost for ever, even worse off than before. Except he already stood to lose her because of the way he felt about her.

If he told her the truth, he might have Tilda at his side as they went through life, loving each other and their child. Children plural. As if. He couldn't deal with the knowledge of one baby on the way, let alone multiple. Face it, he wasn't dealing with anything very well right now.

Go talk to her.

And say what? He wanted to protect her, make her life

easy so that she wasn't at risk of miscarrying again because of added stress. She'd already lost one baby; she'd suffer badly if she lost this one too. So he had to look out for her. That was who he was, unless it came to protecting his heart. He'd stuffed up there. He'd already given that to her. And she didn't know it. Nor did she probably want to know now. He'd started retreating emotionally from her the moment it dawned on him she might be pregnant. The commitment and involvement of being a father wasn't the problem. It was the overwhelming love he'd have for her and his child and the fear of losing them that was causing the pain in his heart and the tension in his gut.

You love Tilda. You'll love the baby the moment you accept it.

That was what got to him. He would love his child from here to the end of the earth and back again if he let it in. As he already did his baby's mother. She'd got under his skin, into his head and heart, and there was no coming back from that. But she didn't want him or his love, did she? She had her baby to love, and he would help her raise it as he'd promised.

His phone vibrated on the bench. Snatching it up, he snapped, 'Yes?'

'Lachlan, I'm Anna, a nurse on the surgical ward. Sorry to bother you on your weekend off, but Millie Jackson's complaining of severe pain at the surgical site. The plastic surgeon on call is in Theatre and I don't think we can wait.'

'I'll come in.' He shoved the phone into his pocket, snatched up the keys to his four-wheel drive and headed for the door. Something else to think about, however briefly, might be good for his messed-up brain. Except he couldn't just walk out on Tilda without saying a word.

Upstairs, he found her in his bedroom collecting her clothes into a pile. No doubt moving into another room. 'I've been called in to see a patient I operated on yesterday.'

'Fine.'

No, it wasn't. But what could he say? At the moment anything that came out of his mouth wouldn't have been thought through enough. He had no clear idea of what he wanted to offer Tilda, other than his love and support, and neither of those was enough, considering how badly he'd already hurt her.

'See you later.'

Her reply was a shrug, as though she'd already moved on from him. And why wouldn't she? He wasn't making anything easier for her. Which wasn't how this was meant to be.

The drive in to the hospital was tedious. He'd done it so often he could probably do it blindfolded. It certainly wasn't distracting his busy mind. Nor did his patient. The pain in her abdomen where he'd done a minor tummy tuck was high, but the reason was not apparent. Until she admitted to bending over sharply to snatch up a mascara brush she'd dropped over the side of the bed. An X-ray showed a minor bleed that had stopped quickly.

'No more bending unless you want to return to Theatre for more surgery,' he said firmly. Too firmly by the look on the nurse's face. But he wasn't having a great day.

Heading out of the hospital, he made a snap decision and grabbed the walking shoes from his vehicle. Going home wasn't an option. It would be too uncomfortable, worrying about bumping into Tilda all the time.

Tilda or Matilda. There was a huge gap between the two versions of her name. One was professional and friendly without being close. The other was his woman, soft and fun and loving. And he'd let her go because he was afraid of losing her. His heart dropped to his feet. He was such a coward. He'd already lost her, so how was this any better?

'I love you, Tilda and Matilda,' he said.

Too bloody late, buster.

Wasn't he always?

His pace increased to almost a jog as he zigzagged around pedestrians out for a stroll. No strolling for him. He was on a mission to quieten the noises in his head.

Tilda was shaking like she couldn't believe. Lachlan was avoiding her.

Sure, he had to go into work. It was part of being a surgeon to be called in even on days off, but today when they had issues to solve? Was she being a little selfish? Of course he had to go in. But at the moment it felt as though he was using it as an excuse to avoid her, and she'd already lost everything. No, not quite. Her hand landed on her stomach.

'I am pregnant.' So she needed to be ultra-careful because she could lose the baby too. To lose this one would be the end of everything. She'd never dream of happy families again.

She stuffed more clothes into the drawer in the spare bedroom. Slammed it shut. Sank onto the edge of the bed. A big bed, not quite as large as the one she and Lachlan had spent so many hours making love in but big enough if he should change his mind and visit her during the night. But there'd be no more lovemaking. She was back to being single. And that had nothing to do with the divorce.

I can't stay here with Lachlan just down the hall. It would only add to her despair. She loved the man to the end of the earth and back. She believed he didn't mean to hurt her.

But she had to stand tall and be accountable for herself. So she couldn't stay here. They'd always be tripping over each other or trying to avoid one another. It would be awkward at the very least.

Not to mention how she'd feel if Faye or John turned up. Or Meredith.

Grabbing a bag, she emptied the drawer she'd just filled. Then she packed some books and shoes and her toiletries. She was out of here.

Where to?

The taxi driver suggested a hotel near Western General when she asked if he knew of anywhere within walking distance of her work. 'It's clean and safe,' he promised.

He was right. The room was rather dark and small but it was clean, and it was her space for as long as she paid the daily rate.

After dumping her bags on the bed, she headed outside for a walk. Anything to distract her from thinking about Lachlan. Of course it didn't work. He was with her every step she took.

He couldn't see how he was such a kind, loving man. His family adored him. Likewise those three boys and Meredith. He had all it took to be the best husband and father ever, if only he could move on from his past. Not that she was doing so well at that either. She knew what it was like to have your dreams stomped all over.

So was she ready to give him another chance? To let him back in, even though he couldn't love her? Was that being strong? She wasn't so sure.

Lachlan picked up his phone and called Tilda.

'Hello.' Her voice was flat. Tired. Full of tears.

'Where are you?' It was after eight and he'd just got home to find her gone. When had she left? After dealing with the patient he'd been called in to see and going for a walk, he'd been called back in to operate on another woman, an emergency this time, requiring a lot of work repairing face and chest injuries after being in a multiple car crash. He was exhausted but he knew sleep would be impossible until he was sure Tilda was all right.

'I've moved out of your place. It's too hard being there at the moment.'

'Where are you?' he repeated. He needed to know she was safe. Damn it, he needed to *see* her. To talk with her. Hug her. Like that was going to happen.

'I'm fine. Promise.'

Relief wasn't flooding him. 'Come back, Tilda. I won't even talk to you if you don't want me to.'

'No, Lachlan. I can't. You're the greatest guy I've known but I can't carry on staying with you. I need to get on with my own life. I have to look out for myself.'

The last shred of hope that she loved him died. But he still tried. 'I want to be there for you and the baby.'

'It's not enough, Lachlan.' She paused. 'Anyway, what happens when your family or Meredith turn up? I cannot look them in the eye and carry on acting as though I'm your fiancée.'

'I'll tell them the truth about that.'

'You need to. We were out of order doing it in the first place. But explaining it doesn't make the situation any better. We're a messed-up pair of individuals who need to sort our lives out, and the sooner the better for our baby's sake.'

'Tell me where you are, Tilda. I'm coming to get you.

Please don't say no. We need to have this conversation face to face.'

'Sorry, Lachlan. It's too late for that. I am not coming back. Ever.' She was gone.

Not coming back, ever? Really? That was what she'd said. Did she mean it? It sounded like it.

He dropped onto a chair and stared up at the ceiling.

He loved her.

Which meant he had to risk it all and take a chance on getting hurt again and let her into his heart for all to see. Not keep his love silent.

He could do that. The question was, did she want to hear it?

He picked up his phone, stabbed her number and listened to it ring and ring until the voicemail picked up. He couldn't tell her he loved her in a message.

So instead he simply said, 'I'll always be here for you, Tilda.' Then he went to bed, lying on her side and breathing in her scent from the pillow she slept with curled around her neck. He didn't get any sleep at all.

I'll always be here for you, Tilda.

She played the message over and over throughout the night, listening to every nuance in his voice, imagining him beside her. If only that was true. Except that would mean she'd gone back on her word to herself—to stay strong. She had to fight her own battles, not rely on Lachlan to be there for her. Not rely on anybody but herself.

It was too much. Throwing the phone aside, she climbed off the bed and dug out some fresh clothes. She'd go and find some breakfast then figure out what to do for the rest of the day.

Breakfast was a fail. It didn't stay down and she returned to her room to lie on her bed until the churning subsided. Then she looked up properties to rent and made three appointments for viewings. Even on Sundays some agents were hungry to make deals. To kill time she walked to Granville Island and had a coffee in the sun before heading to her first appointment.

The apartment was small and smelt of cats.

'No, thanks.'

The next one was clean and spacious and overlooked a nightclub.

'No, thanks.'

She didn't even bother looking at the third one. She was too tired, and couldn't keep Lachlan out of her thoughts.

She loved him.

But she was being strong and staying away.

It was so unbearably tempting to call a taxi and go back to his house. To tell him she loved him and beg him to try to put the past behind him and take a chance with her. That was not being strong.

She looked up jobs in other cities before sighing and switching her phone off. Avoidance was not the right tactic. She wouldn't keep father and child apart.

At eight o'clock she climbed into bed and pretended to sleep the night away. At least she'd be busy at work tomorrow and her mind would get a chance to quieten down.

As long as she didn't bump into Lachlan.

Only he was away at a day conference that she'd forgotten all about. Which made her feel lonelier than ever. She missed him so much every fibre in her body ached with the need to see him. This being strong wasn't going at all to plan.

Had she got it wrong? Would it make more sense to face up to her love and do something about seeing if they could make it work? If he could ever love her back? For their baby's sake, shouldn't she try?

Her heart thumped.

Could she?

The house was cold and quiet when Lachlan got home, dashing the small hope that Tilda might've returned. Throughout the day, when he was supposed to be listening to speakers talking about the latest in breast reduction procedures and scar repairs, he'd heard nothing other than Tilda saying she wasn't ever coming back to him.

Leaving his laptop on the bench, he headed upstairs for a shower, taking a detour to the spare bedrooms to check in case she had returned and was lying low. In the second room he looked in he found a small pile of books she'd left on the bedside table, but no clothes or make-up or shoes.

Spinning around to head for that shower, he saw a packet on the floor half under the bed. Bending down, he picked it up. A photo fell out onto the bedcover. A young Tilda was standing with an older woman, smiling as if her world was perfect.

He sank down onto the bed, unable to take his eyes off the two women. The likeness was incredible. The woman had to be Tilda's grandmother. They had the same twinkly eyes, identical smiles, and while Tilda's hair was dark and the other woman's grey, they both wore it in a ponytail that fell over their left shoulder. Two beautiful women. Two very strong women. One had no doubt passed that trait onto the other.

Shaking the packet, another photo slid out. In this one

Tilda was holding up her nursing certificate and her grand-mother was hugging her. The love in both faces touched him deeply.

'You were loved so much.'

'Yes, I was.'

His head shot up.

There she was, standing in the doorway, apprehension warring with determination in her beautiful face.

His heart began pounding, hard and fast. 'You dropped these.'

'I hoped they were here. I left in a bit of a hurry.'

'I can see where you get your strength from. Your grand-mother was quite special, wasn't she?'

'She was, and she still is in here.' Her hand tapped her breast. 'I wish she was here now to know about the baby. About...' She paused, swallowed and locked her beautiful but sad eyes on him. 'I'm not as strong as I thought I was, Lachlan.'

He stood up and faced her. 'Yes, you are.'

'No. If I was, I'd have understood before now that being strong means showing my weaknesses to you. All of them.'

The pounding got louder and his mouth dried. 'That's not necessary.'

She stepped nearer, still watching him, as if she was beg-ging him to see into her, to understand her. 'I thought I was being strong by standing alone, looking out for myself and ignoring what my heart wanted and needed.'

His pulse went into overdrive. Something momentous was coming. Good? Or terrible?

'I was wrong. It's hard for me to say this, but I need to. For me, for you, and for our baby.' Her shoulders rose and fell. 'I love you with all my being, Lachlan. I believe in you, trust you not to hurt me. I want to spend the rest of my life with you. If you'll have me,' she whispered. 'I don't want to raise our child alone. I want to show you how much I love you every day. And I want you to love me in return.'

He went to speak but nothing came out. Tilda loved him. He'd been longing to hear those words but hadn't expected to. If his tongue wasn't functioning his arms were; snatching her to him, he brushed the tenderest of kisses on her cheek, then her forehead and finally her lips.

'You're not taking all the blame for what's gone wrong between us. I was afraid to tell you I love you so much that my heart actually hurts, but the old fears wouldn't go away and then I thought I was too late anyway.' His heart was quietening, relaxing as the enormity of what Tilda had said finally sunk in. 'I should've been less of a coward and told you earlier anyway.'

'Are you still worried about losing someone again?'

'Yes, but I'm ready to take the chance and make the most of the time we've got together. I don't know about you, but I'm planning on for ever.'

Her lips lifted at the corners, making his heart melt all over again. 'I can't believe we were both madly in love with each other and neither one of us was brave enough to confess. I know we were both trying to protect ourselves, but we were going the wrong way about it. It nearly ended in disaster.'

'From now on, no more secrets.' He couldn't imagine not telling her he loved her every day from now on.

'Agreed.' Her mouth returned his kiss before she pulled back and eyeballed him. 'So? Are we going to spend the rest of our lives together? For ever?'

'Try and stop me.' He beamed. 'Yes, Tilda we are.' Taking

her hands in his, he dropped to one knee. 'Will you make our engagement real? Marry me?'

Leaning down, she kissed him. 'Yes, Lachlan, I will.'

Then she was in his arms and they were kissing as if their lives depended on it. Which they did really. Without Tilda his life would be a cold, sad, barren wasteland.

As he laid her on the bed she looked up at him and laughed. 'Guess this means I'll have to let your mother organise our wedding and talk to that dressmaker.'

'Fine, but I'm the one taking you shopping for an engagement ring.' If there was even one out there that he'd consider being good enough for her.

EPILOGUE

'LACHLAN, WHEN CAN Vicki play soccer with me?'

'Not for a couple of years at least, Lenny.'

'That's not fair. I want her to play with me now.' Stamp, stamp went his feet on the lawn at the back of their house. Meredith had dropped them off so she could spend the day with her new man, who was turning out to be a dream come true for her. Everyone was waiting with bated breath to see where this relationship went. Something that had Tilda laughing because it was a rerun of Lachlan's life before she'd arrived in it.

Tilda looked at Lenny. 'She's only a baby. Babies can't walk or run, and the ball is too big for her to hold.' The boys had taken to Vicki like frogs to water. They adored her but got impatient at times with her lack of activity. Gurgling and slopping milk out the corner of her mouth didn't cut it with them.

Grandma Faye handed Vicki to Tilda, nothing but love in her eyes. 'Think she needs the one thing I can't provide.'

Vicki's little face was screwed up in concentration, obviously about to tell everyone she wanted milk—now.

Latching her daughter onto her breast, trying to be discreet when the boys did their yuk faces, she leaned back against Lachlan's knees and smiled at the wonder of her world. Little more than a year ago she'd walked out into the arrivals hall at Phnom Penh Airport and up to the man holding a piece of card with Matilda Simmons written on it. Now she was Matilda McRae, though no one called her Matilda around here. She was strictly Tilda. And she was a mother to this gorgeous bundle of joy named after the woman who'd shown her how to be strong enough to let Lachlan into her heart. Her grandmother, Victoria.

'Want me to make some tea?' Faye was getting to her feet. At times the woman smothered her daughter-in-law with love, but she meant well and, along with John, was so happy for Lachlan. And therefore Tilda was more than happy to be spoilt.

'Not for me, Mum. I'd better be the sub for Vicki in the soccer game or there'll be bedlam on the pitch.' Lachlan had put up a goal net at each end of the lawn for the boys, admitting on the side that he'd only made his weekend mornings busier because they were determined to play there all the time. 'The ref's out of control.'

Tilda grinned up at him. 'John's loving every minute of it. And they're keeping you fit.'

Glancing around to see where his mother was, he then leaned down and whispered, 'You do that all on your own, Mrs McRae.'

Her heart sped up at the memory of what they'd got up to in their bedroom when Vicki had finally fallen asleep last night. 'Think you had something to do with it, Doctor.'

'Might've added my two cents' worth.'

'Cheap at the price, if you ask me. I might need to go a bit more upmarket.'

'A dollar?' He grinned. 'Love you, Tilda McRae. Vicki's one lucky little girl to have you for a mum.'

Her heart stuttered. She had taken to motherhood without

hesitation. She'd been surprised at how natural it all seemed when she'd grown up with no one to observe. Of course Faye had been on hand from the moment she'd managed to sneak into the delivery room and meet her granddaughter for the first time but, to be fair, she didn't try and take over, merely acted as a guide if Tilda had any questions or doubts.

'Her dad's not too bad either.' In a lot of ways, not all to do with raising his daughter.

'Lachlan, hurry up,' Campbell shouted from the left goal net. 'We're waiting.'

'There's my cue.' He bent down again and brushed the softest and sexiest kiss over her mouth, then touched his daughter's back lightly. 'Love you both.'

'Love you too,' Tilda managed to say through the tears at the back of her throat. 'To the end of the earth and back.'

* * * * *

NURSE'S
PREGNANCY
SURPRISE

AMY RUTTAN

MILLS & BOON

For my dear friend Desiree Holt.
You once said I brightened your life,
being your friend. You brightened mine.
When I was a new writer, you were one of
the first big authors to befriend me.
You never competed…you only shared your knowledge.
You were a light. I shall miss you.
Fly free, my dear sweet friend.

CHAPTER ONE

Barcelona, Spain

"SHARON, THAT HANDSOME stranger is staring at you again."

Sharon looked up from her book and glanced up to where her roommate at the medical conference she'd been attending was pointing. Her heart skipped a beat as she found him, sitting at the bar.

Everywhere she went this week she ran into him. He said his name was Gus, when they first met in the hotel elevator. She knew he was in the medical profession. This was a medical conference after all, and they were in several workshops together.

They always chatted, always compared notes after a workshop, and whenever she saw him she would feel a bubble of excitement inside her.

He was the most handsome man she'd ever seen.

Sharon had to remind herself that she was at this conference for work and not pleasure, but when she saw him, Gus the stranger with the sparkling dark eyes, her insides melted just a bit.

He made her feel things and think of things that were totally out of character for her.

Angelina grinned and elbowed her. "I know you're leaving tomorrow, but you should totally talk to him."

"I have talked to him before," Sharon replied, trying to tear her gaze away from his piercing blue eyes.

Angelina looked shocked. "What?"

"We've been in the same workshops. Infection control, postanesthesia care...another one about infections."

Angelina wrinkled her nose. "I remember those workshops. Kind of gross."

Sharon chuckled. "I thought you were a nurse?"

Angelina ignored her. "So, is he a doctor or a nurse?"

Sharon shrugged. "Not sure. The only thing I know is he's from Latin America. Somewhere."

"Did he tell you?" Angelina asked curiously.

"No, but we both figured out our Spanish accents are similar. Though his is more like my family's than mine is. Mine is tainted by New York." Sharon smiled at that. Although she hadn't divulged she was from Argentina to him, she'd been born there, but her Spanish was a mix of United States and Tierra del Fuego where her mother's family came from. Her father was Italian and she could speak that fairly well too.

When you traveled a lot, which she did for work, it was handy to know multiple languages.

Gus had been impressed when she mentioned that, but they didn't go too deep into personal stuff. That wasn't what she was here for.

What are you here for, then, besides work? He's the first guy you've noticed in years. Maybe you should have some fun.

She shook that thought away.

Heat crept up her neck and she really hoped that the blush didn't reach her cheeks. She had been planning to spend these last few days in Barcelona after this conference. She never really entertained the notion of a fling, but she had been feeling a bit lost lately.

She wanted some things in her life to change. She wanted to live a little.

A fling with a handsome stranger in Spain was definitely out of the ordinary.

As far as Sharon was concerned, Mr. Right was never coming, because she wasn't looking for him. She didn't believe in happily-ever-afters or love.

It's not like she had to do anything tonight.

It might be nice to flirt with him one last time.

And Gus wasn't a complete stranger. She knew his name. She knew he was smart, quiet and focused about medicine.

Things she appreciated and admired.

They didn't need to get into specifics.

"So you know him. Go talk to him!" Angelina urged.

"I don't know," Sharon said.

Angelina rolled her eyes. "Oh, come on. You told me you wanted a holiday fling once. Here's your chance. Don't be RPN Sharon Misasi tonight. Seduce him."

Sharon snorted. "Seduce him? What're you talking about? I can't."

"Sure you can. He clearly likes you, and what's there not to like about him?"

Angelina was right. Gus was very easy on the eyes.

He was tall, athletic, with a dark brown mop of curls and a strong bronzed jaw. Though that wasn't what did it for her the first time they met in that elevator. It was his eyes. His dark brown eyes not only sparkled, but when they settled on her it felt like she was the only one he could see. They mesmerized her, drew her in and made her blood heat with the promise of something more.

Every time she met his gaze he made her melt.

Just a little.

Every.

Single.

Time.

Yet there was something behind that facade of confidence, something sad that drew her to him. Like they shared something deep. She didn't know what, but she couldn't find out. No matter how good-looking or charming or appealing he was, she didn't have time for relationships or the opposite sex. Her career was too important, which had been the main complaint of the couple of men she'd dated for a short time.

Besides, she'd seen the negative effects of loving someone so much and how it could shatter your whole world when that person was gone. It was devastating. Even to the point of abandoning your own child because they reminded you too much of your deceased partner.

Sharon sucked back the memories of her childhood that were threatening to cloud her mind.

Romance was not for her.

So why was Gus so different? Why did he make her want to take a chance? She wasn't sure.

She wanted to find out though.

It would only be for one night. She'd be gone ~~onto~~ her next job and he'd move on as well.

Sharon stuffed her book into her purse and picked up her drink, with Angelina silently cheering her on. She trembled slightly as she made her way through the crowded hotel bar toward him.

He grinned when he saw her, those dark eyes sparkling.

A dark curl on his bronzed forehead escaped between his fingers as he raked his hand through his thick hair.

"Gus?" she asked, hoping her voice didn't crack with nerves.

"*Hola*, Sharon," he replied, brightly.

"Yes." She liked the way he said her name. It rolled off his tongue. "Mind if I join you?"

"No. Not at all." He got up, pulling out the bar stool next to him. She caught a whiff of his cologne. It was a crisp, clean scent. Subtle, but still manly.

Warmth crept up her neck and she cleared her throat as she sat down. She turned her back to him to try to regain composure.

"Thank you," she said, hoping her voice wasn't shaking.

Why did he make her so nervous? What was it about him?

"So how are you enjoying Barcelona?" he asked.

"It's great. But I haven't seen much of it with work."

He cocked an eyebrow. "What?"

She shrugged. "I've been busy."

He nodded. "I do understand that. Work is my life too."

"That sounds depressing, doesn't it?"

He grinned. "It does rather."

"So would you like to grab a drink?"

He turned and motioned to a waiter. "Yes, I like that."

"Maybe we could not talk…" Sharon trailed off as she noticed the waiter coming toward them. He was sweating profusely. It was a warm day, but not hot enough to be that sweaty.

Gus seemed to notice too, because his gaze narrowed and he sat up straighter.

"Are you okay?" Sharon asked the waiter gently.

"I'm fine," the waiter stated, but his balance was off and he was teetering to one side.

"I don't think you're fine, my friend," Gus said, standing up.

"Señor..." The waiter winced and then stumbled over, collapsing.

Gus helped him down on the ground. Sharon crouched down.

"Is he okay?" she asked.

"I think he's having a heart attack." Gus went over the man's vitals.

"You're a doctor?" Sharon asked, calmly.

"Sí." Gus frowned. "He's not breathing." He started compressions as she asked a nearby waiter to call an ambulance. Another staff member rushed over and gave her an AED device. She quickly began to work around Gus's compressions.

"What do you do?" Gus asked, glancing up.

"I'm a registered nurse practitioner. I've worked many a triage."

Gus nodded as he continued his CPR. "Excellent."

He stopped compressions as Sharon hooked up the last of the electrodes to allow the AED to do its work. The device instructed her to shock the patient.

"Clear," she stated, making sure no one was touching the patient.

The AED shocked him, then instructed on its screen for Gus to continue compressions.

They continued in this way until the waiter's heart started and he was breathing again. The paramedics arrived and Gus and Sharon stepped back to let them do their work to transport the waiter to the hospital. The bar had been cleared out and shut down.

"It's good he had a heart attack in a bar with a doctor," Sharon remarked.

Gus nodded. "He was very fortunate. Not many are."

"No," she said, quietly.

"Should we go elsewhere for a drink?" he asked.

"Yes. Please." She could definitely use a drink after the excitement.

Gus opened his mouth to say something further when his phone buzzed. He frowned and cursed under his breath at the message.

"Sharon, forgive me, but I have to run."

Sharon was disappointed. "No problem."

"How about dinner in an hour? I know a great place and it's not far from here."

"Dinner?" she asked.

"If you're not busy."

"I'm not."

He grinned. "Great. Cafe Pacífica by the waterfront at eight o'clock."

"Okay," she said, nodding quickly.

He stepped closer to her. She pulled her cardigan tight around her and her heart began to race. He towered over her, which was strange as she was fairly tall herself at five foot nine.

"I'll see you then," he whispered huskily.

That dark promise laced in his voice made her weak in the knees—there was a part of her that was imagining all sorts of things in that simple answer.

It felt like he stood there for an eternity, before he stepped away from her and left the bar.

When he was gone, she took a deep breath to calm her nerves.

Gus made her nervous like no one had before. In a good

way, but also in a way that scared her, because she was curious. She thought maybe she shouldn't show up to dinner.

Go out to dinner with him.

This was her chance at having a fling. A no-strings-attached night of passion. Something she could look back on fondly as a moment where she took a chance.

What harm could that do?

This was a big mistake. She wasn't going to come.

Agustin wasn't sure what had come over him.

Usually, he would casually date, but it never meant anything. He wasn't interested in finding a happily-ever-after. He'd had that before.

Once was enough.

The idea of loving another as much as he loved his late wife was unfathomable, because the thought, the mere idea of the pain he felt when she died and he was powerless to do anything was something he never wanted to feel again.

It was why he'd left Buenos Aires and opened a practice in Ushuaia.

He'd put his whole past life behind him and started fresh.

Women he had affairs with, they were pretty, but he had nothing in common with them. Sharon was gorgeous, but there was something different about her. He had noticed that at the first workshop they attended together. He had ascertained she was American, but also sounded like she came from somewhere in Argentina, but he wasn't one hundred percent sure.

He couldn't help but wonder if she was from Argentina.

Like him.

Only he didn't want to know. He tried to keep her at a distance, but it was hard. She was intelligent, smart, beautiful and sexy. She had long, soft, chestnut hair that was always pulled back and he pictured over and over again what it would be like to undo her hair and run it through his fingers.

He often thought of that when he saw her.

Actually, if truth be told, he often fantasized about that, and of kissing her luscious pink lips. It thrilled him when she would smile, her gray eyes focused on him and the hint of pink in her olive skin.

It had been a long time since he'd been so enticed, so enraptured by a woman. Not since his late wife, and that was ten years ago.

There was a passionate creature hiding under that prim and proper facade of Sharon's. She was a mystery and despite everything, all the protections he put up to protect himself, he was drawn to her, and she didn't seem to care one iota that he was flirting with her.

Which made him want to know her all the more.

You're here on business. Not to flirt.

It had been a year since his late father had died and he'd stepped in to take care of his half sister. That was when his world changed again, and he was struggling.

This conference was supposed to be a quick trip to Spain. A medical conference to help boost his private luxury plastic surgery clinic back home in Tierra del Fuego. He wanted to make his clinic the premier spot for people to fly in and get surgery.

He hadn't expected to run into an intoxicating woman at the same hotel—or to continue running into her.

He was glad she'd come over for a drink. It was bad timing when that poor waiter had a heart attack, but she had acted so quickly. They worked seamlessly in that moment. Two strangers. She'd kept her head and worked with him.

That waiter had survived. Then he got a message from his half sister, who was hating the boarding school in Buenos Aires he'd sent her to and had banned her boyfriend Diego from visiting. Again.

Agustin was annoyed he couldn't get to know Sharon in that moment, which was why he'd suggested dinner and he hoped she'd actually come. He wanted to do more than talk shop with her.

Although there was a part of him that didn't want to get to know her either.

Still, he hoped she'd come.

He wasn't sure if she would. Every time he heard a click of heels on the cobblestone or saw a tall woman with her hair color, his heart would catch.

Agustin kept hopeful but really, did he expect Sharon to actually show up? They were strangers in a foreign country.

"Hi," she said, catching him off guard.

She stood beside the table in a pink dress, her long dark hair falling over one of her bare shoulders. She wore flats, which explained why she had snuck up on him.

She was absolutely stunning. It took his breath away for a moment.

Then he remembered his manners and stood. "You came."

"I told you I would," she responded sweetly, cocking her head to the side. "I don't usually go back on my word."

"I'm glad to hear it." He pulled out the empty chair so she could sit down.

She sat down and his knuckles brushed the bare skin of her back. It sent a shiver of electricity through him, just that brush of his flesh against hers.

"I'm sorry if I'm late."

"No. You're not and it's quite all right."

He would've waited all night. Only he didn't say that out loud. He was just glad that she was here. He took his seat across from her, just staring at her—it was hard not to in the moonlight.

"This is a beautiful little café," she said. "You've been to Barcelona before?"

"*Sí.* Not for a few years. This place is one of my favorites."

"I haven't explored the city much."

"How long have you been in Barcelona?" Agustin asked.

"Just the week. For the conference."

"Same as me. Just a short trip for the conference," he said.

"So we're both here for the conference." She smiled and dropped her head in her hand. "This is the most tedious conversation ever."

He chuckled softly. "It's utterly boring."

Sharon laughed. "I suppose so, but it's not. I like work."

"I believe we were talking about that before the waiter collapsed," he said.

"How is he?" she asked, gently.

He admired her empathy. "Alive. You were brilliant."

"Hardly. It's what I'm used to. Besides, you're the doctor."

"I get it, but let's not talk about our work anymore."

"Good idea," she agreed.

Work had been his life for far too long.

Except when his late wife had been alive. Then he had been able to find the balance, but when she died, he gave every moment he could to work, until he burned out.

His spine stiffened.

He didn't want to discuss his late wife or think about her.

Not tonight.

Not here.

The waiter came over and Agustin ordered them some wine and tapas.

"I hope you don't mind me ordering," he said.

"No. It's fine. You know what's good. I'll trust you."

"Do you travel a lot?" he asked.

"Only for…" She blushed. "Work, which we agreed not to talk about."

He smiled. "That's right."

Sharon was charming.

"I've often thought of taking some time off and visiting family I haven't seen in a while."

"Why don't you?" he asked.

A pink blush tinged her cheeks. "I don't know. I guess I really never just gave much thought to it."

"Maybe you should. The soul needs time to rest."

Her lips quirked in a smile. "Oh, I didn't know you were so poetic."

"Are you teasing me?"

"Perhaps."

He grinned and leaned across the table. "I have layers of depth. If only you were staying long enough to get to know me."

"Are you trying to blackmail me into staying, Gus?"

His eyes sparkled. "And if I was?"

"You don't know me," she said, the blush on her cheeks deepening. "I could be a monster."

"Are you?"

She smiled, but didn't say anything. The waiter came and poured them wine, then discreetly left. Sharon took a sip out of the wineglass. He was mesmerized by the way her lips parted and he really wished for that fraction of a second that he was that glass of wine and that her lips were on him.

"I seriously doubt that you're a monster," he said, breaking the spell that she was weaving over him.

"You doubt that?"

"I do. I would like to get to know you. Perhaps see more of you. You're one of the most beautiful women I have seen in a long time."

"You're leaving soon too," she said.

"True," he remarked. "Still…it is the truth."

"Beauty is skin-deep," she said quietly.

"I know, but there's something more I see in you."

"Well, that may be…but unfortunately more is something I can't give."

Agustin understood that too, but he did want to get to know Sharon better and that did terrify him slightly. He didn't want to open his heart to anyone else. Not after losing Luisa, his wife, and their unborn child—not after having his life shattered.

He didn't trust the fates not to be cruel again.

Sharon was dangerous to every careful wall he put up to protect himself from ever being hurt again. Still, there was just something about her. Something he couldn't keep away from. Perhaps he was a sucker for punishment.

Maybe he was just lonely?

He dismissed that thought.

"I understand," he said, quickly. "I am not looking for a relationship either. Just…you were someone I wanted to get to know. I am attracted to you, Sharon. I can't deny that."

She seemed relieved. "I am attracted to you as well, Gus. It's just…"

"Just what?" he asked.

A blush returned to her cheeks. "I'm not used to this. I'm not very good at this."

He grinned. "Well, I am."

She looked down, her hair sliding over her face in a sweet, endearing way. He longed to brush her hair away, touch her chin and drag her gaze back to him. He was surprised at how much he wanted to touch her all the time.

"Are you?" she whispered.

"Yes, so let's enjoy this night together. No promises. No deep conversations. Let's enjoy the city so when you leave Spain you'll have more than just memories of work to remind you of this beautiful place."

Sharon smiled, her eyes lighting up. "I like that. Yes. Let's do that."

They held up their wineglasses and cheered to their decision. A night of fun. He wanted to show her everything that Barcelona had to offer. For one night, he wasn't going to think about how to protect his heart or how much he desired her.

Tonight was going to be about fun, and if a little romance happened along the way, then he wouldn't be opposed to that.

He just couldn't promise her forever, but it seemed like Sharon didn't want that either, which was a relief.

Agustin secretly wanted a chance at forever again. There was a hole in his heart that longed for family, for love and forever, but he just couldn't open his heart to that again.

He wouldn't lose at love again.

So tonight would have to be enough.

CHAPTER TWO

SHARON COULDN'T REMEMBER when she'd had so much fun.

Actually, she really didn't have much fun. There was her work and then home. She had a few friends, but it was hard to trust people, to open up to people. Her work, her career as a registered nurse working all over the world was what she could count on.

So going out with Gus, a stranger she had met at the conference, was highly unusual for her. It was also kind of liberating and fun. She enjoyed the workshops with him, but this was so much better.

Sharon was the kind of person who liked to plan things out, so it was a bit different for her to let go and go with the flow.

She certainly didn't go off with people she hardly knew, but with Gus she felt safe.

It was a bit unnerving.

Just relax.

And that was what she had to keep telling herself.

She just needed to breathe and relax.

This was her one chance to live.

She never planned to get married, and she didn't plan on settling down. She liked her life traipsing across the world as a nurse.

No one let her down and she didn't let anyone else down either. Even if she was a bit lonely.

So even though this wasn't her usual modus operandi, she was glad to be here just the same. It was a memory that she knew she was going to keep forever.

So that she could say, later on, that she'd lived.

After their tapas and wine at the Cafe Pacífica, Gus took her on a whirlwind tour of Barcelona at night.

Just like New York City, where she grew up, Barcelona had a nightlife.

The city was lit up and there was music and laughter.

It breathed with life.

How long have I been asleep?

"Where would you like to go?" Gus asked as they walked the bustling streets.

She was getting slightly overwhelmed with the crowds. "I don't know. Somewhere quiet?"

As if sensing that she was a little anxious about being in a big group of people, he slipped his arm around her wait. She could feel the heat of his body through the thin cotton of her dress and she hoped she wasn't trembling under his touch.

She liked his hand there, in the small of her back, protecting her.

You don't need protection.

Sharon ignored that thought.

"How about the beach?" he asked. "We can take a moon-lit stroll down by the water."

"The beach? Which one?"

"Platja del Bogatell is nice." He stepped toward the street and hailed a cab.

A taxi pulled off and Gus rattled off instructions to the driver and then opened the door. She slid inside and then he climbed in beside her. His body pressed against hers in the back of the tiny cab.

"It won't be crowded there, will it?" she asked, as the cab driver raced through the streets of Barcelona.

"Not at this time of night. No sun for the sun seekers, but there will be people. You don't like crowds?"

"I should, shouldn't I. I'm from New York."

He cocked an eyebrow. "Really? I wouldn't have taken you for a New Yorker."

"And why is that?" she asked, curious.

"Your accent. It's American but also…something else."

"My mother was from South America. We moved to New York when I was very young. So yes, I guess you're right. I'm not really a New Yorker."

He smiled at her lazily, making her heart skip a beat. "See, not a New Yorker. Not at heart."

She laughed. "Well, I don't have a lot of happy memories there."

"Then we won't talk about that. Tonight is not a night for unhappy memories."

She smiled appreciatively. "What's it a night for then?"

"Fun." He grinned and he slipped his arm around the back of the seat, close to her shoulders. It was comforting to have it there. "Maybe we can catch the last of the sunset."

"That would be nice."

He smiled.

The cab driver wound his way through the Gothic Quarter, past the Parc de la Ciutadella, and let them off near the stone walkway that ran along the length of the beach.

Sharon helped pay for the cab driver, who thanked them with a simple "*gracias*" before driving away to find another fare.

Gus was right, the beach wasn't completely deserted. There were a few dusk volleyball games happening and several people walking along the shoreline.

They wandered down to the water's edge. Gus kicked off his shoes and she set hers down next to his on the sand.

They were just in time to see the sun sink over the western horizon of the Mediterranean Sea. It was red and emitted an orange hue over the turquoise waters and the white sand beaches. It had been some time since she really stopped and watched a sunset or even a sunrise.

She couldn't remember the last time she did.

"Beautiful," she whispered.

"It is."

She glanced up to see that Gus was not looking at the sunset, but her. Warmth spread through her body again. She was overwhelmed and shy at the moment, which was also unlike her. The water lapped at her toes.

Her heart was racing and she wasn't sure about what she was thinking.

All she knew, in that moment, was she wanted him to kiss her.

He leaned in and she closed her eyes, his body thrumming with anticipation. His hand on her upper arm as he brought her close, her stomach fluttering, her body trembling. Her mouth was going dry and it felt like her heart was in her throat.

She wanted this.

Just once.

It only had to be once.

"*Querida*, I would very much like to kiss you," he murmured, brushing his knuckles gently over her cheek.

"I would very much like it if you did too," she responded,

her voice shaking. It was against her better judgment. There was a rational side of her that was telling her to run, that this wasn't for her, but there was another part of her that was telling her that this was right.

This would be good.

This was worth it, even just for one moment in time.

Gus tipped her chin, so their gazes locked, and he bent down to press a light kiss against her mouth, sending a jolt of heat through her blood. Right down to the tips of her toes. It was almost too much, the heady sensation coursing through her.

She wanted more.

So much more.

She wrapped her arms around his neck, tangling her fingers in his hair at the nape of his neck to draw him in closer.

Deeper.

She was losing herself in this kiss.

She wanted to lose herself in this kiss.

For one night, she didn't want to be herself.

She broke off the kiss to get some air. He was still holding her close, but for her it was not close enough. She wanted more.

"Querida," he whispered, kissing her again.

"Shall we go back to the hotel?" she asked, her voice breaking.

"Are you sure?" he asked.

"Sí. Very much."

"Querida, I don't know… I can't promise you anything beyond tonight. You said so yourself, you're going home tomorrow and I leave to go back to my home in a couple of days. I can't give you a relationship, if that's what you're looking for."

"I'm not looking for a relationship, Gus. I just want to-night. That's all. So yes, I'm sure about going back and seeing where this takes us for tonight. I'm not looking for forever."

Gus nodded. They slipped on their shoes and she took his hand as they quickly walked back to the street to hail a cab and head back to their hotel.

She was nervous, but she wanted this more than anything.

Something to remember.

And she wanted it to be Gus.

Sharon seemed nervous.

He was nervous too and he didn't know why. He'd been with other women since his wife died and there was no emotional attachment to it, but with Sharon there was something else and he couldn't quite put his finger on it.

It made him want to be protective of her.

To comfort her and care for her, and those kinds of thoughts scared him. He wasn't going to let himself feel that way about anyone else. He wasn't going to open his heart and love someone else again.

He just couldn't do that.

Tonight though, tonight he wanted to be with her.

When she let him kiss her on the beach, it had been magical. Even just holding her lithe body in his arms and having her pressed against him had overwhelmed him. He wanted to lose himself in her arms, to drown himself in her kisses.

She was intoxicating.

He had been thrilled when she wanted to come back to the hotel, but he was also nervous, because of the way she was affecting him.

Sharon didn't say much on the cab ride back to the hotel.

Nor when they took the elevator, where he'd first laid eyes on her, to his room.

He opened the door and she stepped in.

Uncertain.

"Sharon, if you're not sure, we can just have a drink and talk."

She turned around quickly. "No. I want this. I have backed out of situations like this one too many times and I've regretted it after, always."

"Are you certain?" he asked.

Sharon sat down on the edge of the bed. "I am. I do want this, Gus, and I want it to be you."

"This isn't like some business transaction."

"I didn't expect so," Sharon stated matter-of-factly.

He ran his hand through his hair. "How about I pour us a drink? I have some wine."

"Okay."

Agustin grabbed two wineglasses from the minibar and opened the wine. It had been a gift from a business associate, but he couldn't take it back home with him to Argentina. He poured Sharon a glass and then himself one.

He sat down next to her.

"Thanks." She took the glass. Her hand was trembling.

"Don't be nervous," he said gently.

She smiled up at him. "I can't help it."

He touched her face gently. "You are sure about this?"

Sharon nodded. "Completely. I meant what I said on the beach, Gus. I don't expect anything after tonight. We'll go our separate ways. I just want to take this memory with me."

Then she reached out and touched his face. It was a light touch, gentle, and her skin felt like silk against his.

He took the empty wineglass from her and set them down.

There was a rational side of him that was screaming not to get involved, but when he looked into her eyes, he was lost.

He wanted to feel her against him.

He just wanted tonight too and he was honored that she chose him.

"We can stop any time you would like."

She smiled and then brushed her soft lips against his. "I appreciate that."

He cupped her face and kissed her deeply, drinking in her sweet taste.

Agustin knew he should stop.

He was in serious danger, but as her arms came around him and they sank against the mattress, he was a lost man.

What harm could come from one night?

CHAPTER THREE

Ushuaia, Tierra del Fuego, Argentina, five months later

IT CAN'T BE.

She had only just arrived in Ushuaia. Yes, she had been feeling off since Spain, but how could she miss this?

Sharon sat down on the lid of the toilet, staring at the pregnancy test in her hand.

This was not part of the plan.

She was supposed to be here to take care of her grandmother. During her last job her aunt had called her and told her that her grandmother had fallen and broken her hip. Sharon knew she was the best one to go down there and see to her grandmother personally. That was what she planned to do.

A baby was not part of the plans.

Sharon didn't know how she was going to break the news to her grandmother.

The news she'd come here pregnant and unmarried.

Her grandmother was all alone in Ushuaia. There was no one to tend to her. Her aunt had her family, a husband in New York.

Sharon was single.

She'd given up her job, flown down to Tierra del Fuego, to the edge of Argentina to care for her abuela.

It was her pleasure.

Her abuela had always been there for her. Even though Sharon had grown up in the United States for the most part, she had been born in Ushuaia. Then her parents had moved to the US, following her aunt and uncle. Then her mother died and her father took off.

Sharon then divided her childhood between Ushuaia and where her aunt lived in the US. It was what gave Sharon her love of traveling.

In the first couple of days Sharon knew she'd have to stay here to take care of her abuela indefinitely. Her abuela's hip was not healing right and there were memory lapses.

Sharon still felt completely run-down, even after being here for two weeks.

Of course, a couple of weeks into taking care of her abuela Sharon got sick. She'd thought it had just been a bug, but the nausea and exhaustion had persisted. Then she'd noticed different things.

Other changes.

Changes she'd refused to believe were happening.

Until now.

Until that little stick had turned positive, letting her know she was indeed pregnant. She'd ignored all the symptoms for so long. Why had she done that? The first time in her life she decided to sleep with someone—using protection— she got pregnant.

"*Querida*, are you okay? You'll be late for work!" her abuela called.

"*Sí*, Abuela." Sharon sighed and continued to get ready in the small bathroom. She had most of the upstairs of the house to herself. Her grandmother couldn't get up the stairs still, but had the main floor set up. Soon her grandmother's day worker would be here.

She zoned out again, staring at the test.

"You'll be late. Remember, it's your first day, *querida*," her abuela reminded her again.

Right.

Her new job.

Sharon needed to work to pay for her abuela's care worker and to support them. It was going to be a great job at the most luxurious private plastic surgery clinic in Tierra del Fuego.

People from all over the world came to this clinic.

It was what had softened the blow of leaving her other job to come here.

Her abuela was right—she didn't want to be late for her first day.

She ran down the stairs and found her grandmother sitting up in her rocking chair and looking out the window.

"It's snowing," her abuela remarked, her voice laced with confusion. "Kind of early, isn't it?"

Sharon leaned over and looked out the window, groaning at the sight of snow. It was summer in the US. Her aunt would be heading to her cottage in the Finger Lakes. Sharon wished she was there right now, because here in Tierra del Fuego it was winter.

"Well, it is June first, Abuela," Sharon stated.

Abuela sighed. "Right. I forgot."

And Sharon knew her abuela was worried about the memory lapses.

Sharon kissed her on the top of her head. "It's okay to forget."

"You start work today at that fancy new clinic, yes?" Abuela asked, changing the subject.

"I do, but the clinic has been there for three years."

"Still new," her grandmother huffed. "When do you think you'll tell them you are pregnant?"

Sharon's blood ran cold. "What?"

"Oh, come on, Sharon. I'm old and I may have forgotten that winter started, but I know when someone is pregnant. I was a midwife for many years."

Sharon's voice shook. "I didn't even know…until now."

"You were too busy working and then moving here to care for me. Of course you didn't notice," her grandmother said, taking her hand. "I appreciate it, by the way. I love that you're here with me. I miss you when you're gone."

Sharon squatted and threw her arms around her grandmother, pulling her slight frame into her arms and holding her close. "I love you, Abuela."

"And I you, *querida*. I hope you know I'm thrilled with the idea of being a great-grandmother. I hope they will be born in Argentina. We have free health care here."

Sharon chuckled softly and got up. "I better get to work. Maria will be here soon to sit with you until I get back from work."

Her abuela nodded. "Have a good first day. I can't wait to hear all about it, and tonight you can tell me all about the father."

Sharon's stomach flipped as she pulled on her winter coat and headed out. There wasn't much to tell. It was an attractive man at a hotel during her last night in Barcelona.

Gus had been so wonderful to her.

It had been hard to leave him, but they'd made no promises.

She took a deep breath, the cold air filling her lungs. It

was a short walk from her grandmother's home to the clinic. All downhill to the center of town.

Sharon was glad for the walk to clear her mind.

Snow was falling gently and the mountains in the distance had white caps, but there was a fog lingering over the city and the harbor.

It had been some time since she'd been back here in the place of her birth. She'd forgotten what it was like to live at the edge of the world. This had been a happy place. Her childhood had been full of tragedy, but coming here had been her happy times.

It was a great place to stay and working at a world-class clinic was a chance of a lifetime.

Maybe she could stay here.

There was a lot to process, and along with all the decisions she had to make, she also needed to somehow get hold of Gus and let him know she was pregnant. She may have been a one-night conquest to him, but he was the father and he had the right to know.

Her blood heated at the memory of their night together.

How he'd kissed her gently, how his strong hands had felt on her body, gently caressing her and making her melt. And when she told him it had been a long time for her, he had been so kind to ask if she was sure and then so patient with her during it all.

Making sure that she felt pleasure first.

And she had.

So much so, she couldn't believe that she had waited so long. It just had never felt quite right until that night in Barcelona. She was glad that it had been him, that she took a chance and listened to her gut that night.

She just hadn't been expecting a baby out of it, especially

when they had used protection. Sharon shook the thought out of her mind. Today she had to give her all to her job. She had to support herself, her grandmother and now her baby.

It was something she was secretly thrilled with.

Even though it had taken her by surprise, she was thrilled with the ideas of being a mother. It was something she'd always wanted, but she never gave time to romance or relationships, so she'd thought it was something that was going to pass her by.

She reached down and cradled the small swell in her belly and smiled, even though the cold was biting at her bare cheeks.

She was happy. For the first time in a long time. It unnerved her how happy she was.

Sharon walked into the clinic and made her way to the employee locker room. She hung up her coat and purse in her assigned locker.

"Ah, so glad you're here, Sharon," Carmen, the head nurse, said brightly as she came into the room. She handed Sharon a set of scrubs. "For you."

"*Gracias,* Carmen." Sharon held the scrubs to her chest. "Where would you like me to start?"

"I'll have you work on the postoperative patients today. The surgeon, Dr. Varela, will be expecting your reports in an hour on their status."

Sharon's heart skipped a beat. There was so much she could learn here.

"Where can I find him?" Sharon asked, hoping her voice didn't crack with excitement.

Carmen smiled. "Agustin will be on the second floor. The offices are there. This is a nonsurgery day. Just postoperatives to take care of and the surgeons are running their clinics today, so they won't be down on the patient floor until later."

Sharon nodded. "Well, I better get changed."

"Find me at the nursing stating once you change. I have your key card and computer passcode so you can access patient files."

"*Gracias*, Carmen," Sharon said again.

Carmen smiled and left the room. Sharon changed into her scrubs. They were a little tight and she was annoyed because again she hadn't noticed the signs.

She made her way to the nursing station on the post-operative floor. Carmen gave her all she needed and she started her rounds.

She didn't need guidance. She'd worked as an operative nurse before. It was one of her favorite jobs.

Her last job had been at a family practice in the United States. This would be far more interesting.

Sharon grabbed the charts and made her way to the first patient, a woman who'd had facial reconstruction after cancer.

She gently knocked on the door.

"Mrs. Sanchez, how are we today? I'm Nurse Misasi. You can call me Sharon."

Mrs. Sanchez stirred slightly, but didn't respond.

"Mrs. Sanchez?" Sharon leaned over. She gingerly touched Mrs. Sanchez's wrist. Her pulse was weak.

Mrs. Sanchez groaned. "Hurts."

"I'm sure," Sharon responded gently. "I'll get your meds."

Sharon took the patient's temperature.

"Hurts," Mrs. Sanchez moaned again.

"I know. Can I check your incisions?" Sharon asked.

Mrs. Sanchez groaned again and slightly nodded.

Sharon checked the incisions under the face wraps and they weren't healing as well as they should. The thermometer beeped and Mrs. Sanchez's temperature was elevated.

Sharon checked the readout of the monitor and then the chart. Mrs. Sanchez should be doing better and she couldn't help but wonder if the patient was allergic to something or was fighting an infection.

She was worried and knew that she was going to have to page Mrs. Sanchez's surgeon for further instructions. This couldn't wait until he made his rounds later today.

"How is my patient this morning?"

Sharon heard the voice and her heart stopped as Dr. Agustin Varela entered Mrs. Sanchez's room. It was like a ghost from her past.

It was Gus.

It was someone she had been thinking about all morning. The man she had slept with in Barcelona. Gus was Dr. Agustin Varela. Her new boss was the father of her baby?

Agustin just stood there in shock as he stared at the new nurse, who was standing beside the bed of his patient Mrs. Sanchez. Carmen had told him when he'd called down that the new local nurse she hired had started today and was going to be doing the post-ops.

Usually, he hired his own staff, but he'd had to travel to Buenos Aires last week and bring his half sister, Sandrine, home from the school he'd tried to send her to, to get her away from her boyfriend Diego.

She had been living with his mother, but Sandrine was unhappy with the school, so he'd brought her home to Ushuaia.

He'd needed a new nurse, had no time to interview, so he'd left it to Carmen.

He trusted Carmen.

Agustin had been so worried about Mrs. Sanchez he hadn't wanted to leave it to chance with a nurse he wasn't familiar with. There was a reason his clinic was world-class: because he insisted on the best care for his patients.

This clinic was his life.

He hadn't been expecting his new nurse to be the woman he couldn't stop thinking about for the last five months.

Sharon.

He'd woken up to find her gone. They had made no promises, yet he was still hurt that she had disappeared like a thief in the night.

It stung, because that night had meant so much to him. For the first time since his wife died, he had felt a connection. A deep, meaningful moment of passion.

And since that night, he hadn't been able to get her out of his mind. When she'd left, it had hurt, but it had also been a relief, because the moment that he'd taken her in his arms he'd known that he had made a huge mistake.

She had ensnared him.

And when he brought her pleasure, she had broken through the ice that he had enshrined around his heart. He wanted more. It was easier to just try to forget her. She was leaving Spain.

For a week he tried to not think about her, but everywhere he looked her memory was lurking. Her kisses were still imprinted on his lips. So to try to put her out of his mind he threw himself into his work, running his clinic and trying to take care of Sandrine, since his father died last year and his stepmother had abandoned her. It was a lot.

The work, his father's messy estate, tracking down Sandrine's mother was keeping his mind off the woman who had left him.

Except in the lonely hours of the night when he would think of Sharon, wondering what happened to her.

He'd just had one of those awful sleepless nights, so he'd come in early to check on his post-op patients and there she was. Like she'd stepped out of his dreams, standing there in the aquamarine scrubs of the clinic, holding his patient's chart.

Her hair was done up in a bun again and she looked like she was staring at a ghost. He felt like he was too.

"How is she?" he asked, finding his voice. Agustin had a lot of questions to ask, but right now he had to focus on his patients.

"Her temperature is elevated and there's swelling at the incision site. The patient's blood pressure is elevated as well and she's complaining of pain, but I can see she's had her dose of pain medication only three hours ago."

Agustin took the chart from Sharon and stood next to her. It was hard to be so close to her. His pulse was thundering between his ears.

"I need a CBC on Mrs. Sanchez. It could be an infection," Agustin said, writing up the order.

Sharon nodded and took the chart back. "I will get the testing done straightaway."

"Have you managed to round on my other patients?" he asked.

Sharon shook her head. "This is just the start of my rounds."

Agustin nodded and checked over his patient. She was sleeping again and as he checked the incision site, he could see what Sharon was worried about. Mrs. Sanchez's incisions were red and swollen still. They shouldn't be this swollen.

"Well, I'm going to finish the rounds and you focus on the blood work of Mrs. Sanchez. I want that test done stat, and then report to me with the findings."

"Of course." She wasn't looking at him as she began to get the supplies ready for the blood test.

Agustin glanced back one more time and watched her moving around the patient's room. He couldn't believe that she was here. He'd thought Carmen had hired a local nurse.

Sharon had said she was from New York, but she'd also said her parents were from South America and she never did specify where. And he hadn't asked, because watching her on the beach at sunset, her parentage had been the furthest thing from his mind. It figured it had to be Argentina, and not even just Argentina, but Tierra del Fuego.

Agustin raked his hands through his hair and tried not to dwell on it. He finished his rounds with his other two surgical patients. Both of them were doing well and there was nothing to worry about. He would be able to discharge them in a couple of days.

By the time he finished with his last patient, it was almost time for his clinic to start and he saw Sharon coming quickly toward him. The aquamarine scrubs looked good on her, but she would look even better out of them.

He was annoyed with himself the moment he thought about her, naked in his arms, or how beautiful she had looked with the white cotton sheets wrapped around her sun-kissed body, her hair fanned out on the bed like a halo.

Almost like she was heaven-sent.

Get a grip on yourself.

"You have the lab results?" he asked, clearing his throat.

"Yes. Mrs. Sanchez has a staph infection. It's common," she replied.

Agustin didn't look at her, but stared at the results. "We need to change her antibiotics."

"Yes. I'll do that straightaway."

Agustin signed off on the orders so Sharon could start the medication. She looked a bit flushed and her cheeks were glowing, like she was sweating.

"Are you okay?" he asked.

"Fine," she said quickly.

"If you're sick…"

"I'm not sick."

"You don't look well. You look pale and tired."

Still gorgeous though.

Only he kept that thought to himself.

"I'm fine. Really," she replied stiffly, but he wasn't buying it. He could tell she was run-down or she was fighting something.

"If you have any kind of sickness you need to tell me. I know it's your first day, but I can't have you putting the patients at risk."

Sharon frowned. "You really think me so foolish as to jeopardize patients, in particular surgical patients?"

"No, but then I don't know you."

Which was the truth. They hadn't talked much that night because neither of them had wanted to talk about work.

All they had was one incredible night together five months ago. Of course, they had both just wanted to have a moment of fun. They'd agreed, or he'd offered, that they wouldn't have deep conversations and that they'd just enjoy themselves.

And they had.

Just thinking about it again made his blood heat, his body thrum with desire, but then he had to remind himself that they weren't in Spain. He was her boss and she was his nurse, or rather the nurse that was working for him.

Sharon sighed. "I'm not sick. I know what's wrong with me."

"What's wrong with you then? Because I am concerned," he said firmly.

"I'm pregnant."

He could feel the blood drain from his face. "Pregnant?"

"Five months," she stated, under her breath and blushing.

"Five…" He trailed off as it hit him.

Sharon nodded. "I just found out today myself."

He took a step back and ran his hand through his hair.

He couldn't quite believe what he was hearing.

She was pregnant and the child was his.

"We used protection," he whispered.

"And you, as a physician, know that doesn't always work."

He wanted to talk to her more about this, but he was also terrified of the implications of it all. He had always wanted to be a father and ten years ago he came so close to that when he and Luisa had found out they were pregnant.

He'd had great aspirations of being a good father, unlike his own.

And that was all ruined.

He'd lost Luisa and he'd lost the child he was desperately excited for. The thought of having children seemed so out of reach to him, especially since he didn't ever plan on giving his heart to another woman.

Now here was Sharon. She was pregnant with his child and she was here in Ushuaia. A local. Like him.

"Dr. Varela, you're wanted in your office," the page came over the sound system.

"I better go," he said, dragging his hand through his hair. "We'll talk later."

"Of course," Sharon replied quietly. "I'll get the antibiotics set up for Mrs. Sanchez."

Agustin nodded. "Right. Keep me posted."

He turned around and made his way to the elevator. He had to put this on the back burner. He had his job to do and he could talk to her later and find out what she was doing in Ushuaia…and what they were going to do about their baby.

CHAPTER FOUR

SHARON HAD BEEN slightly disappointed that Agustin hadn't said much of anything to her, but then again she couldn't blame him.

She was still in shock that the father of her baby was here in Ushuaia and not who she thought he was. Although they had never really talked about anything.

She'd known he was a doctor, but she'd had no idea that Gus was a plastic surgeon. She'd figured Gus was a cardiothoracic doctor or a cardiologist, something to do with hearts, because he had seemed to know about heart attacks.

And she'd suspected that Gus was from somewhere in South America, but they hadn't talked much about it. It just figured he was from Argentina, from Ushuaia, and he probably knew her abuela too.

This felt like some weird comedy of coincidences.

Gus had been a sexy stranger she had flirted with all week at the conference. Her one-night stand. That had been it.

Now he was her boss? Dr. Agustin Varela.

She was relieved when he was called away to the clinic. He'd mumbled they would talk later and left.

That was fine by her.

She didn't want a relationship. That hadn't changed.

If he wanted to be in the baby's life then great, but she wouldn't allow him to abandon her child and break its heart.

You need to focus on your work.

She shook out all those foggy thoughts.

She was a professional and she had a job to do. She couldn't think about the fact her boss was the father of her unborn baby or that he was her one-night stand.

The man who had awakened passion deep inside her.

Get a hold of yourself, Sharon.

She couldn't let thoughts of that night intrude on her work. At least he now knew about the baby and she wouldn't have to worry about figuring out how to get hold of Gus to let him know that he was going to be a father.

At least that was taken care of.

Sharon made sure Mrs. Sanchez got the antibiotics she needed and started a central line. She continued her duties for the day and finished her charting.

Agustin hadn't come back to the postoperative floor, not that she could blame him. She was sure it had been a shock to see her here, his new nurse, who was pregnant with his child while he had a world-class practice to run.

When they had dinner in Barcelona at that café he'd told her that he put his all into work as well. That was the only thing he'd divulged.

It was one of the things that she admired about him.

He had the same passion for his career as she did. Though she hadn't known who he was at the time.

Work was her life too.

She understood that.

She respected that.

Except work would soon have to take a back seat to the little life growing inside her. She reached down and touched her abdomen. Overwhelmed was an understatement for how she felt right now.

There was a lot to do.

One step at a time, Sharon.

That was how she'd gotten through her mother's death and her father's abandonment.

She took her life one step at a time.

She took a deep, calming breath and finished her shift. The night nurses to care for the postoperative patients came in and she handed over the charts gladly. She went to the locker room and changed back into her street clothes.

The night nurses said it was snowing hard and the temperature was dropping. She was glad for the warm parka that she had. She just wanted to get home.

As she walked outside, she saw Agustin, under a streetlamp leaning against a black sedan, bundled up against the cold snow of June.

"Hey," she said, surprised. "You look like you're freezing."

"I am. I drive so I don't need a parka like you are smartly wearing."

Sharon chuckled. "I don't have a car, so I walk."

"Can I give you a ride home, or perhaps we can go somewhere to talk?"

Sharon glanced at her watch. She had to relieve Maria and her grandmother couldn't be alone for too long just yet. "I'm sorry, I can't. I really need to get home."

"Don't you think we should talk?" Agustin asked.

"I do, but I have to get back home and relieve my abuela's care worker."

He looked confused. "I thought you were from the States?"

"I am, but also here. My grandmother lives here. I was

born here." Sharon glanced at her watch again. "I want to talk about what's happening. I do feel bad for springing it on you, but you had the right to know, it's just I really have to get back home."

"Fair enough. I'll drive you."

"You don't have to," she argued. Although, her feet were aching and she wouldn't mind the ride home.

"No. Let me, and then maybe tomorrow at lunch we can go somewhere and talk?"

"I'd like that."

Agustin nodded and opened the door to his car. She slid into the passenger seat. He got into the driver seat. "So where am I driving you to?"

"Near Los Guindos. It's not far from here."

A strange look crossed his face. Just a brief flicker of confusion and shock.

"I know that neighborhood well," he said stiffly.

She didn't know what to say. A tense silence fell between them.

"So, I thought you were in Spain?" she asked, breaking the silence.

"Spain is not my home. Ushuaia is," he stated. "I was there for the conference. As were you if I recall."

"Yes. I didn't actually ask where you were from, did I?"

"No. We didn't really deep dive into too much, other than you were from New York."

"So we're both from Ushuaia and met in Spain?" She chuckled. "Seems a bit…odd. Way too coincidental."

"Yes. Very odd," he agreed and then he had to laugh. "Like a bad comedy."

"Yes. I suppose. I did think the same thing." She chuckled nervously.

"Well, that's a relief you were thinking it was odd too."

An awkward silence fell between them. Sharon stared down at her hands. This was certainly not how she'd pictured telling Gus, or rather Agustin. It was easier this morning to think of him still in Spain.

On the beach.

In that hotel room.

In her arms.

Heat crept up her neck. She had to get control of those thoughts. They weren't in Barcelona now. A lot had changed and she had to remember that.

In fact, there was a part of her that didn't think he would care too much that she was pregnant, and that would be fine by her, but she wasn't not going to tell him and keep her pregnancy a secret. That wasn't her jam.

It certainly had never been in her wildest dreams that he would be her boss and that she would be working side by side with him. Why did he have to be from Ushuaia too? Argentina was big, but she rarely ran into people who were from Ushuaia. Actually, most people had never even heard of Tierra del Fuego.

Of course, the one man she decided to spend a night with the one time she let down her guard and decided to taste that forbidden fruit of passion happened to be a man from Ushuaia, and he happened to be a surgeon. And now they were working together.

Her grandmother was going to think this was funny.

Thankfully, it wasn't a long ride to her grandmother's home. The moment they pulled up on the street, Maria was pacing outside, wringing her hands.

"Oh, no," Sharon murmured.

"A relative?" Agustin asked.

"No, it's my abuela's care worker."

Agustin parked the car and Sharon got out and made her way to Maria.

"Maria, what's wrong?" Sharon asked, fearing the worst.

"It's your abuela. She's being stubborn," Maria said hastily.

Sharon groaned inwardly. "She can be. Tell me what happened?"

"She fell, hit her head and is insisting it's a scratch, but it's bleeding. It's her forehead. I doubt she has a concussion, but you know how much head wounds bleed. She took away my phone, didn't want me to call you and bother you since you were on your way home, and I can't call an ambulance. Then she didn't remember me. I tried the neighbors and no one is home. The teenager who lives there is still at school."

"She'd better be at school," Agustin said stiffly. "I'm your neighbor and that teenager is my half sister."

Sharon was shocked. "You're my neighbor?"

"Apparently, though I've been in Buenos Aires for the last two weeks."

Sharon pinched the bridge of her nose. This was just getting more and more complicated. She took a deep breath. "Where is my abuela now, Maria?"

"She locked herself in her room. The fall literally just happened," Maria said.

"I'll retrieve your phone and then I'll take care of her so you can go home and try to relax this evening."

Maria chuckled. *"Gracias."*

Sharon walked into the house and made her way to her grandmother's room. She knocked on the door. "Abuela, open up."

"Querida?"

"Yes. I need Maria's phone back so she can go home."

"I don't need to see a doctor!" her abuela shouted.

Sharon sighed, not sure what had come over her grandmother, and of course it had to happen right now, with Agustin outside and on the day she found out she was pregnant. She heard the click of the lock turning.

The door opened and Abuela held out Maria's phone, just through the crack of the door. Sharon took the phone and ran it outside to Maria.

Maria thanked Sharon and said she would be back tomorrow at the same time, so Sharon was relieved that her abuela hadn't scared off her care worker.

Sharon headed back inside and saw that her abuela had opened the door, was sitting on her bed, and that Agustin was kneeling down in front of her, examining her head wound. Sharon was confused.

When did he come inside?

Her grandmother looked over at her. "Sharon, this is Agustin Varela. His father was my neighbor and he's our neighbor too!"

"I am aware," Sharon said stiffly.

Agustin didn't smile, but then again if his father had recently died then she could understand that he was grieving still. She didn't know when Mr. Varela died. She'd only been here a couple of weeks.

And clueless to a lot of things.

Sharon sat down next to her grandmother and took her hand. "How bad is it?"

Agustin looked up at her. "Superficial, but it's still bleeding. She would benefit from some stitches. We should get her to the hospital."

"No," her abuela stated. "I won't go there. I don't need to."

Sharon sighed. "Abuela…"

"No." Her grandmother took back her hand and sat up straighter, crossing her arms, but Sharon knew she was becoming agitated.

Agustin stood. "I could do it. We could take her to the clinic and I can stitch her up there."

"You don't have to do that," Sharon said gently.

"It's no problem. It's the least I could do for the woman who delivered me thirty-five years ago." He winked at her grandmother.

Abuela smiled. "Yes. I did deliver you, and I delivered your father, Theo, too."

Agustin's smile, which had extended to a twinkle in his eyes, changed at the mention of his father. "Did you deliver my half sister, Sandrine?"

"No. Sandrine's mother insisted on a fancy clinic in Buenos Aires," her abuela said. "I never liked that woman and I liked her less after she left her daughter. I am sorry about that, Agustin. I'm glad you take care of her."

Agustin nodded curtly. "Well, let's get you to the clinic."

He left the room to wash his hands in the small bathroom on the main floor. He came back with fresh dressings and Sharon took them from him. He barely looked at her. It was almost like he was ashamed that she knew his secrets.

Not that she could blame him.

Abuela wasn't a woman to keep secrets. Especially lately as she aged and her memory went. She was grateful for Agustin's gentle hand. She made sure her grandmother's wound was covered and then helped her abuela get up and put on her outside gear.

Agustin held the door for them and then took Abuela's arm on the other side, and the both them walked her to the front seat of the car, settling her in for the short drive to the clinic. Abuela was grinning the whole time they drove to the private clinic.

Sharon wasn't sure what this new fear of the hospital was, but at least her grandmother would have that wound stitched up and taken care of without too much of a fight. It was worrying her, this change in her grandmother's behavior.

Agustin parked in his parking spot, which was near the door of the clinic. He went inside and got a wheelchair as Sharon helped her grandmother out of his car.

"I don't need that," Abuela stated. "I can walk."

"I insist," Agustin said firmly. "Clinic procedures."

Abuela nodded and sat down.

Sharon followed Agustin numbly, feeling like she was out of place. Agustin took the elevator straight to clinic floor, which was empty at this time of night. He wheeled Abuela into one of the exam rooms, which had a nice bed and was completely fitted out.

Agustin helped her grandmother up onto the bed and then took off his coat. Sharon slipped off her coat.

"I want to help," she said. "I mean, this is my job."

Agustin smiled and nodded. "Well, if you can get a suturing kit from the supply closet, I'll prep the anesthetic."

"I can do that." Sharon wanted to keep herself busy and not think about the fact that Agustin suddenly seemed to be inserted into her life. More than she ever imagined him to be. Just this morning he was someone who was far away and she was trying to figure out how to get hold of him to let him know that she was pregnant.

Now here he was, her boss, her grandmother's neighbor, and he was about to suture up her grandmother's head.

Sharon headed back into the exam room.

Agustin was talking to her grandmother and making her laugh.

"Here's the suture kit," Sharon announced.

He turned and smiled. That dazzling, charming smile that had won her over five months ago. "Great. Thanks."

"Can I do anything else?" Sharon asked.

"Nope. Just sit with your grandmother," Agustin said as he readied his tools. "I numbed her up and gave her something to calm her down. She may have a nap here."

"I'm very comfy," her abuela murmured sleepily.

"It's okay, you can nap here for a bit. Sandrine will be fine on her own, as she tells me often," Agustin groused.

Her grandmother closed her eyes.

Sharon sat there in a chair next to her grandmother, feeling absolutely useless.

"So that's your sister. I've met her. She's nice."

"Yes. Her name is Sandrine." Agustin continued to work on her grandmother's head.

"I know," Sharon said softly. "She never mentioned you."

"I'm not surprised. She's sixteen and keeps to herself. For the most part."

"You mean for a teenager?" she asked.

"Precisely. I had her at a good school in Buenos Aires for a time, but she loathed it. I suspect she's still mad at me."

"When did your father die?"

Agustin tensed. "A year ago."

"Where's Sandrine's mother?"

Agustin shrugged. "My stepmother? No idea. She left, abandoned Sandrine to my care."

Sharon's heart sank.

She knew that scenario well.

"Querida," her aunt Sophia had said, choking. There'd been tears in her eyes.

Sharon had stood there, staring up at the police officers.

There'd been so many people in her home. She'd clutched her doll tight to her chest. It was like a shield. That was what she'd been telling herself for days, since she'd woken up and realized her father had gone.

She'd kept her dolly close to her as she'd eaten what she could, because she hadn't been allowed to use the stove.

I think she's in shock, ma'am. We'll have her taken to the children's hospital to check, a police officer had said.

Her aunt had nodded, kneeling down next to her. *Querida?*

Is Daddy dead? she'd asked, her voice hollow, because now she was recalling when her mother had died. All the police and people had been there then too.

No, her aunt had said, smiling. *No, we don't know where he is, but we're going to take you to the hospital and you can come sleep over at my house. Would you like that?*

Sharon had nodded. *But Daddy said to wait. He always told me to wait. Should I still wait?*

No, querida. *Come.* Her aunt had held out her hand. *Come.*

Sharon shook those memories away, her throat thickening. She hated that that memory had been triggered. It was something she kept locked away tightly. She didn't want it to intrude on her life.

"Well, to be honest, I did think it was rotten she left Sandrine alone. I had no idea. Sandrine said she was used to being on her own for bouts of time…"

Agustin sighed. "Yes. Well, I didn't have much to do with my father and didn't know much about my half sister. My mother in Buenos Aires found out and called me. Sandrine reached out to her when her mother didn't return. Thankfully, I was here and not traveling at the time."

Sharon's heart melted. It was clear Agustin had no feelings toward his late father or his stepmother, but he cared enough about his half sister to put his life on hold and come and do the right thing. Sharon was all too familiar with having hard feelings toward one's father. Hers had left. Agustin was a decent, honorable man who was here for his sister who'd been abandoned after a parent's death. Much like Sharon had been left.

She had been younger than Sandrine and thankfully had her aunt and her abuela to step in. Her aunt had been in the States and her abuela had flown up from Tierra del Fuego to work out an arrangement to take care of her.

Sharon had always appreciated that.

Sandrine had been alone.

"There. Your abuela will be right as rain." Agustin finished putting the dressing on.

"Thank you. I don't know what came over her." Sharon sighed. "She's had small brief episodes since her fall, but she's never taken to stealing someone's phone, locking herself away and refusing medical help."

"She didn't refuse me." He grinned, winking.

Sharon chuckled. "True."

Agustin was hard to resist. She should know.

"I'm glad to help." Agustin stood and disposed of the used suture kit, removed his gloves and washed his hands.

"How long will she sleep do you think? I'm asking because I have no idea what you've given her."

"Maybe an hour or two and then I'll take you home. I

told Sandrine I'd be home late. She responded with 'k.' Not 'okay' or 'all right,' but 'k.' Just the letter."

Sharon smiled. "She sounds like my preteen cousins."

"Shall we grab something to eat? Your grandmother will be fine. I can get us a couple of takeaways from the food cart outside?"

She should say no, but she was starving. "I would like that."

He nodded. "I'll be back in a few."

He left the exam room and Sharon leaned back in her chair. It had been a long day. She wished she was at home in bed. That had been her plan once she settled her grandmother for the night. She was going to have a bath, get into comfy pajamas and watch television.

This was the most surreal first day of her life.

There was a part of her that wanted to quit because working with Agustin would be awkward and weird, but she was no quitter and she needed to support herself and her abuela.

She was staying in Ushuaia for the foreseeable future to give her baby stability. This was a great job. One she could come to love. She'd make this work with Agustin. They were both adults.

This would have to work.

There was no other choice.

Agustin's head was pounding slightly and he was distracted as he bought a couple of meals from the cart outside the clinic.

Of course, he'd been completely distracted since he discovered his new nurse was Sharon and she told him she was pregnant. It secretly thrilled him, but also unnerved him too. They had used protection, though he knew that wasn't always a sure thing.

He had given up hope of ever becoming a father. Especially after what happened to Luisa and their unborn child. It nearly ended him when he lost them, so he'd made peace with the idea that he'd be alone for the rest of his life because it was easier this way.

Easier to eke out the rest of his existence alone.

No feeling.

No pain.

And then Sharon came along.

Pregnant and apparently his neighbor!

Sharon said she had been here two weeks, but he had been in Buenos Aires and then trying to conduct other business when he brought Sandrine back to Ushuaia. He hadn't noticed Sharon was right under his nose this whole time.

Why don't you like the school? Agustin had asked.

Because I'm lonely. Your mother, she's amazing and I've always loved her. She's never treated me bad for what my mother did, but it's not the same. It's not home.

Agustin had sighed. *You mean because Diego isn't there.*

Sandrine had looked sad. *You never listen. You never pay attention.*

Fine. You can come home, but I have lots of work coming up.

Right. Work.

His life revolved around work so the grief of losing Luisa wouldn't eat away at him. Work was a balm to soothe his shattered heart. Sex was a distraction move.

Until Sharon.

It boggled his mind how their paths seemed to be crossing. When they had their night together neither of them shared too much about themselves. They'd both agreed to that because neither one of them could promise more than one night.

Now, within a span of a day, they both knew far too much about each other.

Dios, her abuela delivered him and his father!

So much for a one-night stand.

Now there were many subtle layers tying them together. Fate was entwining their paths and he wasn't sure why. All he could do was laugh about it, although maybe he would laugh about it later. Right now, he wasn't thinking about that—he was thinking about his heart. He made his way back upstairs and found Sharon dozing in the chair next to her grandmother.

Sharon looked so peaceful and tired. His gaze traveled over her, remembering with exquisite detail her body under his hands, and then he saw the slight swell, just ever so slight, and it looked like she was cradling it.

It made his heart skip a beat.

She's off-limits. She works for you.

And he had to keep reminding himself of that.

Both of them had made it clear they didn't want a relationship, but they could both be involved with their child's life. He could see his baby every day.

What if she doesn't plan to stay here? What if she went back to the States?

Agustin didn't like that niggly thought at the back of his mind.

Then the ever-darker thoughts of fate snatching this child away from him too.

Please don't tell me, Agustin had said, choking back the tears.

The trauma surgeon's face had been somber and Agustin had been pulled into one of those rooms. A room where they gave patients' families bad news. A place that was private and hidden away from everyone else.

Please... Agustin had begged, hoping that if he kept saying please then the truth wouldn't come out, but he knew it to be true.

He could tell.

Luisa was gone.

His child was gone.

I'm sorry, Dr. Varela, the surgeon had said. *They were brought to the emergency room without vital signs. We tried everything, but she was gone.*

Agustin had fallen to his knees and wept.

Everything had been taken away from him.

Everything had gone and was broken...

Sharon stirred and opened her eyes. "Oh, you're back."

He plastered a fake smile on his face, to keep back the sadness that was threatening to overtake him. "Come to my office. It's just next door. We can eat, talk and leave the door open to keep an eye on your abuela."

Sharon nodded and followed him to his office.

"What would you like?" he asked. "I got empanadas and asado. I bought your abuela provoleta because I remember hers at community picnics."

"I'll have asado please. It's my favorite."

Agustin nodded and handed her the Styrofoam takeaway box.

"I guess I am getting my way," he said teasingly, sitting down and digging into his food, though he couldn't really taste it.

"How is that?" she asked.

He smiled. "Dinner and a chance to talk."

Her dark brown eyes twinkled. "I suppose so."

"I am glad to talk, but I would've preferred not to have your abuela fall in order to have this chance to talk to you tonight."

"I know."

"So you've been back here for two weeks?"

Sharon nodded. "Yes. I was taking care of my abuela. I spent a lot of time getting her out of the hospital and settling her back at home. I upended my whole life to come here."

"You weren't working before?" he asked. "Because this was your first day I believe."

"No. I quit my previous job when I understood the nature of my abuela's fall and the help she'd require. I'm here now."

"Permanently?" he asked, trying to feel her out.

"For now," she said.

Agustin didn't like her vague answers.

"For now" wasn't a definite yes. It was not cut-and-dried.

"You said you only found out today?"

"Yes." She groaned. "I've been so busy with my grandmother, the move and finding work I ignored the signs."

"So I am assuming you haven't got an obstetrician yet?"

"No. This is a lot of questions," she said.

He grinned. "Sorry, but we're beyond the point of mystery now that you carry our child."

Sharon nodded. "True."

Her grandmother moaned and called out for Sharon, so she went to her while Agustin cleaned up. He poked his head into the exam room. "I'll get the wheelchair and we'll take your grandmother home."

"Thank you. For dinner and your help tonight," Sharon

said quietly. "I really appreciate it… Agustin. Or should I call you Gus?" she asked, a smile playing on her lips.

"Agustin or Gus, doesn't matter."

A blush tinged her cheeks. "I like Agustin."

She said it shyly and it warmed his heart.

What was it about her?

Be careful.

And he had to be. He couldn't take another heartbreak.

He just nodded and closed the door between his office and the exam room. He had a lot to figure out. Not only with Sharon but with Sandrine and her insistence that she be with that boy Diego. It was all so complicated.

Life had been easier when he was alone, working to build his clinic.

When he didn't have to think about grief or loss or family.

Things he'd accepted he'd never risk again after Luisa died.

It had been so much better then.

Hadn't it?

CHAPTER FIVE

THERE WAS A crick in his neck when he woke up and he was confused as to where he was. Then it all came rushing back to him as his eyes adjusted to the dim light. He was at home, but he had crashed on the couch. A bunch of work was scattered around him.

After he had taken Sharon and her abuela home, he'd gone home to see Sandrine. Only she hadn't been there.

She'd been out with that boy again.

When Sandrine got home she'd marched straight upstairs. There was no point in yelling at her, but he was annoyed all the same.

Agustin sat up slowly and stretched. He hadn't realized that he'd fallen asleep on the couch. He hadn't realized how tired he had been. He was used to working late into the night.

"You're awake. I was going to poke you with a pair of tongs to see if you were still alive," Sandrine said from the kitchen.

"Thanks," he groused.

"Where were you last evening?"

He ran his fingers through his hair. "I know where you were."

She shrugged. "Look, you're never around. Always working. I need to live my own life."

"You're sixteen."

"So? I was fifteen when Dad died and you came here. Nothing has changed. I can fend for myself."

Agustin felt bad.

"So where were you?" she asked.

"My new nurse, she lives next door. Her abuela fell and…"

"Theresa fell?" Sandrine gasped.

"You know her well?"

Sandrine made a face. "Everyone around here does. She's the neighborhood grandma."

He remembered that then.

He'd buried those memories, but it all came flooding back to him.

After his father left his mother when he was in university in Buenos Aires, he never came back to Ushuaia. He preferred his mother's home. He distanced himself from his father, although his father tried to reach out.

When Luisa died, Agustin came back to Ushuaia, as Buenos Aires held painful memories of her, but he avoided his childhood home and his father as much as he could. Now that his father had died, he was back living at home with his half sister.

There were even some brief memories of Sharon, although he was a teenager when she was a young child.

How long had Sharon and his life been intersecting?

Agustin shook that thought away.

"You ready for school?" Agustin asked groggily.

"Yep." Sandrine stared at her phone.

Then he remembered all his suits were at the dry cleaner since he'd been in Buenos Aires these last two weeks. He'd planned to pick them up, but got sidetracked yesterday.

"You didn't happen to go to the dry cleaner?" Agustin asked.

"Nope," Sandrine replied.

He groaned. "Great."

He really needed to hire a maid. Maybe then he could keep better tabs on Sandrine and that boy.

"You know, Dad's room is full of suits," she remarked.

His stomach turned. He and his father had never had the best relationship. His father had left his mother for a younger woman, Sandrine's mother.

When his father died Sandrine's mother vanished and Agustin stepped up.

It was weird moving back into his childhood home, but it had been left to him.

Agustin wondered if Sandrine's mother would ever come back, but it was a touchy subject.

It was hard being surrounded by good memories of his parents, but also painful ones of their divorce and his estrangement from his father.

He lived here for Sandrine's sake, but he didn't like being here.

"I'm going to clean up."

Her lips quirked in a small, brief smile. "'Kay."

Agustin groaned and made his way to the bathroom. He was pretty sure that he could find a dress shirt that would be acceptable for work and then he'd get the dry cleaning.

He opened the door to his father's room.

Even though it had been a year since his father died he could still smell him in that room, which was strange. He made his way to the closet and found a blue dress shirt that would match his trousers and suit jacket.

He peeled off his clothes and headed into his father's en suite bathroom, turning on the hot water. He was hoping a nice hot shower would let him think. He'd thought his whole life was figured out.

He just couldn't ever forgive his father.

He finished his shower, dried off and put on the fresh shirt and the rest of his suit. He picked one of his father's ties and headed out for the day. Sandrine had left for school. He had a few appointments today and some inpatient surgeries that he was hoping Sharon could assist him with.

As he made his way outside, he met Sharon heading out the door. She looked adorable bundled up in her winter wear. It made him smile.

"Good morning," he said brightly. "Would you like a ride?"

"It's not a long walk and I need the exercise. You could walk with me," she said teasingly.

He groaned inwardly. "Fine, but you're just going to make me walk back here again and then I have to drive back into town to get my dry cleaning."

"You don't have a personal assistant or a maid for that?" she asked, surprised.

"I am an adult. I'm quite capable," he groused.

"Except you're still not dressed for winter." She smiled.

He glanced down. "No, but as I said I drive everywhere."

"Still no excuse. So are you walking with me or driving?"

"I'll walk. I guess I can take a cab later." He shoved his hands into his pockets.

He had no idea how she'd convinced him to walk. He was grumbling about his decision but he liked to be around her. That hadn't changed since Barcelona.

He'd liked being with her then, the beautiful stranger, and now he was slightly protective over the fact she was carrying their child.

"I remember you, you know," he said, breaking the silence.

"Well, I hope so," she teased.

"I mean from years ago. Your abuela, she was sort of a neighborhood grandma. And I remember this small, shy girl with pink ribbons in her hair. I was a teen then, but I remember your abuela's American granddaughter."

Sharon laughed. "Yes. The pink ribbons. I'm sorry I don't remember you."

"I am a lot older." He winked at her.

"Not that much," she said quickly. "My summers here were a bit of a blur."

There was a hint of sadness in her voice. He wanted to ask her why, when she pulled out a candy from her pocket, unwrapped it and popped it into her mouth.

"Are you okay?" he asked.

"Just a bit of morning sickness."

"You're at twenty weeks though. You should be over it." Although, this summation was completely based on his brief time as an intern when he had to work different specialties to become and surgeon and the small window of time Luisa had been forcing him to read all those pregnancy books.

He really had no idea. And Luisa had never made it that far into her pregnancy.

He'd been a young surgeon then too, just starting out, and wasn't completely engaged with Luisa's pregnancy.

He'd worked to support Luisa and the baby. That had come first.

Always.

And the guilt of that still tore at his wounded heart.

"Tell that to the fetus," Sharon groused.

"You really need to book an ultrasound and an appointment with an OB/GYN or a midwife. Someone who specializes in prenatal care. You're halfway there and haven't seen anyone."

"I know. I am so frustrated with myself."

"Why?" he asked quizzically.

"I didn't see the signs. I even missed the quickening." Her voice caught in her throat and he hoped that she wasn't going to cry. He wasn't sure how he could deal with her heart breaking.

"You can feel the baby now?" he asked, hoping his excitement didn't show through. He wanted to give her space, yet the thought of the little life growing inside her excited him just as much as it terrified him.

His child. A second chance.

Words he never thought he'd ever think or say since the crash and losing Luisa and their unborn baby. He fought the urge to reach out and touch her belly, to see if he could feel his child moving, but he resisted.

"So that's why you have the candy then?" he asked.

"Ginger candy. It's not perfect, but it helps with the nausea," she mumbled. "Truth be told, I really detest ginger..."

They continued their walk to the clinic, not saying anything, but in that moment they didn't need to. It was easy walking with her. He didn't mind the cold so much when he was with her.

It felt right.

Which was alarming.

"Have you worked in an operating room before?" Agustin asked. "I have seen your curriculum vitae, but I can't recall if you have scrub nurse experience. I just remember you mentioning triage."

"Yes. I'm quite adept at all forms of nursing and I really do enjoy the aspects of being a scrub nurse."

He smiled at the way she talked about her work. She was so formal and so logical a lot of the time, but her eyes would light up when she talked about work. She was clearly passionate about it.

He wondered if her formality was a way that she kept people out, kept people at bay, and he wondered what she was holding back from him.

Why does it matter? She's not yours, so it's not your business.

He was holding back too.

He didn't want to let her in. So why did he want *her* to let *him* in?

What was happening to him?

"I have some outpatient surgeries today. Since you're on my rotation I would like your assistance in the operating room."

"Are you testing my abilities?" she said teasingly.

He grinned. "Perhaps. Just a bit."

"Well, I will rise to the challenge gladly." And she nodded her head for good measure, the parka hood sliding forward a bit.

"Good." Agustin unlocked the door to the clinic and held it open for her. "I will meet you in my office in twenty minutes and then we can go over what's expected today and the surgical procedures."

"That sounds good."

She pushed back the hood and he caught the scent of her subtle shampoo. A simple, clean smell he remembered vividly.

How he'd longed to run his fingers through her hair that night they were together, and he could recall achingly still how it felt.

An errant strand of her hair blew around her face and without thinking he reached down and brushed it away.

Her skin was as soft as he remembered. Her cheeks flushed.

"Thanks," she said, tucking the strand behind her ear. "So twenty minutes?"

She was obviously changing the subject, which was for the best.

"Yes."

"See you then, Agustin." She didn't look at him as she stepped inside.

Agustin took a deep breath and followed Sharon inside. They were both trying to keep this professional, but he couldn't help but feel this unwanted attachment to her and her wellbeing growing inside him.

Try as he might, he couldn't deny that night in Barcelona had been more than a regular one-night stand. More than he wanted to admit.

Sharon was trying to keep the nausea at bay. She wasn't sure if it was stress after the events of yesterday or what was going on. One of the things she loved in nursing was working the operating room. She loved getting those jobs. She found it comforting and challenging.

Right now, the smells were getting to her. She was able to get the patients prepped. A lot of the outpatient procedures today had been things like the removal of moles or skin tags or injections of some sort.

This was the final procedure of the day and it was one that required anesthetic and working in the operating room. She wasn't sure if it was the cautery or something else that was causing her to feel awful. She stood next to Agustin as he worked on the liposuction of the patient. The sound of the machines was bothering her and making her ears ring.

She tried to ignore that sensation and focused on the procedure steps—by doing that she could keep all the stomach churning at bay and do her job.

She was determined to keep things professional but it was hard to do that when she was feeling ill and thinking about Agustin brushing away a strand of her hair.

It wasn't turning her stomach, but it made her stomach flutter in a different way.

In a way that was not professional at all.

She liked that he seemed to care for her and the baby, yet he was holding something back and it terrified her.

What if he walked away like her own father had?

It made her anxious to think of her baby feeling the pain of abandonment.

All of this just added to her nausea, her anxiety.

Sharon rolled her shoulders and ignored those racing thoughts. Focusing on work was what she'd done yesterday when he'd sutured up her abuela. He was excellent at suturing and she admired his handiwork.

"Sharon, can you hold this clamp for me?" Agustin asked.

"Of course." She stepped in and took the clamp, and, as she did so, their gazes locked and her pulse began to race.

The anesthesiologist cleared his throat and she cursed inwardly. It was the last thing she wanted, for everyone to suspect there was something going on between her and Agustin. She had to be careful. No one could know.

That time had meant nothing.

Or did it?

Sharon ignored that little voice. Sure, he had been her

first time and it had been so magical and yes, she was carrying his baby, but she couldn't get attached to him.

People left. Hearts were broken when you allowed yourself to get attached to people. Even Agustin knew that with his own parents. There was no such thing as love. Except now, here with him, she had all these warm feelings.

Watching him work, getting to know him. Watching him with her abuela. She wasn't sure what was happening to her. She knew one thing: she didn't particularly like it.

Sharon closed her eyes as another wave of nausea washed over her.

She was able to gain some control to continue with her work.

"There. I think we can close up," Agustin announced. "Sutures please."

He held out his hand and Sharon retrieved what he needed to close up the small incision from the liposuction.

The scent of the operating room was getting to her again, but she focused on all the tasks as the patient was closed and taken to the postanesthetic unit. She gripped the edge of the instrument table, which she would have to take to be sterilized.

"You did well," Agustin remarked. "I'm pleased with your abilities."

She turned her head slowly to see him at the operating room computer, sitting on a swivel stool and typing up his operative notes.

"Thanks," she said weakly, feeling very hot even though the operating room was not a warm environment.

"I definitely would have you work in the operating room with me again."

"I would…" She tried to focus on a source of something,

anything that would keep her grounded, but her vision was narrowing at the sides.

"Sharon?" Agustin called out, his voice like an echo.

She was feeling very overheated as her source of light faded away and her knees gave out.

The last thing she saw was Agustin leaping up, his arms outstretched as the world went black.

"Sharon?" It was Agustin's voice. He was pressing a cold something to her forehead and it felt good.

"Hmm?"

"You fainted."

She opened her eyes and looked up at him. "I…what?"

"You fainted," he said gently. "I've called for an OB/GYN friend of one of my colleagues."

Sharon groaned. "So they all know I'm pregnant."

"Who are 'they'?" he asked.

"The others in here," she moaned.

"What would you have me do? Yes, you're pregnant. Even you can see the logic in my decision to call for someone who is more skilled than I am!"

She groaned again. Her head was hurting. Agustin was right, but it was no good him making sense right now, which sort of irritated her. She was frustrated the secret was out, but really how much longer had she thought she was going to be able to keep it? Others would soon notice.

"Can you sit up?" he asked.

"I think so," she murmured.

Agustin's arms came around her and he gently helped her up off the operating room floor. "Let's get you to an exam room for Dr. Perez to check that everything's okay."

Sharon nodded and let Agustin hold her, but she was still

wobbly on her feet and couldn't stand upright. Before she could say anything or even protest, Agustin scooped her up in his arms and carried her from the operating room.

She was mortified, but also felt safe.

Being in his arms brought back the memory of their night together, making her blood heat and her nipples tighten under her scrubs, and she really hoped she wasn't blushing. She would hate for him to see how she still reacted to his touch.

She was trying to keep things professional. It was hard to do when your boss was carrying you through the halls though.

Agustin carried her into an open exam room and gently set her down on the exam table, the paper crinkling.

"There. I'll stay with you if that's okay?" he asked.

"You don't have to," she said. "Remember, there is nothing between us."

A strange expression crossed his face for just a moment. "I know, but it's my baby and I want to be involved."

Of course. The baby.

Good.

She was glad he was focused on that and not her.

She didn't want a relationship.

Don't you?

She ignored that voice.

"Okay, yes. Please stay."

There was nothing about this whole situation that would ever be permanent. She wasn't hurt by that, or at least she didn't think so. They had both agreed five months ago to just one night.

Not a lifetime.

There was a knock on the door. They both turned their heads to see a doctor in the doorway.

"Is this the right room?" she asked, brightly.

"Are you, Dr. Perez?" Agustin asked.

"Yes," she replied. "I understand that someone fainted in the operating room?"

Sharon blushed. "Me."

"You're twenty weeks?" Dr. Perez, asked setting down her bag and taking off her coat as Agustin shut the door to the exam room so they could have some privacy.

"Yes," Sharon said. "I didn't know I was pregnant."

Dr. Perez cocked an eyebrow. "A nurse not knowing she was pregnant?"

"Stress has…interrupted my normal cycle before," Sharon said.

"Ah. I see," Dr. Perez replied. "That is normal. Especially if it's your first too."

"My grandmother, Theresa Gonsalves, had a fall, breaking her hip. I took a leave of absence from my job as a locum nurse and I've been caring for her. I decided to stay in Ushuaia to be with her and I just didn't notice my pregnancy before now." Sharon felt foolish when she said it out loud, but it was the truth.

"Theresa Gonsalves is your grandmother? She's a respected midwife." Dr. Perez smiled.

"Yes," Sharon replied.

"She delivered me," Agustin quipped.

"And me," Dr. Perez stated, grinning. "I hope she's doing better."

"She is. I take care of her and I have workers sit with her while I work," Sharon said.

"And who is taking care of you?" Dr. Perez asked sternly. "The father?"

"I am...the father," Agustin responded. "I only just found out as well."

Dr. Perez was stunned, but only for a moment.

"Ah, well, how fortunate you're here. Let's take your blood pressure and check your sugars. We'll book an ultrasound, but I have my Doppler here to listen to the heartbeat."

Her ears pricked up at that. "Really?"

Dr. Perez smiled. "Yes, well, you would've heard it via Doppler by now had you been to a checkup. You can sit up and I'll check your blood pressure."

Sharon sat up as Dr. Perez put the cuff around her arm. She took a deep breath as the cuff squeezed her arm.

"Your blood pressure is a little high, but that could be from the fainting spell and the situation you have at home. We'll check your sugars and then I'm going to send you out to get a bunch of blood tests."

"Okay," Sharon said. There was no point in arguing. Not that she would.

She was pregnant and knew the tests needed to be done. Her blood sugars were measured through a finger prick.

"Blood looks good," Dr. Perez said, writing down the info. "You were complaining of nausea?"

"Yes."

"She shouldn't still have morning sickness, should she?" Agustin asked.

Dr. Perez looked up at them. "She could. She may also have hyperemesis gravidarum, but we'll know for sure after some tests. I think Sharon was a bit dehydrated and that's why she fainted. You need to take breaks, Sharon."

Agustin gave her a knowing look and Sharon tried not to chuckle.

"Still, I want you to have a fasting glucose test," Dr. Perez said.

"Okay, when?" Sharon asked.

"As soon you can arrange it." Dr. Perez pulled out her Doppler. "If you lift your shirt we can see if we can find the heartbeat."

Sharon lay back. Agustin was close by, hovering and looking worried.

"Cold gel," Dr. Perez warned, squirting it on Sharon's belly. Sharon winced, because she forgot how cold that ultrasound gel was. She hoped the heartbeat was strong and she was blaming herself a bit for not knowing she was pregnant sooner.

How could she be so obtuse?

Then she heard static, then there it was: something she heard whenever she worked on a job in obstetrics. The rapid beat of a heart, and it wasn't hers. Her eyes filled with tears at the sound making the reality of this pregnancy all the more real to her in this moment.

She was going to have a baby. She was pregnant.

"Strong heartbeat!" Dr. Perez exclaimed.

Agustin grinned from ear to ear. He murmured, "I can't believe it."

"Believe it." Sharon laughed nervously.

Dr. Perez wiped off Sharon's belly and then her Doppler.

"I will see you tomorrow at nine in the morning, Sharon. I'll have the lab requisitions and we'll book a proper dating ultrasound." Dr. Perez gathered up her equipment.

"We'll be there," Agustin announced.

"If I can get someone to sit with abuela," Sharon argued. "Maria has tomorrow morning off."

"Sandrine will sit with your abuela," Agustin said.

"You're sure?" Sharon asked.

Agustin nodded. "She will be glad to."

Sharon didn't say anything else, but she was annoyed he was overstepping his bounds and the boundaries she had set up, making decisions without consulting her.

"Good," Dr. Perez said. "See you both tomorrow."

"I'll walk you out," Agustin said, leading Dr. Perez out of the exam room.

Sharon sat up, feeling frustrated. Sandrine had sat with her abuela before, or so Maria had told her. Still, he'd just decided and Sharon didn't like that one bit.

She didn't want Agustin interfering in her life, especially if he was just planning on leaving her and their child anyway.

Sharon could take care of herself. She always had. She was the one she could rely on.

Only her.

CHAPTER SIX

AGUSTIN MADE SHARON wait for him at the clinic as he walked back home to retrieve his car. She thankfully didn't argue with him about the importance of prenatal exercise, like she had that morning, especially after her fainting spell. It was for the best she didn't walk home to her abuela's.

He wasn't taking no for an answer and she wasn't fighting.

In fact, he was getting the feeling that she was a bit miffed at him for carrying her out of the operating room. Usually he didn't carry staff out of the operating room, but he'd acted first and hadn't really think about the impact.

He needed to take care of her. *thought*

Agustin just wanted to get Sharon back home and settled. When he saw her collapse it had scared him to his very core. He'd tried to get to her in time, but all he'd managed to do was keep her head from smacking the floor.

Dr. Nunez, the anesthesiologist, was the one who knew Dr. Perez the OB/GYN and called her for him. Agustin did have to explain that Sharon was pregnant, but he hadn't told anyone that he was the father.

Although, he was sure that others in the clinic would soon find out, since he'd carried her out of the operating room and stayed for the examination.

Agustin was very relieved that she was okay and that

Dr. Perez had set up an appointment to see her tomorrow. When he heard that heartbeat over the Doppler it had completely upended his world. He knew then that nothing would be the same.

It melted his own heart to hear it.

It had scared him to hear that little flutter, knowing that it was his child, but still he treasured that moment. He never got to experience that with Luisa. She wasn't very far along when she died. So to finally hear the heartbeat of a child of his was a bit world-shattering for him.

He had to do better. He had to protect them.

When Dr. Perez had asked her who was taking care of her, he hadn't hesitated in stepping up and taking over. He was part of this pregnancy. Even though Sharon didn't want a relationship, she had made that clear, they were bound together by that little baby.

When he pulled into the driveway, Sandrine was there and she wasn't alone. She had her arms around a young man and Agustin knew exactly what they were doing. His fingers curled into a fist.

Diego. Again.

He knew the boy well and wasn't a fan of his.

His mother had told him all about Diego because it was something his father had grappled with before he died. Sandrine was too young to get so serious over a boy.

Agustin cleared his throat as he came up the path. Sandrine and Diego startled. Agustin just glared as the boy ran down the steps and past him, waving at Sandrine as he left.

"You scared him off," Sandrine complained.

"He's not supposed to be here," Agustin stated.

"He's my boyfriend."

"I don't trust him."

"Why?" Sandrine asked. "You don't know him."

"Father didn't like him either," Agustin said gruffly.

"How would you know that? You never came around when Father was alive."

It stung, but it was true. His father hadn't told him that because they hadn't had a relationship. His father had tried, but Agustin hadn't been interested and now it was too late.

It was no lie he blamed his father for the breakup of his parents. His father had cheated and broken his mother's heart.

It had been hard to forgive his father and easy to ignore he existed when he'd been in Buenos Aires and happy with Luisa.

Even when he came back to Ushuaia, he'd tried to be in his father's life to get to know Sandrine, but he had still been angry at his father.

So Sandrine was right. He was never around.

Agustin crossed his arms. "Father told my mother and my mother filled me in. She loves you, even though she's not your mother, and she wanted to let me know what was happening."

Sandrine rolled her eyes and he knew that she was thinking something like *as if you cared*, but she didn't say the words. He did care, but it was hard to reach and establish a relationship with a younger sibling who he'd only seen a couple of times when he was a young man.

It had nothing to do with Sandrine's birth and everything to do with their father destroying his mother's heart by leaving her for Sandrine's mother. It wasn't Sandrine's fault. It was just hard to reach out.

"Why are you here without your dry cleaning?" Sandrine asked.

"I came to get my car. I walked to work with Sharon this morning and now I have to go pick up Sharon."

"Is Sharon okay?" Sandrine asked, genuinely concerned.

"She is. You know she's pregnant?"

Sandrine nodded. "Yeah, but I don't think she did. Her abuela knew though. Theresa is smart and told me."

Agustin smiled. "She is. Well, I'm the father."

Sandrine looked confused, her eyes wide. "What?"

"Five months ago Sharon and I met in Barcelona and…" Agustin could feel the heat rising up his neck and he ran his fingers through his hair. "Needless to say, I'm the father. The baby is mine."

Sandrine smiled, her eyes twinkling. "I'm going to be an aunt! That's so awesome."

Agustin was stunned. "You're excited?"

"Of course. I love kids." Sandrine clapped her hands. "This is so great!"

Agustin shook his head, but secretly he was happy that Sandrine was happy about this whole thing. "I'm going to go pick her up and bring her home. Can you sit with Theresa tomorrow so I can take Sharon to a prenatal appointment?"

Sandrine nodded. "Of course! Can I go over to Theresa's house now for a visit and tell her?"

"She doesn't know I'm the father yet. Maybe we should let Sharon tell her, but you can definitely go over there and sit with her and Maria."

Sandrine nodded and clapped her hands as she ran next door. He hadn't seen his sister this happy in…well, ever.

At least with Sandrine at Theresa's she wouldn't be with Diego.

Agustin went inside and grabbed his keys, then headed to his car to drive back to the clinic to get Sharon. Sharon was sitting outside and looked miserable. He hoped that she wasn't still feeling that morning sickness.

He parked the car and then ran to the passenger side and opened the door for her. "Are you okay?"

"I'm fine," she said quietly as she climbed in.

Agustin got back into the driver's seat and started the ignition. Sharon wasn't saying anything, she was just staring out the window, and he had the distinct feeling that she was mad at him.

"Sharon?"

"You're going to ask if I'm mad at you?" she asked.

"Yes."

"Not mad. Annoyed, but not mad." Yet she still wouldn't look at him.

"You can't even look me in the eye."

She turned her head slowly. "That better?"

"What has got you annoyed?"

"You spoke for me. Made the appointment, arranged for care and didn't ask me anything. What if I don't like Dr. Perez?"

"You don't like Dr. Perez?" he asked.

Sharon sighed. "I never said that. She seems great, but the point was you spoke for me. I don't go for that macho attitude or whatever. I am in charge of my life and I make the decisions regarding my body, my baby and my abuela. Got it?"

"Understood. I'm sorry, I overstepped and got a little bit excited. Would you like me to call and cancel?" he offered.

"No. I'll go if Sandrine can sit with Abuela."

"She can. And I told her you're pregnant with my child. She knew you were pregnant, but didn't know I was the father."

Sharon groaned. "Great. Everyone is Ushuaia is going to know my business."

"Because I told my sister?"

"No, my abuela," she chuckled. "Oh, and carrying me out of the operating room."

"Sharon, you're starting to show, and if I hang around you too much people are going to put two and two together."

Sharon laughed softly, breaking the tension that had been in the car since he picked her up. "I suppose you're right. This time."

He grinned. "Thank you for conceding to me, this time."

They shared a smile.

"I am glad you were there when I fainted. I'm so mortified I fainted in the operating room." She shook her head.

"Don't be embarrassed. I'm glad I was there too."

They didn't say much after that and he was relieved that she was no longer annoyed with him. He remembered his late wife getting upset with him too.

Why are you always working? Luisa had said, sobbing.

To build a life for us. I need to work. I'm the low man at the hospital, he'd explained.

Work is more important than me.

He'd pulled Luisa close. *No, never.*

The thing was, she hadn't been totally wrong about that. He had worked a lot and he'd missed a lot. It was why she'd gotten into that car by herself. If he had been with her... Well, there was nothing he could've done to stop the accident.

There was no changing the past.

When they got to Sharon's house Sandrine flung open the door and was all smiles as Sharon walked up the path.

"I didn't say anything to your abuela about my brother

being the father, but I am so excited about becoming an aunt," Sandrine said excitedly. She threw her arms around Sharon and hugged her, which surprised him and caught Sharon off guard as well.

Sharon chuckled softly and patted Sandrine's back, still in a bit of shock. "Well, I am very glad to hear it and I want to thank you for giving up your time tomorrow to sit with my grandmother while I go to my appointment."

"Any time I can help out Maria or you, just ask. I really like your grandmother." Sandrine was beaming and her hazel eyes were twinkling. Agustin couldn't ever recall seeing Sandrine this happy since his arrival back in Argentina, and from what his mother had told him it seemed she wasn't exactly a happy child, except when she'd been around his father.

They all walked inside and Sharon's abuela was sitting up at the kitchen table with a puzzle. Sandrine sat back down at the table, working on the puzzle with the elderly lady.

"*Querida*, you're home!" Abuela cocked her head to one side. "You have something to tell me."

Sharon smiled nervously and hung up her coat. "I do. You remember Dr. Agustin Varela?"

"Agustin? Of course, I delivered him. I may have hit my head but I can still remember," her abuela said, pointing to her temple. "I'm only eighty. I'm not dead yet."

Agustin chuckled softly to himself and Sharon rolled her eyes.

"Abuela, Agustin is the father of my baby. We met in Barcelona, before I moved here. I was at a conference and… well, I didn't know he was from Ushuaia and he didn't know I was either…"

Sharon's abuela grinned. "Well, that's excellent news.

I don't know what kind of medical conference includes hanky-panky, but I understand why it happened."

Sharon's face flushed red and Agustin couldn't help but laugh.

"Abuela, really," Sharon warned.

Abuela just waved her hand in her direction, dismissing her as she turned to Sandrine. "How do you feel about being an aunt?"

"I'm thrilled," Sandrine exclaimed. "We're going to be family. A real family, finally!"

Agustin felt a twinge of guilt at what Sandrine said about family. Wasn't he family enough for his half sister? Only, he knew the answer. He had never been around for her before because of his strained relationship with his father.

He felt bad that Sandrine was obviously missing something.

"Now you can call me Abuela for real," Theresa stated.

Sandrine gave the old woman a side hug and Sharon just crossed her arms and shook her head.

"You need to rest," Agustin whispered.

"Yes," Sharon agreed.

"I'm going to pick up my dry cleaning and I will get some dinner."

He wanted to put some distance between all this. He wasn't sure what he was feeling right now. He just knew he had to clear his head.

Sharon worried her bottom lip. "You don't have to do that…"

"I want to and I'm not taking no for an answer. I'll be back in a while."

Sharon sighed, but nodded.

He left the house to head back to his hotel.

It was a very cozy scene. Sandrine was happy and bubbly. Sharon's abuela was thrilled, although Sharon still looked a bit out of sorts. Not that he could blame her—he was still feeling a bit out of sorts about the whole thing too. It was like they were forming this little family, and he liked that a lot, but then Sharon didn't want a relationship with him and he couldn't have a relationship with her.

The idea of family was scary. There was no certainty of a happily-ever-after. All he had to do was look at his parents or think about what happened to him and the pain he felt when Luisa died. He had fallen for that ideal of happiness and love once before.

The fairy tale hadn't ended well for him.

Sharon had been so angry at Agustin for making decisions without consulting her, but she was glad she was able to talk to him about it. She was having misgivings about how involved he was trying to be in her life. She wasn't used to that.

Their baby's life, fine, but now he was picking up dinner for them? Sandrine and her abuela looked extremely happy together and Sharon was glad for that, but what was going to happen to them when Agustin decided he'd had enough and found someone to create a real family with? Someone who wanted that happily-ever-after?

It was all too much.

Don't stress yourself out.

Sharon was worried that her blood pressure reading was high, higher than usual for her, and she had been a big ball of stress since she came back to Argentina. Not only navigating all the old memories of her past, but also trying to help her grandmother heal.

"Your mail is on the table there," Sandrine said. "There's a large pile of it. I think Maria forgot to get it the other day."

"Thanks, Sandrine," Sharon said. She made her way to the table and picked up the stack of letters and cards and then saw something that made her blood run cold. A statement from the bank that looked ominous and was addressed to her abuela.

Sharon took the letter into the small sitting room to read it over. Her stomach knotted as she read about back taxes on a property her abuela owned in Buenos Aires and overdue legal fees. Sharon glanced over her shoulder at her abuela sitting there. It was a lot of money, money that Sharon didn't have ready.

Sandrine left the room and Sharon went to her grandmother, sitting next to her.

"Abuela, you own property in Buenos Aires?" She handed her grandmother the letter.

"No. I don't think so." Abuela stared at the letter. "I don't understand. I sold this five years ago."

"You did?" Sharon asked, confused.

"*Sí.* Five years ago. My accountant back then took care of it. Arranged Realtors and everything." Her abuela rubbed her head. "At least, I think so. I remember paying taxes on it before."

Sharon took back the letter. "Well, try not to worry. We'll figure it out."

Abuela nodded. "I'm sorry to burden you with it."

"I might have to get a power of attorney."

Abuela frowned. "Okay, but talk to your aunt too. Maybe she knows."

"I will."

She was going to have to talk to her aunt and see if there

was any kind of paperwork and try to work this out. She knew her abuela would sign over a power of attorney so Sharon could talk to the bank in Buenos Aires.

She had some time to get this figured out, but the threat was clear and it was exactly what she didn't need right at this moment. Sharon took the letter and slipped it into her purse.

Sharon would take care of it, just like she'd taken care of a lot of things throughout her life since her mother died and her father abandoned her. She could rely on herself. She didn't need to rely on anyone else.

It was better this way.

She leaned her head back against the couch cushions and could feel the baby moving inside her. It was the first time she'd really ever paid attention to it and she smiled as she felt it whiz under her skin. She placed a hand on her slightly rounded belly. The baby moved under her fingers, but she wasn't sure if she could feel it through her belly or if it was just because she could feel the baby moving within her. Either way, it made her smile even more.

"I will try," she whispered to the baby. "You won't want for anything and you won't be alone."

The baby nudged her and she laughed, fighting back the tears that were threatening to spill. It annoyed her how much her emotions were going up and down today. It was not like her at all and she really did hate this loss of control, especially when it came to Agustin.

There was a knock and the door opened as Agustin came back in with takeaway bags. A swirl of snow followed him in.

"It's really snowing out there," he panted.

Sandrine helped him with the bags and brought them into the kitchen. Their gazes locked across the room.

"Are you okay?" he asked, his voice full of concern, which made her heart melt just a bit. She couldn't let herself fall for him.

He'd leave her. He'd made it clear he didn't want a relationship, just as she had, and she couldn't risk her heart.

"Fine," she replied, plastering a fake smile on her face. "Thanks for bringing dinner."

He nodded and slipped off his shoes and took off his coat.

She sighed and stood up. She had to keep reminding herself this little bloom of happiness, in this moment, with Agustin, his sister, her abuela and her was temporary. Happiness never lasted forever and she had to be ready when the bubble burst.

CHAPTER SEVEN

SHARON WAS LOOKING out at the window absently, staring at the snow when she saw Sandrine coming down the street.

She was with Diego.

A local boy.

Someone Agustin seemed to detest. It was a good thing Agustin wasn't here.

Actually, she hadn't seen him in a couple of weeks. It had been that long since she'd collapsed in the operating room and her first checkup with Dr. Perez.

Sandrine kissed her boyfriend goodbye outside and then came bounding up the steps into her abuela's home.

The young girl had taken it upon herself to come over and visit them after school, which Sharon didn't mind in the least.

It broke her heart to think of Sandrine lonely.

Sharon keenly remembered how it had been for her as a young child.

Abandoned.

Her aunt liked to think she'd forgotten, but Sharon hadn't. Although Sandrine hadn't been abandoned the way that she had, their situations were still similar. It was like looking at a younger version of herself.

A parallel.

The difference between Sandrine and her: Sandrine was older than she had been.

Sharon wasn't sure that made a difference. Maybe Sandrine hadn't been so blindsided when her mother had left her, because she mentioned often that her mother was never around.

No matter how it had happened, it was wrong.

It was heartbreaking.

Something she knew firsthand.

"*Hola*, Sharon," Sandrine said brightly. "Is Abuela asleep?"

"She is," Sharon said. "How was school?"

"Good. We've been talking about careers." Sandrine set her bag down and slipped off her shoes to come sit in the living room.

"Any thoughts?" Sharon asked, interested.

"Gus wants me to be a surgeon," Sandrine responded, using the name Sharon had first known Agustin by.

"How do you feel about that?"

"It's a lot of schooling. Diego wants to be a mechanic and stay here."

Now it made sense why Agustin was wary of Diego's influence. Medical school was far away and trade school was here in Ushuaia.

"Is that why your brother dislikes Diego, because he might be swaying you?" Sharon asked.

Sandrine blushed. "Maybe."

"Look…"

"You're not going to hate on him now too, are you?" Sandrine asked, hurt.

"No. I don't know him. He seems nice."

Sandrine nodded. "He is. You'll see when you get to know him properly."

The problem was Sharon wasn't sure that was possible. With the back taxes her abuela owed on a property she'd thought was sold, Sharon was considering the real possibility of selling the house. It was clear the accountant had absconded with the money and the property was never put up for sale. Her abuela's memories were hazy and Sharon was struggling to find out information.

She would have to go to Buenos Aires, as the property was there. Each province had their own set of rules, so she couldn't figure this out in Ushuaia.

The legal fees were high and if she sold this home as well as the property in Buenos Aires she could discharge the back taxes and pay the legal fees. The only way to do both was to sell this home though. Once that was all done, then she'd have to find a small apartment or affordable small home for her, her abuela and her baby to live.

Which might mean they'd be on the other side of town.

It worried her how she was going to break the news to her abuela as well.

Her grandmother seemed to be getting attached to the idea that Agustin and Sandrine were going to be part of their lives going forward.

Which was not a certainty.

Her abuela was too trusting, too caring, which was why everyone in the community loved her so much and probably why she'd been taken advantage of five years ago.

Sharon felt her stomach dip, a wave of nausea hitting her as she thought of the mess her life had become since Barcelona. How complicated and involved with others it had become.

She'd talked to her aunt in New York and her aunt had referred her to a lawyer so she could get a power of attorney to deal with the back taxes, but it was a mess and stressful.

Between her work, caring for her abuela and her pregnancy, it was hard to conduct it all over the phone and email in Ushuaia.

"Sharon, are you okay?" Sandrine asked.

"No." And she didn't feel okay at all. Her head was pounding and she felt so nauseous. It was worrying. She got up and checked her blood pressure. It was high.

A bunch of scenarios ran through her head, but her head began to ache. She knew one thing: she had to get checked out. "Can you call an ambulance for me, Sandrine?"

"Sí." Sandrine made a call and Sharon sat on the floor. The room was spinning. Sandrine was talking to other people and she felt a blast of cold air as the front door was opened.

"What's wrong?" Agustin asked, his voice panicked.

"The ambulance is on its way," Sandrine said, but it sounded like she was far away.

"Keep Theresa calm." Agustin dropped to her side. *"Querida?"*

Sharon could hear her abuela panicking in the background and Sandrine comforting her.

"I feel dizzy again." And that was all she could manage to say before everything faded to black.

Agustin was beside himself as he paced outside Sharon's hospital room door. He had kept away for a couple of weeks and immersed himself in work, because he thought it was for the best to put some distance between them.

Sharon also seemed off since the operating room incident.

He didn't want to scare her away by being too involved in her life, but it was killing him to keep away.

Sharon threw up some emotional wall after that night and he'd gotten the hint to back off. So he'd gone back to the thing he knew well, where he didn't have to think about emotions or anything.

Work.

Then Sandrine had texted him.

Sharon was ill and an ambulance had been called.

It was like a nightmare. He couldn't even ride in the ambulance with her because he wasn't related to her.

So, all he could do was pace.

Dr. Perez came out of the room.

"Well?" Agustin asked.

"Her blood pressure was a bit high, but it's under control. She's still having morning sickness and she's dehydrated. She's staying here until the bolus of fluids is done and then she needs to go home and rest for a couple of days."

Agustin was relieved. "Can I see her?"

"For a little bit. I'd like her to rest until I'm happy with her electrolytes. I'll let you know when I'm discharging her."

"*Gracias*, Dr. Perez."

Agustin entered the room and Sharon was scowling at the ceiling.

"How are you now?" Agustin asked.

"Annoyed," she stated. "Dr. Perez wants me to rest."

"And you should." He sat down in the chair.

"I like to work," she stated.

"I understand," he chuckled.

"What's so funny?" she asked indignantly.

"Doctors are not the only ones to make lousy patients."

She smiled, the annoyance melting away. "I suppose not.

I like control. It feels like I have none of that in my life right now."

"I understand."

"Sandrine said they were talking about careers at school. She said you wanted her to be a surgeon."

"*Sí.* I do," he responded.

"Why?" she asked.

He groaned inwardly. It seemed to personal. He wanted Sandrine to be independent and not like her mother.

"She's smart," he said.

"Agreed."

He ran his hand through his hair. "She's capable and it would give her freedom."

"Is that why you wanted to be a doctor?" she asked.

"These are a lot of questions," he groused.

Sharon shrugged. "What else have I got to do."

"Fine. Yes, partly. I just loved helping people, saving lives…" He trailed off as he thought of Luisa and how he couldn't save her.

Sometimes medicine failed.

"So why did you become a nurse?" he asked, changing the subject to her.

"Same. I wanted independence and a nurse was…was kind to me when I was young. I wanted to help others."

"Very noble." He smiled and took her hand without thinking. It was so small in his.

So fragile.

Just like the little life growing inside her.

He let go of her hand and stood up. "You need rest."

She nodded. "Okay. My abuela?"

"Sandrine is holding down the fort. I'll go check on them too. I'll come back to pick you up when you're discharged."

"Thank you," she said.

He nodded and left the room. He was getting too attached to Sharon.

It was clear this pregnancy was hard on her.

He was terrified something was going to happen to the baby, to her.

He wasn't sure his heart could handle it if something did.

Sharon had been off work for a week since her episode, which required her to get intravenous treatment for dehydration.

Finally she was given some shifts.

It had been worrying her she hadn't been working. She needed to work as much as possible before the baby came.

She wasn't even annoyed she got light duties at the clinic, which was dealing with a lot of patients who were there for Botox or consults.

She was working and that was all that mattered.

Agustin was keeping his distance too. Which was fine on one hand, but on the other, she missed him.

Something had changed in her hospital room and she wasn't sure what it was.

"You ready for the ultrasound?" Agustin asked, coming into the office where she had been working on her final preoperative assessment reports.

"What?" she asked, shaking her head of all the thoughts that were going around and around inside her.

"It's four o'clock. Our ultrasound is scheduled in fifteen minutes. Are you ready?"

"Right." She shook her head again and closed the file she was working on. "Sorry, I just zoned out there for a moment."

"You're not dizzy, are you?" he asked, worry in his voice.

"No. And no nausea either. Just preoccupied."

Which was true.

She was.

There was a lot going on.

"If you're sure," he hedged.

"I'm fine. Let's go," she responded.

She wasn't too pleased with this babying. She knew how to take care of herself.

Agustin had her coat in his hand. It was just a quick walk to the building next door. It was the same building Dr. Perez worked out of and where she had her blood work done. They walked outside and it was snowing and hazy out.

It had been a stormy June so far.

She slipped a bit on an icy patch and Agustin reached out and steadied her. His hand on her back, even through her thick winter coat, was warming. She could feel her body responding to his simple touch.

"Thank you," she whispered.

"No need to thank me." Agustin opened the door and they made their way inside. They were taken straightaway to a room and Sharon was made comfortable on exam bed, while Agustin stood next to her.

He was very tense.

Or maybe that was her stress.

"Are you okay?" she asked, lying there with her hands folded on her chest.

"Fine," he replied stiffly.

"I don't think so."

He didn't look at her. "Okay. I'm not."

She wanted to ask him why he wasn't when the ultrasound technician walked into the room.

"*Hola!* My name is Mariposa and I'm your ultrasound technician today." She was readying her equipment. "Sharon, you drank all your water?"

"Yes. I'm ready to burst."

Mariposa laughed gently. "Everyone says that. Now if you could lift your shirt and slide your pants down, I've got some towels here."

Sharon and Mariposa exposed her rounder pregnant belly.

"You're about twenty-two weeks?" Mariposa asked.

"Twenty-three," Agustin responded.

"Yes," Sharon said. "Just twenty-three."

"Oh, then we may be able to tell the gender. Would you like to know the gender?" Mariposa asked.

Sharon glanced over at Agustin. "Well, would we?"

"I would like to know," he said.

Sharon smiled. "So would I."

"Great! Just going to put some gel on your belly and we'll get started." Mariposa squeezed the ultrasound gel on her belly and Sharon watched the monitor, waiting for that first glimpse of the little surprise that she had never been expecting.

It only took a few moments for the blurry black-and-white image to show a small staticky-looking baby on the screen. Sharon's heart caught in her throat—she never really had understand that expression until this moment, but now, looking at the baby she never thought she'd ever have, she felt it.

Just like that night after she collapsed and felt the baby under her fingers.

It was magical.

"Looks very healthy," Mariposa remarked, taking pictures and measurements.

Sharon glanced over at Agustin, but he wasn't saying

anything. His face was unreadable, but he reached down and took her hand and squeezed it, his gaze fixed on the screen. She wasn't sure what he was feeling in that moment seeing their child, but she knew what she was feeling and that was love.

Love for that little life.

Her child.

She would never let anyone hurt her child. Her child would never face the trauma she had. Her child would always know love and never loneliness. She made that vow silently to herself.

"Would you like to know the gender now?" Mariposa asked, interrupting her thoughts.

"Sí," Sharon whispered, holding her breath.

"It's a girl. Congratulations," Mariposa said brightly.

A tear slid from Sharon's cheek and Agustin knelt down beside her and touched her face, wiping the tear away with the pad of his thumb. They locked gazes and her heart felt like it was going to burst, sharing this special moment with him. It meant so much to her, but she had to remember to guard her heart and not melt for him, but here she was in this moment doing just that.

"I'll get you both a picture," Mariposa said brightly. She handed Sharon another towel to clean up and then she left the room.

Agustin helped her sit up as she wiped the gel off her belly.

"How do you feel?" he asked, finding his voice.

"Great. I am happy, but I would be happy whatever it was as long as it's healthy."

Agustin nodded. "Same, but I can't help, in this moment,

feeling just a little bit happy at the thought of a daughter. Especially if she looks like you."

The tender comment caught her off guard and she could feel the blush creeping up her neck. "Thank you."

"Shall we go out to dinner and celebrate? Sandrine is with your grandmother tonight."

"Did you preplan dinner?" Sharon asked.

"I did." He grinned and winked. "Come on, I know the perfect little place just outside of town. It's a hotel, but serves a great little dinner overlooking the Beagle Channel."

Sharon cocked an eyebrow. "You want to drive down to the channel in this weather?"

"It's clearing up. We'll be fine and it's early. Come." He held out his hand and even though she thought the idea of going to have dinner out of town seemed silly, it was Friday and the clinic was closed tomorrow and she wasn't on duty.

It might be nice and relaxing to have dinner down by the water. There wouldn't be as many tourists as that road out of town that headed to the national park of Lapataia and in June it wasn't the busiest of roads.

It would be peaceful.

Still, the thought of being alone with him unnerved her. She was trying to distance herself from him and if she went with him, she was hardly doing that. Instead of listening to her rational side though, she took his hand as he helped her stand up and get her coat on.

"I'm not really dressed for a fancy place," she remarked.

"It's not that fancy. You're fine. It's just a gorgeous spot." He put his hand on the small of her back and they walked back to the clinic parking lot and he opened the door to his car. She settled into the passenger seat.

The snow had stopped and the sun was going down.

It was one of her favorite times of the day in the winter months. The sky had warm orange tones as the sun set below the western edge, over the mountains that separated Chile and Argentina, but there were various grays and blacks in the sky, signaling a storm and the cold of the winter months.

A time of darkness.

It was the time of year that always made her feel cozy. She just wasn't quite used to having this feeling in June, which for her had always been the mark of summer.

"I have forgotten what a June winter feels like. I'm going to have to get used to the idea of a warm Christmas," she said brightly.

"I'm used to it. It's the cold I struggle with. Always have."

"Your mother is in Buenos Aires?"

"Yes. She's originally from there, so when her marriage to my father ended...not by her choice, she went back home, and that's where I went to medical school. I was in university when they split up. I was at school in Buenos Aires and I stayed there for a long time. I only came back to Ushuaia about five years ago."

"I'm sorry about your parents."

"What about your parents?" he asked.

Sharon swallowed the lump in her throat. She knew this conversation would come eventually, but it was one she didn't want to have.

Burying the pain of her childhood was easier than talking about it constantly. It helped her to move on and create a life for herself.

"My mother died when I was nine, and about six months after that my father walked out of our home in New York City and never came back. Thankfully, my maternal aunt

Elisa lived in White Plains, just up the Hudson River with her husband, and she was called."

"Oh, my God…how long were you left on your own?" he asked, shocked.

"A week," she whispered, as the memories of that horrible time came flooding back to her. Her fear of the policemen and not understanding what was wrong. The concerned neighbors. She had lived on cereal and whatever she could reach for that week.

Her aunt had been beside herself, trying not to cry as she spoke to the policeman. Sharon had just clung to her dolly, not sure of what was happening.

"I'm sorry that happened to you, *querida*," he whispered.

He'd called her that before. She never paid it any mind until now.

After sharing that bit about herself, the word meant something else now.

She wasn't his dearest.

"What?"

"Querida," he said again. "Dearest. I think it's fitting. You are the mother of my child, or rather my daughter."

She liked when he said it and she shouldn't.

It's what her abuela and her aunt had called her. Everyone in her family, and it just seemed right. She really hoped that he couldn't see the warmth spreading in her cheeks. Still, she was annoyed she was letting him affect her like this.

"Did they ever find your father?" Agustin asked quietly.

"No. I don't know what happened to him. My aunt did obtain guardianship, so he sent in something, but there was no return address. I have no idea what happened to him and I really don't care. You don't know where Sandrine's mother is, do you?"

Agustin sighed. "No. I don't. She left that poor girl all alone, but Sandrine was older and she's told me that she was used to being left. It was just her and our father. She would care for him. I had no concept of how sick he was."

"You didn't come to see him?"

"I never forgave him for what he did to my mother, but my mother is kind. She did forgive Father, probably when she remarried. She was the one that told me Sandrine had been abandoned and the house in Ushuaia was mine. Thankfully, I was there and not still living in Buenos Aires."

It grew darker as they headed west and away from the lights of Ushuaia. It was then that she saw blinking lights in the distance.

"What's that?" Sharon asked.

Agustin slowed the car and leaned over the wheel. "It looks like a car in the ditch."

"We better pull over and check."

Agustin nodded and slowed down more, pulling in behind the car, which was slightly in the ditch, but not completely. As they pulled to a stop a man in his twenties waved at them frantically.

Agustin rolled down his window. "What's wrong?"

The man looked confused, like he didn't understand. "*No hablo Español*. Not very well, that is," the man mumbled.

"American?" Sharon asked, switching to English.

"Yes. Are you American?" the man asked.

"I am. What's wrong?" Sharon asked.

"My wife, we were hiking by Lapataia. We decided to head back to the hotel, but our car hit some ice and we slid off the road. We were okay, but they said it was going to be over an hour to get a tow, and she's in labor and I can't get another cell signal to call an ambulance. Do you have a working cell phone?"

"What's wrong?" Agustin asked, confused.

"His wife is in labor and their cell phone is dead." Sharon turned back to the man. "He's a doctor and I'm a nurse. We'll call an ambulance and then we'll come and check on your wife."

"Oh, thank God," the man said. "I'm Kevin, by the way. My wife is Dana."

Sharon smiled. "I'm Sharon and this is Agustin. Well, Kevin, lead me to your wife and Agustin here will call the ambulance."

Kevin nodded and jogged off, to where she saw his wife had gotten out of the car and was panting, hunched over and leaning on the hood.

Assessing her, Sharon said, "Call an ambulance. I think she can't wait, judging by the pain she's in."

Agustin nodded. "Be careful yourself."

"I will."

Agustin pulled out his phone and Sharon carefully got out of the car. She made her way over to the couple and that was when she noticed the child in the back sleeping. It was a minivan and she knew from stories in the States that they weren't always the most reliable vehicles when it came to icy roads.

"You have another child? Are they okay?" Sharon asked.

Kevin nodded. "Oh, yeah, they're sleeping. Our son sleeps through anything."

Kevin's wife, Dana, snorted in pain, as if agreeing with him.

"Dana, this is Sharon and she's a nurse."

Dana's blue eyes were glazed over in pain. "Oh, thank goodness."

"Let's get you in the back of your van. Do you have blankets?" Sharon asked.

Kevin nodded. "Yeah, we have our whole life in that van. We drove down from Alaska."

Sharon's eyes widened. "Wow. So, no prenatal care?"

"I gave birth to Dylan at home," Dana panted. "I'm fine."

Sharon nodded. "Okay, well, let's check on you."

Kevin and Sharon managed to get Dana into the back of the van. There was a bed set up and she was so thankful that there was a place to get Dana comfortable.

"Did your water break?" Sharon asked, climbing into the back of the van as she got Dana settled.

"Yes," Dana said breathlessly through contractions.

Kevin helped his wife remove her trousers and covered her with a sheet. Agustin came over then with a first aid kit.

"Thought you might need this, or rather *we* might need this." He smiled. "The ambulance is on its way."

"What's he saying?" Kevin asked.

"Agustin said the ambulance is on its way," Sharon said. "Agustin, can you help me?"

Agustin nodded. He peeled off his jacket and opened the first aid kit. They quickly sanitized their hands and put on disposable gloves that were supplied. It wasn't much, but it was something.

"I'm going to check you now," Sharon said to Dana.

Dana nodded. Kevin held her hand. Agustin shone a light for Sharon to see. She felt and could feel the baby's head and it was right there.

"Oh," Sharon exclaimed. "Your baby is getting ready to crown, so I think it's okay to start pushing."

"Really?" Dana asked.

Sharon quickly translated for Agustin, who smiled that charming smile that would put anyone at ease. His sleeves had been rolled up and he handed the flashlight to Kevin as he squatted and got ready to catch the baby.

"Have you delivered a baby before?" Sharon asked Agustin.

"I have. I don't think you can kneel down here in your condition," Agustin remarked.

She didn't even bother arguing with him—he was right. There was no way that she could get down there in such a confined space, in these conditions.

"You're right," she murmured.

"Dana," Agustin said.

"Yes?" she asked.

"Push...next...contraction," Agustin managed in English. "Baby is here."

Dana nodded and Sharon urged her to push as the contraction tightened across Dana's belly. Dana cried and Agustin encouraged her in Spanish. It didn't matter, it was translating well as the little baby was in a hurry and wasn't waiting for any ambulance to make its way from Ushuaia to here.

It only took a couple of pushes. The baby's shoulders were free and the rest of the little boy slipped out and into Agustin's arms.

The baby didn't cry.

"I need a blanket," Agustin said, keeping his voice calm, but she could hear the stress, the serious undertone.

This baby might die.

"Why isn't the baby crying?" Dana asked.

Sharon scrambled down next to Agustin, handing him

clean blankets as he flipped the baby and massaged his back, trying to keep him in the warmth of the back of the van. He slapped the baby on the back as Sharon knelt down, rubbing the baby's face and body, trying to coax a cry.

"He's not breathing," Agustin whispered. He flipped the baby back over and set him down, tilting the little head back and checking the baby's airway. He began giving rescue breaths and Sharon could see the baby's little chest rising. Agustin then started compressions with his fingers.

He only had to do it once and the baby let out a gasp and screamed.

Sharon hadn't realized that she was holding her breath. She held out the blanket as Agustin grinned and clamped and cut the cord, using what limited supplies were available, before placing the baby into the blanket.

"Bueno," Agustin proclaimed, giving a thumbs-up to the worried parents.

"You have a boy," Sharon proclaimed, placing the little boy in Dana's arms.

Dana was crying and held her boy, but then her face contorted and Sharon had a sinking feeling that it wasn't the placenta.

"She's contracting again," Sharon told Agustin.

"Again?" Agustin asked, checking. "There's another head."

"She didn't know. She didn't have prenatal care," Sharon explained.

Agustin said nothing. Just frowned as he went to work.

Kevin took his son and a little girl entered the world just as quickly, but the moment she was free of her mother in Agustin's arms she screamed lustily.

Agustin chuckled and looked at Sharon tenderly.

Sharon was fighting back tears, watching Agustin with those little babies that were in such a hurry to be born on the side of the road in Tierra del Fuego. They were so small in his strong arms and she couldn't help but think of their own little girl as he handed the baby over to her mother.

Sharon just smiled at him in awe and they heard the wail of the ambulance coming up the road. Kevin, Dana and the now awake little Dylan were all cuddled in the back of the van, a happy family.

Sharon envied them.

She wished she had what they had. Maybe not a roadside birth, but Agustin's love, their children.

A family.

Agustin was finally able to make it to the place he wanted to take Sharon for dinner, but they were a little worse for wear after helping deliver a baby in the tight confines of the car, so he ordered takeout and then drove down to a secluded spot that overlooked the channel.

It was not what he'd envisioned, but he was glad they'd both been there to help that family.

When that little baby was born and wasn't breathing, he'd had a flashback to the moment he lost Luisa.

The same terror that gripped him when Sharon collapsed twice.

Thankfully, the baby had pulled through, and Sharon had been a huge help in making that happen. She'd been as steady as a rock through it all.

They had been true partners in that moment.

That little American family seemed like a tight-knit group. They were so full of love. He had that kind of love from his mother, but not really from his father.

Although there were blurry memories from his past that were starting to creep back out from where he'd tightly locked them away.

There'd been some happy times.

He wanted that.

He wanted that loving family, that tight-knit group.

It's why he got married all those years ago.

Love and the hope of happiness.

He was a bit more jaded now.

He glanced over at Sharon, whose eyes were twinkling as she ate her dinner out of a cardboard box in his car, and his heart swelled.

There were a lot of emotions running through him at the ultrasound today. When he saw that little fetus on the screen, he was filled with emotions that he hadn't experienced in a long time, but the sense of dread was still there.

He couldn't help it.

All he could think about was losing Luisa. All he could think about was how much she had been looking forward to her ultrasound and seeing their child and he couldn't seem to let go of Luisa's accident. How work had taken priority that night and she'd driven in bad weather alone.

He'd paid the price by losing them. Now he was here in Ushuaia and had this second chance. Agustin didn't feel that he deserved it. He was afraid to feel happy or excited, even though he was.

And when he saw Sharon help that mother, as they delivered those twins, Agustin was just caught up in the love and the happiness and the pride he felt for having Sharon carry his second chance at his dreams.

Only, Sharon wasn't his.

"You're really quiet," Sharon said. "Are you all right?"

"I think I'm still in shock from that set of twins," he said, which he was, but that wasn't what was on his mind tonight. "I wanted you to have a nice dinner, a sit-down dinner, and yet all I can seem to manage is to get you takeaway dinners."

Sharon laughed softly in the dim light. "I really do like takeaway dinners. And you have managed to take me out before, you know."

"Oh?"

"The café in Barcelona. I believe we had some lovely sangria and tapas that night."

He grinned. "That's right, we did."

"You forgot about that?" she asked.

"About that night, no, but the café is a dim memory compared to what happened later that evening," he said huskily. It was true—he remembered every exquisite inch of her.

"It's in the forefront of my mind as well," she admitted, and then she reached down to touch her rounded belly. His gaze followed her movement.

"May I?" he asked.

"Touch my belly?" she asked, with a hint of hope in her voice.

"*Sí*. I would like that very much."

"Of course."

Agustin reached over and gently placed a hand on her belly, feeling the fullness of the swell and knowing there was a little life growing in there. His daughter. It was hard to wrap his mind around that idea, that it was his daughter in there and that he was going to be a father in less than twenty weeks.

It was then as he rested his hand on her belly that he felt a little push. Just ever so slight, a nudge against the palm of his hand. His daughter was alive and thriving.

She was real.

He knew logically she was real, but his little girl was reaching out to him and letting him know that she was there. All he felt through his veins in that moment was love, and he wanted to protect her and Sharon.

"Did you feel that?" Sharon asked, her voice excited.

"I did," Agustin responded.

Sharon placed her hand on her belly too and there was another nudge and they both smiled at each other.

"She seems to like your dinner as well," Sharon said teasingly.

"It's good food. I'm glad she has taste." He leaned over the console of the car and touched Sharon's face gently. She closed her eyes. Sharon was so beautiful, that hadn't changed. He pressed a kiss against her forehead. "Thank you, *querida*."

"For what?" she whispered breathlessly.

"For taking good care of our baby."

Sharon smiled and then she leaned over, pressing a kiss against his lips, featherlike, but still like the first time she had kissed him. The memories of that first kiss and then the kisses that had come after that came flooding through him. He cupped her face and deepened that featherlight kiss.

Sharon melted under him, parting her lips. He slipped his tongue into her mouth, tasting her again. He had missed her. Even though she wasn't his, he had missed her and missed this, but then he remembered they had made no promises and he wasn't staying here.

Agustin pulled away. "I'm sorry."

"No, don't be sorry. I encouraged that. It was just…the baby kicking and that delivery tonight. I got a little caught up in the moment."

His heart was aching as he looked at her, her eyes twinkling in the dark. "We can't let that happen again."

"It won't. I want us to be friends and I want to be able to work together without everything being so awkward."

"I promise. Friends."

Sharon nodded. "Well, we better get back to town. It's getting late and I'm exhausted."

"You're right." Agustin moved back into his seat and fastened his seat belt. "I did have a great time with you today."

Sharon smiled. "Same."

He didn't say anything more as he started the ignition and slowly made his way back to Ushuaia. His blood was still burning, his body still craving her, and a little voice inside him was questioning why he had to leave when everything he wanted was here, but that little voice had forgotten that he'd once had everything, and he couldn't bear the thought of losing that all again.

CHAPTER EIGHT

WHEN THEY GOT back to Ushuaia, Agustin was still struggling with all these emotions and the pain of Luisa dying was suddenly raw and fresh again in his heart. He was torn and didn't know what to do.

This was not what he'd planned when he decided to come back here and deal with his father's estate and his half sister. It was supposed to be easy, but he didn't know why he'd thought that and he could only chalk it up to his optimism. But the moment they walked back into Sharon's abuela's house he didn't have a moment to even think about it, because they were bombarded with questions from his sister and Sharon's abuela about the baby.

It was all a blur as he stood there, and Sandrine was so happy to find out the baby was going to be a little girl.

All he could do was stand there stunned.

What he needed to do was get some space.

"I have a phone call to make," he said quickly. "I'll be back in a bit."

Sharon nodded. "Okay."

He nodded and slipped out the door. He made his way across the yard and unlocked his front door. He took off his jacket, hanging it up, and then made his way over to the bar to pour himself a shot of fernet.

It was then his phone rang, buzzing in the pocket of his trousers.

He pulled it out and it was his mother.

"*Hola*, Mama," he answered. "You're calling me late."

"It's not late," his mother said.

He smiled. "It's late for you."

"Ah, yes, true, but I can't sleep. I thought I would check in on how you and Sandrine are getting along since she left school here."

He chuckled. "You really called because you knew today was the ultrasound."

His mother laughed softly. "I care about Sandrine and you, but yes, I am also curious about how that went."

"It's a girl and she's healthy," Agustin stated.

"A girl?" His mother's voice quivered. "I am so happy."

"I am sure."

"How are you feeling?" his mother asked.

"Fine."

"Come on, I know that you have always had big emotions and you're just like your father and really good at squirreling them away."

Agustin was annoyed that his mother was comparing him to his father. He was nothing like his father, who'd left. His father who had put work above all else.

Aren't you doing the same?

He ignored that little voice in his head, because he didn't have the emotional strength to deal with it right now. There were a lot of emotions going on inside him and he really didn't want to talk about it right now.

His phone buzzed again, but this time it was the postoperative care unit at the clinic. It was a call that he had to take.

"Mama, I need to go, the clinic is calling about one of my patients."

His mother sighed. "Very well. I will call you later in the week. I am very happy about the baby and I can't wait to meet Sharon. Please bring her to Buenos Aires when you can."

"Night, Mama." Agustin ended the call and then answered the call from the clinic. "Agustin speaking."

"Agustin, it's Pilar from the clinic. I'm calling about your patient, Alondra. She's running a very high fever. We tried to get it down, but then the stitches are coming loose and we need your assistance. The patient's family refused to allow anyone else to work on their mother."

"I'll be there." Agustin ended the call.

He grabbed his coat. He opened the front door and found Sharon standing on the front step. She had changed out of her clothes and had braided her hair back. Had he really been on the phone for that long with his mother? He glanced at his watch—he had left Sharon's place over an hour ago.

"Sharon!" he exclaimed.

"You were gone for a while and Sandrine was getting worried. She made a cake." Sharon chuckled.

"Sorry. Phone call and then the clinic called. Alondra is having problems and the family only wants me to deal with it."

"Okay, well, Alondra is a patient I took care of, so can I come and help you?"

Agustin cocked an eyebrow. "Are you going to be okay?"

"I'm fine. I feel great and this is my job. Alondra is my patient too and I want to be there to help."

Agustin nodded. "Very well. Grab your things and we'll head over there."

Sharon scurried over to her abuela's house and was back outside within ten minutes with her purse and a clean pair of scrubs. They got into his car and they headed over to the clinic, neither of them saying much.

When they got there, Sharon headed to the nurses' locker room to change and Agustin went straight into the attending lounge to change into his scrubs. He wasn't sure what they were dealing with, but with symptoms such as pain, high fever and stitches not holding he was worried about some kind of infection.

He wouldn't know until he got in there and examined Alondra.

When he got to Alondra's room Sharon was waiting and had the chart. She was talking to the nurse on duty for the evening.

"What did you notice, Pilar?" Agustin asked the nurse as Sharon handed him the chart.

"Alondra's temperature spiked to one hundred and five and we just couldn't bring it down. I examined the wounds from her tummy tuck and that's when I noticed the stitches coming away. There was some drainage and loss of feeling."

Agustin frowned. "Did you start her on antibiotics?"

Pilar nodded. "I did, but I thought you better take a look. Her husband was quite adamant that you come in and check. He didn't want just a nurse."

Agustin tried not to roll his eyes. He knew Alondra's husband well, or at least knew his reputation well. He'd flown his new wife down from Buenos Aires just to see him. Agustin was good at what he did, but there were days that he missed working in a hospital and being a plastic surgeon that dealt with scalp lacerations or cleft palates.

Working in this private clinic, he didn't often get a chance to work on cases like that and he was beginning to miss it. He was getting tired of the privileged, although sometimes he did get to work on patients that needed construction after cancer, and those patients were always grateful and he was in awe of the battles they'd fought and won.

This patient was privileged and they didn't let him forget it, which was why he was here.

He knocked on the door and entered her private room. "Alondra, I understand you're having some problems."

"That's an understatement," her husband muttered.

Alondra winced. "I don't feel well, Dr. Varela."

Agustin came over to her and checked her vitals. Her pulse was rapid and her heart rate was elevated. He frowned.

"Sharon, I need you to check on the status of her labs. Pilar did a blood draw, and I need a CBC panel to check for signs of infection."

Sharon nodded. "Right away, Agustin."

Sharon slipped out of the room.

"I'm going to examine your incision," Agustin said, gently. "Is that okay, Alondra?"

"Yes." Alondra nodded weakly.

Agustin carefully removed the bandage and saw the signs. Redness, stitches dissolving and the drainage. There were also hard lumps and as he gently palpated she wasn't reacting unless he got near one of the bumps.

It was some kind of bacterial infection, but Agustin had seen this in hospitals. He was pretty sure that it was necrotizing soft tissue. He would have to know which bacteria was causing this and then he could effectively treat it.

"Well?" Max, Alondra's husband, demanded.

"She has an infection. We've ordered blood work and I'm awaiting the results. She's on a dose of penicillin and that will help with the infection, and once I know what strain of bacteria is causing these symptoms then I can tailor the treatment. I will need to do surgical debridement of the wound."

Alondra started to cry softly to herself. "More surgery?"

"The good news is that I think we caught it early," Agustin continued as Max comforted Alondra. "I will keep you posted and I will be here for the rest of the night to check on you. I promise, my nurse Sharon is going to look after you. I understand she was taking care of you before?"

Alondra nodded. "I like her."

"We both do," Max added.

"Good." Agustin left the room and shut the door. Sharon had the lab report and handed it to him. Her face had a grim expression. He read through it and his suspicions were right. It was a bacterial infection and it was one of the ones that often caused necrotizing soft tissue infections.

He sighed and dragged his hand through his hair. At least he knew what it was and how to treat it. "It's Staphylococcus aureus."

Sharon nodded. "You think it's causing her soft tissue in her wound to necrotize?"

"Yes. The drainage from the wound was not healthy. All the signs are there, but we run a sterile operating room, so I'm concerned about how it got in there, unless she already had it and it hadn't appeared yet. Sometimes it can slip blood screens." Agustin tapped his chin, thinking. "She's on penicillin, yes?"

Sharon nodded. "Yes."

"I want her on vancomycin until we can send this off to be cultured and get the correct strain. We also have a hyperbaric chamber. I would like her to start treatments in that."

Sharon raised her eyebrows. "You have that here?"

"We are a top-notch private clinic," Agustin reminded her gently. "I'm going to prep the operating room. I need to clean and debride the wound before the infection spreads and damages any more tissue. Are you feeling up to assisting me in the operating room tonight?"

Sharon nodded. "I can. I feel good. I swear."

"Please page an anesthesiologist. I will get her into surgery after she's had a proper dose of the vancomycin with her penicillin."

"Right away."

Agustin watched Sharon leave to get the lab to culture and find out which strain of Staphylococcus aureus they were dealing with and to start her treatments.

He would send Alondra down to the hyperbaric chamber after the surgery. Necrotizing infections in the soft tissue could spread fast and he needed to get in there and make sure that everything was cleaned up before it did worse damage.

If they let it go too long it could get into her heart and cause endocarditis and kill her. Agustin also wanted to find out how she got this infection and he would have to make sure that everything involving Alondra and this surgery would be sanitized heavily so that no other patient would catch it.

It was a nasty bacterial infection.

He was worried about Sharon being in the operating room with him, especially in her condition, but she was safe. His daughter was safe and Sharon was a capable scrub nurse, when she didn't faint. There was no one else he wanted by his side tonight.

He just wanted her.

* * *

Don't faint. Don't faint.

Sharon was repeating that mantra over and over in her head as she scrubbed in to enter the operating room. Other than being a little tired, she felt fine. The nausea was gone, and she didn't have a headache. She actually felt okay today.

When she had a moment after prepping Alondra for her surgical debridement, she took a rest. She got off her feet and made sure she had small snacks and drank lots of fluids. The baby was kicking like crazy. As much as she wanted to revel in every second of that, she didn't have time, but whenever her little girl kicked she thought of that moment in the car when Agustin had asked to touch her belly and he felt that kick too.

His eyes had sparkled in the dim light of the car and then he'd called her *querida* and touched her face, kissing her on top of her head. It was sweet, but in that moment she wanted more than just a peck on the head, she wanted to touch his lips again.

She wanted to feel him and share in that moment of connection between him, her and their little girl. She forgot herself completely in that moment when she kissed him and it turned into something more.

Something she knew couldn't continue, but she wanted it to.

Sharon was glad when he ended the kiss, but since then she noticed that he had put a wall up. There was something eating away at him and she didn't know what. She knew that grief did funny things to people, and even though he didn't have a great relationship with his father he was still grieving him nonetheless, but there was something else that troubled Agustin.

And she didn't know what.

It's not your business.

Only she couldn't shove that thought to the side, because the more time she spent with him and Sandrine, the more and more she wanted to be around him. The more she was liking him and the more her feelings were melting for him.

It had her thinking, briefly in the dark hours of the night alone in her bed, that maybe a relationship wouldn't be a terrible thing. Agustin was a good man—but that meant nothing. Her mother had thought her father was a good man.

Maybe if her mother hadn't died he wouldn't have left because she, a child, reminded him too much of his late wife. So much so he couldn't stand it.

Sharon finished scrubbing up and headed into the operating room. Dr. Nunez the anesthesiologist was there and they were prepping a very terrified Alondra on the table. Sharon was gowned and gloved. She headed over to the patient.

"How are you, Alondra?" she asked gently.

"I'm scared. I was scared during the tummy tuck and I'm scared now." Her voice trembled.

"It's okay. You are in very good hands. Dr. Varela is one of the best. You will be right as rain."

Alondra nodded. "I shouldn't have gone swimming before we flew down here. That lagoon didn't look right, but Max insisted."

Sharon and Agustin shared a look across the surgical table.

"Brackish water, Alondra?" Sharon asked.

Alondra nodded. "My abuela told me to never swim in water like that. She knew too many people in her village that died from infections after swimming in that water and having an open wound."

"You had a wound?" Agustin asked.

"A paper cut," Alondra said. "I put a plaster on it."

"That wouldn't keep out the bacteria," Sharon said gently. "At least we now know how you got it. Thank you for telling us."

Alondra nodded.

"Now take in a deep breath and count backward from ten," Dr. Nunez said, placing a mask over Alondra's nose.

Alondra began to count backward from ten, but she didn't even make it past the number seven before she was unconscious. Sharon assisted the anesthesiologist as they taped Alondra's eyes shut and inserted a breathing tube down her throat.

Then Sharon was free to assist Agustin on the wound.

"Thankfully, we caught it early enough," Agustin stated. "It could've done so much more damage."

Sharon nodded and handed him the instruments he needed. She didn't want to say much, because she didn't want to overly focus on the surgery. The last time she did that she fainted. Instead she focused on the equipment he needed like sponges to repair the damage, holding the suction when he needed it held.

She winced slightly as the baby began to kick.

"Are you feeling well, Sharon?" Agustin asked, not looking up as he finished the task at hand.

"The baby is kicking and it's making it hard to concentrate. I'm fine though," she said.

Agustin nodded. "Good, we're almost done here. We need to watch her overnight and I would like to continue her regimen of penicillin and vancomycin. Tomorrow afternoon I will instruct staff to place her in the hyperbaric chamber."

"Sounds good." Sharon handed him the suture kit before

he asked. He looked surprised, but nodded his appreciation as he finished up with their patient.

When it was all done, Sharon cleaned up and took the instruments off to be sterilized. She was glad that Agustin wanted her to work with him, but there was a part of her that hated this professional distance too, especially after what happened today.

She shook those thoughts from her head.

What she needed to do right now was focus on her work and then go and find a quiet place to curl up before she went to check on Alondra again. Right now, she had to take care of herself first rather than wrestling with the conflicting emotions she was feeling about Agustin and their situation.

Right now, to do her job and to take care of her health, she needed to have a nap.

CHAPTER NINE

SHARON WAS DISAPPOINTED that she and Agustin didn't get to talk right after Alondra's successful treatment of her necrotizing soft tissue infection. Instead, Agustin threw himself into his work and so she did the same.

It was like it was before the ultrasound.

They just seemed to settle into this happy existence of working and going home together. It was like they were neighbors, but then there were some times during the day she would look up from where she was working and she would see his gaze fixed on her, smoldering, just like that night long ago in Barcelona.

It was hunger, but then again she might be wrong, because she was feeling that way about him. Thinking about that night and thinking about their kiss in the car. Just one simple kiss and it enflamed her senses and brought it all right back, sharp into focus. And she wanted more.

So much so, she couldn't stop thinking about it for weeks.

At the time, she was glad he had ended the kiss. Now she wasn't so sure.

It's hormones. That's it. Hormones.

Only she didn't think that was the only thing. She had a feeling that her traitorous heart was falling for him and she wasn't thrilled with that.

It's not what she wanted.

She didn't want a relationship.

She didn't want to start having more than friendly feelings for Agustin and she hated that she was getting used to seeing him around, that he was slowly starting to mesh himself into her life. She worried about what would happen with Sandrine and her abuela if it all came crashing down.

It wasn't only the situation with Agustin that was causing her undo stress. It was the bank in Buenos Aires and this whole legal issue about her abuela's back taxes on that property that was eating away at her. She was going to have to make arrangements with Maria to stay with her grandmother and take some time off work to fly up to Buenos Aires before she got too big to travel and sell the property.

Sharon could feel her cheeks heat and she pulled out her portable blood pressure monitor. She was worrying about this too much today. It was her day off at the clinic and she needed to relax. The last checkup she had with Dr. Perez, her OB/GYN, there had been a slight elevation of proteins in her urine and she was threatening to put Sharon on bedrest. Which was the last thing she needed.

Her aunt always used to say that Sharon tried to solve the world's problems, but never her own.

Maria was puttering about in the kitchen doing some cleaning. Her abuela was moving around well with her walking frame and outside Ushuaia was in a blanket of snow.

"Sandrine will be home soon," Abuela remarked. "I have a new puzzle for us."

Sharon smiled weakly. "That sounds like fun."

Only she couldn't really put any enthusiasm into that thought. Not when she had to get herself to Buenos Aires.

"*Querida*, you're quiet today. Is it the baby?" her abuela asked, coming over to touch her forehead and then her belly.

"I'm okay. Just feeling a little down. I think it's the winter weather. I've been away too long in the northern hemisphere. I'm used to this being my summer."

Not a total lie, but the winter wasn't what was really bothering her.

"Are you sure your blood pressure is fine?" Abuela asked, in a very clear moment.

"Positive," Sharon responded.

She was twenty-seven weeks along and yes, her blood pressure was elevated, but Dr. Perez wasn't overly concerned.

Yet.

"As long as you're sure," Abuela said carefully.

"I might have to go to Buenos Aires for a couple days, Abuela," Sharon blurted out. "As soon as I can make arrangements."

"Why?" her grandmother asked, concerned.

"To sell that property," Sharon stated.

"What property?" Abuela asked.

"Remember the one you thought was sold, but wasn't?"

The one you thought was gone, but your accountant stole that tax money and fled, and it took the government five years to track you down because the accountant had used your name but not your address because the accountant was profiting off it?

Only Sharon didn't say that. It had cost a lot of money to find that information out.

She kept all that to herself, because it would upset her grandmother, but it ate away at her, made her stomach twist.

Her abuela frowned. "I don't understand."

"Just some business stuff, Abuela," Sharon said, gently

because it was easier to calm her grandmother down than agitate her. "I better go now and take care of it before I won't be able to fly."

"I wish you weren't going alone. Maybe ask Agustin to go with you?" her abuela suggested.

"Agustin is my boss, not my boyfriend."

"He's the father of the baby," Abuela stated firmly before wandering away to check on Maria in the kitchen.

Sharon just sighed.

She should let Agustin know where she was going. She pulled out the letter again and stared at it—it made her stomach turn just looking at it.

The last thing she wanted to do was get sick again.

She could tell him why, so he wouldn't worry.

Rely on yourself, a voice reminded her.

Only she didn't want to.

Maybe he'd have some good advice.

She had managed to get her nausea under control for the last month and she was very hopeful that it wouldn't make a comeback, but anytime she thought of something stressful, the sickness returned and her blood pressure rose.

It was decided—she needed to deal with this all now rather than later.

"Maria, can I speak with you?" Sharon said, standing up.

Maria came out of the kitchen. "Of course, what do you need?"

"I have to make arrangements to fly to Buenos Aires for some business before the baby comes. Would you be able to stay overnight with my abuela for a couple of days? I would pay you time and a half of course."

Maria nodded. "That's perfectly acceptable. I can do this weekend?"

Sharon was relieved. "That's great. I will just make arrangements."

Maria nodded. "No problem."

Sharon collected up her purse and grabbed her coat. She needed to go to the clinic and talk to the head nurse in charge of scheduling to let her know what was happening. Talk to Agustin. Then she would go buy a ticket.

"I'll be back in a couple of hours, abuela!" Sharon called out as she headed outside.

It didn't take her long to navigate her way to the clinic and she went straight to the head nurse and asked for the weekend off, explaining she had to take care of some personal business before she got too large to travel.

The nurse in charge of rotation had no issue and Sharon could already feel the stress melting away. She had two hurdles taken care of. She had someone to sit with her grandmother and now had the time off work.

As she was leaving the nursing station she ran straight into Agustin. The moment she saw him, her heart skipped a beat and she could feel her whole body respond to him.

"Sharon, what're you doing here? I thought you had the day off?" he asked, shocked.

"I did, but I came to ask Carmen if I could get some time off," she responded quickly, hoping that would end the conversation.

"You're going on leave?" Agustin asked.

She frowned. "I'm not going on leave. Dr. Perez hasn't said anything to me about going on leave. I have to go to Buenos Aires for a couple of days."

Agustin frowned. "Buenos Aires? Why?"

"That's what I want to talk to you about. Can we talk in private?"

He nodded and led her into a private office and shut the door behind them.

"Tell me," he said.

"My abuela owes back taxes on a property she thought she'd sold, but she was swindled. We're still trying to figure it all out, but it's mostly sorted, but I need to go to Buenos Aires to sell the property and sign some papers with my lawyer. I'm going to have to sell her house if I can't get a mortgage or work out a deal. I've spent a lot of money dealing with this and selling Abuela's home will help with some mounting legal fees after the property is sold." She handed the letter to him. He read it.

"Back taxes from a property?" he asked.

"*Sí*. So I'm now her power of attorney and I'm going to talk to the bank."

It felt like such a relief to tell him.

"Perhaps I can loan…"

"No," she said, quickly cutting him off. "I can handle this on my own."

He handed her back the letter. "Very well."

"I appreciate the offer, Agustin, but I can manage. I've just got to go to Buenos Aires to meet with an agent and sign papers. After what happened to my abuela, I need to see it through in person."

So she'd know it was all done with and taken care of.

"What about your abuela?" Agustin asked.

"Maria is going to stay with her this weekend."

"You're going to Buenos Aires this weekend?" he asked, stunned.

"Yes. So if you're around, could you check in on my grandmother or at least send Sandrine over?"

Agustin worried his bottom lip. "Actually, I'll be in Buenos Aires this weekend."

"What?" Sharon asked, carefully.

"I've tracked down Sandrine's mother, my stepmother," he said, with an air of contempt.

"Oh," Sharon said. "Does Sandrine know?"

He shook his head. "She does not, but I have to go to Buenos Aires and… Sandrine's mother is signing over her parental rights. To me."

Sharon instantly felt sorry for the young girl and sat down in a chair.

At least Agustin had found Sandrine's mother. No one knew what'd happened to her father.

As far as she knew her father was still wanted on charges of abandonment and endangerment in New York state.

"Oh. That's awful."

"Sí," Agustin said stiffly. "It's why I've been so preoccupied."

"Right. So, you're going to Buenos Aires too. I was just going home to buy my ticket."

"I leave tonight, but I'm staying there until Monday. I can meet you at the airport when you get in on Friday and take you to your hotel, and perhaps you can meet my mother."

Now Sharon was really shocked. "You want me to meet your mother?"

"Sí. She knows about the baby and she's thrilled."

"She knows that we're not together, right?" Sharon asked carefully.

"Of course," he said. "She wants to meet you."

"She's not going to hate me for ruining her son?" Sharon said teasingly.

He shook his head. "Hardly."

"Okay, I would like to meet her. She is our daughter's grandmother."

Agustin smiled and nodded. "Good. I'm glad that's settled. Are you sure I can't help you?"

"I told you, no."

"I see."

"I really have to get to the airport and book my flight."

"Of course, and I have to get back to work." Agustin opened the door. "You have my number, text me when you land on Friday and I will come for you."

"Thank you," she said. Sharon had traveled extensively— she knew how to get a cab and transportation in larger cities. She'd grown up in New York, after all. But she was still appreciative that he would be there. It calmed her to know she would have a familiar face in Buenos Aires, but also she couldn't help but wonder if there was some kind of destiny trying to throw them together.

Agustin sat in his rental car, waiting for Sharon to come out of the airport. It was still winter here, but Buenos Aires was farther north and milder than Ushuaia in the south. It was nice to not worry about snow and this weekend in July it was even warmer than usual. He was glad there was no cold snap.

It would make it safer for Sharon to be here, especially when she was staying at a hotel on her own.

She's a grown woman. She's traveled the world.

Still, he couldn't shake that worry that something could happen to her or the baby. All he could think about was Luisa and getting the call that he had lost her and the baby.

All that dread that he'd suffered through came clamoring back and he had to shake it away.

Sharon was not his wife.

She wasn't even his girlfriend. She was just the mother of his child and he had to remind himself of that. But the thing of it was that he had to keep reminding himself of that over and over again lately, because even though he tried to tell himself that their friendship was platonic, the truth was he was falling for her. And it was brutally hard to be falling in love with someone who'd explicitly stated that she wasn't interested in having a relationship.

He was beginning to think of her and her abuela as family. They were forming some kind of tight unit together. It was solidified even more when his stepmother signed over her parental rights.

He was now Sandrine's guardian.

Officially.

Not just her brother.

Agustin sighed thinking about that encounter with his stepmother's attorney. He hadn't even seen the woman and that was probably for the best, but there was a part of him that wanted to ask why she was giving up on her child.

He'd lost a child before and now he couldn't even imagine giving up his unborn daughter.

Maybe they could be a real family. Even if he and Sharon weren't together. She was staying in Ushuaia. Then he remembered her vague answers.

She hadn't confirmed that.

What if Sharon took another job that involved travel again after her abuela died?

It tore his heart out to think of her leaving.

This was why he didn't want a relationship.

It hurt too much.

The car door opened and Sharon popped her head in. "Ah, here you are. I was texting you."

Agustin shook his head clear of all the thoughts running around and around in his mind. He glanced down at his phone, which had unread texts from Sharon. "I'm sorry, I was somewhere else completely. Just zoned right out."

He got out of the car and grabbed her suitcase, putting it into the trunk. Sharon had climbed into the passenger seat. He shut the trunk and got back into the car.

"Did you have a good flight?" he asked.

"Yes. But it was hard to be cramped in a seat for almost four hours and the baby was kicking furiously. The food was awful too."

Agustin chuckled. "Yes. Well, you're here now. Where am I taking you?"

"The hotel Blanca. It's downtown."

Agustin nodded. "I know it well."

He drove away from the airport with a sense of relief that she was here, with him, and he could see that she was safe.

"Did you meet up with your stepmother?" Sharon asked, carefully.

"No. She didn't show up, but her attorney did. She signed over parental rights to Sandrine. Apparently, she's moving to Rio with a new husband and wants a clean break."

Sharon sighed sadly. "Abandoning your kid as a clean break, that's so sad. I should know."

He knew she was thinking of her past and he wanted to comfort her.

He resisted.

"Your father?"

She nodded. "Though my aunt never knew where he

went really. Just that she was handed parental rights to me. I don't know if he's dead or alive and I'm not sure I care. He needed a clean break too, I suppose."

"I'm sorry he did that to you. I don't know how I'm going to break it to Sandrine." He sighed.

"If she needs someone to speak to I would be more than happy to talk to her about it," Sharon offered.

His heart warmed. "Would you?"

She nodded. "Yes. Of course. Sandrine is our baby's auntie after all, and it's a role she takes very seriously."

"Yes," Agustin said, smiling. "I'm glad she's been going over to visit your abuela instead of hanging out with that so-called boyfriend she has. That boy is nothing but trouble and I don't trust him."

"They're just teenagers."

"Exactly," Agustin grumbled.

"Why don't you like him?"

"I don't want Sandrine to make life decisions based on love."

"I get that," she said softly, with a hint of sadness in her voice.

He didn't want to stress her out or worry her.

He knew why she was here and he didn't want to add to it.

"Well, if you don't have plans for dinner tonight I was thinking I could pick you up around seven and then we could head over to my mother's apartment in Recoleta."

Sharon cocked an eyebrow. "Wow, she lives there?"

"My stepfather is from old Buenos Aires money."

"Seven?" Sharon asked as Agustin pulled up to her hotel in the Microcentro.

"*Sí*. I'll wait in the lobby for you."

A porter came up and opened the door for Sharon. Agustin got out and handed the porter Sharon's suitcase.

"See you then." Sharon waved and the porter followed her into the hotel lobby.

Agustin sighed and got back into his rental. He was staying with his mother and Recoleta, thankfully, was only about twenty minutes away. When he got to the apartment, he parked the car in the underground parking lot. He grabbed his jacket from the back and then noticed the letter had fallen out of Sharon's purse.

He folded the letter up and slipped it into his trouser pocket.

She didn't want him to loan her the money, but her abuela had touched so many lives in Ushuaia.

Maybe she wouldn't turn down help from the community. They could help cover the legal fees?

Maybe it would give her an inkling of home and roots so she wouldn't be tempted to leave.

It was the least he could do for the mother of his child.

You could convince her to stay.

Only he wasn't sure he could. She'd made it clear she didn't want more than a friendly relationship with him.

Against everything his broken heart was telling him, he was falling in love with her.

CHAPTER TEN

AGUSTIN WAITED IN the lobby for Sharon. He was there twenty minutes early and he had the letter safely in his sport coat pocket. When he got a chance, at his mother's, he was going to slip the letter back into her purse.

He had made a few calls. Sandrine was having residents of Ushuaia, in particular their neighborhood, help so that Sharon wouldn't have to move. Their legal fees were high, but people were willing to pitch in to keep Theresa in her home.

He wasn't sure what could be raised, but at least the community was rallying behind Theresa and Sharon. Any little bit would help.

Then Sharon would see you could trust others.

Hopefully, it would allow Sharon to relax and not have to worry about anything. Having her stressed out was not good for the baby and he was sure she was worrying about this. Who wouldn't?

He just wished she'd let him help.

He knew she still didn't fully trust him and borrowing money complicated matters, but he would give it to her, no problem. Still, he understood her misgivings about it.

It was hard to let her through his own barriers.

It was hard to let anyone in.

Agustin heard the elevator ding and glanced over to see

Sharon come off the elevator. She was wearing a pink dress. It wasn't the same pink gown that she was wearing the night at the café in Barcelona. This was more of a winter dress, but it was a similar shade of pink, which he thought suited her to perfection. His breath was taken away at the sight of her. Her hair was up in a low chignon. She was stunning and looked flawless.

Graceful.

His blood heated at the sight of her walking toward him and he couldn't help but feel a sense of pride thinking that she was his.

Only she wasn't.

Though there was a part of him that wanted her to be.

Even after all these months since he'd met her and telling himself that his heart couldn't take it, watching her now and knowing that their baby was growing inside her, he wanted her to be his.

Only his.

"You look beautiful," he said.

She blushed. "Thank you. I don't feel very comfortable. I'm really quite nervous."

"There's nothing to be nervous about. My mama loves everyone. She never even hated my father for what he did. She embraced Sandrine as one of her own too and she'll do the same for you."

Sharon smiled shyly. "I hope so. I have never been in this position before, of meeting the parents, probably because I never dated anyone for that long before."

She blushed.

She had said dating.

Are we?

He shrugged it off.

"It'll be fine. Though I remember being nervous meeting Luisa's parents the first time."

The truth slipped out so easily. It was always so hard to talk about Luisa, but it came out and didn't sting as much as it had before.

Agustin wanted to tell her.

"Who is Luisa?" Sharon asked.

"My late wife. I am a widower." It was the first time he was admitting it to her. It was the first time in a long time he had mentioned Luisa to anyone outside his family.

He never talked about her.

Even his partners at the clinic didn't know about her, because he'd met them after Luisa died. All they knew was he was widower. It was always just too painful to think about it and the guilt that ate away at him for not going with her to visit family.

If he'd been with her, then he could've been spared the pain of losing her or could've stopped her.

"You never told me that," Sharon said softly.

"I know. I keep it to myself."

And he did. He and Luisa had lived in Buenos Aires. No one knew she had been pregnant. People in Ushuaia knew how it pained him to talk about his late wife, so they didn't ask questions.

The baby was his secret.

It was easier to keep it all to himself.

"How did she die?" Sharon asked.

He nodded. "She died visiting her family. See, she went on the trip alone. I was too busy to go with her. Work came first."

"You being there might not have changed anything," Sharon replied.

He knew that, but his grief and his guilt over not being there for Luisa told him otherwise. He didn't want to dwell on this anymore. His mother would be anxiously awaiting them and he wanted Sharon and his mother to meet.

"Well, let's go to my mother's. She'll be waiting, probably outside on the street by now, she's that excited."

Sharon nodded, but didn't say anything else. It wasn't how he'd wanted to tell her, but he had been trying to figure out a way to bring it up for some time. It had just come out.

Agustin reached down and took her hand. Sharon didn't pull away, but he could feel her trembling.

"*Querida*, trust me."

Only how could he ask her to trust him, when he was still withholding secrets from her? But he wanted her too.

The more time he spent with her, the more he wanted her to be his, and that was a scary prospect indeed.

Sharon couldn't believe what Agustin had told her.

He had been married and his wife had died tragically. She understood him a bit better now. She understood tragedy.

Although not the kind where you lose the love of your life, and if she had her way she would never.

She knew what grief made some people do.

What it made her father do. At least she thought she did.

There was a niggling worry in the back of her mind that she and their daughter would never be enough for Agustin.

Would the grief over his late wife drive him away like it drove her father away?

Would her daughter be left to the wayside because he was reminded of what he lost before? Or maybe he'd feel like he was betraying his late wife's memory by starting a family with a new woman?

Agustin is not like that.

Sharon ignored that anxious little thought the moment that it crept into her head. She didn't have the space for it now, but she was appreciative that Agustin had shared that with her. It was an odd moment for sure, but she was glad that he had nonetheless.

It also meant that he was beginning to trust her, and maybe she could trust him, even though the idea of doing so was scary. There was a reason she protected her heart.

You're just nervous because you're on your way to a posh neighborhood of Buenos Aires and you're going to meet his mother.

And that was what she had to keep telling herself.

It wasn't the fact that she was falling for Agustin, a man who could very well leave her and her baby. A man who obviously was still grieving his late wife.

It wasn't the fact that the moment she got off the elevator and saw him there in his business casual clothes that her heart beat just a bit faster and she reminisced about their one night together and that kiss they shared a couple of weeks ago.

And it certainly wasn't because when he looked at her it was like she was the only woman in the room. His eyes would sparkle and he would smile only for her.

She was falling for him hard.

This was her first time really falling for someone and it was a terrifying process, but it was exhilarating too.

They didn't say much in the car on the way to Recoleta, but the moment they entered the neighborhood Sharon was in awe at all the French-inspired buildings. It was like she had been transported back to a golden age, when Eva Perón was the first lady and it was all glitz, glamour and romance.

At least that was what Maria, her abuela's care worker, often would say, but Sharon couldn't help feel she romanticized that time period just a bit.

He pulled into an underground car park for one of the larger apartment buildings on the street. As they walked to the elevators, he held out his hand and she took it. It was comforting, his strong hand around hers.

"You're still shaking, *querida*. I told you there's no reason to be nervous."

"No, I'm just knocked up with her son's illegitimate child," Sharon groused.

Agustin chuckled. "That doesn't matter to her, I swear it. Come."

Entering the elevator, he punched in a code and Sharon watched the numbers roll by until they were on the second-to-top floor. The doors opened straight into an art deco and French-inspired apartment.

Sharon gasped at the large floor-to-ceiling windows directly in front of her across the lounge area, looking out on the Atlantic Ocean. She could see all the lights from the boats and the cruise ships glittering in the darkness.

"Oh. wow," Sharon whispered.

"I know, it's something, isn't it?" He took her purse for her and set it down in the entranceway table.

It was at that moment his mama came floating around the corner.

"Agustin, you finally brought her." The woman was willowy and elegant. Her silver hair was pulled back tight into a bun and her clothes were high-end, and Sharon couldn't help but think that if Eva Perón had aged and was still alive, then Agustin's mother could be her doppelganger.

"Mama, this is Sharon. Sharon, this is my mother, Ava."

Sharon could see where Agustin got his warm, twinkling dark eyes from. Ava smiled, holding open her arms wide and embracing her in a warm hug that caught Sharon a bit off guard.

"It is a pleasure to finally meet you," Ava said, her voice catching. She took a step back and her gaze traveled over Sharon, resting on her bump. "I can't tell you how excited I am that you're making me an abuela. Finally! And that it's a girl!"

"It's a pleasure to meet you too," Sharon said, still a little overcome by the warm welcome. "Thank you for inviting me into your beautiful home."

"Of course! Why don't I give you a tour. It's two floors! Come." Ava grabbed her hand, not taking no for an answer. "Agustin, are you coming?"

"I'll be there shortly, Mama. Show Sharon around," Agustin said. "Is Javier coming tonight?"

Ava nodded. "Your stepfather will be here soon. He wouldn't miss meeting the mother of his future grandchild! Come, Sharon, I want to show you everything and then I'll take you out on the terrace. It's unseasonably warm this time of year. I still find it cold, but you come from Tierra del Fuego and New York City, so you probably think this is warm!"

Sharon couldn't help but smile around Agustin's mother. She usually didn't like to be led off with strangers in a strange place, but Ava seemed to have this way of just welcoming you. Agustin was right, his mother didn't seem to care one iota that she and Agustin were not married or that her grandchild would be illegitimate.

She was glad that Ava was open-minded.

They walked up a spiral staircase to the second floor. "These are the bedrooms. There are fourteen up here."

Sharon's eyes widened. "Fourteen?"

"Yes. I want to dedicate one of them to the baby, so that when you come visit me with the baby you'll both have your own rooms." Ava stopped in front of a door and opened it. "I'm afraid I got excited and already started decorating, but you can tell me if you don't like it."

Sharon walked into the dimly lit room and was taken aback by the large room that was decorated in soft pastel colors. There was a round crib in the center of the room and a matching change table and dresser. There were also toys, and everything reminded her of a fairy princess kind of dream.

Her eyes filled with tears.

This was too much.

What if things changed and didn't work out?

"If it's too much, I'm sorry. I am an interior decorator and I'm just so excited about this little girl and for you and Agustin. Agustin lost his wife and child, you know, and I know he's always longed for a family."

Sharon's heart stopped for a moment.

His child?

Agustin had told him about his wife, but he hadn't mentioned a child. It broke her heart to think about that kind of pain. She wrapped her arms around her belly. She was giving him what his late wife couldn't. What if he resented her?

What if after all was said and done she couldn't give him what he'd lost?

"I love it, Ava," Sharon said, choking back tears. "It's beautiful and very generous."

Ava beamed happily. "Oh, I'm so glad you like it."

"Mama, the caterer has questions," Agustin said, coming into the room.

"Oh, okay. I'll be back. Show her around the rest of the place, Agustin." Ava hurried away and Agustin stepped into the dimly lit room—there were no light fixtures set up yet.

"I'm sorry she went a bit overboard. She does that sometimes," Agustin said.

"Are you okay with this?" she asked.

"Why wouldn't I be?" Yet there was something in his voice that let her know this was hard for him.

She turned to look at him. "Why didn't you tell me about your other child?"

"What?" he asked, choking back emotion.

"Your mother told me."

He sighed and ran his fingers through his hair. "It's too painful."

"I'm so sorry she did this. Are you okay?"

"I told her to. I want our child to feel welcome here. I won't lie, it was hard, but I did pick out some things."

"Like what?" she asked, curious at his hand in this nursery.

Agustin walked over and picked up a doll. It reminded her of the doll she had when she was abandoned.

He handed it to her and she gingerly held it against her chest.

"It's lovely." The tears flowed down her cheeks.

She felt like she didn't deserve this.

She didn't deserve any of it.

"Querida," Agustin said, gently closing the distance between them. He wrapped her up in his arms and held her. "Don't cry."

"I should be comforting you. No wonder work is your life."

Agustin nodded. "It was ten years ago. She was pregnant, just newly pregnant so I didn't even know if the baby was a boy or a girl, but it crushed me. I didn't think that I would ever have children. Not sure I wanted them to be honest."

"And now?"

Agustin smiled and tipped her chin. "Well, now it can't be helped. No tears. Please don't feel sorry for me. We need to take care of you and our little girl, yes?"

Sharon nodded, swallowing the lump in her throat, but there was a part of her that couldn't shake her heartache over Agustin and his loss. She couldn't even begin to fathom the pain of losing a child. Or the fear he might change his mind and leave because the grief was too much.

Because she reminded him of his late wife, and their daughter of the child he never got to hold.

Her baby kicked in her belly.

Agustin chuckled.

"What?" she asked.

"I felt that." He was grinning and reached down to touch her belly. "Maybe she's hungry?"

Sharon laughed softly. "Maybe. I am."

"Then let's go downstairs. Javier has arrived and I'm sure the appetizers are out. Apparently a couple of old family friends are coming tonight too to meet you. It's quite the party my mother organized. I'm sorry, I had no idea. I just knew about this room."

Sharon wiped the tears on the back of her hand. "It's okay. We can socialize. Your mother is so sweet. I think I can manage this for her."

Agustin grinned and held out his hand. "Good, because there is no escaping now."

She laughed and took his hand. It felt like it was natural, like it was the right thing to do as he led her from that beautiful nursery and down to meet a bunch of strangers. The problem was, all she could think about was Agustin and his pain.

She remembered her father's pain clearly. It haunted her.

It all made sense to her now, and in this moment all she wanted to do was comfort him and assure him that everything would be okay.

Their baby was fine.

They would be okay, provided she was able to talk to the bank tomorrow and work out some kind of arrangement for the legal fees. At least the property in Buenos Aires would be up for sale soon. She was dealing with a reputable Realtor.

Sharon had met with them after she checked in. The property in question was run-down and she wasn't sure if there would be anything left over after the sale and the taxes to pay the legal fees she racked up. She was still pretty sure they would have to sell her abuela's home in Ushuaia.

It didn't sound like Agustin ever wanted to take another chance on love, and it was all well and good to have a beautiful nursery in someone else's home, but Sharon had learned at an early age that the only person you could rely on was yourself.

And for that reason, she had to make sure Abuela and her were taken care of if Agustin ever thought their presence in his life was too painful.

Her heart was already breaking, because in spite of all this, she was falling for him.

CHAPTER ELEVEN

SHARON HAD A lovely dinner with Agustin's parents Ava and Javier and their friends.

She tried to forget, though, the niggling thoughts in the back of her mind about Agustin's loss.

It reminded her of her childhood and her father's grief and the abandonment.

Then there was the nursery and the doll he bought for their daughter.

It meant so much to her, but she was still completely overwhelmed. There was a part of her that thought maybe she could have a happily-ever-after, after all.

And yet, it was hard to believe.

She hated the fact she had become so indecisive. What was happening to her?

Love? a little voice suggested, but she shook that thought away. There was no way it could be that. She was vigilant about keeping the idea of love out of her heart.

After dessert Agustin discreetly excused them, much to her relief, and took her back to her hotel. She thanked him for a wonderful night and they made arrangements to meet for lunch after her appointment at the bank.

She should say no, but it would be nice to see him because she wasn't looking forward to talking to the bank tomorrow.

What she needed was a good night's sleep. The problem was that she didn't get that. All night long she thought about the bank appointment as well as Agustin's loss.

She was worried he'd be so torn up with memories that he would leave her and the baby behind to escape the ghosts of his past.

She also hated that this was keeping her up all night.

She didn't have time to think about this.

She needed rest.

Then the pain hit her. Hard. In the center of her back and tightening around her front.

Oh. God.

She rolled over and grabbed her phone, calling Agustin and hoping that he was awake.

"Querida?" he asked, confused.

"Something is wrong. I'm having…pain and tightening."

"The baby?"

"Sí," she said as another wave hit her.

"I'm on my way. I'll be there in fifteen minutes."

"Hurry. I'm going to call the concierge for an ambulance."

"I'll call an ambulance. Stay put."

"Okay," Sharon said, through another bout of pain. She was trying to think of all the things it could be, but through the pain she couldn't rationalize any options. She had spent all her career using that calm, logical mind to help patients.

Right now, with her baby on the line and pain coming in waves, she couldn't think of what it could be.

She wasn't sure how long she was lying there for, but it wasn't too much longer until Agustin and the hotel manager were opening her door. She let out a cry of relief as Agustin came to her side, and behind the hotel manager she could see an ambulance crew.

"*Querida?*" Agustin asked softly. He was kneeling beside her, stroking her face gently.

"It feels like contraction, but it shouldn't be a contraction. It's too early."

Agustin didn't try to tell her that she might be foolish. Instead he helped her sit up and the paramedics took over.

He fired off instructions to the paramedics on which hospital to take her to and then never left her side. Sharon held his hand as she was wheeled out of her hotel room and into the waiting ambulance downstairs.

Agustin climbed into the back of the ambulance with her, never letting her go and holding on to her.

"Thank you," she said over the sirens as they made their way through Buenos Aires.

"For what?" he asked.

"Staying with me."

He smiled and caressed her face. "Where else would I be?"

She didn't want to think about where else he could be, because the important thing in this moment was he was here with her right now.

Agustin wasn't allowed in the room when the obstetricians on call were examining Sharon. Just like what happened in Ushuaia.

He wasn't her husband and even though he was the father, it didn't seem to matter. Sharon hadn't told anyone he was allowed to go in, so therefore he had to wait outside. It also didn't matter that he was Dr. Varela. His name and reputation as a plastic surgeon, a world-renowned one at that, didn't matter in the least. It was a bit maddening.

He was sent to the waiting room on the obstetrical floor and all he could do was pace. He also hated this. He was a doctor and he was used to being on the other side of the curtain, as it were. It also reminded him of a different waiting room.

One where he was alone.

Waiting on the status of his wife, but knowing that she was already gone when they put him in a private waiting room.

Here, there were others.

He wasn't alone, but all those old feelings came rushing back to him. The moment that Sharon had called him, frantic, telling him that she was scared, well, it'd sent an ice-cold shiver of dread through him.

He was glad that he was there with her and this hadn't happened when he was in Buenos Aires and she was in Ushuaia.

If something had happened to her or the baby in Ushuaia while he'd been here, he never would've forgiven himself. He couldn't bear it if he lost another child. Another woman he cared for.

Agustin glanced at the clock on the wall.

It had been three hours since Sharon had been brought in. *What is taking so long?*

"Dr. Varela?" a doctor questioned, sticking his head into the room.

"Sí." Agustin made his way over to him.

"Miss Misasi is doing fine. She was not in labor. It was Braxton Hicks, they were particularly strong though and we are concerned that her blood pressure was slightly elevated, but it has come down. I think it was due to the stress of the contractions."

"Braxton Hicks. Well, that's good news," Agustin said, relieved.

"She's going to be discharged, but I would like her to rest today and I don't want her to be on her own. Would you be able to stay with her?" the doctor asked.

"Of course. I will take care of her and I will take her back to Ushuaia myself. That is if it's okay to travel?"

The doctor nodded. "She was very vexed about being admitted. She explained about her grandmother. I would like her to rest for a couple of days before she flies home."

"That makes sense, and I'll make arrangements for her grandmother so she won't worry about that," Agustin said.

The doctor nodded. "Very good, Dr. Varela. You can go in and see her now and take her back to her hotel."

Agustin shook the doctor's hand and made his way to the room that Sharon was in. She would not like the idea of remaining in Buenos Aires for a couple of extra days, but it was doctor's orders. He would call Maria himself and make sure she was compensated well, and there was Sandrine to stay with Sharon's abuela at night.

He would tell Sandrine what was happening.

Sandrine already knew about the situation with Sharon's abuela. He knew he would have to ease her worry about the bank. The bank could wait. Right now all that mattered was her health and the baby's health.

"Come in," Sharon called out.

Agustin opened the door. "I'm told I can take you back to the hotel."

Sharon sighed. "I feel kind of foolish right now."

"Why?" he asked.

"Braxton Hicks. I know what those are." She rubbed her abdomen. "I really know what those are now."

Agustin chuckled. "It's different when it's you going through them and not in a textbook."

She nodded. "He wants me to stay in Buenos Aires, but my abuela..."

"All taken care of, or will be. I will handle arrangements and you can fly back to Ushuaia with me on Monday."

"That's too kind, but I really can't have you stepping in like this."

"And why not? We're friends, coworkers and neighbors. We also share a baby who is the reason you're being afflicted right now."

Sharon smiled, her eyes twinkling. "I suppose so."

"You suppose nothing. I'm right, aren't I?"

"Okay, but I have a meeting with a bank. I am here for things regarding my abuela's property."

"When we get back to the hotel you can call your lawyers and tell them what happened. If you feel up to it on Monday we'll reschedule the meeting. No one will blame you for missing it due to health reasons. Right now, you need to rest so we can get you back to Ushuaia."

Sharon looked mollified. "You're right."

"Of course I am." He grinned.

The nurse came in, bringing the discharge forms. Sharon signed them and a wheelchair was brought into her room.

"Normally, I would object to a wheelchair, but as I don't have my shoes, I think I'll ride in this."

Agustin smiled. "A taxi is downstairs waiting for us as I left my car at your hotel."

"Thanks again for coming with me."

"You need to stop thanking me. This is my baby too."

Sharon climbed into the wheelchair. Agustin took Sharon out to the waiting cab. He scooped her up in his arms and carried her to the vehicle.

"You're being ridiculous." Sharon chuckled.

He grinned. "Just taking care of my..."

"Your what?" she asked quietly.

He didn't know what to say. She wasn't his wife, and she wasn't his girlfriend.

The woman you're falling in love with?

"The mother of my child," he quickly said.

"Oh." She looked slightly disappointed, but it was a fleeting expression. "Right."

He climbed in beside her in the back of the cab and gave the driver instructions on where to go. When they got to the hotel he carried her into the lobby. They made it back up to her room with the help of a spare keycard, as hers was inside the room with her purse.

It was four in the morning and now the adrenaline was wearing off.

He was tired.

Sharon made her way to the bed and climbed in under the covers.

"You look exhausted," she said.

"I am. Are you hungry? Do you want room service?" he asked.

"No. Just sleep."

"Sounds good," he said, relieved. He made his way over to the chair in the corner.

"What're you doing?" she asked.

"Sleeping. The doctor at the hospital doesn't want you to be alone."

"I know that. What I mean is why are you sleeping there?

This is a king bed. You can sleep next to me." She patted the empty spot.

His pulse thrummed. The last time they shared a bed no sleeping had happened.

"Are you sure?" he asked, looking at the bed longingly, but worried about the implications.

"Of course. That chair can't be comfortable."

"No. It's not." He got up and climbed on top of the blankets lying on his back. Now, lying here in bed with her, he wasn't as tired as he had been. He was more terrified of giving in to how his body was reacting being in bed with her.

Being so close to her again. He could just reach out and touch her. She wasn't just some random memory that he had been clinging to since their night in Barcelona.

She was here. So why didn't he reach out to her?

Agustin rolled onto his side and he could hear the even breathing of her in sleep.

It hadn't taken her long to fall asleep and he was glad for that.

He closed his eyes and tried to resist the pull of snuggling closer to her. He resisted the urge to hold her in his arms. The urge to make her his. Like he wanted to.

He woke with a start when he felt the mattress move.

He saw Sharon pacing by the window. She had changed and it looked like she'd had a shower.

"What's wrong?" he asked groggily.

"Sorry, did I wake you?" Her voice sounded agitated.

"It's fine. Are you okay?"

"Yes. I'm fine."

"What time is it?" he asked.

"One in the afternoon."

Agustin balked. "One?"

It felt like he'd hardly slept at all. He hadn't dreamed and he felt even more tired than usual.

"I woke up at eleven. Talked to my attorney then had a shower to figure out some things." She worried her bottom lip.

"Is everything okay?" he asked.

"Yes," she murmured. "I'll talk to a Realtor when we get back."

"You don't have to," he said.

"I can't get a mortgage for Abuela's house and the sale of the property will be a loss. It was in shambles. The legal fees I had to pay… I tried to get an appeal on the taxes as she'd been swindled, but unless I spend more money to track down the thief and wait for his extradition…" She sighed. "This is just easier. I sell Abuela's house and I find a more affordable place."

"But I can help."

"No," she said softly. "I can't let you do that, Agustin."

"Why?" He wanted to know. He wanted to help her. He wanted to be there for her and it was hard to have her push him away.

"It's something I have to do."

He understood that. He didn't like it, but he understood it.

"Are you hungry?" he asked, changing the subject.

"Yes. Starving."

"Okay. I'll clean up and we'll go out since your business has been taken care of. The doctor wants you to stay until Monday and your abuela's care has been arranged, so now we'll have some fun."

"Fun?" she asked in disbelief. "Not sure I know the

meaning of that. Last time I let loose and had fun I ended up pregnant."

He chuckled. "Well, I can't get you any more pregnant than you are, so we'll just have a nice time."

Sharon shook her head, but was smiling. "Okay, but hurry up. I'm hungry and I'm buying since you're staying with me."

"Right away, Nurse." He headed into the bathroom to have a quick shower and freshen up. He would have to stop by his mother's place and grab his clothes. He'd let his mother know what was going on and she would insist on him staying with her.

And Agustin was glad that Sharon seemed to be in better spirits. Maybe now she would relax, and that was the goal for today. To help her de-stress, which he hoped would keep his mind off wanting to help her relax in a completely different way by staying put in bed.

Sharon was glad for the distractions. She needed some light and happiness, especially after last night and talking to her lawyers this morning.

She had been so scared and then felt absolutely foolish for not recognizing Braxton Hicks contractions. She was thankful for Agustin though, and that he'd come to take care of her. It was nice to have him there soothing her, telling her it would be okay and holding her.

She was a strong, independent woman, but she liked he'd been there last night, and she'd slept so calmly with him next to her. It had felt right.

Like she belonged by his side.

It was nice to depend on someone, but it was something

she couldn't get used to. The only person she could rely on was herself.

As much as she wished she could take him up on his offer to help, she couldn't.

It wasn't right.

They weren't together and what would happen if he changed his mind?

She'd be left with nothing.

It was better that she handled it.

She had a lot to do when she got back to Ushuaia. The doctor at the hospital had made it clear that he didn't want her stressed out.

Agustin had made that clear too.

And it might be nice to have some fun. Enjoy a mild winter's day in Buenos Aires.

Agustin took her to a café that overlooked the water and they talked about his mother and her friends. There was just an ease to their conversation. It was light and it felt like they had been talking this way for a long time.

After their late lunch they decided to go for a walk downtown. The sun was shining and it was almost warm out. It felt like a spring day in New York City.

"Sandrine just texted that it's snowing in Ushuaia," Agustin groused.

"Did you rub it in that it's light jacket weather here?" she said with a smile.

"Why would I rub that in?" he asked.

"You're her older brother. That's what brothers do...apparently."

"Well, I'm more like her father now," he said sadly.

"Good practice for you," she remarked, touching her belly.

"Yes," he said. "Especially when it comes to boys. Sandrine is still seeing that boy I don't trust."

"Diego, you mean. Not *that boy*," she corrected.

He grunted. "Whatever."

"I still don't know why you don't like him. He seems nice enough."

Agustin shook his head. "I know what he wants with her."

Sharon chuckled. "You've got to be fair with her or you'll drive Sandrine away."

He grumbled. "I suppose."

"I guess…" She trailed off as her gaze landed on a group of teenage boys skateboarding. One of them was skateboarding down a set of steps, specifically the railing part of the steps. She knew what was going to happen before the boy did. He was flung high into the air and landed smack down on his face. Blood pooled under him.

"Good Lord." Agustin raced over as the boy's friends formed a stunned circle around him.

Sharon knelt down to the unconscious boy and checked his ABCs. His airway, breathing and it was clear his C for circulation had failed. The boy was bleeding profusely.

"I need a towel," Agustin shouted, turning to his friends. "Or a T-shirt."

"Here," a boy said, handing him a towel. "Are you a doctor?"

"I am. Do you have a cell phone?" Agustin asked.

The unconscious boy's friend nodded. "Yeah."

"Call an ambulance." As soon as Agustin said that they all ran away. (world)

"What in the word?" Sharon asked, stunned.

"Drugs," Agustin murmured. "I can smell it on him."

"Oh, no."

Agustin handed her the towel. "Hold pressure to his wound and I'll call the ambulance."

Sharon applied pressure on the boy's head wound while Agustin called for an ambulance, then he checked to see if the boy had identification. He did not.

There was nothing. They didn't know who he was or who he belonged to. The boy was alone.

Sharon was heartbroken.

"We can't leave him," she said quietly.

"No. You're right. We'll follow the ambulance then," Agustin said.

The ambulance came and took over. Agustin and Sharon followed the ambulance to a different hospital than she had been take to the previous night. The hospital had an overflowing emergency room. The emergency doctors let Agustin in as they were so overrun, and the boy was alert by the time he was being rolled into a trauma room. After a nurse took his blood to check for illegal drugs and do a CBC panel, the boy was left alone.

He was conscious and therefore not a priority at the moment.

Agustin leaned over the boy. "*Hola*, what is your name?"

"Pedro Gonsalves," the boy answered.

"That's good you remember who you are," Sharon said gently.

"Pedro, do you remember what happened?" Agustin asked.

"No, but my head hurts," Pedro whined.

"Pedro, do you have parents we can contact?" Sharon asked.

"Yes." Pedro gave his number to a nurse who came in

with some painkillers for him. The nurse was going to contact his parents.

The ER doctor came in. "Are you his parents?"

"No," Sharon said. "Witnesses. His parents are being called."

"I'm Dr. Varela," Agustin said, stepping forward. "We were on the scene."

The ER doctor was impressed. "Dr. Varela the plastic surgeon?"

"*Sí.*" Agustin nodded at Sharon. "This is Nurse Misasi."

"He's lucky you both were there," the ER doctor said as he examined the boy. "Most likely a mild concussion. I'll send a nurse in to do the sutures. Tox screen shows a low dose of marijuana."

The ER doctor left and they waited for a nurse to come and repair the scalp laceration.

"How old are you, Pedro?" Sharon asked.

"Sixteen," Pedro replied.

"You know you shouldn't do drugs and skateboard. You could've died," Sharon gently chastised him.

"I know," he sighed. "It was foolish. Thanks for helping me."

"Of course. I'm a nurse. It's what I do."

The nurse arrived and went to work stitching up the boy's head wound. A pressure bandage had just been placed on Pedro's head when his parents came in. Agustin spoke to them and they both thanked him profusely.

"Well, not the most relaxing after-lunch walk," Agustin stated as he and Sharon left the hospital.

"No, but I do like watching you work."

"You know, I'm glad you were there with me," he said.

"Are you?"

Agustin nodded. "When we work together...it's like you're an extension of me. I can't explain it. You're so talented."

She could feel the blush in her cheeks. The warmth. It meant so much he valued her work. That he liked working with her. She wasn't used to compliments like that.

"I am bit tired," she responded, steering the conversation away from compliments.

"Let's go back to the hotel." He said it so easily, almost like saying, *Let's go back home*, and it made her heart skip a beat.

"I could use a nap."

"Me too." Agustin reached down and took her hand. It sent a zing of pleasure through her. He made her feel warm and secure. She wanted to hold on to the moment for as long as she could.

For the first time she was contemplating the idea of relying on someone, of falling in love with someone, but she was too scared to ever really give in to that thought.

She was scared of all the things she was feeling about him and all the things she wanted.

CHAPTER TWELVE

THEY GOT BACK to the hotel and both climbed into bed. Only now, being in bed with him, she couldn't sleep. All that exhaustion she was feeling vanished. Agustin lay there on his back, with his eyes closed and his hands folded across his chest.

"I feel like you're watching me," he murmured.

"I'm not."

Only she was. She couldn't help it.

She was falling for him, even though she didn't want to admit it. Something she never thought she'd do. She should try to stop herself, but it was hard to. There was a part of her that didn't want to stop this rush of feelings she was having for him.

There was a part of her that wanted a happily-ever-after. Even if she didn't quite believe in them still.

Agustin rolled over. "I thought you were tired?"

"I am." She grinned. "I didn't thank you."

"For what?" he asked.

"Taking care of me last night."

"Of course, *querida*. Why wouldn't I take care of you?" he asked, astonished.

"We made no promises that night," she whispered.

"Things have changed."

"Have they?" she asked.

"Haven't they?" he asked back. "You trust me, enough to call me when you need help."

"It's hard to trust. Especially after my father left."

"I'm not your father."

"I know." Although she couldn't completely trust him. Yet she couldn't stop thinking about him. Any walls she put up to protect her heart would come crashing down.

He was the only man ever to get through her defenses.

It would kill her when he left, because it was hard not to think of him staying, but maybe he could change his mind. Maybe she could convince him to stay and that little secret dream of having a family of them, the baby, Abuela and Sandrine in Ushuaia would become a reality.

She could have the family she'd always dreamed of.

Maybe they both needed something worth fighting for.

She leaned in and kissed him like she had before. Gently, but then she wanted to feel all those same feelings she had felt back in Barcelona when she had surrendered to his charms. When she was vulnerable to him.

And she wanted that same vulnerability again. She desired Agustin like no other man.

If this wasn't going to last, she wanted one more night of passion with him.

She deepened the kiss, pulling him close to her, pressing her body against his. Agustin's hands skimmed over her, causing her body to tingle in anticipation.

"Querida," Agustin mumbled against her neck. "When you kiss me like that I lose control."

"I know. I want you too."

Agustin kissed her again. "Are you sure?"

She nodded. "I want you, Agustin. Just like I did in Barcelona. I just want to be with you. Here. Now."

Agustin kissed her all over, his hands over her body as they hastily removed their clothes. Her skin was on fire, wanting to be touched by him. Her blood was singing. Soon it was just them, nothing between them, just their bodies pressed together, skin to skin.

Warmth spread through her, melting her right down to her toes and making her wet with need. His lips trailed over her sensitive skin, down her body to her breasts. Sharon cried out as his tongue swirled around the peak of her sensitive nipples.

Every bit of her reacted to his touch, his tongue. Her body remembered the way he felt under her fingers. The strength of his muscles, the power of his hands on her and the erotic hold he had on her.

She remembered him.

As he nipped at her neck his hand slipped between her legs, stroking her folds, bringing her so close to a climax she arched her hips in response. Her body aching with the need for him to be buried deep inside her.

She wanted all of Agustin.

She wanted more.

So much more.

"What do you need, *querida*?" he whispered against her neck. "Tell me what you want."

"You," she said breathlessly.

Their gazes locked as he entered her. She cried out in bliss.

"Am I hurting you?" he asked.

"No. Don't stop." Sharon didn't want him to stop. She wanted more.

So much more.

She wanted him always, but she knew that was a folly

and the pain she felt later would be her fault for letting him in and loving him.

Right now, she didn't care about any of that.

Right now Sharon wanted Agustin deeper. She wrapped her legs around his waist, begging him to stay, wanting him pressed against her, which was impossible because of her belly.

"*Querida*, let's try another way." Agustin pulled out. "Lie on your side."

Sharon obeyed. He took her leg and draped it over him as he entered her from behind.

"Touch yourself," he whispered in her ear. "I want to feel you come around me."

Sharon began to stroke her clitoris. Her body lighting up as pleasure washed over her.

Agustin quickened his pace as she came around him, heat scorching through every fiber, every cell in her body.

It wasn't long before Agustin came. She was in a pile of goo as he eased her leg down, kissing her shoulder.

"*Querida,*" he whispered.

Sharon wanted to tell him that she was in love with him. That she wanted him to stay with her. That she wished he wouldn't go. Only she couldn't say those words because she was so scared of trusting him and her heart enough.

Agustin just lay there after she fell asleep. He was still curled up against her back and he had his hand on her belly, gently caressing her and feeling each little kick from his daughter. He hadn't felt this happy in a long time.

Not since Luisa, and he never thought he would ever feel this way again.

It was unnerving.

And he was scared, but still there was nowhere he would rather be. Just lying with her and feeling his baby kick. His eyes stung with tears, but he quickly swallowed the lump in his throat. He wasn't sure that he deserved to be this happy.

He wasn't sure that he deserved this second chance with a beautiful woman like Sharon. He got up slowly, as to not disturb her, but she rolled in his direction, reaching out.

"Agustin?" she asked sleepily.

"I'm just going to my mother's to get my bag. Go back to sleep, I'll be back in an hour."

"Promise? You're not leaving?"

His heart melted and he kissed her gently on the top of her head. "I will be back."

Sharon didn't open her eyes. Just nodded and slept, her brown hair fanning across the pillow again. Just like he remembered. Her body tangled in the sheets, but she was shivering so he took an extra blanket from the hotel closet and covered her up, tucking her in, and then kissed her on the cheek.

It was almost like he had been doing it for some time.

Except he hadn't.

He got dressed and grabbed the extra key card. He made his way to his car and took the short drive over to his mother's apartment in Recoleta.

When he got into his mother's place, she was up and pacing. Instantly, the hair stood on the back of his neck.

"What is it?" he asked.

"Oh, I was just about to text you when I saw you come into the lobby. There's been an accident in Ushuaia," his mother said, her voice shaking.

It was like he was in some kind of parallel universe. Has he been transported back in time? "What do you mean?"

"Sandrine, she was in a car accident, from a landslide. She's in the hospital. That's all I know, that's all they'd tell me because you're her legal guardian. They called here looking for you."

Sandrine had been alone. He was doing what he had done to Luisa when he'd worked so much. He felt terrible and knew that they had to get back to Ushuaia as soon as possible.

"I have to take Sharon with me. She's supposed to stay in Buenos Aires since her Braxton Hicks scare, but her abuela will be alone now."

"Maria is with her abuela, I checked," Ava said. "Sharon's abuela was my midwife. I still keep in touch with her."

"Of course you do." Agustin smiled. Theresa was in everyone's life. Maybe it was supposed to be that way.

"You need to take my private jet," Javier, his stepfather, said. "I made a call."

"Thank you, Javier." And he was grateful. He needed to get to Sandrine. It was eating away at him that he hadn't been there again.

What kind of brother was he?

The worst.

If he couldn't be there for Sandrine, how could he be there for his own daughter? It was a terrifying prospect. It chilled him to his very core.

Javier nodded. "Go to Ushuaia and take care of your family."

Agustin just nodded.

His family?

They weren't a family. They were… He didn't know what they were, but family? Did he deserve a family when he couldn't even take care of Sandrine? He had left her alone and she'd been in a car accident and he didn't even know her status.

He was failing.

Again.

Sharon slept on the plane. He hated to wake her up, but when he told her that Sandrine was in the hospital after a car accident, she got up and packed her things. He didn't say much to her as he drove the rental car to the airport where Javier's private plane was waiting.

Once they were settled the pilots got clearance, and when they were in the air Sharon curled up in her seat, her head against the window, and slept.

He wished he could sleep.

It was three-hour flight, in good weather, but all he could think about was how he had failed his sister. He had guardianship over her until she was eighteen, but did he really deserve that? He shouldn't have left her in Ushuaia. He should've brought her to Buenos Aires, but Sandrine had been so insistent on staying in Ushuaia for school and for Sharon's grandmother Theresa.

Sandrine thought of Sharon and her grandmother as family already and he wished that he had that same kind of optimism. He was struggling to connect with his sister too, but the thought of losing Sandrine was too much to bear.

He had issues with his father and didn't have a good relationship with Sandrine's biological mom, but Sandrine was his sister. Besides his mother and Javier, he had no one.

You have Sharon.

Only he didn't. She wasn't his and he was terrified to reach out and make her his, because the idea of losing her the same way that he'd lost Luisa was almost too much to bear.

Yet when he took her in his arms, when he was with her, he wasn't scared.

But in this harsh reality of accidents, the thought of losing Sharon was too much to bear.

"You should head straight home," Agustin said as they collected their luggage.

"No, I'm a nurse. If it's a multi-vehicle accident they'll need all the help they can get," Sharon stated.

"You really think you should be working?" he asked tensely.

"I'm fine."

Agustin was frustrated. "You need rest."

"I'm going." She crossed her arms and there was no point in arguing with her.

They went to the emergency room. It was full and Dr. Reyes, who was Agustin's friend and head of the emergency room, appeared relieved when he caught sight of him.

"Agustin! Sandrine is in room three, but if you can spare some help we have a lot of injured here and a lot of burn victims."

"Of course," Agustin said. "I just need to check on my sister."

"Room three, down the hall," Dr. Reyes said.

"I'm a nurse, a registered practice nurse. Can I help?" Sharon asked.

"Of course," Dr. Reyes replied enthusiastically.

Agustin paused. He wanted to stop her, but she wouldn't listen to him. She wasn't his. There was nothing he could do as she walked off with Dr. Reyes. He wanted to tell her to be careful. Only the words didn't come.

She wasn't his.

Agustin took a deep breath and headed to room three. His heart was hammering as he entered the room. Sandrine was lying there, staring at the walls, her arm bandaged up.

"Sandrine?" he asked tentatively.

She startled and her eyes widened. "Agustin? You came back?"

"Why wouldn't I?" Agustin asked. "I'm your brother, right?"

Sandrine's eyes filled with tears. "No one ever comes for me. Except Father, but he's been gone… I've been so alone."

She began to sob and Agustin took his sister in his arms, holding her.

"It's okay, I'm here," he reassured her.

Sandrine clung to him, crying herself out. Agustin just held her. He was glad she was alive and angry at himself for not being there, for being just as guilty for letting her be alone as her biological mother had done. He was mad at himself for putting his work first, like he did with Luisa and thinking Sandrine needed space.

"I'm here now," Agustin said. "What happened?"

"I was driving with Diego—"

"I knew that boy Diego would get you into trouble."

Sandrine pulled away. "Diego didn't cause the landslide. That's what caused the accident. He pulled me from the burning car."

Agustin felt awful. "Where is he?"

Sandrine's eyes welled with tears. "I don't know. He went to help the others, the cars that were buried."

"Why were you driving with him?"

"Taking the money we raised for Theresa to the bank.

We were coming back. We almost raised enough to pay those legal fees."

"What?" Sharon asked.

Agustin spun around to see Sharon standing in the doorway, her arms folded. She looked confused and hurt.

"Sharon? I thought you were helping Dr. Reyes?" he asked.

"I am, but I decided to see Sandrine before I changed into scrubs. What do you mean money was raised for my abuela?"

"The community raised the funds," he said.

"Not the full amount," Sandrine piped up. "Enough that you don't have to move."

Sharon was still confused. "I don't understand."

"You didn't want my help," Agustin stated.

"No. I don't want charity either." Her voice was raised.

He glanced back at Sandrine. "Can we speak in the hall? Sandrine, I'll be back. Rest."

Sandrine shook her head and rolled her eyes as Agustin ushered Sharon out into the hall. He closed the door behind him.

"So you told the community about Abuela's financial troubles?" Sharon asked.

"I did. Theresa needed help. As did you."

"You had no right," she snapped. "That was too much. I have money…"

"Not enough. You were going to sell the home. Move away."

"Only across the city. I'm not poor. It was for me to take care of."

"What does it matter? I took care of it. It was a way for me to help."

"Help? You mean a way to ease your conscience when you leave us eventually."

He knew she was lashing out because she was afraid.

"You're the one leaving by moving away," he countered.

"I'm not really. I'm moving across the city," she said quietly. "You can still see us."

"You don't sound so sure," he snapped. "What happens when your abuela, God forbid, dies and you go back to your old job as a traveling nurse?"

"What happens when you feel guilty about moving on from your grief and leave us?" she asked, trembling. "Just like my father."

"I'm not your father."

"I'm sorry your wife died, but you can't run from your problems."

That struck a painful chord with him. "Look who's talking. You took a job where you never settled. You were running from your pain just as much as I was."

Sharon's lip trembled. "I'm here now and you're abandoning us."

"I am not. You are leaving me by pushing me away, not allowing me to help," he said hotly.

"I'm not."

"Then let it go. Let's leave this all behind and you can accept the money."

"I can't," she whispered.

"What're you afraid of?" he asked.

They didn't say anything for a moment. Just stared at each other. He could see the hurt and anger in her eyes.

He'd put it there.

"I will pay you back, everyone back," Sharon replied coldly.

She turned to leave.

"I'm not your father. I'm not leaving you. You're choosing to leave me."

She looked back over her shoulder. "And I am not your wife, and I'm safe here. I won't have my child left behind. I won't allow her to feel that pain."

He stood there shaking as he let her walk away.

He went back into Sandrine's room, but she was obviously angry with him too.

"Did you make it right?" Sandrine asked.

Agustin ran his hand through his hair and sighed. "It's complicated."

"No. It's not. You love her. I know you do. I was only small when Luisa died, but she would want you to be happy, Agustin."

"I may love Sharon, but she doesn't love me. If she did, she'd trust me."

"Her love is predicated on that?" Sandrine asked. "Seriously. How immature."

"What?" Agustin asked.

Sandrine cocked an eyebrow. "And how do you know she doesn't love you? Just because she is struggling to trust after her trauma? You are too by the way."

Agustin was stunned. "You know about that?"

Sandrine nodded. "She told me. I was struggling with abandonment too. You were always working and…it was a lot."

Agustin pulled her close. "I'm sorry you were struggling, and that I didn't notice."

"You bury your grief in work. It was hard for me to trust you with you putting your work first, but that doesn't mean I don't love you, you blockhead."

"She's never said she loves me," Agustin said.

"Have you asked her?"

No. He hadn't.

He just heard her say that she didn't want a relationship, so that's how he'd interpreted it.

"It's complicated," he said, again, knowing it was just an excuse for his fear.

Fear of falling in love.

Fear of losing.

The problem was, he was in love with her and he was ruining it.

"It's not complicated," Sandrine said. "It really isn't. Make it right, Agustin. Or it won't just be me coming after you, but your mother too."

The threat was clear.

He just hoped he hadn't ruined it all.

Sharon was fuming and hurt, but she swallowed all those feelings of pain and betrayal as she assisted the nursing staff in the hospital as they cared for all the victims of the major pileup. The emergency crews were still digging people out of the rubble.

It was a mess.

Sharon focused on work and not her broken heart.

Has he really broken your heart, though? Aren't you to blame too?

Agustin wasn't completely to blame. She was too.

All he'd done was something kind to ease the burden off her. Yes, she had the means to solve it, but was she so untrusting that she had to push everyone away? Even the community that loved her abuela as much as she did?

As she glanced around the full emergency room, she could see a community rallying together in the face of tragedy.

Just like her aunt had come for her, and that nurse who had been so kind to her as a child, the nurse who had inspired her to help others.

Her aunt and her abuela always said she took too much on. She never let anyone in and tried to solve every problem herself.

It was true.

She could rely on herself and had always done so.

She couldn't accept any help and she was terrified he was leaving. It was easier to push him away, except there was a part of her that didn't want him out of her life.

A part of her that wanted to rely on him and trust him.

Despite the terror of loving and losing, she was in love with him.

"Victim is male, approximately sixteen to eighteen. Pulled from under a pile of rocks. Burn and crush injuries to the face and neck," a paramedic shouted, pushing the gurney into the trauma bay. He was listing out vitals as Sharon went to help. The boy was lucky to be alive. Then she recognized the shoes. They were distinctive cross trainers Sandrine's boyfriend wore.

Oh, no.

"Victim has identification," a doctor said. "He's Diego Santos. Someone contact his next of kin."

Sharon's stomach twisted. "I know him."

The doctor turned to her. "You do?"

"He's my neighbor's boyfriend," Sharon said.

The doctor nodded. "His face is partially crushed. He needs surgery. Stat."

"I can help," Agustin said, not saying anything to her. Not that she blamed him.

They had both said things. Hurtful things.

Agustin examined him. "He needs surgery. Now. I need an operating room prepped."

"I can help," Sharon offered.

"It'll be a long surgery. You shouldn't be standing that long."

"I'm fine," she said quickly. "This is my job. I can handle it."

"Of course," he replied. "You don't need approval. Prep the patient."

He moved out of the trauma room to get ready for surgery. It hurt and she wanted to talk to him, but right now they needed to save Diego's life.

Sharon could feel the sweat trickling down her spine under her scrubs. The surgery was grueling and she was getting tired. She was annoyed that she had lost control of her body in this moment. It was a surgery she had never witnessed before and Agustin was a master of it.

"Are you okay, Sharon?" Agustin asked, not looking up from his work.

"Fine," she responded. Only she wasn't completely sure.

"You can take a break," he offered.

She wanted to retort back that she didn't need to, but that seemed a little hotheaded and she wondered where that thought had come from. Her feet began to ache and it felt like her shoes were too tight. She felt off.

"You know what, that might be wise," she admitted.

"Abril, can you take over for Sharon?" Agustin asked.

"Of course, Agustin," Nurse Abril said.

Sharon stepped away and exited the operating room. She scrubbed out and realized she'd been standing there for eight hours. No wonder her shoes were feeling tight—her feet were aching and swollen.

Her head spun, just for a moment, and then she got control of it again. She left the operating room floor and made her way to Sandrine's room.

"Can I come in?" Sharon asked, knocking.

"Sure!" Sandrine said. "You look tired."

"We were in surgery." Sharon didn't want to tell Sandrine who it was. That was up to Agustin. Sharon sat on the edge of Sandrine's bed. "How are you?"

"Fine." Sandrine sighed. "I'm sorry if I had a part in upsetting you, Sharon. It's just we all love your abuela. She delivered most of the neighborhood and beyond, and the community loves you too. I love you."

Sharon smiled. "I love you too, Sandrine. No matter what happens."

"So you're not mad at me?" Sandrine asked.

"No. It's all fine. I was being stubborn. I got it in my head not to receive any help."

Sandrine nodded. "About my brother…he just lost a lot… you know?"

Sharon nodded. "I know. It's just hard for me to trust after my father left."

"Like my mother left." Sandrine sighed. "Not that she was much of one when she was around."

Sharon laughed to herself. "So many coincidences. So many parallels."

Sandrine smiled. "Fate. We're meant to be a family."

And Sharon wanted to believe it, but she still had doubts.

"Agustin loved his wife. What if I'm not enough?" Because she hadn't been enough for her father to stay.

Sandrine shook her head. "He's being stubborn. He won't

leave. Please, Sharon, you love him. I know it. Don't be mad at him. He means well."

"I know…" The room began to spin, and her head began to throb with the start of a headache. An excruciating one that was like hot, blinding pain. A knife slicing through her head, stealing her vision. She clutched her head, groaning.

"Sharon?" Sandrine asked.

"Call for help," Sharon managed to get out before everything went black.

Agustin came out of Diego's surgery. He would be fine—he would have some scarring and require physical therapy, but he would live. Agustin had learned from Sandrine and others about Diego's heroics. He had been really wrong about Diego. He'd been wrong about a lot of things.

Now he was looking for Sharon. They had some things to talk about and he hoped that she wasn't still so angry at him.

He wasn't angry with her. It was just a misunderstanding.

He knew she'd needed rest, but that was two hours ago. He'd thought she would've returned to the operating room.

She never did come back and now he was worried. When he came out of the scrub room Dr. Perez, Sharon's OB/GYN, was in scrubs and approached him.

Immediately his heart sank.

Oh, God. No.

"Dr. Perez?" he asked, hoping his voice didn't crack.

"They told me you'd be here. It's about Sharon."

"What's wrong?" he asked, cursing himself inwardly for having let her work, but there had been no way to stop her.

"She has preeclampsia. I've been trying to bring down her blood pressure. It's not budging. The baby is in danger and so is Sharon. I'm prepping the operating room for an emergency C-section."

Agustin's stomach knotted.

The baby could die.

Sharon could die, or would if they didn't proceed with the surgery.

He couldn't lose Sharon.

Not after just finding her. Not after truly realizing after all this time he loved her.

"The baby is twenty-eight weeks," he numbly said, trying to process it all.

"And Sharon's been given some injections to help the baby's lungs. Twenty-eight weeks is not ideal, but it's better than twenty-seven or twenty-six even. Every week matters."

"Can I see her?" Agustin asked.

He needed to tell her how he felt before she went into surgery. She needed to know that he loved her in case… He didn't even want to think about the *in case* because he refused to let it happen.

"Quickly," Dr. Perez said. "She's in the preoperative area."

Agustin ran to the preoperative ward and found Sharon behind the curtains in a bed, crying softly.

"Querida," he whispered, pushing back the curtains, hoping his voice didn't crack. He was trying to remain strong for her.

She turned to him. "Oh, Agustin. I'm sorry for everything I said."

"Hush." He sat down next to her and took her hand. "No apologies. I'm sorry."

"I'm so worried. She's so small," Sharon whispered.

"She's strong, like her mother." He touched her belly.

Please live, his heart was saying.

Pleading to God and the universe that he hadn't ruined everything by not seeing his second chance when it had been staring him right in the face. He wanted to weep and beg for her survival, for the baby, but right now he had to be strong for her.

"About…everything," she said, mumbling as the medication began to work on her.

"We'll talk later. I'll be here waiting for you, *querida*. I will not leave."

Sharon drifted off as the sedatives began to take over.

"I love you," she whispered.

"I love you too." He kissed her hand as the nurses came to take her into surgery.

His eyes stung with unshed tears. His heart was breaking, watching her being wheeled away and knowing there was nothing he could do.

He was powerless.

He'd sworn he'd never let his heart be hurt again, and here it was breaking, but he wouldn't change anything. Sharon was his second chance at happiness. He could make his home with her.

Anywhere she was, was home.

But now the very scary realization that he may lose her and their baby—it was too much.

Please.

It was a simple prayer.

Just let her live.

He paced outside the operating room. She was under general anesthetic so they wouldn't let him in. Even though he was a surgeon and would be used to seeing a patient under general, because she was his partner, they wouldn't allow him to be there.

So he waited.

And he hated every excruciating minute of it.

Finally her doctor came out.

"She made it," Dr. Perez stated. "She lost a lot of blood, but she'll recover."

"And the baby?" Agustin asked.

"Go in and see for yourself. They're readying her for her transport to the neonatal intensive care unit."

Agustin put on a mask and headed into the operating room. Sharon had been taken to the postanesthesia recovery unit, but the pediatric team was working on his tiny daughter.

She was in an isolette, already hooked up to machines, but one little eye opened as he squatted to peer in through the glass.

A sob welled up in his throat.

"*Hola*, little one," he murmured, touching the glass and wishing that he could touch her delicate little arm. So tiny, so fragile, but his.

"She's strong, Dr. Varela," a pediatric nurse said.

"Like her mama," Agustin responded, not tearing his gaze from the little life he'd made with Sharon. His daughter was everything, and just as beautiful as her mother. She was love, hope and family.

Everything he'd always wanted but never thought he would have.

And the moment that little baby looked at him through the glass of the isolette, she was his world. Sharon and the baby were his world and he was never letting them go.

* * *

Sharon woke up. She felt pain, but she was confused as to why. Then she remembered.

Oh, my God. My baby.

She struggled to open her eyes under the influence of anesthetic. She drifted off again and then woke, not remembering why she was agitated.

"Agustin?" she called out.

"I'm here. Don't worry. I'm not going anywhere."

She sighed and her vision came into focus. He was by her bedside.

"What happened?"

"You had preeclampsia. You had an emergency C-section."

She shook her head. "No. I was working with you on Diego."

"He's fine. He'll live," Agustin said.

All the memories came back to her—the headache, her swollen feet and dizziness. Sandrine calling for help.

"Our baby? You said I had an emergency C-section."

"Yes, you did, and our baby is fine. She's alive and strong."

"Really?" Sharon began to cry. "You saw her?"

"Sí." He took her hand and kissed it. "We can go see her when you're ready."

"I want to go."

He nodded. "I'll get a wheelchair."

Sharon was in pain, but none of that mattered. She wanted to see her baby. She took her time and slowly sat up.

Agustin helped her out of bed. She used a pillow to brace her incision. He helped with her IV bag. She slowly sat down. Once she was settled, he tucked a blanket around her and wheeled her through the halls to the other end of the hospital where the neonatal intensive care unit was.

Her heart was swelling with joy and fear. All these emotions going through her. She was trying to hold them back. To be strong.

Agustin took her to the isolette in the corner of the unit. Under all the wires and lines, there was a tiny baby.

Her baby.

So small, with just a whisper of dark hair.

"See our daughter, *querida*. She's strong," Agustin said proudly.

"I see," Sharon said, her voice trembling as she tentatively reached out and touched the glass, wishing that she could hold her.

"Would you like to hold her, Sharon?" the nurse asked. "Skin to skin, or kangaroo care, is great for preemies. She's doing well."

"Yes," Sharon whispered.

Her heart ached to hold her, because holding her meant that she would be okay. At least in her mind. Holding her daughter would let her little girl know that she hadn't left her. She wasn't alone and she would never feel that longing, that pain for want of a parent who didn't want them.

The nurse gently took her tiny baby out. Sharon moved her hospital gown aside and her little girl, who curled up in the palm of the nurse's hand, was placed on her skin. A tangle of cords, but warm as Sharon cradled her close to her heart.

"Her stats are already improving," Agustin remarked.

The nurse smiled. "Kangaroo is the best. I'll leave you two. Let me know when you want to take Sharon back up to her room and I'll put the baby back. Sharon needs to rest too. She just had major surgery," the nurse reminded them, because Sharon knew that the nurse knew that doctors and nurses made the worst patients.

Agustin knelt down beside them. He was smiling, his eyes twinkling. A tear slid down his cheek and he brushed it away quickly.

"Agustin, are you crying?" Sharon asked.

"*Sí.*"

"Why?"

"Because this is the most beautiful thing. It brings me joy that I didn't think was possible again. I almost ruined it. I will do better. I love you, Sharon. I can't lose you."

"What about your work and your grief?" she asked, stunned.

"The only plans I have involve you, our baby, your abuela and Sandrine. And I guess my mother and Javier, but those plans are here in Ushuaia. Luisa has been gone a long time. I will always love her and miss her, my heart will always hold her, but there's room for you. For more love. She would want me to be happy. I believe she sent me to you."

Sharon grinned. She couldn't hold back the tears. "I love you and I tried to push you away. I thought it would be easier if I pushed you away instead of waiting for you to leave."

"I'd never leave you, *querida*. Both of you are my life." He leaned over and kissed her. "Say you'll marry me?"

"Yes." Her heart overflowed with joy. "I love you, Agustin, and I'm sorry too. I just want you. I'm scared about the future, but I am more terrified about a future without you."

"Agreed. I can't live without you or her." Agustin kissed her again and they both gazed down at the little life squirming and moving against her chest. "What shall we name her?"

"How about Ava Theresa after your mother and my abuela? Both strong women."

His eyes twinkled. "Perfection."

"*Sí.* Perfection." She gazed down at her little miracle and then to the man that she loved. It was all a little too much and she really couldn't hold back the joy she was feeling, sitting here holding her little girl.

She couldn't quite believe that she was here. That this little surprise had happened to her. This was never in the plans. She never thought that love would find her or come looking for her like it had, but she knew one thing—with Agustin and her little daughter in her arms, she was home.

For the first time in her life she felt like this was really home. She was no longer that little girl, scared, living on cereal in an apartment waiting for her father to come home, moving between her aunt's and her abuela's. Her whole life she had been lost and floating, but now this was home.

Finally, she was home.

It had taken so long to get here and there'd been many surprises along the way, like a pregnancy, but they were good surprises. They were what she'd needed to find her path and wake up from that nightmare of her past that had held her heart captive for too long.

She was finally home.

She had finally found her family.

She had found her forever family at the end of the world.

EPILOGUE

Six months later

SHARON GLANCED OUT the window at the shared garden between her abuela's house and Agustin's house, which had been his childhood home. There was construction to join the two homes together and expand so that they wouldn't have to walk outside to visit her abuela, who was doing so much better and didn't require as much care.

Abuela's home would be a small, contained apartment, but without a kitchen. Abuela would be coming across to the main house and having dinner with them, which suited her abuela fine.

Her abuela reveled in her great-granddaughter and namesake.

Sandrine loved having the homes connected.

She would be off to Buenos Aires in a year to go to school and living with Ava and Javier at Agustin's insistence.

Sandrine was going through school to be a surgeon, like her big brother. This time, it was her choice.

For now, Sandrine soaked up every moment of being a doting auntie. Sharon smiled at Sandrine curled up next to little Ava Theresa, who was trying to learn to crawl. She was up on all fours and rocking back and forth as Sandrine coaxed her from the other side of the blanket.

Her abuela was sitting outside under the pergola Agustin had installed so they would have some shade from the sun. She was clapping and cheering little Ava Theresa on too.

And Agustin's mother, who was down for a visit, was setting out a light lunch. They were going to have a picnic when Javier showed up.

A family picnic.

Sharon never thought she would ever really get to experience that with her own little family unit, but that was what she had here in Ushuaia and it made her heart burst with happiness watching them all.

It was the perfect late summer day.

Agustin came up behind her and slipped his arms around her. "What're you looking at?"

"Just enjoying the view," she remarked, wrapping her arms around his.

He leaned his head on her shoulder. "Is she trying to crawl?"

"I think so."

Agustin moved away, panicked that he was going to miss a milestone. "I don't have my camera."

Sharon laughed. "Sandrine has it. Don't worry, she'll catch it all. Between you and your sister, Ava's life is going to be completely documented from dawn to dusk for the next twenty years."

Agustin chuckled and then spun her around to face him, touching her face. "How did I get so lucky?"

"I believe it was the elevator at the conference hotel where we first met," she said teasingly. "Of course, it could've been that workshop on infections."

"I do remember that, but I mostly recall the kiss on the beach and afterward." He grinned.

"Oh, I remember that too. Fondly."

He chuckled. "Have I told you lately that I love you like crazy?"

"Not lately."

He kissed her, but their kiss was interrupted by the sound of the doorbell. Agustin groaned. "It's probably him."

"Be nice. You saved his life. Besides, I thought you liked him now. He's a hero."

"I know, I know, but I can't let him know that."

"You need to be nicer. Show him that you like him."

"Am I supposed to like the boyfriend?" Agustin groused.

Sharon crossed her arms. "Yes. Especially when he adores you for what you did. He's here today because of you."

Agustin groaned, but smiled and opened the door. "Mr. Santos, you're right on time."

Diego smiled brightly. It was only a half smile as he had some nerve damage and he walked with a slight limp, but he no longer needed his cane thanks to Sharon helping him as much as she could when he was over visiting Sandrine.

"My mother sent asados," Diego said, holding up the plate.

"Those look delicious!" Sharon exclaimed, taking the plate. "Have you been practicing your walking in the pool downtown?"

"Yes, Sharon," Diego replied, smiling.

Sharon nodded. "Good. Sandrine is outside with Ava… or both Avas."

Diego grinned and made his way through the house and through the new sliding glass doors out into the back garden.

Agustin's mom got Diego a chair and fussed over him. Sharon watched as Sandrine stood up, bent down and gave him a kiss. She could see the love there. They were young, but it was undeniable.

Sandrine had been crushed when she learned Diego had almost died, but he'd pulled through and Sharon couldn't help but wonder if in a few years' time they would be having a little wedding out there.

"What're you thinking about now?" Agustin asked.

"Weddings," she responded dreamily.

"You don't mean my little sister and Diego?" Agustin groused.

Sharon laughed. "In a few years. Once she's a surgeon. Then she can have two flower girls, or a flower girl and a ring bearer."

Agustin's eyes widened. "What're you telling me?"

Sharon had taken the test that morning. They'd had the all-clear from Dr. Perez that they could try for another baby. Initially Sharon had missed the signs again, but thankfully she'd figured things out quicker this time around—only six weeks this time. She held up the test for him.

"I'm six weeks. At least I'm not twenty. By next June or July we should have a full-term addition to the family."

Agustin kissed her. "I think I'm in shock. Another winter baby!" He smiled. "I'm extremely happy."

"Are you?" she asked.

He scooped her up in his arms and she squealed as he kissed her passionately, making her blood heat in anticipation.

"Let me show you exactly how happy I am," he said huskily.

"Yes, show me, but be quick about it…we have guests."

"Quick? I don't do quick," he murmured against her neck.

She melted a bit. "Okay, fine, but we don't have all day."

His eyes gleamed. "Who says we don't?"

Her knees went weak. "I can't resist you, Agustin."

"And I can't resist you either, *querida*." Agustin winked and carried her up the stairs to their very private, newly finished master suite and the large king bed. He showed her exactly how he was feeling about the new baby. The new surprise they weren't expecting, but one that was welcome all the same.

Just another person to add to their family.

A family full of love.

* * * * *

COMING SOON!

We really hope you enjoyed reading this book. If you're looking for more romance be sure to head to the shops when new books are available on

Thursday 6th July

To see which titles are coming soon, please visit
millsandboon.co.uk/nextmonth

MILLS & BOON®

Coming next month

BROUGHT TOGETHER BY HIS BABY
Kristine Lynn

"Why don't you stay here?"

He hoped the look he shot her—confusion mixed with something less inhibited—implied that it wasn't a good idea. And if he was an artist, he'd commission a whole piece in the shade of red her cheeks turned as she realized how her question had come across.

"I mean in the cabin I have on the property. It's not being used, and you can make it your home as long as you need."

"Why would you offer that to a stranger?"

"You aren't a stranger; you're Emma's dad. And you're trusting me to help raise her. For now," she added when he opened his mouth to reply. "And if I'm being honest, it serves my designs, too. I don't know how to be away from her for very long, and if you're here I won't have to. And if you ever need help with her, I'll be next door."

He considered that. It checked a lot of boxes. It would probably be cheaper than any of the dumps he'd find in town. He knew the landlady already—and trusted her. But the stone tipping the scales was that he'd never be far from Emma either.

"I'll insist on paying rent."

"Fine. If that's what you need. It's furnished, but you can make it your own."

"And, to be honest, I'm not sure I'll be comfortable taking her overnight—not until we find our rhythm, anyway."

"That's fine. Just let me know when you're ready."

Liam sipped at his water, looking out over the expansive deck to the ocean below. It was more than he deserved.

"Thank you. I've put the end of my marriage behind me, but I know I've still got work to do to build your trust—and Emma's, too. I don't take that lightly."

"Good. Me neither. Now, let's talk about getting you a job. Are you set on downtown?"

Liam smiled so hard he felt it in his cheeks. He hadn't been sure at all about coming out here, about meeting Emma and what would come of that first meeting, but now, deep in his soul—the one he'd built from scratch after the first one had been obliterated in combat—he rejoiced.

Things were shaping up for the better for the first time in his life, and he had a feeling he owed a lot of it to the beautiful woman holding his child.

But imagining her as more than that was as off-the-table as imagining how he was going tell his dad to find someone else to fill the Everson Health board seat. Because Liam wasn't going home anytime soon.

Continue reading
BROUGHT TOGETHER BY HIS BABY
Kristine Lynn

Available next month
www.millsandboon.co.uk

LET'S TALK
Romance

For exclusive extracts, competitions and special offers, find us online:

- **MillsandBoon**
- **@MillsandBoon**
- **@MillsandBoonUK**
- **@MillsandBoonUK**

Get in touch on 01413 063 232

For all the latest titles coming soon, visit
millsandboon.co.uk/nextmonth

MILLS & BOON

THE HEART OF ROMANCE

A ROMANCE FOR EVERY READER

MODERN
Prepare to be swept off your feet by sophisticated, sexy and seductive heroes, in some of the world's most glamourous and romantic locations, where power and passion collide.

HISTORICAL
Escape with historical heroes from time gone by. Whether your passion is for wicked Regency Rakes, muscled Vikings or rugged Highlanders, awaken the romance of the past.

MEDICAL
Set your pulse racing with dedicated, delectable doctors in the high-pressure world of medicine, where emotions run high and passion, comfort and love are the best medicine.

True Love
Celebrate true love with tender stories of heartfelt romance, from the rush of falling in love to the joy a new baby can bring, and a focus on the emotional heart of a relationship.

Desire
Indulge in secrets and scandal, intense drama and sizzling hot action with heroes who have it all: wealth, status, good looks…everything but the right woman.

HEROES
The excitement of a gripping thriller, with intense romance at its heart. Resourceful, true-to-life women and strong, fearless men face danger and desire - a killer combination!

To see which titles are coming soon, please visit

millsandboon.co.uk/nextmonth

MILLS & BOON
True Love
Romance from the Heart

Celebrate true love with tender stories of heartfelt romance, from the rush of falling in love to the joy a new baby can bring, and a focus on the emotional heart of a relationship.

MILLS & BOON

MODERN

Power and Passion

Prepare to be swept off your feet by sophisticated, sexy and seductive heroes, in some of the world's most glamourous and romantic locations, where power and passion collide.

MILLS & BOON

Desire

Indulge in secrets and scandal, intense drama and plenty of sizzling hot action with powerful and passionate heroes who have it all: wealth, status, good looks…everything but the right woman.